Praise for the nove

"The best thing about the second book of the Granger series is the setup for the next one. The romance is classic Jackson storytelling, but the hints dropped about the murder mystery are tantalizing and delightfully frustrating."
—*RT Book Reviews* on *A Man's Promise*, 4 1/2 stars

"Welcome to another memorable family tree created by the indomitable Brenda Jackson, a romantic at heart."
—*USA TODAY* on *A Brother's Honor*

"Jackson's series starter proves once again that she rocks when it comes to crafting family drama with a healthy dose of humor and steamy, sweaty sex. Here's another winner.... Bring on the Granger brothers!"
—*RT Book Reviews* on *A Brother's Honor*, 4 1/2 stars, Top Pick

"This deliciously sensual romance ramps up the emotional stakes and the action with a bit of deception and corporate espionage.... [S]exy and sizzling."
—*Library Journal* on *Intimate Seduction*

"Jackson does not disappoint...first-class page-turner."
—*RT Book Reviews* on *A Silken Thread*, 4 1/2 stars, Top Pick

"Jackson is a master at writing."
—*Publishers Weekly* on *Sensual Confessions*

BRENDA JACKSON

A LOVER'S *Vow*

MIRA

ISBN-13: 978-0-7783-1800-2

Recycling programs
for this product may
not exist in your area.

A Lover's Vow

To the man who will always and forever be the love of my life,
Gerald Jackson, Sr.

To everyone joining me on
the 2015 Brenda Jackson Cruise to Bermuda to celebrate
my 20th anniversary as an author, this one is for you!

To all my readers who enjoyed reading Books 1 and 2
of the Granger Series and waited patiently for Dalton's story,
I appreciate you!

To my Heavenly Father, who gave me the gift to write.

A bowl of vegetables with someone you love
is better than steak with someone you hate.
—*Proverbs* 15:17

A LOVER'S *Vow*

One

Dalton Granger glanced around, noting the hundreds of people assembled in the rose garden of the Granger estate. What had happened to the small wedding Shana Bradford had originally planned? Granted, the pregnancy wasn't obvious, but he thought the huge wedding along with the white gown was a bit much. But then, even he would be the first to admit that Wonder Woman looked jaw-droppingly stunning.

Wonder Woman was the nickname he had given Shana, and she'd proven more than worthy of the name after performing more than one impossible feat. The main one of which was capturing his oldest brother Jace's heart. Dalton had honestly thought Jace would avoid marriage like the plague, especially after his first failed marriage to the woman Dalton still thought of as Evil Eve.

Stay focused.

Easier said than done, Dalton thought, shifting his gaze from the bride to her maid of honor, her sister, Jules Bradford. She was the one woman on this Earth he despised with a passion. Unfortunately, his major problem was that he desired her with that same degree of passion. Yes, he would own up to it, although he wished things were otherwise. There were times when he'd even concluded that his attraction to Jules was too obsessive to be considered normal. However, he could deal with it as long as she stayed in her space, because he certainly intended to stay in his. Today would be an exception, since her sister was marrying his brother. He'd been warned by Jace to be on his best behavior, which was an effing challenge. And nothing could have prepared him for last night's rehearsal dinner. It wasn't his behavior but his attraction to Jules that had tested his level of control.

She'd shown up wearing a pair of skin-tight black leggings and a long-sleeved white dress shirt with tails fanning across her shapely hips, thighs and curvaceous backside. And she'd worn a tie of all things. Was that a new trend or something? Mixing masculine with feminine? Business with casual? You had to have balls to make such a bold fashion statement. But the one thing he'd discovered about Jules was that she thought nothing of pushing the damned envelope to do whatever she pleased. However, he would admit, even grudgingly, that when she'd worn what he considered outlandish attire, she'd managed to look totally feminine and sexy as hell.

A frown curved Dalton's lips. He needed to get a grip. The last thing he wanted was to think about how Jules looked last night. But then, today wasn't much better with her hair pulled up tight in a bun with a few curls left to frame her face. She had skin that looked soft and flawless, and her eyes were a dark chocolate. Then there were those beautiful, high cheekbones and lips that looked enticingly kissable and were painted a beautiful shade of red.

It was damned torture standing here and looking at her when he should be paying attention, listening to whatever asinine wedding vows Jace was making to Shana. It was a known fact that Dalton didn't believe in that forever-after, until-death-do-us-part BS. Being cynical was a character flaw of his, one he embraced wholeheartedly. He prided himself on never doing anything he'd regret later. But there had been that one time he'd been stupid enough to let his guard down, *and* it had been with Jules.

Damn, he needed a drink. Thinking he needed one was better than thinking he needed to go over to her, unwind her hair and run his fingers through it before kissing that lipstick right off her lips. Hell, since he was thinking of being so effing bold, he might as well strip her naked, too. He could imagine the wedding guests' reactions to that, and the last thing his family needed was another Granger scandal.

He couldn't help but recall the first time he'd seen Jules. He'd been feeling so fucking horny and had gone to this nightclub to make a hit. He hadn't been impressed with the prospects until she'd walked through the door. At the time he'd had no idea she was Shana's sister and, to be quite honest, it would not have mattered had he known. All he'd cared about was that she'd looked hot, and he'd wanted a piece of her. No, not just a piece, he'd wanted the whole thing. Head to toe and especially all those areas in between. He saw. He liked. He got. Things had always been that simple for him. Quick, easy and hassle-free.

Anger suddenly rushed through him, and he fought the emotion by breathing in deeply when he remembered how things had actually gone down that night... definitely not the way he'd planned. Jules Bradford had turned his life into a damn circus, where he was a clown one minute and walking a tightrope the next. No other woman could make his blood boil while at the same time rev his libido up to the point of making his groin ache.

He should have more control, but unfortunately, at the moment, he didn't. He couldn't help but be grateful for the little ring bearer who was standing directly in front of him, blocking any telltale signs of his aroused state. By rights, all eyes should be on the wedding couple, anyway, and that included his own. But some things were unavoidable, and his fixation on Jules today fell into that category.

He slid his gaze down to her feet and then back to her face while wondering whose idea it was for the maid of honor and the bridesmaids to wear short dresses. At any other time, he would have appreciated seeing so many gorgeous pairs of legs, but since one of those pairs belonged to Jules...the pair he was transfixed by...he would have preferred otherwise.

"By the power vested in me by the great state of Virginia, I now pronounce you man and wife. You may kiss your bride."

The minister's words collided with Dalton's thoughts. Had he been standing there and staring at Jules the entire time Jace and Shana had exchanged vows? He quickly slid his gaze away from Jules in time to see Jace kiss Shana.

Dalton then shifted his gaze to his other brother, Caden, who was standing beside him and grinning from ear to ear. Both he and Caden had served as Jace's best men. He loved his brothers, although at times they got on his last nerve. And lately, he couldn't understand what drove them to do some of the idiotic things they did, like getting married, for instance. Jace tied the knot with Shana today, and a few weeks ago Caden had eloped with Shiloh Timmons, whom Dalton referred to as the Wine Lady, since she owned a wine boutique in town. It was quite apparent that both of his brothers had been p-whipped out of their ever-loving minds.

He returned his gaze to Jules at the same exact moment she glanced over the heads of the kissing couple. Their gazes clashed, and *bam*, he swore he could hear cymbals banging in his ears. Her eyes were frosty as hell, and she was probably calling him all kinds of names under her breath. And then, as if she suddenly recalled they'd both been warned to be on their best behavior, she parted her red lips, showing perfect white teeth in what he knew was a fake smile. Was she trying to taunt him while staring him down? He'd be damned if he'd let that happen, but she was welcome to try. Moments later, he saw she'd given up when her phony smile was replaced by a frown, and her eyes went back to being frosty again. Now it was his turn to smile, and his was more fake than hers had been.

The music began playing, and it was time for the newlyweds and their wedding party to exit the garden. At least Shana had the good sense not to pair him with Jules. Instead, he was coupled with her best friend and neighbor, Gloria McCabe, the perky, blue-eyed blonde he'd met last night. She smiled as she took his arm, and he escorted her from the rose garden.

He'd managed to get through the wedding and hoped the same would hold true for the reception.

Jules loved her sister immensely, which was why she had promised Shana that she would try like hell to be civil to Dalton Granger even if it killed her. Already, she felt like she was taking her last breath because it *was* killing her.

She'd been aware of him the entire time he'd been staring her down during the wedding ceremony, but she'd refused to glance over at him. Feeling the heat of his gaze scan every inch of her body, lingering in places it should not have, made her think how totally disrespectful he was, but then she wasn't surprised. The man was so full of himself it made her teeth ache. He assumed he could get any woman he wanted and, on two occasions, she'd proven him wrong by ignoring his schoolboy pick-up lines. Of course, he was still furious about it and had placed her on his shit list. Good. No sweat off her back if he kept her there.

Snagging a glass of champagne from the tray being carried by a passing waiter, she glanced around the wedding reception. The botanical garden that overlooked Mammoth Lake was nice—pretty damned impressive, in fact. But then, so was the rose garden where the wedding had taken place. The moment she'd driven onto the sprawling grounds of Sutton Hills, the Granger estate, she'd been captivated. Shana had warned her, but she'd still been stunned by the two hundred acres of lush and beautiful countryside near the foothills of the Blue Ridge Mountains.

She'd never ventured into this part of Charlottesville, Virginia, but she'd really had no reason to do so. People who lived in this area had money, and she was a plain old working-class girl. The number of people who'd attended the wedding—college friends of Shana or her close business associates—were mesmerized by the wealth surrounding them in the same way Jules was. She knew her sister was taking it all in stride, since she had married for love and not money. But Jules felt Shana had been lucky to get both.

She glanced to her right and saw Dalton talking to Gloria, no doubt trying to make a hit. She knew that Gloria was already in a committed relationship, so he was wasting his time. Good. But what if she was wrong about that?

Releasing a long breath, she wondered why she cared one way or the other. She couldn't stand him. The very ground he walked on. The air he breathed. Whatever food he ate. The clothes he wore. The—

For some reason, her thoughts refused to move beyond his clothes. Okay, he wore them well; she would give him that. Each and every time she saw him; he looked like he'd stepped off the pages of some fashion magazine. But then, she had to grudgingly admit, it was more than the clothes. A lot more. For starters, he had the looks—chiseled features that were handsome beyond reason, eyes that could draw you in, a pair of fascinating brows…and lips that promised more sin than anyone could possibly indulge. Those things alone should have been enough. But unfortunately, they weren't. He'd found favor in someone's eyes, because on top of all that, he was so arrestingly male, so strikingly masculine with muscles in all the right places, broad shoulders and perfect abs—and he was tall, at least six-two. He had the ability to take any woman's breath away and increase her pulse rate just by walking into a room.

He'd gotten a lot of feminine attention last night at the wedding rehearsal and was getting a lot of attention now. She noticed several women hovering on the sidelines, waiting for his conversation with Gloria to end so they could take their turn. Honestly, did they have no shame? Apparently not, she thought, noticing that as soon as Gloria moved away, another woman had taken her place.

This time it was Rosa Larimore. The divorcée was one of Shana's friends from college and someone Jules had never cared for. She liked her even less now. The woman had been married twice already, and after eyeing the Granger wealth, was probably contemplating Dalton as a third prospect. Since Rosa was a known man-eater and Dalton a woman-lover, they should be great together. But Jules didn't like the thought of that for some reason.

She frowned. Was that a twinge of jealousy she was feeling? No, it couldn't be. There was no way she would ever succumb to such an emotion for Dalton Granger. The bottom line was that it bothered her when women acted so desperate for a man, wealthy or otherwise. There was absolutely no way she would sink that low. No man was worth it.

Deciding she had been standing in the same spot too long, she was about to turn to go find her father when Dalton suddenly leveled his gaze at her over Rosa's head.

Jules drew in a slow breath. She couldn't stand him, so why did just looking at him make her feel all hot inside? Why had her throat suddenly gone dry? It was as if his gaze were a heated caress, some kind of physical connection that was drawing her to him. She fought the sensations consuming her, sucking her into a sensual abyss. She shouldn't be reacting to him, or any man, this way. It had to do with control, something she liked having; and she refused to let any man take it away from her. Especially a man like Dalton Granger. She knew all about him, including the fact he'd been a cub to numerous cougars while living in Europe. Yet, at the moment, her body didn't care what she knew. It was operating on hormones and a need long overdue. And it was that need that had heat sliding up her spine, making it difficult for her to draw a full breath.

What finally broke the spell was the conceited gleam in the depths of his eyes along with a smirk. The arrogant bastard thought he had her, but she intended to prove otherwise. No man had her, now or ever. She was a woman who didn't tolerate bullshit and, as far as she was concerned, he was full of it.

"You and young Granger are trying to stare each other down again, I see."

Jules blinked and quickly broke eye contact with Dalton to glance up at her father. "Again?"

Ben Bradford smiled down at his youngest daughter. "Yes, I noticed you and him doing the same thing during the wedding ceremony."

Jules wondered if the others had noticed, as well. "The man is simply horrid. Totally despicable. I hope Shana knows what she's doing by marrying into that family."

Ben took a sip of his champagne. "I think your sister knows exactly what she's doing. She loves Jace. He loves her. I'll be a grandpa come spring. I think you're the only one not happy with the match."

Jules moved quickly to correct her father's assumption. "I *am* happy with the match, Dad. I like Jace. He's wonderful and a dream come true for Shana. They were meant for each other."

"Oh. Then it's Jace's brothers you don't like."

She knew her father was toying with her. "Of course I like Caden. Who wouldn't? He's a sweetie pie."

"That leaves Dalton, and I know the whole story involving the two of you."

She didn't say anything, although she was tempted to tell her father he was wrong. He didn't know the whole story, not even half. He only knew what she'd told him, and she had left out a few details he didn't need to know about.

"So where's Mona?" she asked, deciding to change the subject.

"She went to the ladies' room."

Jules raised a brow. "Alone?" Mona, who was legally blind, was the woman her father had been seeing for a few months.

"Yes. Alone. She's very independent."

"Obviously. And she looks beautiful today."

Ben smiled. "I think Mona looks beautiful every day."

Jules nodded. Her widowed father had fallen in love, and he'd made that clear to both her and Shana. He'd also made it clear that he intended to make Mona a permanent part of his life, and that anyone who had a problem with that needed to get over it. Since Shana had easily accepted Mona's role in their father's life, that comment had been mainly directed at Jules, and they both knew it.

"You know what I think, Juliet?"

She knew that line, especially when he referred to her by her full name. Her father was about to point something out to her that she would rather not hear. But she wouldn't dare tell him that. She would do as she'd always done, just grin and bear it. "No, Dad, what do you think?"

"That there's a thin line between love and hate."

She hoped her father wasn't intimating the possibility of something happening between her and Dalton. He was totally wrong if he thought there was a chance that she and Dalton Granger could ever be anything other than enemies. Just in case he was thinking that way, she knew she had to squash that assumption. He was so far from the truth it wasn't funny. "You have it all wrong, Dad, trust me. I wouldn't fall for Dalton Granger if he were the last man on Earth. Even if I were threatened with jail time, I would gladly take a life sentence. I would choose hell over heaven if I thought for one minute that he had already passed through the pearly gates."

Her father didn't say anything; he merely stood and stared at her for a long moment. She could handle his stare as long as it meant he accepted what she said as gospel. She knew he was thinking, giving what she'd said much consideration…a little too much to suit her. When he finally nodded, she released the breath she'd been holding. Had it been anyone other than her father who'd suggested such a thing, she would have given him the tongue-lashing he deserved.

"I can understand why you might assume that," she said, breaking the silence after taking another sip of her drink.

Ben lifted a curious brow. "You do?"

"Yes. You're in love with Mona, and Shana got married today. So, in your mind, love and happiness are ruling the day."

"Possibly," he said, still giving her that in-depth Ben Bradford stare. "Nevertheless, you and Granger need to resolve this issue and make permanent peace."

Permanent peace? She doubted that was possible. In fact, she knew it was highly unlikely. "Why?"

"For your sister's sake."

Jules shook her head. She couldn't see herself doing

it, not even for that reason. "Dad, Shana's fine. Besides, she married Jace, *not* Dalton."

"He's Jace's brother."

"And I'm her sister."

Her father paused a moment then asked, "Do you want to force Shana to take sides?"

"Of course not."

"You are twenty-six, not six. You and Granger need to stop behaving like children and start acting like adults."

She had news for him. Acting like an adult is what had landed her in this mess with Dalton. As a fully grown woman, she'd never been aware of a man the way she was aware of him…and that wasn't good.

"There's Mona. I'll talk to you later," her father said, moving away. "Come to breakfast in the morning," he threw over his shoulder.

Jules watched as he walked swiftly across the room to where Mona Underwood stood. Jules glanced down at her watch, and although she didn't want to, she glanced over to where Dalton was standing and saw him glancing down at his watch, as well. Like her, he was probably counting the minutes before the newly-weds left for their honeymoon so he could split.

Dalton glanced up and snagged her gaze. Jules tilted her head, lifted her chin and regarded him with all the loathing she could muster. The bastard had the nerve to smile. She shook her head in disgust as she turned, deciding to check out the live entertainment. If he wanted to stare, let him stare at her back.

The jazz band sounded great, and everyone appeared lively and festive. She was glad Shana had ditched the idea of a small wedding and had gone all out. She deserved it. Like Jules had told her sister, she wouldn't be the first pregnant bride or the last. Besides, few people knew about her sister's condition, and frankly, it wasn't any of their business.

"Nice band, isn't it?"

Jules froze. She cut her gaze away from the musicians to the man who'd come to stand beside her. The rough, manly texture of his voice grazed her insides, suddenly making her feel so hot that she was tempted to fan herself. His eyes were penetrating, and it felt as if he were looking at her naked. She'd never felt self-conscious about anything she wore; she liked dressing up and showing off her body. Knowing she looked desirable to a man was no big deal to her. But not with this man. She didn't need or want his attention.

"The day is almost over," he added after getting no response from her. His voice had shifted to a smooth yet husky tone, sending shivers up her arm. "We pulled it off, being on our best behavior and all, so I thought I'd come over and say hello."

She was tempted to tell him what he could do with his hello. Instead, she took a sip of her wine to help fight off the sensuous dominance radiating off him. It took every ounce of fortitude she had to hold his gaze, pretending nonchalance when she was so aware of him. Her body's reaction to him made her livid with him as well as with herself. "I can't believe your audacity," she said in a low, cutting tone.

His smile was slow and seductive. "Yeah, I do have balls, don't I?"

Now why did he go there? Her gaze lowered to the area below his well-proportioned waist. He had an incredible masculine build that not only made her speculate about his balls but also about every single inch of him. She snatched her focus back to his face and watched his eyes darken at the same time his mouth spread into one of those *gotcha* smiles. He'd realized what she'd been thinking when her gaze had dropped.

"Look, Dalton," she said in a stern voice, while trying not to make a scene. "In case you haven't figured it out yet, I don't like you."

He chuckled, and instead of irking her, the sound sent a small quiver humming up her spine. "Then that makes us even, Jules, because I don't like you, either."

Although he might not like her, he did want her, Dalton admitted, staring at her with an intensity he hoped she found unnerving. He could envision all the things he would do to her if he ever got the chance. She was the cause of many sleepless nights and the loss of his peace of mind. Even worse, she was stopping him from desiring other women. Whenever he saw Jules, her level of femininity struck a blow to his libido, mainly because what he saw in her was something he would never get.

Bullshit.

He refused to acknowledge she was different from any other woman he saw, wanted and got. He knew women, could read them like a book. Although he would be the first to admit there were a few of Jules's chapters he'd rather skip. The bottom line was that she wanted him, probably just as much as he wanted her. She could pretend otherwise. She could fight it. She could even deny it. But a woman's scent didn't lie. She wore Amarige like no other woman, and the way it mingled with her body's chemistry was so damned mind-blowingly hot, like some aphrodisiac that was drugging him senseless, making him act like a boor when he should be a gentleman. It was revving up his sexual awareness of her, and he was convinced the feeling was mutual.

"Since our total dislike for each other has been established, why are you here, in my face?" she asked, cutting into his thoughts like a sharp knife.

She hadn't seen anything yet, he thought, leaning in closer to that same face, breathing against her ear as if he were about to let her in on a little secret. In a way, he was. "I like riling you, like seeing you flustered and all hot and bothered. I can tell, although you might deny it. I could remedy things easily, to both our liking. I could put smiles on our faces that could last a lifetime. The animosity between us ends here if you come home with me tonight."

There was a brief moment of silence. "Dalton?"

"Yes?" He'd heard a catch in her voice. Why did it have to sound sensuous, so unbearably sexy, causing his breathing to stop as he hung on, waited in lustful anticipation for her response?

"Go fuck yourself."

Those three words had been whispered low but spoken clearly, direct, definitely matter-of-fact, no holds barred. His eyes narrowed as anger ran up his spine. Instinctively, he took a step back, refusing to let what she'd said affect him. And he rejected the idea that the strange tight feeling in the middle of his chest meant anything. Her snubs were becoming commonplace, like oil rolling off his back, because in the end, they would make her capitulation that much sweeter.

He pulled back and smiled down at her, saying with none of the calm he actually felt, "I'd rather do you than myself. Sorry you're missing the opportunity."

She rolled her eyes. "I'm not missing any opportunity, trust me. And—"

The clapping of hands drowned out her next words. They both turned when Jace and Shana appeared holding hands. They had changed into traveling clothes. It was time for them to leave on their honeymoon—two weeks on the beaches in Cape Town, South Africa.

Dalton shifted his gaze from the smiling couple and back to Jules. She was still looking at Jace and Shana with genuine happiness on her face. But he saw beyond her happiness for her sister and his brother. She was clearly not a romantic at heart, and he'd picked up on her cynicism a few times. They thought alike in some ways, and Dalton figured that if given a chance, they would set a bedroom on fire. He would see to it. But there were a few things about Jules he was determined to find out. Unravel. Sink his teeth into. And then he would sink his body into hers. Make her scream. Holler. Bite him a few times. Come unglued and put an end to this shitty attitude she wore like a suit of armor. The thought of taking her on in the bedroom made a tingling sensation spread through him. Right now she was made of ice, and he couldn't wait to see her melt.

"You're a difficult person, Jules Bradford."

She glanced at him, her smile gone. "You're still here? I thought you would have seized the opportunity to leave."

"With my tail tucked between my legs? No woman will ever drive me to such madness."

"Really? And as far as my being a difficult person, I disagree. I just refuse to tolerate bullshit."

He leaned in closer again. "Then I don't understand why we don't get along, since I refuse to tolerate bullshit, either." He straightened and smiled down at her. "See you around, Juliet."

And then he walked away.

Two

"Do you ever get the feeling you're being followed?"

Caden Granger glanced up from the file he was reading and watched his brother Dalton walk into his office to plop down in the chair across from his desk. He figured it was going to be one of those days. When Jace had left for his honeymoon, he had deliberately assigned Dalton projects guaranteed to keep him busy. Now that the two-week honeymoon was over, Jace was back and Dalton…was being Dalton.

"No, can't say that I have," Caden said, leaning back against his chair. "But if you are being followed, it wouldn't surprise me."

Dalton pursed his lips in a hard line. "Why would you say that?"

"Because I'm your brother. I know you. You've probably pissed somebody off. A jealous husband, perhaps?"

Dalton glowered. "I don't do wives, so there shouldn't be any husbands out for blood." He paused a moment and said. "Unless…"

Caden lifted a brow. "Unless what?"

"Nothing."

The single word was spoken too quickly, and Caden

eyed his brother speculatively. "Well, if you're not worried about jealous husbands, then maybe Jules Bradford has put a hit out on you."

The edge of a wry smile appeared on Dalton's lips. "If I haven't put one out on her first."

Caden rolled his eyes. "Seriously?"

Dalton nodded. "Seriously."

"I meant that as a joke."

Dalton shrugged broad shoulders. "Can't say the same."

"Then you have issues. And, from the sound of it, they are rejection issues."

The smile dropped from Dalton's face. "I can handle rejection, Caden. What I can't and won't tolerate is a woman who tries to play me."

"Play you?"

"Yes. Play games with me."

"Is that what she did?"

"Hell, yes. That night she brushed me off, but then told me to find her. So I did. I hired a private investigator to find her, and when I did, she acted all shitty, like my finding her was no big deal, and she didn't want to be bothered when she knew the score. I found her for a reason."

"And that reason?"

Now it was Dalton who rolled his eyes. "Damn it, you know the reason, and she did, too. I found her, and she didn't deliver. Her entire attitude sucked. And then she showed up at that club a second time just to remind me about what I wasn't getting."

Caden didn't say anything for a long moment. He knew his brother. He was still hot behind the collar about an incident that happened a few months ago. Dalton took holding a grudge to a whole other level. Unfortunately, the woman he loathed was Shana's sister.

He drew in a deep breath, glad that Jace was back from his honeymoon and would be coming into the office tomorrow. There was only so much of Dalton that Caden could handle at times. When he, Jace and Dalton had left Charlottesville years ago for college, all three had sworn never to return permanently, only for visits. Having their father charged with their mother's death years earlier had left deep scars. After college, Jace had settled in LA and worked for the state of California as an attorney; Caden had pursued his dream of making it big in the music industry. His love for his saxophone had earned him his first Grammy at twenty-seven. He'd spent most of his time touring the country and playing his sax to sold-out crowds. And as for Dalton, after a stint in the NFL, he left the US for Europe and made a name for himself as a playboy and boy toy. Because of good investment decisions, Dalton was the one who'd become the billionaire. The one who believed a person should work smarter, not harder. And the one who liked to whine about practically anything. Like he was doing right now.

The three of them had returned to Charlottesville when their grandfather, Richard Granger, had suffered a fatal heart attack. What they hadn't counted on was making a deathbed promise to him to take over the family business, Granger Aeronautics. They hadn't expected a failing company, one deep in the red. But they had made the promise and rolled up their sleeves. Hiring Shana's crisis management firm had been the smartest decision they could have made. She'd discovered employees divulging trade secrets and helped expose someone they thought was a family friend as a killer.

"Caden, are you listening to me?"

No, he wasn't really. But he knew he should. This issue Dalton had with Jules wasn't good and could cause lots of problems in the long run. "Yes, I'm listening," he lied. "You were talking about Jules. Let's look at this logically for a moment, Dalton. Have you considered the possibility that when you did find Jules that you came on a little too strong? That maybe you were too focused on what you expected? You probably walked into her office with a hard-on." The look that suddenly appeared on Dalton's face let Caden know he'd guessed correctly.

"So what if I did? Like I said, she knew the score," Dalton countered.

"And you would have taken her right there in her office."

Dalton shrugged unashamedly. "I had no problem doing that. It would have saved time."

Caden shook his head. It was hard to believe the audacity of his brother at times. As the youngest Granger, Dalton had grown up spoiled and pampered…especially by their mother. Things came easily for him, at times too easily. As a result, he often had an air of entitlement about him. "And you assumed she would feel the same way you did?"

"Don't see why not. She did challenge me to find her. Besides, spontaneity is the spice of life, Caden. But I wouldn't expect you to understand that. You've been living in Shilohville for too long."

A smile couldn't help but touch Caden's lips. "And what does Shiloh have to do with this?"

"Admit it. You've loved your wife forever, even when you were kids and didn't know what love was. Granted, the two of you were apart for a few years, thanks to her bastard of a father, but you never hired anyone to find her. You didn't go to bed every night dreaming about what you would do to her when you did. You never—"

"Okay, Dalton, I get the picture, although I don't agree with everything you're saying. No man should expect a woman to put out on their first date. Hell, it wasn't even a *date*. You just showed up at her office. I can just imagine how surprised she was to see you there."

"She should have known I would eventually find her. She should have expected it, and she should have been ready—definitely more accommodating. Instead, she all but gave me her ass to kiss, and for that reason…"

Caden listened as Dalton continued with his tirade; coming out with crap he hoped like hell his brother would regret saying later. One thing was for certain; Jules Bradford had pissed him off big-time, ruffled a few of those manly feathers. He wouldn't be surprised if she had been the first woman to do so, definitely to this degree.

"I happen to like Jules," he broke in to say. When Dalton gave him a look that was sharper than glass, he added, "After all, she did find out who tried to kill me. And it didn't take her much time to do it."

"Fine. Shana's Wonder Woman, your wife is the Wine Lady and Jules is Miss Whirlwind. If she hadn't figured things out, someone else would have."

"Not me, for sure," Caden said, remembering the period of time he was trying like hell to forget.

"Then you owe her. I don't," Dalton said, easing out of the chair.

"Shana's dinner party this weekend should be interesting with both you and Jules there."

Dalton glanced over at Caden. "No, it won't be, because I don't plan to attend."

Caden frowned. "Why?"

"We just discussed it. I tolerated Jules's presence at the rehearsal and the wedding, but I'll be damned if I'll be in the same room with her again when I don't have to."

"But this will be Shana's first dinner party that she'll be hosting as a Granger."

"Won't be her last. Maybe she should have stayed a Bradford."

Caden just stared at Dalton. He knew that although Dalton wouldn't admit it, he liked Shana a lot. And he probably disliked her sister just as much. "At some point, you and Jules need to forget the past and move on. Shana is her sister, and Jace is your brother."

"So?"

"So you're both driving us all crazy. And since she probably dislikes you as much as you dislike her, I can just imagine what Shana is dealing with."

"Not my problem. Like I said, I won't be coming."

"Now that Jace has married Shana, we're all practically family."

"Like hell. That's like saying that now you're married to Wine Lady, your in-laws are family, as well. There's no way Sandra Timmons or Dr. Sedrick Timmons will ever be considered family to me."

Caden didn't say anything for a moment because he was finding it hard to consider them family, too. "I hope that you reconsider coming on Saturday night, Dalton. It would mean a lot to Jace and Shana if you did."

Dalton shoved his hands into the pockets of his slacks. "If they feel that way, then I hate to disappoint them. But I will have to." He glanced at his watch again. "I have a meeting with my security team. I'll see you later." He turned to leave.

"Wait. When you came into my office, you said you thought you were being followed."

Dalton turned back around. "I'm sure I'm just imagining things. Both you and Jace recently came within an inch of losing your lives, so I'm starting to get a little paranoid. And I don't like it worth a damn."

An hour later, Dalton entered his own office at Granger Aeronautics, the company his great-grandfather, Sutton Granger, had founded. He was sure that when the old man had done so, he'd believed he was starting a legacy for all Grangers to follow. And they had for a while. As expected, his grandfather, Richard, had followed in Sutton's footsteps, and Dalton's own father, Sheppard, had done likewise, working beside Richard to build a dynasty to pass on to his three sons—Jace, Caden and Dalton.

There was no doubt in Dalton's mind that things would have continued that way if his mother, Sylvia, hadn't been murdered, and his father arrested for the crime. Jace had been sixteen, Caden fourteen and Dalton only twelve. His mother's death had hit him hard, but his father's imprisonment had been even harder. Neither he nor his brothers believed their father capable of killing their mother, but a jury had found him guilty and sentenced him to thirty years.

Dalton drew in a deep breath. Instead of sitting down at his desk and diving into some of the emails that were mounting up, he walked over to the window and looked out. Nice view, although he thought the ones seen from Jace's and Caden's windows were better. Every once in a while, he enjoyed ribbing them about that.

He stood there a moment, staring out the window and remembering his conversation with Caden. Leave it to Caden to bring out Jules's one redeeming quality. She was a private investigator and was good at her job. So what? Maybe he did owe her for that, just like he owed Shana for her part in saving Jace's life. Shit, he didn't like owing anyone anything. But he did love his brothers, and the thought of anything ever happening to them was too much to think about.

And it was time for him to pay his father a visit. Jace had gone to see him right before the wedding, and Caden had gone just last week. Caden said their father had asked about him. Dalton needed to go before his father got some crazy idea about why he hadn't been visiting.

In a way, Dalton felt guilty. He'd known about his mother's affair with another man, but he'd never told his dad. He'd been only eleven when he'd found out, and Sylvia had sworn him to secrecy. That had been a huge secret for any kid to carry around, but he loved both of his parents. He often wondered whether his parents would have divorced had Dalton told his father about the affair. Then he could have gone his way, and she could have gone hers and…

Dalton shook his head. With those thoughts, one would assume he believed his father was responsible for his mother's death, and that a divorce might have spared her life. That wasn't the case, since he knew his father was innocent, and that he'd already spent fifteen years behind bars for a crime he hadn't committed.

Dalton and his brothers had fulfilled one of their grandfather's deathbed promises, and now it was time for them to take care of the other. They needed to find out who had really killed their mother so their father could finally be freed.

He moved away from the window to sit down at his

desk. The first thing he needed to do was to call Shana and thank her for the invitation to dinner this weekend and let her know he wasn't coming. Knowing Shana, she wouldn't ask why, but she would know the reason. The bottom line was that he didn't have to put up with anyone he didn't want to put up with and, at the moment, her sister topped his list.

A couple of weeks ago at Jace's wedding, he'd considered putting a plan in place to play Jules the same way she'd played him. Although that idea wasn't completely off the table, he didn't want to have anything to do with Jules for the time being.

Go fuck yourself. She had a lot of damned nerve. No woman had dared ever tell him something like that. He knew he needed to get her out of his mind because, honestly, Jules Bradford really wasn't important. What he needed to spend his time doing was concentrating on the important business at hand, namely, Granger Aeronautics, and finding his mother's real killer.

Jace would be back in the office tomorrow, and Dalton intended to meet with both him and Caden to discuss strategies about the latter issue. Getting their dad out of prison was the most important thing on his mind.

Three

Jules slid her car into the first available parking spot in front of the condo where Dalton lived. She called herself all kinds of fool for being here, even though she knew it was necessary if she wanted to talk to Dalton. He'd never answer his phone if he saw her name on the caller ID. "It's not about you," she muttered to herself. "It's about your love for Shana—that's the only thing that could make you even think about putting up with this bullshit."

She and Shana were two years apart and had always had a close relationship. Shana had been just months from turning fifteen and Jules thirteen when their mother had died of pancreatic cancer thirteen years ago. Their father had raised them alone while working as a police detective in Boston. He had retired a few years ago, wanting a quiet life, and had decided to settle in Charlottesville, the place where he and his wife had met while attending college. Jules had been the first to follow their father to Charlottesville, where she established a private investigation firm. Shana had relocated to Charlottesville a few years later.

The three of them always managed to do things together, even when Jules's busy work schedule took her out of town, as it often did. But things were somewhat different now. Shana was married, and Jace was now the main planet in her universe, which meant he would be taking up a lot of her sister's time. And Ben was involved with Mona, something Jules knew she had to get used to. Mona was the first woman her father had been seriously involved with since her mother died, and he rightly deserved to be happy.

She had called Shana earlier today to welcome her back to town and to find out how the honeymoon had gone…like it would have been anything but great. During the conversation, Shana reminded her about Saturday night, which would be the first dinner party she would give as Jace's wife. Shana was excited but somewhat disappointed, because she had gotten a call from Dalton saying he wouldn't be coming. No one had to figure out the reason behind that decision.

What Jules loved most about her big sister was that at no time did she try to make her feel guilty because Jace's brother wanted to act like an ass. Shana knew the whole story, from start to finish, and refused to take sides. In fact, she wouldn't give her opinion one way or the other, even when Jules had asked for it.

But still, Jules knew that Dalton's refusal to come to dinner was a letdown, although Shana tried not to show it. Her sister didn't deserve that. She deserved better than having Dalton Granger as a brother-in-law.

And Jules felt that she herself deserved better than having to come here, seeking him out to talk about it. Why she was even wasting her time, she wasn't sure. History had shown on more than one occasion the man had a one-track mind. He had this entitlement complex that needed to be knocked down more than a few notches. All they ever did when they were within five feet of each other was argue. Dalton Granger brought out the worst in her. Most of the time, intentionally. But at least she could try to convince him that it wasn't about him and her, but about Jace and Shana. They didn't need their siblings on the warpath. For Jace's and Shana's sakes, they should try to at least be civil to each other. They'd almost succeeded during the wedding weekend. Had almost made it to the end, but of course, he'd felt the need to rattle her, piss her off bigtime. And what made her even madder was that she'd let him. Why did he have the ability to get under her skin?

She killed the ignition of her car and sat there a moment. She didn't see him or that red two-seater sports car he drove around town. But she felt something. The air surrounding her seemed to be spiked with intensity. Maybe it had something to do with the fact that she was invading his space. And now it seemed as if his space were invading her.

How could that indescribable masculine aura that seemed to cling to him surround her now, even when he was nowhere to be seen? But it didn't take much to remember how he'd looked at the wedding. The visual suddenly shot heat up the full length of her spine, making her hot inside.

Jules refused to believe her sudden rise in body temperature had anything to do with Dalton. After all, he was just a man. But she would admit he had this predator side that was powerful at times, almost overwhelming. Of course, she staunchly refused to let that happen, although the very idea sent a shiver through her body. That quiver prompted her to turn the car's ignition back on to generate some heat. It was October, and there was a definite chill in the air. Everyone had begun wearing overcoats weeks ago and was anticipating the season's first snowstorm before the end of the month.

She glanced at her watch. It was almost ten on a weeknight. It was too much to assume that Dalton, like most normal people who worked the next day, would have the sense to be home at this hour. But then, he had a reputation of being a party animal. He'd definitely left his mark on the women over in Europe. She'd done her research and knew that he preferred older women. He'd had no problem being their boy toy.

But to give him credit…something she didn't like doing…he'd been smart enough to capitalize on his money by investing wisely. He'd become a billionaire without the Granger name or money. He'd done so in his own right. If it had been any other man, she would admire him for achieving such brilliant success. But since it was Dalton, hell would freeze over before she held him in high esteem for anything.

Deciding she would leave if he didn't come home in the next ten minutes or so, she relaxed her head against the headrest and stretched out her legs as far as they could comfortably go while glancing out the car's window at her surroundings. This was a pretty exclusive section of Charlottesville, not too far from town. After seeing the Granger estate at Sutton Hills, she could understand his choice—when you were used to wealth, why settle for anything less? Although his condo wasn't in a gated community, it still had that old-money, country-club feel all wrapped in modern architecture. Even the streetlamps spelled prestige with their intricate, wrought-iron design. Although it was dark, the landscape lighting revealed a luxurious building with immaculately manicured grounds.

Of their own accord, her thoughts shifted to Dalton

and the last time she'd seen him at the wedding, a little over two weeks ago. She would admit, but only to herself, that she'd been aware of every single thing about him, every fine line and manly curve. Then there had been the way he'd stared at her with so much heated lust she'd felt exposed, vulnerable and so unbearably hot that when she'd gotten home she'd stripped off every inch of her clothing and taken a cold shower.

After wrapping up her last case, she'd decided that for the remainder of the year she would take it easy and stick around home, refusing new cases until after the holidays. But now she was considering doing the opposite just to get as far away from Charlottesville as she could. And all because of one man.

The thought that Dalton Granger could make her run sent anger flowing through her limbs. Why was she aware of him in a way she'd never been aware of any other man? Why did he have the ability to creep into her dreams at night, engaging her in all kinds of kinky acts? Even now, she could feel a line of heat licking across her skin, thinking about some of them.

She drew in a deep breath. Lately, her arsenal of sex toys wasn't doing a damned thing for her. It was time to call in the big guns, the real guns. Her personal little red book, which she hadn't used in months, was tucked in the bottom drawer of her nightstand. It was time to pull it out and flip through the pages. Most single people had little black books, but hers was red. Intentionally. It meant danger. Fire. Heat. The first name from the book that popped into her mind was Ray Ford. She wondered if he was still in town. Last time they'd talked…around this time last year…he was thinking about relocating to Baltimore to be closer to his little girl. At the time she'd only smiled, thinking that, in truth, it was probably his ex-wife he wanted to be close to. No harm there, and if that was the case she hoped they had reconciled and remarried.

Jules was about to consider another name in her little red book when she saw headlights approaching. It was easy to tell they were from a sports car. A sudden, low heat began spreading in her belly, and she frowned. Why was Dalton an ache even when he was a good twenty feet or more away, tucked safely inside his own vehicle? Just the thought of him approaching was making her body feel some pretty weird stuff, and that wasn't good. Maybe this wasn't the best night to have any type of conversation with him, after all. Tomorrow would be better, perhaps, when she could get control of her senses. Or maybe *after* she'd gotten laid.

As she watched his car turn into the condo complex, she knew excuses wouldn't work. She was here and fired up to talk, and she wouldn't back down. She needed to say what she wanted to say now, whether he wanted to hear it or not. She could handle this. She could handle him.

But as she watched him open his car door to get out, one leg at a time, and saw how each powerfully built thigh eased from the red two-seater, her throat suddenly went dry. And got even drier when he began walking toward his front door with that sensuous strut he could do so well, full of cool sophistication and overflowing with sexiness. He was wearing an Armani suit, and there was that air of natural confidence and casual arrogance that he exuded like no other man she knew. It turned her on when it should be turning her off. It was at times like these when she really got frustrated with herself. The very thought that her body would respond to anything about him was totally exasperating.

And here she was, outside his house, sitting in her car, determined to follow through with her mission to set the tone for a peaceful truce. She despised him; that couldn't be helped, nor would it ever change. But for her sister and his brother, they could at least tolerate each other during those few times they were in each other's company. She was willing to make the sacrifice and hoped he would be, too.

Knowing she needed to get it over with, confront Dalton and have her say, Jules was about to unbuckle her seat belt when she noticed a car pull up, a black sedan with tinted windows. Its approach was timed perfectly to when Dalton reached his door, opened it and went inside his condo. Only then did the driver slide the vehicle into a parking spot that provided a perfect view of Dalton's front door. Maybe the driver lived in the complex, as well, but she had a gut feeling that something wasn't right…so she waited.

When the driver of the vehicle killed his engine and didn't make a move to get out of the car, she knew Dalton had been followed. Jules had been on enough investigations to recognize a tail when she saw one. Why had someone followed Dalton home just to sit there parked? Watching? Waiting?

She knew all about the Grangers' background. About how their father, Sheppard Granger, was in prison serving time for killing their mother, although all three sons were adamant he was innocent. Just over a month ago someone had kidnapped Jace and was intent on killing him—not to mention that it was only a few weeks ago that someone had tried to run Caden down and kill him, as well. All were unrelated incidents but with the same purpose. Based on these facts, the idea that someone was following Dalton was highly suspicious.

And why should she care? He was definitely not her favorite person, and if someone had it in for him, then that person could stand in line behind her. But in reality, she knew there was logic and there was reason, and her mind couldn't separate the two. Despite how she felt about him, if Dalton was in any kind of danger, she had to react. She blamed it on her days of being a cop, when protecting someone's life had been her calling.

On instinct, she scanned her surroundings, this time with a different eye. If she got out of her car, whoever had followed Dalton would see her. That meant she couldn't circle around on foot and catch the person off guard. She didn't know if she was dealing with a man or a woman. All she knew was that not only had the person followed Dalton home, but also it seemed as if he had Dalton under surveillance and was settled in for the night. She knew she was right a short while later when Dalton had turned off all the lights, yet the vehicle did not move. Did the driver assume Dalton would be leaving again to go elsewhere?

Jules glanced at her watch. Although she had no earthly idea about Dalton's social calendar, it was after eleven. Most people who worked the next day would be settled in for the night. But then, she wasn't dealing with most people. She was dealing with Dalton Granger, who thought his single status and good looks gave him the right to any woman he wanted. The man who frequented nightclubs to pick up women, regardless of the day of the week or the time of day. The same man who could make her see red faster than any man she knew.

She scanned up and down the street again. Her car windows were tinted, but if the driver of the vehicle was observant, he would have noticed her car was running. It wouldn't take long for him to begin wondering the same thing about her that she was wondering about him. Why was she just sitting in a car and not getting out?

Jules nibbled on her bottom lip as she came up with a plan, one that could expose the person who'd followed Dalton home. Reaching under her seat, she retrieved her gun. Once she had her loaded Glock securely in her hand, she tucked it inside the inner pocket of her coat. Now she was ready to handle business. She would pretend to be one of Dalton's late-night visitors. For Dalton, that would definitely be believable. After quickly apprising him of the situation, she would leave his condo through a back entrance. That way, she could circle around the building and catch the person in the black car by surprise.

Dalton hugged the pillow to his head to drown out the insistent ringing of his doorbell. What the hell? He'd been in the middle of the most sinfully erotic dream and didn't appreciate having it come to an end. Who in their right mind would be at his door at this time of night?

He hoped Jace and Shana hadn't had their first big fight so Jace wanted to sleep on his sofa. That wouldn't be happening, so he might as well take his ass over to Sutton Hills. Dalton would love to be there when his brother explained to their long-time housekeeper, Hannah, why he was back already.

But then, it might not be Jace. It could very well be Caden at his door, Dalton thought, angrily getting out of bed and grabbing his robe. Then Caden's ass could go to Sutton Hills, as well. Nobody told them to get married, and he wasn't running a damned boarding house.

When he reached his front door, he peered through the peephole and blinked. Jules Bradford? Shit, he must be seeing things. There was no way the very woman he'd been dreaming about moments earlier was standing outside on his doorstep. He looked through the peep-hole again. Miss Whirlwind? She wasn't an illusion. His porch light was clearly shining on her.

He cautiously opened the door, and the moment he did, she threw herself in his arms and whispered, "Pretend you're kissing me."

That request earned a brazen chuckle from deep in his throat. *Why pretend?* Unable to resist, he pulled her into his arms, lowered his mouth to hers and used his foot to slam the door shut behind her.

Four

Jules heard a throaty growl just seconds before Dalton's mouth connected with hers. She had been about to push him away, but that was before his tongue had tangled with hers, before his scent had filled her nostrils, before she could feel the brush of his fingertips across the side of her neck.

This kiss was only supposed to be pretend. So why were they locking lips? Why had that greedy sigh slid from her throat, and why on Earth was she kissing him back? It might have everything to do with the way his tongue was dominating hers, stroking it into submission while sending erogenous shivers through her body. What kind of kiss had the ability to do that?

Before she could answer, he shifted his body and she felt him, even through her leather coat. His hard thighs definitely had an erection between them, and that erection was sending one hell of a need spiraling through every part of her body, making their mouths devour each other even more greedily.

Pangs of sensual hunger shot through her at the same time a powerful rush of emotions thrust her into deeper submission. It would not have been so bad if she hadn't spent the past three months dreaming about kissing him, fantasizing about how he tasted, how he would use his tongue. She'd imagined his manly scent was imbued into his skin, and she knew the only way to find out would be to taste him. The thought of her tongue coming into contact with his flesh sent sensuous shivers escalating all through her. This was her punishment for allowing him to invade her dreams at night. Now that she was sampling what she'd fantasized about, she was finding it hard to regain control.

He sank his mouth deeper into hers, and before she could wonder how he'd managed to do such a thing, she heard herself purr. *Purr?* No man had ever made her purr.

The kiss suddenly ended, and she felt herself swept off her feet into strong arms. He stared down at her with eyes glistening with lust, and his mouth curved into a sexy smile. "I figured you'd come to me sooner or later, when horniness got the best of you," he said before leaning down to take her mouth again.

This time she did have the sense to push him away and quickly scrambled out of his arms. "I told you to *pretend* to kiss me, you ass." She was tempted to lick her lips but refused to give him the satisfaction.

Before she could blink, he had her body pinned to the door, holding her arms above her head. How had that happened? Her reflexes were normally good, right on point. His move had been too swift and had caught her off guard. She could lift her leg and knee him in the balls but, for some reason, damaging him there was something she just couldn't make herself do, especially after coming into contact with such a robust erection.

He was glaring down at her with eyes filled with anger. "I don't know why you showed up here at this hour, Jules, with a fucking request about pretending to kiss you, but I'm warning you of two things. Never call me an ass again, and never ever tell me to go fuck myself."

She glared back. "And if I do?"

He leaned in, his face just inches from hers. "It would be a real shame, since that beautiful mouth should be used in far more interesting ways than saying unladylike things. I'd love to let you try it out on me." He grinned, a little of the predator showing through, but well in check.

She drew in a deep breath while slowly raising her knee, deciding maybe she should shove him in the balls, after all. "And I wouldn't do that, if I were you," he warned. "I happen to like my jewels and would retaliate if any harm came to them."

However, to be on the safe side, he released her and took a step back as piercing dark eyes stared up at him. "So if you aren't here to give me the one thing I want from you, then why are you here?"

His question made her remember why she was here, and she pulled the Glock from inside her coat.

"Damn! Why do you have a gun?" he asked, backing up even more. "This anomisity between us isn't that serious. Let's talk about it."

"I don't have a lot of time to explain things, Dalton. I need to use the back entrance to your place and—"

"What the hell is going on?"

Already, her eyes were scanning his condo. It was as elegant on the inside as it was on the outside. She spotted the kitchen and moved toward it. "Can't talk now. I'll fill you in later."

He blocked her path. "Like hell you will. You can't show up at my place at almost midnight, ask me to pretend to kiss you, pull out a gun and then ask to see my back door."

She had to agree the situation did seem weird. "You've been followed."

"What?"

"I said, you were followed tonight."

Penetrating eyes stared down at her, and she had to fight against just how achingly handsome he was standing there in his silk bathrobe. She couldn't help wondering if he had any clothing on underneath it.

"I was followed?"

"Yes."

"And you know this how?" he asked, crossing powerful arms over his chest, making his robe rise a little, exposing powerful legs, hard thighs and an erection that hadn't gone down.

"I was parked outside, waiting for you to come home." When she saw a semblance of heat flare in his eyes, she decided to explain herself before he thought the wrong thing. "Shana mentioned earlier today that you weren't coming to her dinner party Saturday night. It didn't take a rocket scientist to figure out why. So I felt the two of us needed to discuss it."

"There's nothing to discuss. If you were going to be there, then I wasn't. Now back to the part about why you thought I was followed."

She was about to call him an ass again but remembered his warning. "I'm a PI, Dalton. I can recognize a tail. In fact, the person is still parked out there. I plan to go out through your back door and catch him by surprise."

Her story sounded too far-fetched to have been made up. *He'd been followed?* Hadn't he been getting an eerie feeling about that lately? He stared at her. "You sure?"

"Positive. Now I need to—"

"Wait."

"Like hell I'll wait, and don't suggest we call the police," she said. "I used to be a cop. I can handle this."

From the way she was handling that Glock, he believed her. But still, if someone was out there, it might be a foe of the USN, the United Security Network. A few years ago, he'd worked as an agent for the United States Government while living in Europe. No one knew…except for Lady Victoria Bowman, one of his former lovers, but his secret was safe with her. His brothers didn't even know of his involvement with the USN, and his identity and role in the agency was never to be revealed. But what if it had been?

"I need to get dressed," he said, moving toward his bedroom. "Your assumption that I was followed might be a misunderstanding."

"Why?"

Jules was asking too many damned questions. "Just sit tight for a second. If the person is just sitting there, that means he won't be going anywhere." He closed his bedroom door behind him and quickly began dialing a number he'd hoped he had no reason to ever call again.

A gruff voice came on the line. "It's late, Granger."

"That's too fucking bad. I was followed tonight," Dalton said, tossing off his robe and grabbing a pair of jeans and shirt from his closet.

There was a pause, and the voice that asked the next question was now alert, attentive. "You're sure?"

"Yes, I'm sure."

"Okay. Give me less than five and I'll call you back."

"All right." Dalton hung up the phone. He finished dressing and was slipping into his shoes when he got a call back…in less than five. "Okay, what's the deal?" he asked.

"Nothing on our end. If you're being followed, it has nothing to do with us."

Dalton wasn't sure whether he should feel relieved or exasperated.

"You must have pissed someone off, Granger."

The only person he knew he'd pissed off was presently standing in his living room. "Possibly."

"Take my advice. Find out what's going on and deal with it before it deals with you. If you need me for anything, let me know."

He nodded. "Okay. Thanks." He then opened the drawer to his nightstand and pulled out his own pistol. A Glock that was just as impressive as the one Jules had. He tucked it inside his jeans as he left his bedroom. Entering the living room, he found her pacing the floor. Even when pacing she had that sexy walk that could make his entire body go hard. He tried not to focus on how good she looked in her black leather trench coat and matching boots. The belt enhanced her small waistline. It didn't take much to remember how she'd looked the two times he'd seen her at that nightclub. He knew how her clothes fit beneath that coat and was tempted to forget whoever was following him, cross the room and strip every stitch of clothing off her body.

She turned around and glared when she saw his gun. "What do you think you're doing?"

"What does it look like? You got your gun, I got mine."

She rolled her eyes. "This is not show and tell. Do you even know how to use that thing?"

"Probably just as well as you."

He could tell that his boast had her curious. "If that's true, then you have some explaining to do."

Thinking he'd said enough, possibly too much, he turned toward the kitchen. "Let's go. I hope you're not making this shit up."

"Why would I do that?"

"Just to find an excuse to make a booty call. You did let me kiss you."

"I told you to pretend. You took advantage of me," she snapped.

"And at what point did you tell me to stop? You could have pushed me away. Bitten my tongue. Scratched my face. But you did none of those things, which leads me to believe you wanted to be kissed."

"Like hell."

"I'd like to think I gave you a little bit of heaven, instead."

Ignoring her curse words, he moved toward his back door. Instead of concentrating on the potential danger outside, he was thinking about their kiss. Why had she tasted so damned good? And her womanly scent had only intensified his desire for her.

"Look, Dalton. Just stay back and let me handle this," she said, quickly moving in front of him.

"If the person was following me, then I want to know who it is and why. We expose him together or not at all."

"Fine," she snapped. "We've wasted enough time already. Just follow my lead."

"Whatever," he drawled, holding the door open.

She slid out the door into the darkness. A quick glance over her shoulder indicated he was right there, close behind. A little too close for comfort, especially when she could feel his heat through her coat.

And like hers, his gun was drawn and ready.

* * *

"Stonewall, I told you that Bobby is handling things, so relax."

Stonewall Courson paused from pacing in front of Roland Summers's desk. Roland was the owner of Summers Security Firm where Stonewall had worked off and on for the past ten years. Although Roland was his boss, he was also a good friend. "I just have a gut feeling that something isn't right."

Almost a month ago, Stonewall and his friends Quasar Patterson and Striker Jennings had taken on the duties of undercover bodyguards for the sons of Sheppard Granger, a man whom they'd met while serving time in prison. Shep had quickly become more than just a fellow inmate to the three of them. He had become the father they'd never had, a role model they could look up to and a mentor they admired. So when word got out that his sons needed protection, Stonewall, Quasar and Striker had volunteered for the job. The hard part was making sure no one knew, not even the sons themselves.

Quasar Patterson, who was in charge of protecting Jace, the oldest Granger son, was still bragging about the two weeks he'd spent in South Africa, although he did say Jace and his wife stayed inside their hotel room most of the time. After all, they had been on their honeymoon. And Striker Jennings was protecting Caden, although nothing was happening there, either. At least not since the attempt on Caden's life last month. According to Striker, Caden had settled into his wife's place over her wine boutique, and when they weren't working, the couple preferred staying inside most of the time.

Stonewall had been assigned to Shep's youngest son, Dalton. He was the real challenge, since Dalton was a party animal who liked frequenting the clubs. He liked women. At times had a restless soul and would eliminate fidgeting by driving that sports car, sometimes breaking the speed limit, on the interstate during the middle of the night when most police officers were somewhere getting their fill of donuts and coffee.

Tonight had been Stonewall's grandmother's seventieth birthday, and his sister had thrown a private party at a local restaurant. She'd threatened to do him bodily harm if he didn't show up. He'd been replaced tonight with Bobby Turner. It wasn't that Bobby wasn't good or dependable, but he was young and not as experienced.

"Your gut feeling is probably nothing more than exhaustion, Stonewall. You, Quasar and Striker have been protecting Shep's sons for over a month now with barely a break."

Stonewall remembered when they'd begun. It was right after Sheppard Granger had received a mysterious email on the prison computer, warning him that his three sons' lives were in danger. He'd told his attorney, Carson Boyett, to hire bodyguards, and she'd called Roland. Since Roland, who'd also been an inmate in jail with them at one time, had known of their relationship with Shep, he had mentioned it to them, and they'd readily taken the job.

"You could be right," Stonewall said, sliding into the chair across from Roland's desk. "But I'd rather not leave just yet. Think I'll grab a few hours of sleep downstairs."

Roland had a cot room for any of his men who needed power naps between jobs. "Okay. You aren't scheduled to switch off with Bobby until the morning. But if it makes you feel better, I'll check with Bobby to see how things are going," Roland said, picking up the phone.

Bobby answered on the first ring, and Roland placed the call on speaker. "Got Stonewall here. We just want to know how your night is going."

"Boring as shit," Bobby replied. "The best part was trying to keep up with him on the expressway and not be seen. He finally decided to call it a night, thank goodness. However, I did notice a car parked across the street with the engine running when we pulled up. I planned to check it out but didn't have to."

"Why?" Roland asked. "Did the person drive off?"

"No, it was a woman making a booty call to Granger."

Stonewall frowned as he eased up out of his chair. "How do you know that's what she was doing?"

"Because he opened the door for her and before she could get inside he was shoving his tongue down her throat." Bobby chuckled.

Stonewall shook his head. "During all my time guarding Dalton Granger, there's never been a woman to show up at his place."

"Then she must be hot enough to earn an invitation," Bobby countered. "Even though she was wearing a coat, I could tell she's hot. Besides, there's a first time for everything, and like I said, she didn't force her way inside. From what I saw, he was already kissing her before the door slammed shut."

"I don't like it. Is she still there?" Stonewall asked, beginning to pace again.

"Yep. And she probably won't be leaving for a while yet. I figured after giving his living room a good work-out they'll head for the bedroom and—"

Suddenly, a commotion and loud voices could be heard in the background. A woman was shouting an order to Bobby, "Get out of the car. Now!"

Roland glanced over at Stonewall, who was already rushing toward the door. "I'll call Carson on the way there. She'll want to know about this," he said, grabbing his gun from the top desk drawer and quickly following Stonewall.

Five

Bobby Turner found it hard to think with two Glocks staring him in the face. What the hell happened? How had his cover been blown? And from the questions the two were firing at him, it had been blown to smithereens. He recognized the man as Dalton Granger, the person he was supposed to be protecting. However, he had no idea who the woman was, other than the one he'd assumed had been making a booty call.

"You have two seconds to tell me who you are and why you were following me," Dalton snarled, eyes locked on Bobby.

Two seconds? He had to be kidding, Bobby thought, sweating profusely. When Dalton inched the gun closer, aiming right between his eyes, Bobby knew he wasn't kidding, after all. "I wasn't following you," he stammered, barely able to get the words out. He hoped Roland and Stonewall had figured out what was going on. At twenty-four, he was too young to die, and from the look in Granger's eyes, he was as good as dead.

"I told you to let me handle this, Dalton," the woman snapped.

Not taking his eyes off Bobby, Granger snapped back, "I can take care of my own business."

"Ha!" The woman gave a snorted laugh. "You didn't even know you'd been followed until I told you."

Bobby watched Granger's jaw tighten. Evidently, he hadn't liked being reminded of that. "Whatever." Dalton's features hardened even more at Bobby. "Are you going to answer my question? Why were you following me?"

Bobby knew he had to think fast. "I wasn't following you. My name is Bobby, and I have a girlfriend who lives in one of these condos. I was just sitting here keeping a watch out for her." He'd given his real first name just in case they asked to see his driver's license.

"Then you're a stalker," the woman accused, inching her gun closer to his forehead.

"No, I'm not a stalker. Just a concerned boyfriend." He knew his story sounded as unbelievable as shit, but for the time being, he was sticking to it.

"What's her name?" Dalton threw the question out at him.

Bobby frowned. "Whose name?"

"Your girlfriend. I want to validate your story."

Bobby rolled his eyes as best he could with two Glocks pointed at him. "Come on, man. You think you know every person who lives around here?"

The woman snorted. "If she's a female, he probably knows her."

Bobby watched Dalton switch his gaze to glare over at the woman. "I told you I had this, Jules, so go home."

"Like hell I will."

Bobby drew in a deep breath. Were these the same two he'd seen kissing earlier? Evidently, they'd never made it to the bedroom.

"I can put you in your car, you know," Dalton snarled over at the woman he'd called Jules.

She lifted her chin. "I'd like to see you try."

Bobby's heart missed a beat. Were they actually standing here having a heated argument while holding guns on him? What if one of their fingers slipped and the gun accidentally fired? Shit. People would be reading about his dead ass in the papers tomorrow morning.

"Excuse me."

Both Dalton and Jules stopped glaring at each other long enough to turn their attention back to him, snapping simultaneously, "What?"

"If you don't believe me, then I suggest you call the police," Bobby said, hoping they wouldn't take his suggestion. "At the moment, I'd feel safer in their hands than yours."

"We couldn't care less how you feel," Dalton snapped angrily. "If you have a girlfriend who lives around here, then give me a name or tell me why you were following me."

"I can answer that for you, Mr. Granger."

Dalton jerked around at the sound of the feminine voice to find a woman standing within ten feet of them with two big guys by her side. Where the hell had they come from? He quickly switched his aim from the man who'd claimed his name was Bobby to the trio, grateful Jules had taken stock of the situation, as well, and, like him, wasn't taking any chances. She kept her gun aimed directly on Bobby while he kept his leveled on the three.

"And just what can you tell me, Ms....?"

"Boyett," she said easily. "Carson Boyett."

Dalton frowned. Where had he heard that name before? He tossed the question around in his mind a few times, and then he remembered. It had come up during a conversation he'd had earlier that day with Jace and Caden. They had been discussing how to go about getting their father freed from jail. Jace had mentioned a man by the name of Carson Boyett...but this was no man. This was a very attractive woman.

"Wait a minute," he said slowly, staring at her. "Carson Boyett is..." He found it hard to get the words out as it hit him just who she was. She took pity on him and completed what he was hesitant to say.

"Sheppard Granger's attorney."

He lowered his gun. Shocked. "But we...my brothers and I assumed you were a man."

She chuckled softly. "But, as you can see, that's not the case."

"Hey, not so fast," Jules spoke up, operating on the side of caution. She glared at Dalton, not surprised he was being taken in by a pretty face. "Let's see some ID. Now!"

Carson Boyett nodded as a wry smile touched her lips. "You're cautious. I like that. I'm going to need to stick my hand into the pocket of my jacket to get it."

"Fine. I suggest you do it slowly and easily, or Bobby here won't live to see tomorrow." Jules inched her gun closer to Bobby's skull. "And I'm warning the two of you," she said to the men standing beside Carson. "I suggest you not try any funny business, either."

If Dalton didn't find it odd that his father's attorney had two large, muscled men in tow, Jules certainly did. And what woman looked this put together in the middle of the night? Not a hair on Carson Boyett's head was out of place. She was wearing a business suit and was well dressed, neat as a pin. It was cold outside, but she wasn't wearing a coat. Jules wondered if that was intentional to show her toughness, her ability to endure what others might find grueling.

She figured the woman's age to be in her midforties, if that. Out of her peripheral vision, she saw that Dalton was checking the woman out, as well…but probably for entirely different reasons.

Annoyed, she leaned over to him and whispered, "I heard you had a thing for older women, but need I remind you that something serious is going on here?"

He had the nerve to chuckle. "Jealous?" he whispered back.

"Hardly."

"Here you are," Carson said, breaking into their private conversation, moving forward slowly and reaching out to hand her driver's license to Dalton.

He took it and scanned it a moment before handing it to Jules. "And who are these men with you?" Dalton wanted to know, feeling comfortable enough that he tucked his gun back inside his jeans.

Carson hesitated a minute before answering. "Roland Summers on my right and Stonewall Courson on my left. They are friends."

Jules, who hadn't reached that level of ease with them, kept her gun aimed on Bobby. "Friends?" she asked with a chuckle, while rolling her eyes. "Surely you can do better than that. Why would *friends* be hanging out at this time of night?"

A smile touched Carson's lips. "I could ask the two of you the same thing."

Dalton snorted. "Trust me. We *aren't* friends."

"They most certainly aren't," Bobby chimed in rather loudly.

Jules glared as she finally lowered her gun, ignoring Bobby's deep sigh of relief. "You claim you can explain why this guy was following Dalton." She decided they needed to stick to the business at hand.

"Yes, I can explain," Carson said calmly. "But I think it would be best if we go inside. And although it's rather late, I believe Jace and Caden Granger should be included in this conversation, as well."

Six

Dalton opened the door to find his brothers standing there...with their wives. He knew Jace and Caden had questions and wanted answers. When he'd called, the only thing he'd said was that he'd been followed that night and that their father's attorney was going to explain why. He wanted them to get their asses over to his place as soon as possible. That had been less than twenty minutes ago, so they'd made good time.

"Come on in," he said, stepping aside. "Boyett will explain everything."

Being the gentlemen they were, of course, his brothers stood back to let their wives enter first. That gave Dalton a chance to pull Jace and Caden aside. "Why are Wonder Woman and Wine Lady here? What Boyett has to say might be private."

Jace rolled his eyes. "Privacy is not an issue when it comes to our wives, Dalton. They're now part of this family, so get over it."

Dalton drew in a deep breath. He *was* over it, since being married was what they'd undoubtedly wanted. But he hadn't gotten used to having additional players in their family business, especially when it concerned their father. Hell, he'd tried sending Jules home, but she had refused to leave. Since she was the one who'd nailed the fact he'd been followed, he had allowed her to stay.

"Jules? You're here?" he heard Shana ask her sister, surprised.

From the look on his brothers' faces, they were surprised, as well. Caden leaned in to whisper, "You questioned us about bringing our wives, yet Jules is here? A woman you claim you can't stand?"

Dalton frowned. "She's not here by choice, trust me. And I can't stand her. Nothing has changed."

"Then why is she here?" Jace asked with a speculative look on his face.

"Not for the reasons you think. All of your questions will be answered soon, so come on and join the club." He couldn't wait to see the expressions on his brothers' faces when they discovered that Carson Boyett was a woman.

Dalton quickly moved to stand in the center of his living room. Deciding not to delay the introductions, he said, "Everyone, I'd like you to meet Roland Summers, Stonewall Courson, Carson Boyett and Bobby Turner. As you know, Carson is Dad's attorney and has information to share with us."

His brothers and their wives glanced at the three men expectantly, having assumed that Bobby Turner was the female. Dalton couldn't help but chuckle when Carson moved forward and presented her hand to Jace. "I'm glad we're finally meeting. Your father speaks highly of his sons."

The shock on their faces was priceless. "You're Carson Boyett?" Jace asked, stunned. "Dad never said you were a woman."

"That must be true since Dalton had the same reaction," Carson said, grinning. "You'll need to mention that to Sheppard next time you see him."

"He fired his former attorney, Jess Washington," Caden said, eyeing Carson curiously. "He never said why. Granddad didn't, either."

Carson nodded. "Yes, he felt Washington didn't do a good job representing him at the trial. And now he's wondering whether it was intentional, since Vidal Duncan was the one who recommended Washington."

Jace shrugged. "Duncan recommended Shana," he said, smiling over at his wife. "And she worked out just great for Granger Aeronautics."

"Yes, but he had an ulterior motive in making sure that I did," Shana reminded her husband.

Caden glanced over at the other three men. "So who are you three?"

"They're friends of mine," Carson said. "They are also friends of your father."

Dalton frowned. "Since when?"

Roland chuckled. "I've known your father since Carson became his attorney. He was going into the slammer just as I was getting out, so our paths never crossed."

"You served time in jail?" Caden asked, beating Dalton to the punch.

"Yes. We all have."

"Not me," Bobby Turner spoke up proudly. "My record's clean."

"Yes, Bobby, it is, and we want to make sure it stays that way," Roland replied.

"You met Dad through Carson, too?" Dalton asked the man called Stonewall. There was something about him that reminded Dalton of several agents he'd worked with while in the USN. Stonewall had very little to say, but Dalton knew not to take his silence lightly. He'd been sizing things up, and in a way, that made Dalton a little uncomfortable. He looked like the type of man you wouldn't want to cross. Although Roland Summers wasn't a small man, either; Stonewall stood at least an inch or two over him. And although both were muscular compared to Bobby's slim frame, Stonewall looked a lot more edgy—dangerous and threatening.

"No, I met Shep when we served time together at Glenworth," Stonewall said.

"You were at Glenworth?" Jace asked, studying the man.

"Yes."

"Why?" Dalton asked, as if he had a right to know. He knew Glenworth Penitentiary, the prison where his father had served time for ten years before being sent to Delvers Prison. It wasn't an Alcatraz but was known to house hardened criminals, those locked up for long periods of time and considered a definite menace to society, like murderers, bank robbers and habitual offenders. Dalton wondered which category Stonewall fell in.

Stonewall crossed his arms over his chest. "Doesn't matter why I was there. Thanks to Shep, I'm no longer a convict," he said in a voice that sounded as dangerous as he looked.

"Dad got you out?" Caden asked.

Stonewall's lips curved at the corners. It was a smile that nobody saw coming. "In a manner of speaking. He kept me out of trouble. Without Shep at Glenworth, there's no doubt in my mind I would have killed several guards and inmates by now."

Shit! What sort of men had Dad associated with while at Glenworth? Dalton knew all about his father's ten years at Glenworth and that Sheppard Granger had been a model prisoner. Hell, he'd even started a number of positive programs for the inmates, such as Toastmasters, Future Leaders of Tomorrow and a GED program. His efforts had been successful and were recognized by the media and even the governor himself. But then, his father had always been a born leader, a man admired and respected. That wouldn't change just because a fucking jury found him guilty of a crime he hadn't committed. Five years ago, on the recommendation of the warden at Glenworth, the governor had approved Sheppard's transfer to Delvers, a prison that housed less-serious offenders.

Dalton knew he wasn't imagining things. The room had grown silent. It seemed that everyone, especially his brothers and their wives, were speechless after the man's blatant admission. However, he did notice that Stonewall's testimonial didn't seem to faze Carson, Bobby or Roland at all. Moments later, after clearing his throat, Jace turned to Carson. "I'm trying to understand what's going on. Dalton said he was followed tonight and that you can tell us all why."

Carson nodded, and a light smile touched her lips. "Yes, and I suggest we all sit down. You are all tall men, and I'll get a neck ache looking up at you guys."

Dalton nodded. Although his condo was a nice size, the living room didn't have seating for ten people. "I'll grab some additional chairs from the dining room."

It didn't take long for everyone to be seated. The Grangers turned expectant eyes to Carson. She was about to speak when Dalton's doorbell rang. "Who in the hell can that be?" Dalton asked, standing.

"That's probably my other two men," Roland offered.

"Former inmates, as well?" Dalton couldn't help asking, considering what they'd been told so far.

"Yes."

Dalton frowned as he headed for the door. His gaze met Jules's, and somehow he could decipher her thoughts, which were identical to his own. *Jeez. What was this? The meeting of the former criminals club?* What type of business was Roland Summers operating with employees…including Roland himself…who were former inmates at Glenworth? And why was his dad's attorney involved with them? Dalton didn't know about his brothers, but he wasn't feeling too good about this. And what was going on with his and Jules's thoughts connecting? How did that happen…and why? That was scary as hell. So far she hadn't had anything to say, but he knew she was listening attentively and carefully observing everything that was going on. So was he. He couldn't wait to hear what Carson Boyett had to say.

He opened his door to find two tall, muscular men standing there. They looked like real ass-kickers. "Yes?"

"We're here for Carson's meeting," one of the men said, seeming to stare him down.

Dalton started to ask for their names and even thought of asking them to present their ID. But what would be the point? It was late. He wasn't in the mood, and he had a feeling they weren't, either. So he just moved aside and said, "Welcome to the party." He led them toward the living room.

The moment they entered the living room, Caden glanced their way and was out of his seat in a flash. "Striker?"

Striker? Dalton glanced at the men behind him, and one of them actually smiled.

"Yeah, man, it's me."

"Wait a minute." Jace stood and glanced at Caden and then back at the man Caden had just called by name.

"Isn't that the name of the guy who saved your life that night Grover tried to run you over?"

"Yes," Caden said, nodding. He then looked over at Carson. "I want to know what's going on."

Carson inhaled deeply. "What's going on is that your father believed your lives were in danger, and he requested bodyguards be assigned to each of you," she said, addressing the three brothers.

"What?" the Grangers and the wives asked simultaneously, not believing what they were hearing.

"Are you kidding us?" Dalton asked. "Why would Dad think that? Was this before or after that attempt was made on Jace's life?"

"After. Someone sent him an email in prison and told him that if the three of you reopened his case, bodily harm would come to you. He felt he wasn't in a position to call the person's bluff, so he told me what to do."

"Trust me," the man standing beside Striker said. "Had I been there, that bastard wouldn't have gotten close to you, Jace."

"But *you* were there," Caden said, staring over at Striker. "And you didn't happen to be out walking like you claimed, did you? You were guarding me that night."

Striker nodded. "Yes."

"You saved my life. You pushed me aside—would have taken the hit to protect me." Caden shook his head slowly. "Amazing. You would have lost your life for a job."

"No," Striker said, holding Caden's gaze. "Not for a job. For Shep. I would do just about anything for that man, especially protect his sons. Your father is one of a kind."

Thinking the mood was getting kind of sappy, Dalton said in a lighthearted tone, "Don't tell us that Dad kept you from killing guards and fellow inmates, too."

Striker moved his gaze from Caden to Dalton. "No, he didn't keep me from killing any of the prison guards or fellow inmates. What he did was keep me from killing Stonewall."

Dalton's throat tightened. *Damn, the man was serious.* He couldn't imagine his father keeping Stonewall and this man called Striker from coming to blows. There was a lull in the conversation in the room, and he understood why…at least with his brothers. They were probably wondering how their father had endured being incarcerated for fifteen years.

He switched his gaze from Striker to the big hulk of a guy standing beside him. "And you are?"

"Quasar. Quasar Patterson."

Dalton decided not to ask what Shep had kept him from doing. Instead, he asked, "And you've been guarding my brother? Jace?"

"Yes, ever since Roland told us what Shep wanted." He chuckled. "Nice honeymoon, by the way. I enjoyed South Africa."

"Let me make sure I understand what you're saying," Jules said.

Dalton rolled his eyes. Why did she feel the need to clarify anything? She wasn't in the family, so she needed to just keep her mouth shut like she had been doing up to this point. He was about to say so, but when he glanced at Jace, he got his older brother's warning glance and held his tongue.

"Are you saying that someone sent Sheppard Granger an email threatening to do bodily harm to his sons if they reopened his case?"

"Yes, that's exactly what I'm saying," Carson said,

meeting Jules's intense stare. "Sheppard immediately requested that I hire bodyguards. I agreed to do so with the understanding that if a situation came up in which I needed to reveal the truth to his sons, I could make that call."

"And you made that call tonight," Jules clarified, understanding completely.

"Yes. Bobby's cover had been blown, so I had no choice."

"Who wouldn't want Jace, Caden and Dalton to re-open their father's case?" Shana asked.

"Sheppard has no idea, but he wasn't writing the email off as a prank. He loves his sons too much to do that."

"So Quasar has been guarding Jace, Striker has been guarding Caden and Stonewall has been guarding Dalton?" Caden's wife, Shiloh, confirmed.

"Except for tonight," Stonewall answered. "I had personal business to tend to, and Bobby was my replacement."

"And I made a mess of things," Bobby said, with regret in his voice. "I should have been more cautious."

"You were cautious," Jules reassured him. "But I'm a private investigator and an ex-cop. I'm suspicious by nature. When Dalton arrived home, it was easy for me to pick up on the fact that you had followed him. Someone else might not have noticed. Dalton clearly didn't."

She *would* have to remind him of that in front of everyone, Dalton thought, frowning. He knew how to fix that. "Had I known you were parked outside in the cold waiting on me, Jules, I would have hurried home," he said in a deliberately seductive tone.

"Yeah," Bobby chimed in, grinning. "If you ask me,

that was some kiss you laid on her before she could even get inside your house."

Dalton frowned. *Well, nobody asked him.* He didn't have to meet anyone's gaze to know their eyes were on him and Jules. Speculating. Wondering. Assuming. He glanced over at Carson. It was time to get the conversation back on track.

"Regardless of that email my father received, we're reopening his case. My brothers and I have already discussed it."

Carson shook her head. "Sheppard won't allow it. Like I said, he won't take a chance with your lives."

"Why would anyone not want Sheppard Granger cleared?" Jules asked, her mind turning with all kinds of questions. Dalton could see it in her eyes. Spinning like a whirlwind. Just like the name he'd given her.

"Only Sheppard can tell you why he assumes that," Carson said after a brief hesitation.

"Doesn't matter," Dalton said matter-of-factly. "Dad has served fifteen years in prison too long. Granddad made us promise to do what we could to get him out."

Carson shook her head. "Sheppard wouldn't want you to do that. He'll be eligible for parole in a few—"

"We don't care about that," Caden interjected. "He didn't kill our mother, and it's time we proved it."

"He does not want the case reopened," Carson stressed again.

"Do you think we're wrong in wanting to clear our father?" Dalton asked.

"No, but my client doesn't want—"

"What do you think?" Jace interrupted.

"It's not what I think. It's what my client wants."

Jace didn't say anything for a moment. He'd been observing Carson closely, especially during her exchange with Dalton and Caden, but mostly with Dalton as she kept repeating her client's wishes. He must still be getting over the shock of learning that she was a woman... a very attractive woman. She was all business. Professional. Straight to the point.

Suddenly, something hit Jace in the gut, and he couldn't help breaking into the conversation to say, "A client you're in love with."

The room fell quiet. Everyone stared first at Jace for having the audacity to make such a bold statement, then at Carson, who had yet to deny what he'd said.

Instead, she drew in a deep breath, met Jace's direct gaze and said, "Yes. I'm in love with Sheppard Granger."

Seven

"I don't like this," Dalton said while pacing Jace's office the next morning. "Dad should have returned our call by now."

Caden, who was staring out the window with his hands shoved in his pants pockets, slowly turned around. "Did you honestly expect him to?"

Dalton stopped his pacing. "Yes, why wouldn't he? You think Warden Smallwood didn't get the message to him like he said he would?"

Caden braced his hip against the window ledge. "Oh, I'm sure he got the message, but it's my guess that Dad's planning his strategy."

"What strategy?"

"How he plans to deal with us," Caden replied, running a frustrated hand down his face.

Sitting at his desk, Jace leaned back in his chair and nodded. "I think you're right, Caden."

Dalton crossed his arms over his chest. "And why do you think he's right?"

Jace stood and came around his desk to sit on the edge. "Think about it. We're dealing with our father, Sheppard Granger. A man who ordered his attorney to hire bodyguards to protect us without letting us know. Bodyguards who even now refuse to back off until he gives the word. We're dealing with a man who would gladly spend the rest of his days behind bars if he thought doing so would keep us safe. I figure Carson has contacted him. She's told him about last night's meeting, and now he's trying to figure out how to deal with us."

Caden left his place by the window to stand beside Jace. "And you heard Carson last night just like we did, Dalton. She was adamant about Dad not wanting us to reopen his case."

Yes, Dalton thought, he had heard Carson; however, he'd been somewhat distracted. Jules's presence had made it hard for him to concentrate for most of the meeting. After all, whether he wanted to give her credit or not, she had been the one to notice that Bobby had been tailing him. More than once, his attention had been drawn to her against his will. She'd taken off her coat last night, and the black skirt and red blouse she was wearing had grabbed his attention. For once, he'd regretted that red was his favorite color. He'd been aware every single time she'd shifted positions on the sofa. Hell, she'd even crossed those gorgeous legs and all he could think about was how it would feel to get between them. And although he hadn't been close to her, that hadn't stopped him from inhaling her scent. And the more her fragrance flowed through his nostrils, the more he'd thought about sex. The-fuck-through-the-night kind.

He jumped when Caden snapped a finger in his face. He frowned. "What did you do that for?"

"Because we were talking to you, asking you a question, and your thoughts were a million miles away."

"Whatever," Dalton said, not wanting to admit that they had been. "What question were you asking me?"

"What was Jules doing at your house after midnight?"

He'd wondered when they would get around to asking him about that. "Evidently, I wasn't the only one not listening to what was being said. I think Jules explained herself. She had been parked in front of my place waiting for me to come home."

Caden rolled his eyes. "We know that, Dalton. We want to know why."

Dalton slid into the chair in front of Jace's desk. He had gotten very little sleep last night and was definitely feeling it. "She heard I wasn't coming to Shana's dinner party and thought we should discuss it. Of course, it would have been a total waste of her time."

"And of course you told her that…after you laid that kiss on her. The one Bobby told everyone about," Jace said, studying his brother.

Dalton's mouth curved into a frown. "That guy talks too damned much. It was a kiss that wasn't supposed to happen. She told me to pretend I was kissing her."

"And of course, you didn't pretend."

A slow smile touched Dalton's lips. "No, I didn't." He couldn't help remembering how kissing Jules had made him feel. After everyone had finally left last night, he'd gone back to bed determined to pick up on his dream where he'd left off. He hadn't been able to, because his mind had been filled with memories of their kiss…how she'd tasted and how she'd felt in his arms.

Realizing his brothers were watching him, he decided to get them off the subject of him and Jules. "Now I have a question for you, Jace."

"What?"

"How on Earth did you know Carson had a thing for Dad?"

Jace chuckled softly. "She doesn't have a thing for him, Dalton. She's in love with him. There's a difference. One day, you'll realize the difference when you come to know love for yourself, and then you can easily recognize it in someone else."

"I agree," Caden chimed in. "I caught on when I noticed the look in her eyes whenever she said Dad's name. I don't know what his feelings are for her, but I can say she has very deep feelings for him."

"I can't believe you called her out on it," Dalton said, grinning. "Surprised the hell out of me when you did."

Jace took a sip of the water sitting on his desk. "I surprised myself. I was out of line in doing that, and I apologized to her before she left last night." Jace rubbed the back of his neck. "My only excuse is that there were so many shockers revealed last night—Carson being a woman, the fact we've had bodyguards for over a month now and that one even went on my honeymoon, and our very professional and business-minded father's close relationship with Stonewall, Quasar and Striker. I guess I had one of those moments when I felt the need to reveal something for a change."

Dalton didn't say anything for a moment, thinking that last night definitely had been one big surprise after another. Carson Boyett was definitely a looker, and he could see his father falling for her. He stood up. "So what do we do about Dad? I think we should just get in the car and drive over to Delvers right now."

"Oh, so now you want to go see Dad when you haven't gone to see him in over a month?"

"Stay off my ass, Caden. I had planned to go see Dad this week, but now I'll do it sooner. Especially since

Stonewall, Quasar and Striker won't let up until Dad gives the word. I was followed to work this morning."

"So were we," Jace said, "so stop whining. We need to let Dad work this out for himself. But regardless, we will reopen the case, and I think he knows it. He's worried, and he has every right to be. Let's give him the rest of the day, and if we don't hear from him by then, we'll go to Delvers tomorrow."

Both Dalton and Caden nodded their agreement.

"Well, I must say, Jules, it sounds like you and Shana had a very interesting night," Ben Bradford said, leaning back in his chair at the kitchen table.

Jules had just finished telling him everything, including the fact that for the past month Sheppard Granger had assigned bodyguards to protect his sons. The ex-cop in Ben thought the three guys were pretty good if they'd gone undetected until now. And he wasn't surprised it had been Jules who'd figured out Dalton was being followed. He knew she was good at what she did.

"You should have seen Shana's face when Quasar admitted to having gone to South Africa with them on their honeymoon," Jules said, grinning.

Ben didn't say anything as he took another sip of his iced tea. He knew Jules was trying to bring a little humor to the situation, but she knew as well as he did that if Sheppard Granger thought his sons needed protection from professional bodyguards, then things must be pretty serious. It didn't help matters that by being married to Jace, Shana could also very well be caught in the line of fire.

"I wonder who doesn't want Sheppard Granger's case reopened."

He met Jules's gaze. He knew that she was doing

more than wondering. Her mind had already dissected every piece of information she had heard last night, and in addition to that, she intended to do her own research. This time she was driven by more than mere inquisitiveness—her sister might be in danger.

"I don't know," he said, placing his glass of tea aside. Having one daughter who could possibly be in danger was bad enough. He didn't need two.

"You researched the case, right, Dad?"

Yes, he had done his research when he'd known Shana was marrying Jace. He'd known Jace's father was in prison for killing Jace's mother and wanted to know more about it. "Yes, and it seemed pretty cut-and-dried. Sheppard Granger's fingerprints were found on the murder weapon, and he and his wife had been having marital problems. There was even evidence presented that he was having an affair…although no other woman was named. All they had to go on were hotel receipts."

Jules rolled her eyes. "Circumstantial evidence. Why wasn't that part thrown out of court?"

"Not sure. His attorney should have been on top of his game. Doesn't sound like he was."

Jules nodded as she took a sip of her lemonade. "The issue of Sheppard Granger's replacing his attorney with Carson Boyett did come up last night. She admitted Mr. Granger felt that Jess Washington, his previous counsel, didn't do a good job representing him at the trial. And now it seems that Mr. Granger is wondering whether it was intentional, since Vidal Duncan, the man who tried to kill Jace not long ago, was the one who recommended Washington."

Ben stood to take his plate to the sink. "Under the circumstances, I would wonder the same thing."

Jules nodded as she ate the last of the fried fish her father had prepared for their lunch. It had been close to three in the morning when everyone had finally left Dalton's condo. Instead of driving home, although it was only another ten miles, she'd come here to spend the night, only to find her father had spent the night elsewhere. Since she had a key, she had let herself in and used the guest bedroom as usual.

She glanced over at her dad. He was loading the dishwasher, smiling and whistling. He'd been doing both things a lot lately, so she couldn't be mad at Mona. She probably should be thanking the woman for her father's jubilant moods. Ben and Mona had met in the grocery store almost six months ago, although for the life of her, Jules couldn't imagine her six-foot-three-inch, sixty-two-year-old father hanging around any store long enough to hit on a woman. In her opinion, her father had always been a handsome man, but during all the years after their mom had died, neither she nor Shana had known him to be involved with a woman. Oh, they knew he'd dated once in a while, since she could still recall the packs of condoms she and her sister had found in his drawer one year. But he'd never brought any of those dates home to meet his daughters.

Now, not only had he brought Mona, a college professor at the University of Virginia, home, but he was bringing her to family functions, too, like Shana's wedding and Sunday dinners. Although Mona was legally blind, there was a fifty-fifty chance she could get her eyesight back, since her optic nerve hadn't been damaged in the auto accident, just her peripheral nerves.

Jules had slept until almost noon that morning, and it had been the smell of the fish her father was frying in the kitchen downstairs that had awakened her. She loved all types of seafood, with fish and shrimp topping the list as her favorites. Luckily for her, her father enjoyed fishing. And no one fried fish and cooked hush puppies like Ben Bradford.

By the time she'd showered and dressed to go downstairs, he'd set the table for lunch. He hadn't provided any explanation about where he'd spent the night, and she hadn't asked. It didn't take a rocket scientist to tell from the smile on his face that he had spent the night with Mona. She'd figured they had become sexually active during their trip to New York last month. But any time she thought about her father having sex when she wasn't managed to grate on her last nerve. Now more than before, she intended to call Ray Ford the first chance she got.

"So what are you thinking about, Jules?"

She blinked, realizing her father had spoken and what he'd asked. It was not the time to be honest and tell him what she really had been thinking, so she said, "About Sheppard Granger and his situation." That wasn't a total lie, since everything that had happened last night was still on her mind when she woke up this morning, especially that kiss. No matter how tired she'd been last night, it hadn't kept Dalton from invading her dreams. Last night had been worse, since she now knew how he tasted.

"And?"

She shrugged. "You tell me, Dad. You've met him." A week before Shana's wedding, Jace had invited her dad to accompany him and Shana to Delvers to meet his father. The only thing Ben had said afterward was that Sheppard Granger was a likable guy. That hadn't told her much, since there were plenty of murderers who'd gone down in history as being likable.

"The meeting with him didn't last long, Jules."

"Doesn't matter. The ex-cop and ex-detective in you would have sized him up pretty quickly. Tell me something other than he was a likable guy."

Ben turned from the sink and met his daughter's intense gaze while heaving a deep sigh. "Apparently, the word *likable* doesn't do it for you."

"No, it doesn't."

Ben moved across the room to take a chair. He knew Jules had questions for a reason, and he didn't particularly like where this line of questioning might lead. "If I had to do a quick character analysis of Sheppard Granger, I would have to say if he wasn't behind bars, he would be an affluent entrepreneur who, although born with a silver spoon in his mouth, is the type of man who doesn't have a problem sharing his wealth and thinking about those less fortunate. He would be an awesome benefactor. Not just of his wealth but of his knowledge, which I believe is extensive. I could tell he's kept himself up-to-date on modern technology, changing trends and world events. I believe that although he's behind bars, he has a special leadership gift that few men possess, which is why he was able to not only form relationships with the three men you met last night, but also become a positive role model, counselor, adviser and confidant to them, as well as to others."

Ben paused a moment to gather his thoughts, knowing that his daughter, the ex-cop, was latching on to his every word. "I was able to pick up on those things about him immediately, the minute I walked into the prison. He's highly respected by more than just the warden. He's earned the respect of the guards and his fellow inmates. They know he's getting special favors, but it didn't seem to bother anyone. In fact, it's as if they know any favors given to him will eventually benefit them. They know that he will look out for them."

Jules nodded then asked the question Ben had been waiting for. The one he had known she would get around to asking. "Do you think he's someone who could have killed his wife?"

Ben didn't say anything for a minute. "I only met him that one time, Jules, and the meeting lasted a little more than an hour. But it's my belief that the only way he could have done such a thing is if he'd been pushed, and I mean pushed really hard. I never knew his wife, so I can't say what he was dealing with. But, according to what Jace and Shana shared with me on the ride to Delvers, the brothers have proof that it was their mother, not their father, who was having an affair."

Jules already knew that. The way the story went was that one night, while working late at Granger Aeronautics, Shana and Jace had discovered a secret compartment inside a sofa in Sheppard Granger's office. The secret compartment held a file containing proof of the affair.

What Jules had found just as fascinating was why her sister and now-brother-in-law were in his father's empty office in the first place. Both Jace and Shana had sealed their lips on that part, but Jules figured they must have been giving that sofa one hell of a workout.

"Throwing that into the mix," Ben interrupted her thoughts to say, "a jealous husband might do just about anything. He might have snapped."

Jules rolled her eyes. "Maybe right then, but not a few months later."

Ben shrugged his wide shoulders. "Maybe not. But maybe he wanted a divorce, and she refused to give him one."

Jules drained the last of her lemonade. "What if Sheppard Granger's suspicions are true and whoever sent that email meant business? That means Shana could be in as much danger as Jace. It also means there might be more behind Sylvia Granger's death than her affair. That may have just been a cover-up for something bigger."

Ben didn't want to hear that, although the same thought had crossed his mind earlier. Before he could formulate a response to his daughter's comments, his phone rang. He stood up, grateful for the reprieve. "Excuse me for a minute. That might be Mona." He quickly left the room to answer his mobile phone, which he'd left in the living room.

When he reached it, he frowned, not recognizing the phone number. "Hello?"

"Ben, this is Sheppard Granger. Is there any way you can pay me a visit? Today, if possible? I might need your help."

Eight

Dalton walked into McQueen's and glanced around. It was happy hour, and the place was certainly lively. He walked over to the bar and slid into a seat, thinking that just a few months ago, he and his brothers would have been enjoying a drink together after a long day at work. Now Jace and Caden were biting at the bit to get home to their wives.

"What are you having, Granger 3?" Myron, the bartender and owner of McQueen's, asked. Myron was a fun-loving guy who managed a nice place. The drinks were good and the food exceptional. Myron had started differentiating between Dalton and his brothers by referring to Jace as Granger 1, Caden as Granger 2 and Dalton as Granger 3.

"The usual."

Myron grinned. "Your usual is coming right up. Where are Grangers 1 and 2?"

Dalton shrugged. "Home with their wives, I suppose. Probably ran red lights to get there."

"Marriage has a way of doing that to you," Myron said, placing a glass of scotch in front of Dalton. "So don't hate them."

Dalton frowned. "I don't. I just didn't expect the changes so soon. Jace, Caden and I were apart for years, living our lives in separate places, but now we're back in Charlottesville, what do they do the first chance they get? Get married. If that's not bullshit, I don't know what is."

Myron shook his head, grinning. "Doesn't sound like bullshit to me but good common sense. Remember, I'm also married—and happily. I played your game for years, different woman every day of the week, a flavor of the month. But at some point that crap gets old. I wouldn't trade being married."

Dalton figured he didn't want to hear anything else Myron had to say. He wasn't in the mood. Taking his drink, he said, "I'm grabbing a table. Talk to you later."

Crossing the room, he saw several women checking him out, some brazenly, not even trying to hide their interest. Surprisingly, he wasn't in the mood for them, either—women throwing themselves at him, probably needing a good fuck as much as he did. So why was he having a pity party when he could probably go somewhere and have an orgy? He felt the answer soak deep into his skin, and he could taste it on his lips. Because he only wanted a certain woman. One who was more edgy than soft, sharp than dull, one who invaded his dreams every night like she had a damned right to be there.

He slid into a booth and took a sip of his scotch, loving the taste. He needed it tonight. His brain was on overload. Last night had been a jolt to his system, and something was still kicking inside him. Anger. Frustration. Horniness. All three. He hadn't liked giving in to Jace's suggestion that they give their father time to decide how he would deal with them. Shit, they weren't children but grown-ass men. What was there to deal with?

"Mind if I join you?"

He glanced up and stared into Stonewall's face. He took another sip of scotch. "Does it matter if I mind?" he asked flatly.

"Not really," Stonewall answered, sliding into the seat across from him. "Now that you know what my job entails, there's no longer a reason for me to be discreet or keep a low profile."

Dalton wasn't sure whether that was good or bad. The fact that he'd been followed around for a little over a month without his knowledge still didn't sit well with him. The USN had taught him how to be on his guard, expect the unexpected and be ready. But over time, once he'd put the agency behind him, he had stopped looking over his shoulder. Now it seemed he would have to start doing so again for an entirely different reason.

Stonewall summoned a waitress to take his drink order, giving Dalton a chance to study the man more closely. He figured Stonewall was in his midthirties and worked out a lot, probably hitting the gym every day. Dalton could tell that even while talking to the waitress, Stonewall was scoping out his surroundings and had taken stock of every single person in McQueen's, somehow making a mental note while not missing a beat. And he was doing so with evident ease and efficiency, which led Dalton to believe he was well-practiced at it.

As soon as the waitress left, that assumption led him to ask, "How long have you been doing this?"

Stonewall's gaze shifted from the backside of the waitress walking away to Dalton. His eyes were filled with male appreciation, and Dalton knew that the smile touching the man's lips had nothing to do with the question but with the woman he'd just ogled.

"Why do you want to know?"

Dalton shrugged. "Let's just say I'm curious."

At that moment, the waitress came back and smiled at them both before placing Stonewall's drink before him. This time, they both watched when she walked off. Knowing they were looking, she put a deliberate sway in her hips for their benefit.

Dalton grinned. "I love coming to this place."

Stonewall nodded. "After my first night of tailing you, it became obvious that you do."

Dalton took a sip of his drink and watched as Stonewall did the same. Just to make sure the question he'd asked earlier wasn't lost in the shuffle, he leaned forward in his seat. "So how long have you been working for Summers?"

Stonewall took another sip of his drink. "Off and on for about ten years, while working on my degree."

"Degree in what?" Dalton asked with a raised brow.

"Education."

Now he'd heard everything. "You ever use it?"

"I sub sometimes."

Dalton shook his head. *Interesting.* The man was full of surprises. He couldn't imagine him being a substitute teacher in any classroom. "One last question."

Stonewall's gaze was keen. "And make sure it's your last."

Dalton stared across the table at him. "When are you going to stop following me around?"

Stonewall held his stare. "Not until Shep gives the word, so whether you like it or not, you're stuck with me."

* * *

Gesturing her sister over to the sofa, Shana eased down in the wingback chair across from it and gave Jules a bright smile. "So you're here to tell me why you were staked outside Dalton's place last night?"

Jules rolled her eyes. "No, I'm here to see how you're feeling. Dad said you texted him to say that you wouldn't be going into the office today."

Shana chuckled softly. "I'm fine, but since I had a late night I decided to stay home and take it easy. In fact, it was really Jace's idea."

Jules laughed. "I guess sleeping with the boss has it perks."

Shana joined in, laughing with her. "Yes, it does, trust me. More than one," she said, leaning back against the chair and lifting her legs to rest on the ottoman. "Although, technically, Jace isn't my boss. I was hired to do a job for his company, and one thing led to another."

It most certainly did, Jules thought, studying her sister. Was she imagining things, or was Shana finally getting a little pudgy in the stomach? It was about time. She was pregnant, so she might as well look it. "When will you find out whether you're having a boy or a girl?"

Shana shrugged. "Not sure if we want to know. I think we just want to be surprised."

It was their choice, but if she were the one having a baby, she would want to know. "Did Dad ever tell you that our maternal grandmother was a triplet?"

Shana frowned. "No, and he didn't tell you that, either, so don't play with me like that, Juliet. And speaking of Dad, I understand you spent the night over at his place."

"Yes, and did he mention he wasn't home when I got there?"

"No, he didn't mention that. It had to be after two when we left Dalton's place."

"Exactly. He didn't come home all night, and I have a feeling it wasn't the first time." When Shana didn't say anything, just sat and smiled, Jules's eyes widened. "You knew?"

"Yes, and I wondered how long it would take for you to figure things out. I believe he began spending nights at Mona's place after they took that New York trip together. So I guess it's now really serious."

Jules waved off Shana's words. "Men sleep with women all the time, and there's not a doggone serious thing about it."

"True. But we're talking about our dad, Benjamin Bradford, the man who has never introduced a girlfriend to us before Mona. Trust me, it's serious."

"Maybe he'll get over it."

Shana glared at her sister. "I hope you're not counting on that happening, and why should you? Dad's happy. I'm happy for him, and you should be, too."

"I am, but..."

"But what?"

Jules didn't say anything for a minute. "But we never had to share him with anyone after Mom died."

Shana nodded her understanding. "I know, but don't you think it's time? We both have our lives, and now it's time for him to have his. It would be selfish of us not to want that for him."

Jules knew Shana was right and would admit she liked Mona. But still...

"Just think of the bright side," Shana said, interrupting her thoughts.

"Which is?"

"He's found someone special. Someone we can both

admire. She's a very strong woman, the kind of woman he raised his daughters to be. Mona hasn't let her blindness stop her from living a fulfilling life. I think that's one of the reasons Dad fell in love with her."

"You're probably right. Good thing we had finished lunch before he got her call. You should have seen the way he rushed out the door."

"Yes, our dad is truly smitten," Shana said with a pleased smirk on her lips. "So tell me. Why were you parked outside Dalton's place last night waiting for him to come home?"

Jules inhaled deeply. She knew how her sister's mind worked and could see the wheels turning in her head. "It wasn't for that, Shana. No matter what that guy Bobby thought, I was not making a booty call. The only reason I was parked outside Dalton's house that time of night was because of you."

Shana's mouth dropped open in surprise. "Me?"

"Yes, *you*. While talking to you yesterday, I could tell how disappointed you were by Dalton's refusal to attend your dinner party this Saturday night because of me. I figured that he and I could talk things out like two sensible and mature adults and learn how to tolerate each other. Needless to say, we never had that conversation."

"But the two of you did kiss?"

Jules frowned. She knew Shana wasn't really asking the question, since Bobby had made a big announcement about the incident the previous night. "He took advantage of the situation. When I noticed he was being followed, I realized that I would have to be creative to find out who it was. I rang his bell and when he answered I told him to pretend that we were kissing, and then he took full advantage."

Shana laughed. "Yes, that sounds like Dalton. He's a 'take advantage' kind of guy, definitely an opportunist. Now you see what you're dealing with."

Jules shook her head as she stood. "I'm not dealing with anything. I can see that discussing anything with him would not have worked. The man is impossible."

"But is he a good kisser?"

Jules shrugged before heading toward the door. "What does that have to do with anything?"

Shana smiled. "For you, a lot. I've known you to drop guys after the first date if they didn't kiss worth a damn. So how did he do?"

Jules paused before she reached Shana's front door. "Truthfully?"

"Yes, truthfully."

She didn't say anything for a moment, knowing Shana was the only person she would admit this to. "On a scale of one to ten, with ten being at the top, I would give him high twenties or above."

Shana's eyes widened. "He was that good?"

"Better than good," Jules said with an expression that indicated the very thought infuriated her. "Although Dalton Granger has many faults, being a lousy kisser is decidedly not one of them."

Nine

"Thanks for coming, Ben."

Ben nodded as he dropped into the chair across the table from Sheppard Granger. Ben had been a cop long enough to see how unusual Sheppard's accommodations were. First of all, most inmates don't get to use a private conference room to meet with anyone, and they definitely aren't offered one as spacious as this one. Ben recalled this room from his previous visit with Sheppard.

He'd noted that the room was adjacent to the prison library. It was a huge, windowless room that Ben figured was some sort of conference room used by the warden and the parole board to determine the fate of inmates.

And the guard, the same one who had been there the last time, and who was the only other person in the room, was only there for show. He hadn't called Sheppard out on any violations, like when they had shaken hands. Under normal circumstances, there would be a no-touching policy.

From what Jace had shared with Ben, he knew that a few years ago the warden had given permission for Sheppard Granger to be alone for any meetings with his attorney or close family members. That privilege wasn't given to all prisoners, just those considered trustworthy. Evidently, Sheppard Granger had found favor with both the warden and the governor, who would have to approve such rights and honors before they were extended to Granger.

Ben got comfortable in his chair while studying the man sitting across from him. He and Granger were the same height, although he figured Granger was probably a few pounds heavier. However, it was obvious he used the gym regularly and seemed fit and healthy. And then there was that same air that had surrounded him the last time. This was a man who had not only accepted his fate fifteen years ago, but had worked hard to deal with it in a positive way, too. Ben doubted most men could have pulled something like that off and seriously doubted that he could have.

"Over the phone, you said something about needing my help," Ben said, breaking the silence in the room.

"Yes. But first I want to say something, and it's something you need to hear straight from me."

"Which is?"

"I didn't kill my wife."

Ben wasn't sure why Sheppard wanted to see him, but with that opening, he knew there was no time for formalities. And there was no time for cat-and-mouse games. "I honestly didn't think that you did," Ben replied.

He saw relief etched on Granger's face when he said, "Thank you."

Ben shook his head. "You've been locked up for fifteen years for a crime you didn't commit, yet you're thanking me?"

"Yes, because you believed me when a jury didn't."

"But to be fair to the jury, you didn't allow your attorney to introduce evidence that could have swayed them." At the lifting of Sheppard's brow, Ben could only smile and say, "Your son was marrying my daughter, so I couldn't help but be curious. You can chalk it up to the ex-cop and the ex-detective in me."

Sheppard didn't say anything for a moment as he stared at Ben. "Had I done that, it would have dirtied my wife's name. She was the mother of my sons, and I couldn't do that to them."

"But you could do this to yourself?" Ben asked. "Take a rap you didn't deserve?"

"Yes, if it meant keeping them safe."

"Or sheltered?" Ben countered.

"Or sheltered." Sheppard Granger paused a moment before saying, "The reason I called you here is about keeping them safe. I understand there was a meeting last night."

"So I heard, since I wasn't invited. I spoke to Shana briefly this morning, but it was my younger daughter, Jules, who filled me in on most of it."

"Your younger daughter was there?"

"Yes. In fact, she's the one who spotted that guy following Dalton. She was parked across the street, waiting for him to come home last night."

"Oh."

Ben chuckled softly. "Trust me. It's not what you think."

"It's not?" Sheppard asked with eyes that didn't hide his interest.

"No. In fact, I'm convinced she hates Dalton's guts... probably just as much as he hates hers. Their first meeting some months back left a very negative and lasting impression on both of them. The only reason she was there was to confront him about his refusal to attend Shana's first dinner party this Saturday night."

Sheppard frowned. "Why wouldn't he attend?"

"Because he knew Jules would be there. It's a long and taxing story. So let's just say we have two kids who love each other, and then there are two who can't stand the ground the other walks on."

Sheppard didn't say anything for a moment. "I assume you know about the bodyguards I hired to protect my sons."

"Yes, and I'm sure you know they aren't thrilled about it."

"So I gather. My warden gave me a message that they called. By then, I had already spoken to my attorney, and she'd given me the details. They are waiting for me to return their call, but I wanted to talk to you first. Get some advice."

Ben lifted a brow. "Advice? Shouldn't you consult your attorney for that?"

"Not for this. I need the advice of an ex-cop, one who was honored as Policeman of the Year four times. And one who would have had a great career as a detective if he hadn't put his daughters first and resign after a couple of years to go back to being a cop to spend more time at home with them."

At the widening of Ben's eyes, Sheppard smiled. "My son was marrying your daughter, so I did some research of my own."

Ben laughed. "Fair enough. So why am I here?"

At that moment the prison guard Ben remembered from the last visit, Ambrose, crossed the room and handed Sheppard a piece of paper. He took it and glanced at it before handing it to Ben. "This is the reason for the bodyguards. I know I didn't kill my wife, but someone else did. And that someone doesn't like the thought of my leaving here anytime soon."

Ben glanced down at the paper and read it. It was an email that had been sent to Sheppard. He didn't like the words. He didn't like the tone and he sure as hell didn't like the blatant threat.

Granger. You don't know me, but I know you. If I were you, I would make sure your sons don't get it into their heads to prove your innocence. Something tragic could happen.

Ben lifted his gaze. "Have you shown this to the prison officials?"

"Yes, Warren Smallwood is aware of it. My attorney was able to trace it to a public computer in the Wesconnett Library."

Ben nodded. Wesconnett was a community on the outskirts of Charlottesville.

"I never wanted them to find out about that email."

Ben shrugged. "So now they have, and according to Jules, threat or no threat, they intended to fight to have your case reopened."

"I can't let them do that."

"Not sure you can stop them."

"I must. They have more than just themselves to think about. Jace and Caden now have wives and we—you and I—have a grandbaby on the way. I don't know who or what I'm dealing with here, Ben. And I don't want anything to happen to my family. Which is now *our* family."

Ben didn't say anything for a long moment as he stared at Sheppard, understanding completely what he was saying. "What is it you want me to do, Sheppard?"

"My sons won't like what I intend to tell them when we meet, but it can't be helped. Their lives are a lot more important than mine. I can't allow them to reopen my case. I'm hoping you will get through to them where I might fail."

Ben lifted a brow. "I don't know your other two sons that well. Just Jace."

"And that's a good start. Jace is levelheaded, and Caden and Dalton respect his leadership. If you can convince Jace of the danger, not just to himself but to Shana and their child, he might see reason."

"And if I can't get him to come around?"

Sheppard heaved a deep breath. "I don't even want to think of that possibility, Ben."

The lone figure stood on the opposite side of the street and glanced up at the impressive building, sizing it up as if it were a person. A person who would eventually have to be dealt with.

Granger Aeronautics.

The weather was cold, and evening would be settling in soon and making it even colder. History was about to repeat itself. Sheppard Granger had been warned, but it seemed he couldn't keep his sons in line. Keep them from sticking those noses where they didn't belong. If the case were to be reopened all the players would be exposed, and that couldn't happen.

Cold eyes watched as Granger employees hurriedly left the building. The workday was over, and it was time to go home. A new plan had been implemented, one more sinister than the last. Before it was over, additional lives would be lost.

Fifteen years had passed, and it was time to once again take care of business.

Ten

Why had he agreed with Jace and Caden that they should ride in the same car to Delvers? Dalton thought to himself while trying to stretch his legs in the confined space. They had put him in the backseat when they knew his legs were longer than theirs. They had the air conditioner turned on full blast when it was cold outside. Were they trying to freeze his ass? This little trip was definitely not off to a good start.

"Are you whining back there?" Jace had the nerve to ask while eyeing him through the rearview mirror.

"What does it sound like?" he snapped, his gaze narrowing.

"Sounds like you're whining."

"Go to hell."

Caden wasn't saying anything, and it only took Dalton a few seconds to realize he was asleep. When his brothers had arrived at his condo to pick him up…thirty minutes late…both Jace and Caden had been wide-awake and in extremely good moods. How dare Caden sleep in the front seat while he was in the back, frozen and miserable? Glowering, he leaned forward and smacked his brother on the back of his head.

"What the hell?" Caden jerked around with a murderous look on his face. He rubbed his head. "What did you hit me for?"

Dalton shrugged. "You were sleeping. If I can't sleep, then you can't, either."

Caden switched his gaze to Jace. "Pull over to the side of the road so I can whip his ass."

Jace chuckled. "Don't have time. Not if we want to meet with Dad at the scheduled time."

"And whose fault is it that we're running late?" Dalton sneered. He'd already figured out the reason for the delay. Jace had been smiling all morning. "I just don't understand you and your wife. She's pregnant already. Give it a rest."

Jace shook his head. "You're really in a bad mood today. Some woman rub you the wrong way?"

"Or didn't rub you at all," Caden suggested with a smirk.

Dalton rolled his eyes, deciding Caden's comment didn't deserve a response. "So how did Dad sound, Jace?" Dalton had gotten a call from Jace around eight last night saying their dad had finally returned his call and wanted to meet with them at ten this morning.

"Agitated. He wouldn't go into any details over the phone, but you can bet he will try to talk us out of reopening his case."

"When doves cry," Dalton snorted.

"Glad we're all in agreement, *Prince*," Caden said, still rubbing the back of his head. "So are we still being followed?"

Dalton glanced through the car's back window. "No reason we wouldn't be. Those three guys take this bodyguard thing seriously. At least Stonewall's no longer hiding. He joined me for a drink yesterday at McQueen's."

"He did?" Jace asked, looking at him through the rearview mirror again.

"Yes, and please keep your eyes on the road and not on me. Jeez. Do I need to drive?"

"Hell, no," Jace and Caden said simultaneously.

"Besides, I don't know why you're whining, anyway," Jace said, turning on the car's blinker to exit off the interstate to the state road that would take them to Delvers. "That little red toy you drive is nothing but a death trap. You probably have more space in my backseat than you do in that entire car."

"Yes, but you can't beat the turbo power. Driving my toy is the next best thing to fucking a woman."

Caden turned around with a silly grin on his face. "If you believe that, then you aren't with the right woman."

Dalton held back the words he really wanted to say. Saying them would be too easy, and he wouldn't waste his time, mainly because what Caden said had struck a nerve. His love life really sucked lately. The women were there aplenty, easy as Sunday morning and ready and willing, but his interest wasn't. It was as if that one kiss with Jules had affected his entire body. Definitely one part in particular. All it took was for him to remember his tongue tangling with hers, and he would get hard and be consumed with a sexual need the likes of which he'd never felt before.

"We're here."

He glanced ahead as Jace pulled through the gates of Delvers Correctional Center. It would be the first time he'd seen his father since admitting to his brothers that he'd known about their mother's affair. It was a secret he'd held for almost twenty years, and it was time to set it free.

* * *

"Good morning, Manning."

"What's so good about it?"

Jules rolled her eyes. Evidently, it would be one of those mornings. Emanuel Carmichael, all six feet three inches and two hundred and five pounds of him, was her administrative assistant and a darned good one. Usually he was in a good mood, but not this morning. He and his partner must have had a tiff. Hell, if anyone should be in a bad mood, it was Jules. She had pulled out her little red book last night only to find that Ray Ford had remarried his wife as she'd suspected, and the next three prospects were now in serious relationships.

"Nothing, I guess. Sorry I asked," she said, quickly moving to her office.

Once inside, she closed the door behind her and immediately headed for the coffeepot. At least Manning's anger hadn't stopped him from making sure she had coffee as usual. What would she do without him? She hoped she never had to find out. He helped to keep her day normal and ran her office like a charm during those times she was away.

They had gone through the police academy in Boston together, but he'd resigned after his first month on the streets, deciding he preferred an inside job shuffling papers to being outside shuffling criminals. Manning was too handsome for his own good and extremely well built, but his sexual preference relegated their relationship to a very close friendship. When she had followed her dad to Charlottesville and opened a private investigator's office, Manning, who had just split from his lover, decided that a change of scenery would do him good. They had opened this office together, and both did what they did best. He shuffled papers, and she still shuffled criminals, so to speak.

After her last grueling investigation, she had decided not to take on any new cases until the first of the year, so her days were spent closing out old files, doing follow-ups and filing reports. She'd also been summoned to court to testify on a kidnapping case she had solved a few months ago. That meant a trip to Miami next week. Hmm...a few days in South Beach sounded nice, considering the weather there and what she was dealing with here.

An hour later, after going over several reports and vouchers, Jules heard Manning's voice come across the intercom on her desk. "You have a visitor, Ms. Sweet." And before he hung up, he said in a low voice, "Sweet Pea."

Sweet Pea was a nickname she'd been given by other local PIs. Her agency was the J.B. Sweet Agency. It wasn't uncommon for private investigators to use fictitious names for privacy as well as protection. The last thing you want is for someone—like a deadbeat dad you've arrested—to show up on your doorstep or in a dark alley. Nothing wrong with playing it safe. And since she was a woman and most people preferred having a man handle their investigative work, she used her first and last initials as well as her mother's maiden name, hence the moniker J. B. Sweet.

Jules frowned. She didn't have any appointments today, so it must be a walk-in. Why was Manning bothering her when all he had to do was tell the person she wasn't taking on any new cases until after the holidays? "You better have a good reason for interrupting me, Manning." She heard his chuckle. *Chuckle?* Hadn't he been in a sour mood just moments ago?

"I do have a good reason," Manning replied. "It's Mr. B."

"Dad?" she asked, surprised. Not that he'd never come to her office, but lately his time had been filled with Mona, Mona and more Mona.

"Yes, the one and only. Can I send him in?"

"Of course." She was already out of her seat when her father opened the door and walked in.

"Dad, this is a surprise. Were you in the area or something?"

Ben shook his head as he sat in the chair opposite her desk. "No. There's something I need to talk to you about."

"Okay," she said, moving to sit back in her chair. Her father seemed intense for some reason. "Is everything okay with Mona?"

He lifted a brow. "Yes, why do you ask?"

"Because you seem bothered by something, and you rushed off quickly yesterday after you got her call."

Ben heaved a deep sigh. "That call I got yesterday wasn't from Mona."

"It wasn't?"

"No. It was from Sheppard Granger."

Jules's mouth fell open. "Sheppard Granger called you from prison?"

"Yes, and he wanted me to come see him."

"Why?"

"To tell me he didn't kill his wife and to explain why he'd hired those bodyguards."

"Why did he feel the need to confess that he didn't kill his wife to you? And as far as those bodyguards go, we already know why he hired them. He thinks his sons' lives are in danger."

Instead of answering her inquiry just yet, Ben added,

"He also showed me the actual email he received. It was traced to a public computer in the Wesconnett Library. Under the circumstances, if I had gotten that email, I would have reacted the same way he did."

Jules nodded. "But why did he request a meeting with you? He could have told you all that over the phone."

"Yes, but it was more a man-to-man sort of meeting. We have a lot in common."

"I doubt that."

"You've never met Sheppard Granger. If you ever get the chance, I think you'd be surprised."

She decided to move on instead of disagreeing with her father. "There has to be more."

"Yes, and I think you know where we're headed with this."

Jules shifted in her seat. "Possibly, but why don't you tell me, anyway?"

"Since Sheppard Granger didn't kill his wife, that opens up a lot of questions about who did."

"I'm listening," she said but really wished she didn't have to. There was no reason to tell her dad that she'd been dissecting what little information she had in her mind already, ever since that night at Dalton's house.

"Whoever actually killed Sylvia Granger is still out there and doesn't want to be exposed. And Sheppard believes it has nothing to do with his wife's affairs."

"Then what does it have to do with?"

"Not sure if he even knows, but he doesn't want to take any chances. He's meeting with his sons this morning and will try to convince them to back off from reopening his case."

"Do you think they will do that?"

"I don't know. What do you think?"

Jules pulled in a deep breath. "They were pretty

adamant about reopening his case the other night, although Carson Boyett told them their father would be against it."

Ben didn't say anything for a minute. "My main concern is Shana. She's married to Jace, so anything that concerns him concerns her."

"True," Jules said, not liking that thought. "Have you talked to her?"

"No, she went into the office today. Besides, I'd rather talk to her and Jace together. But I'll wait to see what Sheppard's sons decide to do. They might go along with his suggestion to back off."

Jules couldn't see that happening and had a feeling her father couldn't see it, either. "And if they don't?"

"He's asked me to talk to them."

Jules snickered. "If he thinks you might have a chance to succeed where he's failed, then he doesn't know his sons. I think their minds are made up, and nothing and no one is going to stop them."

After giving each of them bear hugs, Sheppard gazed into the eyes of the three men he was proud to claim as his sons. When he'd left them in the care of their grandfather fifteen years ago, they had been young—too young to fully understand the impact his incarceration would have on their lives. Unfortunately, they'd had to learn the hard way that some people they had thought were friends truly weren't, and that when the going got tough, those fake friends were the first to get going. But through it all, they had survived. They had bright futures ahead of them, and he couldn't risk anything happening to those futures just to prove his innocence.

"Dad," Jace said in a soft tone, filled with emotion. "It's good seeing you."

"Yeah, Dad, it's always good to see you," Caden tacked on.

"Dad, I—"

He held up his hand to stop whatever words Dalton was about to say. "Doesn't matter, son. You're here now, and that's all that matters to me. It's good seeing all three of you. Come, let's sit down. We need to talk and agree on a few things."

"We'll talk, Dad, but we're not sure we'll agree," Jace said, moving forward to take the first chair.

Sheppard waited until all three sons were seated before taking the chair across from them. As usual, Ambrose Cheney stood at the door. The man was more to Shep than just a prison guard. Over the years, they'd become friends. Ambrose had three sons who were the same ages Shep's sons had been when he'd been sent away. Ambrose never enforced the "no touching" policy whenever Shep's sons came to visit, because he fully understood the need for bear hugs.

"I guess you know we've met your new attorney," Dalton didn't waste time saying. "She's a very nice-looking woman, and it's obvious she's smart."

Sheppard smiled. "Yes, Carson is very attractive and a superb attorney. She's also intelligent and trustworthy."

"She's also in love with you," Dalton said, ignoring the kick to the leg he received under the table from Caden.

Sheppard stared across the table at his sons, who were staring back. "I'm in love with her, as well." As if his relationship with Carson was a closed subject, he quickly moved on to the next. "I understand you've met Striker, Stonewall and Quasar."

Caden nodded. "Nice guys."

"No-nonsense types," Jace chimed in.

"Real badasses," Dalton added. When his brothers frowned over at him, he raised his chin. "Well, they are."

"They're good men," Sheppard said, his gaze moving from one son to the other. "I would trust them with my life, though I wish I didn't have to trust them with yours."

Dalton thought that statement said a lot. "You should have told us about them."

"I couldn't. I needed to keep the three of you safe."

Caden shook his head. "We aren't kids who need protecting, Dad."

Sheppard nodded. "Not kids, but you do need protecting."

"Why?" Jace asked. "Because of some email you received?"

"Yes."

"Then we'll protect ourselves. Thanks to you and Granddad, we've gone hunting enough times to know how to handle firearms."

"That might not be enough. You have no idea what your mother was involved in."

Dalton lifted a brow and met his father's gaze. "Do you?"

Eleven

The entire room grew quiet, and all eyes were on Sheppard, studying his expression to see what sort of reaction Dalton's question had engendered. Sheppard drew in a deep breath, deciding to be completely honest.

"No, and trust me, I've had fifteen years to ponder it, replay the weeks, months and days leading up to Sylvia's death. Trying to remember her actions, recall anything unusual she might have said or done. But my mind goes blank."

He paused a minute and then said, "I do know that it was during that time when Granger Aeronautics was at its peak. We had government contracts coming in from left and right, and we'd just finished work on our first supersonic combustion engine. The model had been unveiled the year before. Everything was going great." *Except for my marriage.* And Sheppard refused to discuss just how terrible his relationship with their mother had become during that time.

"There are a lot of unanswered questions, Dad. So we hope you understand why we want to reopen your case," Jace said, leaning forward in his seat to stare directly into his father's eyes.

Instead of answering, his father handed him a slip of paper that had been lying on the corner of the table. "I don't want you to do that for this reason," Sheppard said.

Jace read the contents on the paper before passing it on to Caden, who skimmed it quickly and passed it on to Dalton. When Dalton saw his father frown, he figured that neither he nor his brothers had reacted the way their father had expected.

"So someone has threatened to kill us," Jace said casually.

"Yes, so hopefully now you understand why you can't reopen the case."

"Sorry, but we don't understand," Jace countered. "The one thing I think the three of us remember before you left for prison is that you always told us when the going got tough, that's when the tough got going. You said never to back away from a fight."

Sheppard nodded. "Yes, and I also recall telling you to choose your battles wisely. I'm taking that note seriously, guys."

"So are we, Dad," Caden said softly. "I would just love to meet the coward who wrote it. Evidently, there's information surrounding Mom's death he doesn't want exposed."

"And if he killed once, what would stop him from killing again?" Sheppard interjected.

"I dare him or anyone to mess with any of us," Dalton said angrily, tossing the paper back down on the table.

"What about your wives?"

Dalton's lips curved into a happy smile. "I don't have one of those."

Sheppard rolled his eyes. "I was referring to your brothers."

"And what *about* our wives?" Caden asked, holding his father's gaze captive.

"If you reopen the case, this demented person, whoever he is, will not just strike at you but might be crazy enough to go after those close to you. Those you love."

"I'd like to see him try," Dalton snarled. His eyes had darkened and seemed to flitter with deadly outrage, though moments before he had been quick to disavow having a wife.

"That's something the two of you need to think about," Sheppard said, addressing Jace and Caden, deciding for the time being to ignore the simmering fury radiating from his youngest son.

"Do you think we haven't, Dad?" Jace asked, rubbing his hands down the front of his face. "Caden and I talked it over with Shana and Shiloh, and they feel the same way we do. We want you out of here, and to do that, we have to expose the real murderer."

When Sheppard didn't say anything for a long moment, Caden asked, "If it were me in here instead of you, Dad, and someone made you the same threat, would you let me stay in here out of fear?"

"Damn it, it's not fear, Caden!" Sheppard said, raising his voice in frustration.

"We know, Dad," Caden responded gently. "And you're right. It's not fear. It's love. You might as well have given up your life fifteen years ago, at least life as you knew it. And if one of us...all of us...have to give up our lives for you, it will be worth it."

"Don't you see that it won't be worth it? If I were to lose any of you, I would lose everything."

"Think of what we've already lost. What we can still lose, Dad," Jace said hauntingly. "My son or daughter deserves to spend the time with you that the three of us lost. I want that for my child. For your grandchild."

Agony shone on Sheppard's face, was etched deep in his features. "Do you know what you're asking me?"

"Yes," Caden said with conviction. "To let us be the men we were raised to be."

Sheppard shook his head. "But not for this. You're a musician, Caden. Jace, you're an attorney." He glanced over at his youngest son and couldn't help the smile that touched his lips. "And Dalton, you're still trying to find your way."

Under a certain woman's skirt, Dalton thought, but his expression showed he was digesting his father's perspective. "You've forgotten to take something very important into account, Dad," Dalton said, leaning back in his chair.

"What?"

"Regardless of how you try to size us up, we're still your sons. Grangers. And I've never known a Granger to back down from a fight...or a challenge."

Sheppard could see this conversation was not going the way he'd hoped. His sons were stubborn. And they didn't know everything. He stood up and began pacing, knowing that everyone in the room, including Ambrose, was watching him.

He finally stopped pacing and faced them. "There's something else. Something you should all know."

Jace stood, as well, resting his hip on the edge of the table. Alert and attentive. "What?"

"It's something your grandfather and I suspected."

"Which was?" Caden asked just as alert and attentive.

"Marshall Imerson."

Dalton raised a brow. "Wasn't he the private investigator Granddad hired to look into your case?"

"Yes."

"I recall hearing he was killed while driving under the influence," Jace said.

Sheppard nodded. "That's what the police report said, but Dad and I never believed it, because we knew Marshall didn't drink. There were even rumors of financial problems within his company, and that he was into something illegal. I think those lies were spread deliberately so no one would suspect anything about his death."

"Anything like what?" Dalton asked, tension within him mounting.

"That he was murdered."

"Murdered?" Jace asked, shocked.

"Yes. He had contacted Dad about some new evidence he'd uncovered and was very excited about it. A few days later, before he could meet with Dad and tell him what he'd found, he was dead."

Dalton was fully aware of how silent everyone had become; even the prison guard appeared to have gone numb. "So you think…"

"Yes," Sheppard said, anticipating Dalton's question. "I believe he was too close to uncovering something, and someone didn't want that to happen. Whoever silenced Marshall is still out there, and that same person doesn't want anyone reopening my case. He'll do just about anything to make sure no one does."

Sheppard paused a minute. "So not only will the three of you be in danger, whoever you hire to reinvestigate my case could find himself in danger, too. Take my advice and let it go. I'll be up for parole in a couple of years and—"

"No, Dad," Jace interrupted in an adamant tone. "We're moving forward. Risk or no risk."

A sliver of daylight from the hallway came into the room, and Dalton saw that his dad was still sitting at the table. It was easy to see his head was lowered in frustration.

"Dad?"

Shep lifted his face to stare at his son. "Dalton? I thought all of you had left."

"Not yet," Dalton said, coming into the room and closing the door behind him. "Jace and Caden are outside in the hallway talking to Ambrose. I convinced him I needed to speak with you privately. He agreed to break another rule for me."

"Ambrose needs to stop doing that...breaking rules. He has a family to take care of, and he needs his job."

A smile touched Dalton's lips. "I know. He's out there in the hallway now, telling Jace and Caden about his sons." He moved to sit down at the table opposite his father. This time, Dalton took the time to study him, especially his features. He looked tired, worn, somewhat defeated. Dalton could just imagine what his father was dealing with right now. In the past, when they were younger, his dad told them what to do and they did it. Now things were different.

"Did you come back because you finally understood what I was saying? The risk I don't want the three of you to take?"

Dalton shook his head. "I got what you said the first time, Dad. We all did. But even considering the risk, I agree with Jace and Caden. This is something we have to do."

"Why? Because your grandfather made the three of you promise that you would?"

"No, because we love you, and it's time we bring you back home." And then, in an attempt to make light of the situation, Dalton leaned in closer and added, "Besides, I don't know how much longer I can handle Jace being in charge. He's a pain in the rear end. So we need to get you out of here and back to running Granger Aeronautics."

Even with anger and frustration consuming his body, Shep couldn't help but chuckle. In typical Dalton Granger style, his youngest son had soothed his ruffled feathers somewhat. But he was still not happy with the situation, mainly their refusal not to reopen his case.

"That might be true, but I'm sure complaining about Jace wasn't why you had Ambrose bend the rules to have a private talk with me." He studied his son intently, watching how his amused features suddenly became serious, intense.

"No, the reason I hung back was to tell you something."

Sheppard lifted a brow. "Tell me what?"

Dalton hesitated a moment and then said, "Something I probably should have told you years ago. About Mom."

Sheppard frowned. "What about your mom?"

Dalton hesitated a moment as he recalled how long he'd been carrying this secret around. The guilt he'd always felt in doing so. "I was young, probably around ten or eleven years old."

When he didn't say anything else, his father coaxed him further. "Go on."

He met his father's stare. "I found out Mom was having an affair."

He heard his father swear under his breath. "I think you need to start from the beginning, Dalton."

Dalton nodded. "It was the year before she died. I was hiding because I had been acting up in class that day, and I figured my teacher would be calling you and Mom to let you know. You'd already threatened to stop me from riding Glory if I got into any more trouble in school." Glory had been his horse, a beautiful palomino his grandparents had given him for his eighth birthday.

"I hid out in the boathouse, hoping no one would find me. I was hiding in the closet. That's when I saw Mom...with a man who wasn't you. She saw me when I sneaked out of the closet, but the man never did. Later that night, Mom came to my room and made me promise not to tell anyone."

Sheppard drew in a deep breath as rage swept through his body. Not because his wife had brought her lover to Sutton Hills, but for what she'd done to their child. How dare she let him be a witness to her treacherous behavior and then hold him to secrecy?

"I should have told you long ago. I should never have promised Mom that I—"

"No, Dalton," Shep interrupted in a soft tone and with a gentle smile. "You did the right thing. If she made you promise not to tell, then you shouldn't have. A promise is a promise."

"Just like a vow is a vow?" Dalton countered angrily. "When the two of you married, you exchanged vows, right?"

"Yes."

"Vows are to be kept, not broken. What gave Mom the right to break hers with another man?"

Now that, Shep thought, was a question he could not answer. But what he could do was release his son from the guilt he must still feel for keeping Sylvia's promise. "It doesn't matter now. You did the right thing in doing what she asked you to do."

"But you'll never know how I felt all those years, Dad. I was young at the time, and at first I thought it was cool having a secret with Mom, one that nobody else knew about. Not you, Jace or Caden. Not even Grandpa. But when I got older and realized what she'd been doing and understood the depth of the promise she'd asked me to keep, I felt sick inside. I knew I had betrayed you."

"You didn't betray me, Dalton." *However, your mother did.*

"I loved Mom, Dad. But what she did to you was wrong."

And what she did to you was even worse, son, Shep thought, reaching out and taking hold of Dalton's shoulder. They stared at each other in silence. He'd known about Sylvia's affair with Michael Greene, but he'd been willing to keep his marriage together, anyway, for his sons. "It's okay, Dalton. That all happened years ago."

"I know. I'll never forget that day. Jace and Caden thought the man she was with was Michael Greene, but it wasn't."

Shep's jaw dropped, startled. "It wasn't?"

"No. I knew Mr. Greene, and the man I saw Mom with that day wasn't him. It was a man I'd never seen before."

If it wasn't Michael Greene, then who? Shep wondered. He would never forget the day he received the pictures Greene's wife, Yolanda, had sent to his office. She'd hired a private investigator and had been more than happy to share what the man had uncovered. There had been several photographs of Michael Greene and Sylvia together in a number of compromising positions.

He had confronted Sylvia about it, and she hadn't denied a thing. In fact, she had laughed in his face and told him that he was stuck with her if he wanted to remain a father to his sons. That had been her leverage. That had always been her leverage.

When they heard two raps on the door indicating Ambrose couldn't bend the rules any longer, they stood. "I feel better now that I've told you," Dalton said, releasing a deep breath. "Every time I came here and saw you, the guilt I felt beat me down."

That explains why he hasn't come here as often as the others, Shep thought, coming around the table to hug his son. "It was not your fault, Dalton. It was never your fault. You did nothing wrong."

"Thanks, Dad. I know this might sound crazy, but after all these years, I needed to hear that."

Twelve

Definitely déjà vu, Jules thought as she sat parked outside Dalton's place exactly three nights after the last time. This time she wasn't questioning her sanity, mainly because she had a plan. She was fully aware of the Granger brothers visit to their father and, thanks to Shana, she'd known things hadn't gone the way Sheppard Granger had hoped. She also knew that yesterday her father, keeping his word to Sheppard, had met with Jace, Caden and Dalton at Granger Aeronautics. From what her father told her that morning at breakfast, the three appreciated his meeting with them but were fully aware of the risks in the decision they'd made. They were determined not to back down and had the blessings of their wives. Jules thought all that might be fine and dandy with them, but one of those wives happened to be her sister, so it wasn't fine or dandy with her. Although her father had stressed it was their decision, and the Bradfords needed to honor it, she wasn't that compliant.

So here she was again, for the second time this week, at Dalton's home, trying to get him to go along with her way of thinking. As far as she knew, he had not changed his mind about attending Shana's party tomorrow night, but the matter she now needed to discuss with him was much more important. To her, it was a matter of life and death.

After the briefest of hesitations, she opened her car door and got out, noticing how much the temperature had dropped since the noon hour. Her leather coat was little protection from the cutting cold and icy winds, the result of an earlier downpour.

There was no need to be concerned with the car that had followed Dalton home tonight. Stonewall Courson was no longer being discreet. He'd parked and was sitting with the window down as if he were enjoying the chilly weather. She could tolerate a lot of things, but cold weather was not one of them. After living most of her life in Boston, she should be used to it, but she wasn't. She was aware that Stonewall had noticed her vehicle the moment he had parked. He had glanced her way, seeming to acknowledge her presence, after which he ignored her, knowing she was no threat.

She decided to speak when she passed by his car. "Stonewall."

He tilted his head in a nod. "Ms. Bradford."

Was that presumption she saw in his eyes, like he knew the reason for her late-night visit to Dalton? At the moment, she couldn't have cared less what he assumed and continued to make her way to Dalton's front door. Suddenly, it began raining again, and she increased her pace when the showers began coming down in earnest.

Before she had time to react, a huge golf umbrella covered her. She glanced up into Stonewall's face and realized she hadn't heard him get out of the car. The man was too much like a panther—sleek, deathly quick and quiet—for her peace of mind. Oh, she needed to include muscular, as well.

"I'm sure Dalton wouldn't want you to get wet."

Honestly? Dalton wouldn't care if the rain drowned me, she thought, forcing back a laugh. Stonewall had the nature of her relationship with Dalton totally wrong, but she didn't have the time or the inclination to explain anything to him. Instead, she simply accepted his gesture of kindness. "Thanks."

"You're welcome."

As soon as her feet touched the floor of Dalton's covered porch, she heard Stonewall say, "Enjoy your night," and then he was gone through the rain and back to his car.

Enjoy her night? In Dalton's presence? He had to be kidding. In fact, he might be a witness to just how much she and Dalton disliked each other when he opened the door to find her standing there. Dalton might slam the door in her face or even refuse to answer it. She knew she was taking her chances coming here unannounced tonight, but she'd also known he wouldn't take a phone call from her if she'd made one.

The rain began pelting down harder, and because of the wind the covered porch did little to shield her from it. She tightened her coat around her with one hand and lifted the other hand to ring his doorbell.

Dalton had stepped out of the shower and begun drying off when he heard his doorbell. Stonewall was parked outside, so if the person had gotten past his watchdog, that meant there was no threat. The one thing he'd figured out about Stonewall was that he pretty much had everything under control. The man was there when he left in the morning and was on his tail when he came home at night. Dalton just didn't get it. It was storming outside—who in their right mind would want to sit in a car all night in the rain? He had invited him inside, but Stonewall had refused his offer, saying he would be fine. He liked the rain and cold, because during those years he was locked up, he'd been without both.

Wrapping a towel around his waist, he walked out of his bedroom toward his front door. Playing on the side of caution, he took a look out the peephole and blinked. WTF? Jules? Again? What the hell did she want?

He opened the door and stepped aside to let her in, telling himself there was no need for him to stand in the doorway and catch pneumonia, even if it looked as if she had a mind to. Why was she out in the pouring rain? "You better have a good reason for coming here at this hour and in this weather."

"We need to talk."

"About what?" he asked despite his irritation, closing the door when she walked in. "I thought I made it clear the other night that I have no intention of going to your sister's dinner party tomorrow night."

'That's not what I want to talk about."

"Umm, let me guess. You've changed your mind and are making a booty call, after all."

She rolled her eyes. "Get serious."

"Baby, I am serious." He tried not to notice how her hair, damp from rain, hung down her shoulders, giving her a sexy look. Too bad the rain hadn't washed away her scent; it was there drifting through his nostrils, inciting all sorts of ideas in his mind. "So if you're not making a booty call, did you come by for another kiss?"

She snorted. "Not on your life."

He frowned, no longer interested in playing guessing games. "So what brought you to my doorstep in the pouring rain, Jules? What is it you want to talk about?"

After a moment's hesitation, she said, "I intend to find the person who killed your mother."

Jules watched. First his eyes widened, and then his lips drew in a tight line while he eyed her like she'd suddenly become a strange phenomenon. And while he was doing all of that, she was studying him, as well. There was no use arguing the point that perhaps *ogling* was a better word as she gave him a long, in-depth perusal from head to toe.

"Now that's an interesting joke," he drawled, crossing his arms over his chest. "I'm curious to hear the punch line."

Somehow, she'd known he wouldn't take her seriously. "No joke. No punch line. I will explain things in detail after you put on some clothes."

He glanced down at himself and smiled as if he found the very idea that she was bothered by what he was wearing rather amusing. But when he met her gaze again, his smile had been replaced with a deep frown. "What makes you think I want to hear anything you have to say?"

Jules thought that was an easy question, one with several answers, but for now, she would give him the one that mattered. "Because you know your father is innocent of a crime he's spent the past fifteen years paying for."

Dalton stood there a moment and stared at her, as if he was trying to decide whether she deserved to waste any more of his time. But she knew as well as he did that what she said had pulled him in. If nothing else, he was intrigued. It wouldn't take much thought to determine what was more important. That towel wrapped around his waist or hearing what she had to say. The towel lost.

"It won't take me but a minute to change into something more appropriate. I would suggest you make yourself at home, but I don't imagine you will be here that long."

He turned and walked away. Was that arrogant strut from the room supposed to be for her benefit? Deliberately done to cause that familiar ache between her legs? It would be her luck that Dalton Granger was sex incarnate on the most luscious pair of legs any man could own.

She removed her coat, hung it on the coatrack and began pacing. It was either that or stand still and lick her lips dry while that ache intensified. Why was she allowing him to get to her this way? Yet she was here, while it was pouring rain outside, to offer her services. But not in the way that could definitely relieve the horniness that had been racking her mind and body for days.

"Ah, you're still here," he said, coming back into the room. Thankfully, he was no longer wrapped in that towel but had slid into a pair of khakis and a T-shirt. She tried not to act surprised when she read the large words emblazoned across his chest. *I lick*. She meant to ignore it, but then she decided that since he'd probably put it on to annoy her, she intended to show him it hadn't worked.

The corners of her lips curved into a barely there smile, just enough to let him know his T-shirt didn't bother her. "Nice shirt. I need to get one for myself, because I lick, as well."

Bam. As she expected, heat suddenly swirled in his eyes. Men. They could try to be cool, smooth and suave. But at hearing the first word connected to sex from a woman's lips, they would become primitive creatures who thought a good lay would ease all of their troubles. She hated admitting it but, at the moment, she was thinking the same thing.

"Then maybe we can have a licking party one of these days," Dalton said, intruding into her thoughts.

She momentarily tightened her lips to refrain from saying, *Yum yum.* Instead, her response was, "Trust me, that won't be happening."

He shrugged as he gestured for her to sit down on the sofa while he sat down in the wingback chair. "I'm listening."

There was no doubt in her mind as she sat down that Dalton knew just what women thought of him. Some would even find him irresistible. Eye candy so sweet it could be considered sinful. She'd watched when he eased down in the chair and noted the way his khakis stretched over powerful thighs. The thought of a female's body being held tight by those thighs while he rode her to glory had her shifting positions in her seat.

"You okay?"

His voice was a rough caress that seemed to rake sensuously across her skin, sending luscious shivers down her spine. But, of course, she wouldn't tell him any of that to feed his already overstuffed ego. "I'm fine."

"Glad to hear it. Now you were saying…"

How could a man look intrigued and sensuous at the same time? She held his gaze, and was it her imagination, or had the air surrounding them taken on a deliriously stimulating aura? And why had it begun feeding her sexual hunger? Forcing the thought from her mind, she said, "As I stated earlier, I intend to find your mother's killer."

"Why?" he asked with obvious annoyance in his

tone. "You never knew my mother, and you don't know my father. As far as I know, you've never met him."

"No, I haven't," she agreed. "But I don't need to meet him to want an injustice overturned. Besides, my father met him, and his opinion is good enough for me."

He waved off her words. "Stop trying to sound so damned noble. I refuse to believe that you don't have an ulterior motive for wanting to find my mother's killer."

She didn't respond immediately but gave him a long, hard stare. "You're right. I do have an ulterior motive. My sister. Your brothers might not have a problem with dragging their wives into your family madness, but I do."

Dalton leaned forward, and the anger that stiffened his jaw was radiating off him. "My brothers do have a problem with it, but I was told that it was those same wives, especially your sister, who reminded them of the vows they took together. That *we promise to love and protect each other* bullshit."

Jules wished at that moment she could say something in Shana's defense, but she couldn't. That's why she hadn't discussed any of her plans with her sister. Since falling in love, Shana's entire attitude and outlook on things had changed. Jace wasn't just her husband. He was now her soul mate…at least, Shana was convinced he was. In Shana's present state of mind, there was nothing she wouldn't do for her husband, including agreeing to place her own life in danger.

And Jules could probably say the same for Caden's wife. She'd seen the pair together and could feel their love and affection, the strong hold of their commitment and dedication to each other. That degree of love for another person was downright scary.

"Okay, we can agree that it's Shana's and Shiloh's

choice, but I intend to do something about it before somebody gets crazy. Somebody like the actual killer."

"And you think you can just walk in and solve a case that's been closed for fifteen years?"

"And you and your brothers don't intend to try doing that same thing? I assume you were going to hire a PI to check things out."

"Yes, but before you get some kind of crazy inkling that the PI should be you, there's something you might want to think about."

"What?"

"Dad is convinced the last person my grandfather hired to prove his innocence ended up dead."

The smooth arch of Jules's brow rose. "Are you saying the man was murdered?"

"Yes, that's exactly what I'm saying."

Jules was pacing.

Dalton thought about saying something about wearing out his carpet. But who gave a damn about carpet when he was getting a front-row seat for the most incredible pair of legs any woman had a right to own?

She was wearing a skirt and blouse, and to say she looked good in both would be an understatement. What he'd told her about Imerson had her thinking. She was in deep thought, and so was he. The woman had such an indescribably sexy force that he was totally captivated. Definitely an amazing sampling of femininity—he'd been hard fifty times over and was still expanding. He'd switched positions on the sofa to relieve the strain on his crotch, and she hadn't even noticed.

But he'd noticed a number of things. Like how that denim skirt was hugging her delectable ass and the way that crimson blouse was shielding what he figured had to be two magnificent breasts. He couldn't help wondering what she was wearing beneath her skirt and blouse. Satin, lace or both. She would be the type of woman whose bra would have to match whatever panties she wore.

She finally stopped pacing and glanced over at him. They exchanged a long look that let him know she was aware of his sexual state. Her gaze left his eyes to drift downward to his zipper. She rolled her eyes before glaring at him. "How can you think of sex at a time like this?"

He gave her a long, slow perusal from head to toe. "Easily. Do you know what I see whenever I look at you?"

She didn't answer. He figured she was afraid of his response. However, he would tell her, anyway. "What I see whenever I look at you is an orgasm just waiting to happen."

He couldn't help but smile at the darkening of her cheeks. Wow. He'd made her blush. And was that heat stirring in her eyes? "Do I need to prove my point, Jules?"

She lifted her chin. "Do you mind?"

"Mind what? Having sex with you? It would be my pleasure."

She closed her eyes and looked up toward his ceiling as if silently counting to ten. Hell, she could count to thirty, and his desire for her wouldn't diminish one iota.

She glanced back at him. "Look, Dalton."

He stood, feeling frustrated and angry all at once. "No, you look. I didn't invite you here. I don't invite women to my home."

She placed her hands on her hips. "My being here is not personal."

"Maybe not on your end, but it is on mine. Do you know how it feels having an itch you can't scratch?"

"That's not my problem."

He crossed the room in a flash, covered the distance separating them, meeting her face-to-face. "It is your problem, because you owe me."

"I owe you nothing."

"You told me to find you, and I did."

"Yes, but you found me for one thing and one thing only. How do you think that made me feel?"

"It should have made you feel special, knowing any man would go to such lengths." No need to tell her of the many nights she had haunted his dreams and that before her, he hadn't bothered running after any woman.

"You just don't get it, do you? I came here with a serious agenda, and all you can think about is getting me in your bed?"

Dalton knew he should back off, put his libido in check, but for some reason, he couldn't. At that moment he was too overcome with horniness to think straight. "Oh, getting you just in my bed isn't my fantasy anymore, Jules. I want to get you on that wingback chair, this sofa, my kitchen table, the kitchen counter, up against my refrigerator, on top of my stove, on my stairs, every damned wall in this house and the backseat of my car, if it had one. What I just named are places. And the various positions I'm imagining will blow your mind. I want you. Bad. Do I make myself clear?"

Her eyes were filled with more anger than he'd ever seen before. "Clear as glass." And then without saying another word, she moved to the coatrack, grabbed her coat, went to the door and stormed out.

Dalton stood there, feeling like a total ass. Every damned encounter with Jules Bradford turned out to be un-freaking-believable. Why did lust get to have a mind of its own and rule a person's senses? She had come here to talk to him about reopening his father's case, and all he'd thought about was jumping her damned bones... in every damned spot in his house as well as his car.

At least it had stopped raining so she hadn't gotten wet when she'd left. He rubbed his hand down his face and simmered with frustration as he remembered her words: *You found me for one thing and one thing only. How do you think that made me feel?*

Shit, any other woman would have felt fucking honored. But then, he wasn't dealing with just any other woman. He was dealing with Jules Bradford, ex-cop, ex-detective, present-day sex goddess, with remarkable eyes, perfectly curvy ass and a pair of gorgeous legs. The same woman who could walk into a room and make heads turn and dicks get hard.

And his was more than hard; it was pounding. He needed to get his mind off what he wouldn't be getting from Jules again tonight, and the best way to do that was by being turbocharged. He grabbed his car keys from the table to take his car out for a spin, but then tossed them back. If he left, that meant Stonewall would follow, and the man shouldn't be inconvenienced just because he was in a horny state.

Dalton sighed as he headed for his bedroom to take off his clothes. This would be another one of those nights when he went to bed feeling needy as hell.

Thirteen

"I must say, your first dinner party as Mrs. Jace Granger was a great success," Jules whispered to her sister while glancing around Shana's home. "I'm impressed."

Shana grinned softly. "Thanks, but I can't claim all the credit, since I had help. Hannah was a godsend. She has all that experience of catering dinner parties for the Grangers over the past many years. And now she's doing it for an entirely new generation."

"How long has she been working for the Grangers? And this is delicious, by the way," Jules said, biting into a mini chocolate truffle.

Shana smiled. "That's another Hannah original recipe, and it is delicious. She's been with the Granger family since Jace's dad was a kid. That's why everyone adores her so much. She's a sweetie pie. In addition to cooking all this food, she volunteered to be here tonight, working behind the scenes to make sure everything runs smoothly."

"Well, just let her know I think she's a wonderful cook," Jules said, smiling. "I told her that at your wedding, but it won't hurt to tell her again."

Jules glanced around the living room. She knew some of the people and surmised the others were either business associates of Jace's or family friends. Of course, there were business associates of Shana's in attendance, as well.

She saw her father and Mona talking to an older couple near the fireplace. "Who is that talking to Dad and Mona?"

Shana followed her gaze. "That's Harold and Helen Owens. According to Jace, Mr. Owens and his grandfather were good friends, and they played golf together regularly. They weren't originally on the list of invitees, but Jace ran into Harold last week at the bank and decided to invite them since they weren't in town for our wedding."

"Well, they evidently have a lot to say. It seems Dad is barely getting a word in. The old woman's mouth is moving a mile a minute," Jules said, grabbing a couple more truffles from the tray being offered by a passing waitress.

"I meant to ask where you were last night," Shana said, taking a sip of her apple juice.

"Last night?" Jules asked, glancing around again, refusing to meet her sister's eye.

"Yes. I called you and didn't get an answer even though it was after eleven o'clock."

Jules knew exactly where she had been at that particular time. But the last thing she would do is let Shana know she'd made a fool of herself yet again by going over to Dalton's place. "Umm, I was probably in the shower or something."

At that moment, Kent Fairfield rolled up. Kent worked for Shana's company as a troubleshooter. A veteran of the Iraq war, he'd been left paralyzed in both legs by the shrapnel from a missile blast. What Jules admired most about him was that he hadn't let being wheelchair-bound stop him from succeeding in life. He was married and his wife, Marsha, was pregnant with their first child. According to Shana, he was good at his job, and she considered him a key player in her organization and a valuable member of her team. It was Kent's discovery of the wrongdoings at Granger Aeronautics that had saved Jace's life a few months ago.

They had been standing, holding a conversation with Kent for a good ten minutes when Shana looked up and said, "Now this is a surprise. I thought he wasn't coming."

Following her sister's gaze, Jules glanced toward the foyer, and her gaze connected to Dalton's.

"I wonder why he changed his mind," Shana mused.

Jules broke eye contact with Dalton, glanced over at her sister and shrugged. "Trust me, I have no idea."

Dalton wasn't surprised when his brothers approached him with wariness lining their eyes. "Dalton, we thought you weren't coming tonight," Jace said, taking a sip of his drink and eyeing him closely.

"You said as much," Caden chimed in.

Dalton shrugged. "Can't a man change his mind?"

"Depends," Jace replied, looking at him over the rim of his glass. "Why did you change your mind?"

Dalton grabbed a drink off the tray on the coffee table. "For a number of reasons, which I don't intend to get into now with the two of you."

"That might be the case," Jace said in a firm tone. "But I expect you to be on your best behavior, because I'm sure you know Jules is here."

Yes, he knew, which was why he'd decided to come,

after all. "Whatever. Now if you guys will excuse me, I think I'll mosey over to Shana and say hello."

Caden touched his arm. "Jules is with Shana."

The corners of his lips tilted into a grin. "I know. Imagine that." And then he walked off, knowing his brothers were watching his every move. He even heard one of them mutter a low curse.

Halfway across the room he was stopped by a couple that knew him, but he didn't immediately remember them until they told him their names. Damn, the Owenses looked *old*. But then he figured since they'd been friends of his grandparents back in the day, they should look old. It had been close to ten years since he'd seen them. How had they aged that much in ten years?

Of course, they had to travel down memory lane and remind him of all those things he did as a kid. Out of respect, he listened and did very little talking. Not that they seemed to notice, since they were the ones keeping the conversation going.

"Is it true what we heard about you?" Mrs. Owens leaned in to ask. He snapped back to attention. He'd been distracted when he noticed Jules was no longer talking to Shana but was now engaged in conversation with some man. Who was that guy? In fact, who *were* all these people here tonight?

He smiled down at Helen Owens. "It depends on what you heard."

"That you're more of a ladies' man than either of your brothers."

He wondered where the hell she'd been living, since that had always been the case. "Yes, I guess that's true," he said, trying to keep his smile in place.

"What about you?" Harold Owens then asked. "Marriage in your future plans?"

Dalton had to bite his lip to keep from saying, *Hell, no. Triple hell, no.* Instead, in a respectful tone, he said, "No, sir. Marriage is not in my future plans." Then, making an excuse about needing to talk to Shana, he quickly moved on.

Shana watched her brother-in-law head over in her direction as if he had fire under his feet. She wondered what his problem was, but with Dalton you could never tell. The reason his features appeared all too serious couldn't be because Jules was here. He'd known she would be. In fact, it was his presence that was a surprise.

She glanced past him to where her husband stood, talking to a group of people. Their gazes connected, and Jace shrugged broad shoulders, letting her know he had no idea what was going on with his brother. That meant it was up to her to find out.

"Shana," Dalton said, giving her a hug.

"Dalton. Glad you changed your mind and decided to come."

He nodded, taking a sip of whatever he was drinking while glancing around. "Nice crowd."

"Thanks."

"Who are these people, anyway?" he asked, frowning.

She countered his frown with a smile. "A mixture of family, friends and both my business associates and Jace's. And, of course, you have those who took it upon themselves to bring a guest. So there are a few people here Jace and I don't even know."

Dalton's frown deepened. "Considering everything, do you think that's wise?"

She smiled. "We're safe if that's why you're asking.

I'm in a house with two ex-cops, two bodyguards and an FBI agent." The FBI agent she was referring to was Marcel Eaton, an ex-cop turned federal agent who had worked with her dad in Boston. Marcel, who had also moved to Charlottesville from Boston, had been the agent who handled the Granger Aeronautics trade secrets violations and embezzlement a few months ago when four arrests were made. More currently, he was investigating a Granger Aeronautics employee, whose death by suicide was now suspect.

"Quasar and Striker are here?" Dalton asked, glancing around again.

"Yes. They thought it would be best if they worked the party from the inside while Stonewall kept a watch on the outside. There they are, coming in off the patio."

Dalton turned, saw the two men in business suits, and chuckled. "Hey, they're blending in well."

"I think so, too."

Dalton's gaze raked over her. "You're beginning to look pregnant."

Was that censure she heard in his voice? Shana held back a laugh. "I look pregnant because I *am* pregnant. It was going to happen sooner or later, Dalton."

"Yes, I suppose," he said, as if he wasn't truly convinced. He glanced around again. "So where is Jules?"

Shana considered his question and couldn't help pondering the reason for it. "Mingling somewhere, I suppose. Why do you ask?"

"No reason."

Shana saw the flash of a smile that touched his lips and wondered whether there was a private joke. "Jules is surprised you came tonight when you said you wouldn't," she said, watching him closely. "And to be quite honest, so am I."

Dalton gave her the smooth grin that she was certain could make some women drool. "You should know by now that I'm a man full of surprises. I think I'll mingle, as well. See you later."

He moved to walk off but turned back and smiled. "By the way, nice party, Shana."

"And how long have you been living in Charlottes-ville, Jules?"

Jules glanced over her glass at the man who'd sort of latched on to her a few moments ago. And he hadn't wasted any time suggesting they take a stroll on the patio that overlooked a beautiful lake. His name was Gary Coughlin. He wasn't bad to look at; in his late for-ties he was slightly older than the men who normally held her interest. But he was a man, and it appeared he had all working body parts. Hell, she'd even allow the blue pill if it came to that.

"A few years," she said, deciding not to get more specific than that. No need to give or receive too much information. "Now, tell me again how you know Jace and Shana." When she'd asked the first time, she re-called that he never got around to answering.

"I never met them before tonight, actually. I'm fairly new to town and came with a friend who's a business associate of Jace's. Ron is CEO of Zimmons Aviation Supply Company."

Jules nodded. "And what brought you to Charlot-tesville?"

"Needing a change of scenery after a divorce. I started a retail company right out of college and re-cently sold it for a nice profit. Now I'm free to just kick back and enjoy life."

And enjoy women. Jules smiled at the thought of that.

"Good for you." She took a sip of her drink and then asked, "So what are your plans when you leave here tonight?" Although she wasn't one who made a habit of indulging in one-night stands, there were times a woman had to do what a woman had to do. Especially when her toys weren't doing their job.

Gary looked at her and smiled, evidently picking up on her hint of what she had in mind. "I don't have any plans for later. Any ideas?"

Do you want to see the list? Being in Dalton's presence twice in one week had worked on certain parts of her body. And then last night, his rattling off all the places in his home where he wanted to have sex with her hadn't helped. And what kind of man would tell a woman that whenever he looked at her he saw an orgasm just waiting to happen? Unfortunately, that's all she'd been thinking about since last night. Orgasms. Multiple ones. Explosive ones. The beat-your-head-against-the-bedpost kind. She needed one of those quick, fast and dirty.

"So this is where you ran off to, Jules."

She muttered a low curse and turned around. Why was Dalton pretending he'd been looking for her? She drew in a deep breath and intended to be pleasant even if it killed her. "I was enjoying a conversation with Gary. Gary Coughlin, this is Dalton Granger. Jace's brother," she said, introducing the two men.

They exchanged handshakes, and it was obvious they were also sizing each other up. She hated admitting it, but she was, too. And as much as she didn't want to admit it, Dalton had taken over the show.

"So you're the third brother," Gary said, smiling.

"Yes, and you know Jace how?" Dalton wanted to know.

Jules rolled her eyes and fought to hold her tongue while Gary provided the same information he'd given her earlier. "Well, Gary, if you don't mind, I need to talk to Jules privately for a minute."

Jules was tempted to give Dalton a few harsh words then and there, but figured Gary shouldn't be party to such a tongue-lashing, so she smiled sweetly up at him. "Gary, we will definitely finish our conversation later. What Dalton and I need to discuss should take less than a minute."

Dalton's piercing brown eyes turned on her, and the message she read in them all but said he'd be damned if that was true. With a lot of effort, she tightened her lips until she was sure Gary was out of hearing range. Then she turned on Dalton. "You've got *one* minute."

Fourteen

Dalton frowned. One minute, his ass. If she thought that was all the time he was going to get, then she was wrong. He had overheard the last part of her conversation with Coughlin. They were in the midst of making plans for hooking up later tonight. He shouldn't really care what she did with her time, but it really irked him no end that she had no qualms about engaging in an illicit affair with Coughlin, but she flatly refused to give him the time of day. Or, preferably, her night. "I think we need to go somewhere and talk."

They stood not even a foot away from each other, appearing to square off. He looked down into eyes that were usually dark brown. But tonight in the lanterns around the patio, they appeared a stormy gray. "What on Earth do we have to talk about, Dalton?"

"We need to discuss what you told me last night about your interest in finding the person who killed my mother."

She glared at him. "Oh, you're interested in that now, are you? Last night all you wanted to do was fuck me."

He glared back. "Oh, don't get me wrong. I still want

to fuck you. But, at the moment, I want to hear what you have to say about finding my mother's killer."

"Too bad, because I don't feel like talking."

"Really? What's wrong? A cat got your tongue?" he sneered, his gaze latching on to her mouth. Why did she have such a luscious pair of lips on that smart-ass mouth?

"Yes, I guess you can say the cat has my tongue," she replied snippily.

Dalton didn't like her attitude. Felt it needed adjusting. "Then by all means let me get your tongue back from the damned cat." And then he drew her into his arms and lowered his mouth to hers.

Pleasure that Jules didn't want...but definitely needed...filled her entire body the moment Dalton's tongue slid inside her mouth. And just like the last time, she was consumed in a kiss that had her purring deep in her throat. But then, in a way, the kiss was different. More powerful. Carnal. Possessive. It was as if he were intentionally claiming a part of her while at the same time wiping her desire for any other man from her mind, soul and body.

Mentally, she tried fighting Dalton's takeover of her senses but found herself sinking deeper and deeper into the kiss. She'd always enjoyed being kissed, and loved the feel of a man's hand touching her backside while doing so. But Dalton wasn't just touching it; he was artfully molding it to fit perfectly against his tall frame so she could feel certain parts of him...like his engorged penis. The size, the shape and the way it was pressing hard in the juncture of her thighs was incredible. It would be easy and pretty damned satisfying to reach out and lower his zipper and get what she wanted, just what she needed, to ease the ache that had been driving her to madness lately. The thought of brushing her fingertips across the swollen head of his penis before lifting her skirt and sliding down her panties so he could slide it inside her brought glints of sexual pleasure to eat away at her, causing a delicious shiver to cascade through her body.

To radiate this much mind-boggling power in a kiss was a gift few men possessed, and it was turning her into a wickedly wanton woman. She was beginning to lose her ever-loving mind and wasn't certain she could turn back.

The clearing of someone's throat was a harsh intrusion, and she pulled out of Dalton's arms and looked over her shoulder to see Jace. "Excuse me, I hate to interrupt, but your father was looking for you, Jules. I think he's about to leave and wanted to tell you goodnight." With that said, Jace turned and went back inside.

Jules drew in a deep breath, and with it came Dalton's masculine scent, which seemed to be all over her, drenching her skin and clothing. "I have to go," she said, trying to move away quickly and regain her perspective as well as her common sense. She could just imagine what Jace thought.

Dalton reached out and grasped her arm to pull her back into him. "Not so fast. We didn't finish our conversation."

She glared up at him. "And whose fault is that?"

"It's not a question of fault, Jules," Dalton said in a husky voice. "For us, it has become a question of sanity. You know what I want, and I know what you want. Why are we fighting the inevitable?"

That was a good question, one she wasn't ready to answer. "I need to go say goodbye to Dad."

He held firm to her hand. "Come by my place later. We do need to talk."

She shook her head. "No, not your place." Not when he'd pretty much spelled out all the areas in his home where he wanted to take her. Just her luck, she'd be weak and needy enough to let him do it.

"Then your place."

That was even worse. He probably wouldn't make it over the threshold before she would be tearing the clothes off his body. Especially tonight when she was so wound up for sex. "No. If we need to talk…and *only* talk…we can do so over coffee at Manning's parents' restaurant. They stay open late on the weekends."

"Who's Manning?"

"My administrative assistant. And the restaurant isn't far from here." She paused. "So far, you're the only one who knows that I intend to find your mother's killer. I don't want anyone else to know just yet, until I finish my preliminary research on the case."

A deep frown covered his face, and she could tell he hadn't liked what she'd said. "I don't like the idea of your getting involved. I told you what happened to the last PI who was hired. You're placing yourself in danger."

She shrugged. "Better me than my sister and her unborn child." She then rattled off the address of the restaurant. "Give me about half an hour, and I'll meet you there." And then she quickly left.

Jules paused briefly to glance over her shoulder and saw Dalton following her back inside from the patio. She glanced around and saw Shana wearing one of those I-know-what-you-were-out-there-doing smirks. Jules didn't have to wonder why. Chances were good that Jace had told Shana about the kiss he'd interrupted.

Fifteen

Sitting at a table in the back of the restaurant, Dalton watched as a smiling Jules entered the establishment and hugged the older couple that greeted her. And then with much too much familiarity for Dalton's liking, she gave a huge hug to the muscular guy who came out from the back. Who was he? A former lover? A present one?

And why do I care? That was the same question he'd asked himself earlier after he'd come in off the patio and scanned Shana's party for Gary Coughlin, who was nowhere in sight. Dalton assumed he must have left.

He sighed deeply, feeling annoyed with himself. When had Dalton Richard Granger begun feeling territorial about any woman? Especially the one walking toward him. The one who looked like she would prefer to be any place other than meeting with him tonight. And she also looked damned good. Too damned good, which is why Coughlin had been all over her. What man wouldn't have been? Her blue wool dress clung to her curves in a way that should be outlawed, and her boots, a different pair than she'd had on the other night, looked good with her outfit, giving her an overall sexy look. Hell, as far as he was concerned, Jules wore sexiness like she outright owned it. She was different from any woman he'd ever wanted to make love to, and for some reason, he felt his desire for her stemmed from more than just her sexiness and beauty. More than the fact he wanted at least one night—one whole fucking night with her, doing just that.

She didn't acknowledge his presence but merely slid into the chair across from him and picked up a menu. "Glad you could make it," he said easily, deliberately drawing in a deep breath so he could inhale her scent.

"Whatever," she responded drily.

For him it was more than just a *whatever*. He had never wanted a woman to the degree that he wanted Jules, which was a fact established months ago. What he was still having a hard time coming to terms with was her attitude toward him. She was so indifferent, although he knew she wanted him probably just as much as he wanted her. Yet she refused to budge. They'd kissed twice, and both times had been initiated by him. At first, he thought she was playing one of those feminine games, but now he wasn't so sure. She was confusing the hell out of him, and a man who was supposed to know every single thing about women should not be confused. He was slowly discovering that lust could be fueled by something more potent than sexual desire, but for the life of him, he wasn't sure what that component was.

"I suggest a glass of wine instead of coffee," he said.

She looked across the table at him. "Why?"

He held her gaze. "Because tonight I'm in the mood to savor something. Slowly. Unhurriedly. Leisurely. And since I can't savor you, the wine will have to do." He watched the way her eyes darkened, the way her lips parted with a heated breath. Yes, she wanted him as much as he wanted her. But she was deliberately holding back.

"Why do you say such things?" she asked, her mouth now set in a petulant frown.

He shrugged. "I only say what I mean, Juliet."

Her frown deepened. "I prefer Jules."

"And I prefer a number of things. The first on my list is—"

"I can just imagine what's first on your list," she interrupted him.

"I doubt that you do. However, I will say it does involve you. But it's not all about *what* we'll be doing. It includes *how* we'll be doing it."

She placed her menu down. "You wanted to talk."

He would allow her to change the subject, satisfied he'd given her enough to mull over. "No, I'm ready to listen. Evidently, you're going to do whatever you want to do, so I assume you have a plan."

They paused when a waiter came to take their order, and it just had to be the guy she'd given an extremely large hug to earlier. "I'd like a glass of Riesling," Dalton said, not taking his eyes off her.

"I'll have the same, please, Manning."

Dalton raised a brow when the waiter walked off. "Manning? I thought you said Manning was your administrative assistant."

"He is. I also said his parents owned this restaurant. He likes helping them out on the weekends."

Dalton knew he should let it go but couldn't. "Have the two of you ever dated?"

She smiled. "I was interested, but unfortunately, I don't think his partner at the time would have appreciated it much."

"Partner?"

"Yes."

Dalton nodded. She didn't need to say any more than that, but he was curious about something. "How did the two of you meet?"

"Manning and I went through the police academy together in Boston and have been good friends ever since. He was going through a bad breakup at the time I made the decision to move here from Boston with Dad. And when I told Manning I was opening my own PI firm, he volunteered to be my assistant. He's good at what he does and makes my job a lot easier."

Manning returned with their drinks, and when he left, Dalton watched Jules take a sip of hers as he sipped his. She even looked sexy sipping wine. At that moment, unadulterated pleasure warmed his blood at the thought of sipping her.

"Mmm," she said, leaning back to get comfortable in her chair. "I needed that."

He wouldn't waste his time telling her what he needed since he was certain she knew. "So what is your plan?"

She shrugged beautiful shoulders. "I don't have one. I plan to investigate your mother's death the same way I do the other cases I handle. Thoroughly. I won't leave a stone unturned. Everyone could be a suspect until I rule them out. When I get back from my trip next week, I plan to—"

"Trip? Where are you going?"

She rolled her eyes. "Not that it's any of your business, but I've been called to court in Miami on a case I solved earlier this year. A kidnapping that happened over two years ago in which the father took his son and faked their deaths. The mother never believed her husband and son were dead and hired me to prove it. I did. The father is going on trial, and I'm a witness."

"When will you be back?" The expression on her face let him know she thought that information wasn't any of his business, either, but she answered. "Friday. I'm due in court on Tuesday and figured I'd stay on South Beach for a couple of days to relax and take in the sun…something we haven't seen much of around here recently."

She took another sip of her wine. "Anyway, as I was saying, when I get back, I plan to check out information Manning will be working on while I'm gone. I'm curious to see whether that PI your father hired left any files around. Although I would think the killer would have been competent enough to make sure any files were destroyed, I've dealt with incompetent killers before. So who knows? A smart PI would have been working with two sets of files, sometimes three, depending on the intensity of the case. Most people don't know that."

"And there's nothing I can do to sway you from wanting to do this?"

"No. Although you and your brothers haven't hired me, I have a personal, vested interest in solving this case."

Dalton didn't say anything for a minute. "I'm reassigning Stonewall to guard you."

She laughed. "You've got to be kidding." When she saw from his expression that he wasn't, all amusement left her face to be replaced with a deep frown. "Don't you dare. I can take care of myself, and I don't need any man following me around."

"And you think I do?"

"Umm, I'm not sure. I admit I was impressed with the way you handled that Glock the other night."

"No need to be surprised. I've been handling fire-arms since I was out of diapers. My grandfather and father were big on hunting trips." There was no way he would ever tell her about his days working for the USN, when he'd learned to handle weapons she probably didn't know existed.

"Then that explains things. But I meant what I said. Stonewall is your bodyguard, not mine. Whether either of us thinks you need him is irrelevant. Evidently, your father isn't taking any chances."

Exhaling deeply, a sudden thought entered Dalton's mind. Neither was he.

The next morning, Jules opened the door to her of-fice. She had enjoyed early-morning church service, and instead of accepting her father's invitation to brunch, she'd decided to come here. Since she was going out of town tomorrow, there were a few things she needed Manning to take care of while she was gone.

The main thing was that today she needed to stay busy and not focus on last night with Dalton. The man had a way of wearing on her last nerve. Over their shared glasses of wine, he hadn't asked to sleep with her, but all the nuances had been there. The way he had looked at her. The subtle things he said. The things he didn't say. Even the way he sipped his wine and licked the rim of the glass a few times, reminding her of his T-shirt the other night and the words written across it.

Jules figured she'd had a sure thing with Gary Coughlin last night, only to find out she was wrong. After bidding her father and Mona goodbye, she had glanced around to find the man gone. Vanished. He evi-dently had gotten tired of waiting for her conversation with Dalton to end. Maybe it was for the best, since impatient men had a way of annoying her in the bedroom.

She preferred a man who knew how to...*savor.* Hadn't that been the very thing Dalton had hinted at last night? *Slowly. Unhurriedly. Leisurely.* She knew better than to think the conversation had only been about the wine. Sitting across from him, she'd seen all that heat in his eyes. At times, depending on what she said or her body movement, it had even turned into a blaze. It didn't take much to turn him on. But then last night, she'd been just as combustible.

It had taken all her senses, common and otherwise, not to break down and invite him to her bed last night. It had been so long since her bed springs had gotten a good workout that even her mattress was screaming for her to get some.

Remembering what happened the last time she hadn't locked the door when Manning wasn't there, she locked the door behind her before moving toward her office. She would never forget how Dalton had walked in and found her alone, and she wouldn't give him the chance to do so again.

Today, she had plans to spend her time doing research, and the first thing on her list was to obtain information on Marshall Imerson. Who was he? Why had Richard Granger selected him as a PI to find Sylvia Granger's killer? Had he been one of Vidal Duncan's picks, as well? Was he part of a PI firm, or had he worked alone?

It wouldn't hurt to call around and talk to some of her buddies in the business who'd lived in the Charlottesville area a lot longer than she had to see if they'd heard or suspected anything about Imerson's accident.

Had it truly been an accident or a staged murder as Sheppard Granger thought?

She had been working for a couple of hours when her phone rang. It was Shana. "Hi, what's going on?"

"We joined Dad for brunch, and you weren't there. He said you told him you had to go into the office today. I thought you weren't going to start a new case until after the holidays."

"Have you forgotten I'm leaving town tomorrow to appear in court? I need to brush up on a few notes." That wasn't a total lie, she thought.

"I'd forgotten about your trip to Miami. What time does your plane leave?"

"Early. And I plan to stay and enjoy South Beach afterward for a couple of days, so don't look for me until the end of the week." She was hoping and praying that while in South Beach she would meet some hunk that had no qualms about indulging in a short, meaningless fling.

"I hope you enjoy yourself."

Jules smiled. "I hope that I enjoy myself, too."

"What do you want with me?" Dr. Sedrick Timmons asked, narrowing his gaze at the person who'd summoned him here to the abandoned warehouse in broad daylight.

"I might need you to arrange another death."

A chill went through Sedrick, but he didn't say anything. Little did this person know, but he hadn't arranged the last one. They believed Richard Granger would have survived his heart attack if he hadn't administered a certain drug to make sure he didn't. Little did they know he hadn't carried out their order to administer the drug. Richard had died of the heart attack, and he'd had nothing to do with it. But the person standing in front of him didn't know that, and he wasn't about to say anything different. Shiloh and Cassie's lives would be in jeopardy if anyone found out the truth. As long as this person assumed he was one of them, his sister Shiloh, and Cassie Mayfield, his longtime girlfriend, were safe. Right now he wasn't sure whom he could trust, and until he knew for certain, he would have to play along. "Whose death are you talking about now?"

"We haven't decided yet whether we want a medical death or an accident, but wanted to put you on notice regardless. We'll keep in touch. When the time comes, just do what you have to do and don't disappoint us."

Sixteen

"Now, this is the way to roll," Jules said, looking out her hotel room window at the ocean below. It was hard to grasp that in Miami the temperature was in the high eighties while, according to The Weather Channel, in Charlottesville, it was in the low forties. That was a big difference, which is why she needed these few extra days in Florida.

She moved from the window and glanced around her hotel room. Usually, to cut costs, she would stay in a modest hotel. However, this time, she'd splurged a bit, deciding to give herself an early Christmas present. This was a gorgeous two-room suite with separate living and dining rooms. She'd already checked out the fully equipped wet bar and Jacuzzi bathtub big enough for two. She could see herself sipping wine while covered in bubbles. This was definitely the type of place a person could relax and feel right at home, and she intended to do just that.

She was to appear in court at nine the next morning, but already she had made plans to spend as much of her free time on the beach as possible. And tomorrow evening after she left the court, she intended to go shopping for the sexiest dress she could find.

She walked across the room to browse the hotel booklet that listed numerous nightlife activities. She was excited and raring to go, and the first event that caught her eye was a jazz night tomorrow. And the nice thing was that the hotel had its own jazz club. How cool was that? She loved jazz, and after spending a day in court, it would be just what she'd need to unwind.

It had been after seven last night when she'd finally left her office for home. She had dug deep into all the information she could find on Marshall Imerson. The internet had been a great source of information, including the details of his auto accident. He was a married man and the father of a son who'd been in high school at the time of the accident.

She had talked to Manning this morning, and he understood just what information she still needed from the police, which meant digging into a bunch of old files. If Manning called requesting the information, he would get the runaround after being placed on hold for no telling how long. But if he showed up in person, the female clerks in the records department would be willing to jump through hoops to give him copies of whatever files he wanted. It happened every time.

Knowing she needed a clear head for court tomorrow, Jules decided to order room service for dinner, go over her investigative notes and get in bed early. But tomorrow night would be totally different. That's when the fun would begin.

"You didn't mention anything about leaving town for a few days," Caden said, gazing sternly across the conference table at Dalton.

"I didn't?" Dalton asked with a straight face.

"No," Jace said, studying his brother as he leaned back in his chair.

"Well, I'm telling you now. I'm leaving in the morning and won't be back until the weekend. There shouldn't be a problem, since both of you have taken trips away from Charlottesville yourselves. This will be my first time doing so."

He knew there was nothing his brothers could say after calling them out on that. Caden had left on two occasions to fulfill concert obligations, not to mention his elopement in Vegas. And Jace had taken two weeks off for his honeymoon.

"I don't recall Jace or me saying we had a problem with it, Dalton. We merely stated this was the first we'd heard of it, so we can only assume it was a last-minute decision. What's wrong? You're headed to London because you're missing your duchess?"

Dalton rolled his eyes. His brothers were razzing him about his long-standing affair with Lady Victoria Bowman. "For crying out loud, Caden, how many times do I need to remind you that Victoria's not a duchess, she's a lady—of English nobility—the daughter of an earl."

"And your cougar," Caden said, grinning.

Dalton sighed. "And she's my good friend." Neither Caden nor Jace could get beyond the fact that Victoria was twenty years his senior. She had been more than just his lover. She had been his close friend and confidante. "And just so neither of you will be surprised when it appears in the newspapers in a few months, I'll tell you right now that Victoria is getting married." He thought the look on his brothers' faces was priceless. Both of their jaws dropped at the same time.

"*You* seem to be taking it well," Jace said.

"There's no reason I shouldn't. I'm happy for her. Sir Isaac Muldrow will do right by her and make her happy. She deserves it," Dalton said, standing to gather up the papers he'd scattered on the table. "Now, if you guys will excuse me, I need to go home and pack."

"You didn't say where you're going," Caden reminded him.

"Didn't I?"

"No," Jace said smoothly.

Dalton smiled. "I thought Florida would be nice this time of year. It's been years since I've been to South Beach."

Jace leaned forward and placed his palms flat on the table. He arched a brow. "Now, isn't that a coincidence? Shana mentioned at breakfast that Jules left this morning for Miami. But I'm sure you didn't know that."

Dalton's smile widened. He couldn't forget it was Jace who'd walked in on him and Jules kissing on the patio, so there was no need to play dumb. But he would do so, anyway. "Why would I know Jules's whereabouts?"

Dalton knew his brother. A part of Jace wanted to call him out, but he wouldn't. If something more was going on between him and Jules than that kiss he'd witnessed, Jace would leave it up to him to 'fess up when he was ready.

"And just in case the two of you try to get cute, I'm turning the tracker off my phone," Dalton said, smiling.

Caden laughed. "We don't need a tracker when we have Stonewall."

"Stonewall?" The smile vanished from Dalton's face. "Stonewall is *not* following me to Miami."

Jace chuckled. "I'd like to see you try to stop him. If

Quasar can follow me on my honeymoon to South Africa, then Stonewall can certainly follow you to Miami."

Dalton frowned; his grip on the papers in his hand was unusually tight. "We'll see about that."

He then turned and stalked out of the room.

Seventeen

Jules stepped off the elevator feeling like a woman on the prowl. A real man-hunter. Never in her life had she taken such drastic measures, but it couldn't be helped. When a woman had gone without sex for as long as she had, it was time to take action.

It didn't take her long to walk across the hotel's lobby to the jazz club. The moment she stepped inside, she felt gazes turn her way as she headed toward the bar. The live entertainment would start in an hour, and until then, she intended to scope out the prospects. She was anxious, but that didn't mean she wouldn't be selective. She loved her life, and when it came to safe sex, she was on top of her game, which is why her purse was full of condoms.

Not seeing an empty table, she crossed the room and slid onto a bar stool before glancing around the room. The lighting in the club was dim, but she could see the room was full of couples, sitting snug, all lovey-dovey and sharing drinks. To her disappointment, she didn't see one man sitting alone. But that didn't stop the guys from checking her out when they thought their female companions weren't aware of it. She shook her head.

Men could be such fools at times. Didn't they know a woman could detect when her man had a roving eye?

"What are you having?" the bartender asked her, smiling and trying not to be so obvious while checking out her outfit.

She smiled back. "A martini. Dirty."

"One dirty martini coming up."

"Make that two."

On recognizing *that* voice, Jules swung around so fast it was a wonder she didn't fall off the bar stool. And then she saw him. Dalton. Standing right there in front of her. Where had he come from? She had glanced around the room just seconds ago and hadn't seen him. But her main question was what on Earth was he doing here, in Miami?

"What are you doing here, Dalton?" At that moment rage began building up inside her. She refused to believe this. It was like a bad dream, and she needed to wake up quickly.

He eased closer, leaning in, and she breathed in deeply, inhaling his manly scent. "Let's pretend, Jules," he whispered in a deep, husky voice. "Forget how we met. Let's start over. Here. Now. Hundreds of miles away from Charlottesville. Pretend we're strangers just meeting for the first time. Strangers who caught each other's attention while here on South Beach. We can even use phony names if you like."

Jules didn't say anything as she contemplated his suggestion. Heaven help her, but she found the idea intriguing. "Pretend?"

"Yes," Dalton said in a seductive tone. "I can pretend to be a salesman in Miami on business, or whatever you want me to be."

Her gaze raked over him. Yes, he could be a salesman. But with the tailor-made suit he was wearing, the CEO of a major corporation would be more likely. "And when we return to Charlottesville, what then?" she asked, not believing she was considering his idea.

"How we handle things after this week will be up to you. I will honor your decision."

Could she trust him to do that? She stared at him, looked deeply into the eyes staring back at her. Already she felt the heat as his gaze burned into hers and knew that his problem was the same as hers. They wanted each other. It was an attraction that had been obsessive, borderline compulsive, from the start. But she had refused to give in to his terms, and he'd refused to give in to hers. Both had wanted things their way or no way at all. And now the concept of *no way at all* had brought them to this. Stalemate.

She could not believe he was actually here. Over wine on Saturday night, she had mentioned she was coming to Miami. How had he known what hotel she would be staying in? How did he know she would be coming to the club tonight? How...

She shook her head, not able to ask herself any more questions. It was obvious that Dalton Granger had managed to find her for a second time. And he wanted them to pretend they were just meeting for the first time. Could they pull it off? It might be to her benefit to dig a little deeper to determine his thought process. "So what name will you go by if I don't want to call you Dalton?" she asked after the bartender placed their martinis on the counter. Dalton reached around her to get his, and her breath rushed from her lungs when their shoulders brushed. He leaned in and whispered, "My middle name is Richard, but more than once I've gone by the nickname Dick."

Bam. The area between her legs began to throb mercilessly. And the nipples on her breasts tightened to buds. *Dick.* That was the name he'd given her the day he'd shown up unexpectedly at her office. Before she'd learned his true identity.

"And if you prefer," he said, taking a slow sip of his drink, "I'll call you Sweet Pea."

She would rather he didn't. "If I were to use a fake name, I think Jane would be perfect for your Dick." *Jeez.* She cleared her throat. "I mean, Jane would be perfect with the name Dick." The throb between her legs increased, almost becoming an unbearable ache.

"*Fun with Dick and Jane.* I recall seeing that movie a few years ago. I enjoyed it." His gaze flickered over her. "So what do you think of my idea to pretend?" he asked in a gentle voice that still managed to stir every single thing inside her.

"I'm thinking." She took a sip of her martini as she stared at him over the rim of her glass. The lighting in the club was perfectly calibrated to manifest how good he looked standing there in his business suit. He had broad shoulders. A trim waist. Tapered thighs. And he was wearing a pair of shoes that probably cost more than Manning's entire monthly salary. The one advantage of going along with the pretend idea was that she would get a full night of sex. Enough to make up for what she'd gone several months without.

"While you're thinking, can I give you something else to think about?"

She shrugged her shoulders. "Depends on what it is."

Dalton smiled, showing perfect white teeth and a too-delicious smile. "I'll let you decide."

He shifted to move closer to where his body brushed against her thigh. And she felt it. His erection. Hard, engorged and ready. The contact sent succulent shivers all through her. She suddenly felt so intensely ravenous that she traced her top lip with the tip of her tongue.

"I'd really like to get to know you, *Jane*. Will you join me at my table?"

"Your table?"

"Yes. I have a private room in the back that overlooks the ocean."

Her heart was pounding hard in her chest. *A private room?* That should not have surprised her, but it did. Why did she have a gut feeling he had prepared well for this night just in case it included her? And why did she believe he knew about any and every secret fantasy she'd ever had, and would have no problem playing each one out to her satisfaction if given the chance?

Jules met his gaze. "Before I join you at your table, I think introductions are in order to get things started off on the right foot." Offering him her hand, she said, "I'm Jules. Not Jane."

He gave her a sizzling smile when his fingers curled over hers. "And I'm Dalton, not Dick."

She couldn't ignore the sparks that shot through her when he held her hand in his. "Nice meeting you, Dalton."

"Nice meeting you, as well, Jules."

He assisted her as she slid off the bar stool. "Nice outfit, by the way," he said, dragging his gaze all over her, lingering in certain places.

Jules smiled. "Thanks." Her dress was definitely an eye-catcher, deliberately and provocatively so. Black, short, sleeveless, razor slashed, exposing a lot more skin than it covered, especially in the tummy and chest areas. She could feel the heat of his gaze move from her navel to her breasts, and the thought of his mouth replacing those eyes had her nearly drowning in lust. If they didn't get to that private room fast, there was no telling what would happen.

"Lead the way, Dalton."

"It will be my pleasure, Jules."

Dalton would never consider himself a possessive man, but the moment Jules had walked into the club wearing that dress, he'd had to step back a moment to linger in the shadows to get his erection under control. Some things a man couldn't hide, and his desire for Jules was one of them. His briefs had gotten tight and had practically cut into his groin. Even now, heat was shimmering in the air surrounding them as well the aura of sex. Much-needed sex.

When he'd seen her enter the club, he had been shocked one second and then totally captivated the next. She was being watched, ogled and desired by a number of men, and the thought of any man approaching her for any reason made him rabid.

Her very short, scandalous, erection-making dress looked as if someone had taken a razor to it, deliberately slashing and slicing it in certain key stimulating places. Like the stomach area, where her navel was clearly displayed. But nothing could compete with the firm and shapely breasts clearly in view. If getting attention had been her intent, then she had reached her goal. There hadn't been a man in the place who hadn't checked out both her and her outfit. And then on top of the dress— or below it—she had the nerve to wear stilettos on those gorgeous legs. She evidently had planned to take care of some serious business tonight.

They rounded a corner with only a few steps left to go to the private room. He picked up his pace, and so did she. The first thing he intended to do when they got behind closed doors was to shred the rest of that dress off her. Since she obviously enjoyed showing her body, he intended for her to show a lot of it tonight…for an audience of one. They reached the door, and he pushed it open. "Have you had dinner?" he asked, standing aside to let her enter.

She gave him a smile that almost turned his brains to mush, and when she licked her lips and said in a sultry voice, "Umm, not yet," he felt a deep throb in his groin.

With anticipation rippling down his spine and rushing fast and furious through his veins, he followed her into the room and locked the door behind them.

Eighteen

Jules's heart thumped like crazy in her chest the moment she heard the lock click in place. And when Dalton reached out for her, she was ready. But she intended to do things her way, in her own time. Instead of falling into his arms, like she figured he expected, she took a step back and glanced around the room. "Nice room, Dalton. So just what do you do for a living?"

He held her gaze, and even with the distance separating them, she saw heat and desire churning in his eyes and felt it emanating from his body. He was staring hard at her, particularly her outfit. "Dalton?" As much as she wanted to feel him deep inside her, they had agreed to pretend, and they would do so…for now. She wanted to test his restraint to see just how far she could entice him before his control snapped.

"Do you really want to know?" he asked, removing his jacket and tossing it on a chair.

She shrugged. "Why not? We can hold a nice conversation while waiting for the live entertainment to begin. We can even stand at the window and watch the waves wash ashore."

He lifted a brow as he removed the cuff links from his shirt. "Hold a nice conversation?"

"Yes."

A throaty growl that was meant to be a laugh permeated the air. "Are you deliberately trying to drive me insane, Jules?" he asked, his attention focused solely on her.

"Why would I do that when we just met and—"

His movement was swift, quicker than she thought, and she found her body wrapped in his, her backside nestled snug against his crotch. "Are you trying to manhandle me, Dalton?" she asked in a tone of faux indignation when they both knew he had her just where she wanted to be. His erection was pressed hard against her backside, causing tingling sensations to travel up through her spine.

"Manhandle you?"

"Yes."

"Now why would I do that?" he asked, easing her dress up over her thighs.

Her ears perked up. Was that the sound of his zipper lowering? She tried looking over her shoulder and couldn't because he had leaned down to place a kiss on the back of her neck. The feel of his lips against her skin had blood rushing through her veins.

"I don't know. You tell me. Are you admitting this game of pretense was just that? A game, to get me in here alone with you?"

She felt his smile against her neck, just seconds before she felt his tongue as he began to lick her. The contact with her skin made her shiver, and all she could think about at that moment was that T-shirt he'd worn last week. *I lick.*

"You taste good," he murmured huskily as the tip

of his tongue slid from her neck toward the underside of her ear. And then he used his teeth to gently nibble her there. "I want to taste you all over, but first I need to get inside you."

"Don't I have something to say about that?" she asked, trying not to home in on the feel of his solid chest pressed against her back.

His chuckle made her entire body tremble. "What do you want to say?"

"That you should never underestimate a woman who needs to get laid."

In a quick movement, she broke free of his hold and in a few seconds flat, he was on the floor staring stunned up at her. She smiled. "Maybe I should have warned you about all those self-defense classes I took in college."

"Yes, maybe you should have," he said, shifting from his back to his side. Knowing he was trying to look under her dress, she spread her legs to stand over his body to make sure he got a good view. "See something you want, Dalton?"

"Plenty," he said, reaching his hand upward, under her dress. Pushing past her thong, he used his fingers to stroke the area between her legs. He moved beyond her womanly folds to massage her clit.

"Beginning with this."

She fought back a moan. His touch was causing a weakness in her knees, and she was wet, true evidence that she definitely needed to be laid. Deciding to waste no more time, she eased her dress over her head and tossed it aside. Except for her thong, she was naked since she hadn't worn a bra.

"I wanted to rip that damned thing off you the mo-

Brenda Jackson

ment I saw you," he grumbled, while his hand continued to stir her wetness.

"If you buy the dress, you can rip it off. But since my money paid for it, you can't—"

That's as far as she got. In a movement she hadn't seen coming, Dalton was back on his feet and grabbing her around her waist. Whatever words of protest she was about to say evaporated from her lips when he buried his head in her chest, and his tongue latched on to a breast, kissing it hungrily. She couldn't do anything at that moment but writhe in pleasure and moan in satisfaction, especially when his fingers ripped her thong off her body. He eased his mouth from her nipple long enough to say, "I don't give a damn who bought those. They were coming off."

And then he was backing her naked body back toward the table. *Not fair*, she thought, since he still had on his clothes, and she was completely naked. "Not so fast," she said when the backs of her legs hit a chair. "One of us still has clothes on." She then reached up and began popping buttons from his dress shirt, trying to get it off him.

"What were you saying a few minutes ago about ripping off someone's clothes when you didn't pay for them?"

Instead of a comeback, her fingers were fast at work at his fly. He'd lowered his zipper earlier, but what she wanted was still in hiding.

"You keep this up and I'm going to think you want me, Jules."

"Do you?"

"Yes. Need some help?" He leaned over and murmured close to her ear, before using his tongue to swipe the side of her face, while his hands fondled her breasts.

"No, I got this," she said as she captured the engorged hardness of his sex in her hand. He was big. Super big. Thick. Mighty thick. And hard. Magnificently hard. She'd dreamed many nights of her hands and her mouth on this. She had also dreamed of this being inside her.

"Need condom," he murmured in a guttural groan.

"Not yet." She glanced down at his erection, jutting proudly from a dark thatch of curls, and began stroking him. She loved the feel of his shaft beneath her fingers, especially the thickness of the veins running along the sides of it. The head was swollen and felt warm in her hands.

"I love the feel of you stroking me," Dalton murmured hoarsely, leaning close and putting his mouth to her ear before licking her there.

Being stroked was just the beginning. She intended to give him the blow of all blows. "Time to savor," she whispered, lowering down in front of him and then easing him into her mouth.

She used her mouth to stroke him even more, to tantalize and to drive him mad. She loved his scent. She was being hypnotized by his taste and mesmerized by the feel of his entire shaft in her mouth while her hands caressed his balls.

"Jules…"

She felt his fingers massage her scalp, holding her head in position as she continued to use her mouth to pleasure him, and just when she thought he was about to come, he surprised her yet again by pulling her up and turning her body away from him while holding on to her tightly. She heard him remove his pants and the sound of his teeth ripping open a condom packet. She managed to look over her shoulder and watched him sheathe himself like a pro. Definitely a man who'd done this more times than either of them could count.

"Grab hold of the table."

She did and immediately felt the fullness of his body over her, felt his fingers reaching between her legs, spreading them. "I love this position," he murmured in her ear.

And then she felt the engorged head of his shaft caressing the area surrounding her feminine folds. Her clit was wet, hot and practically begging to be taken, but he held back, evidently deciding to torture her a little first.

"Dalton, please…"

"Please what, baby?" he asked, leaning to lick her neck again. "Do you need to get laid?" he asked, reminding her of what she'd said earlier. "Tell me what you want."

"You know what I want."

"Is it the same thing I want?" he asked, as if he needed her to acknowledge it, anyway. "The same thing we both wanted the first time we saw each other and every time since? Even when you want to hate me and I, you?"

Why was he bringing all that up now? The only thing she wanted was to be filled by him in a way she'd never been filled before.

"Jules?"

He obviously wanted her response, and if it would hurry the process, then she would give him one. "Yes."

Holding tight to her thighs, he suddenly thrust inside her, plunging hard, going deep. Then he began pounding into her so hard that she almost found it difficult to breathe, the pleasure was that keen and intense. But that didn't stop her body from taking him in, greedily expanding for more, contracting her muscles, holding tight to his shaft and attempting to pull everything out of him. He could penetrate her so well, as if he'd been tailor-made just for her.

Groans filled the room, both his and hers mingled with the sound of flesh slapping against flesh. She needed this. Her entire body ached for release, and she knew at that moment that no other man but Dalton could have done this, given her the degree of release she needed.

She was convinced had it been any other man, she would have returned to Charlottesville after experiencing a fling that left her unfulfilled. But now, tonight, she was getting everything she wanted and then some. Satisfaction had never felt so good.

She loved the feel of him thrusting in and out of her with an intensity that drove her to lose all control. The raw hunger that he was not holding back was absorbing her, consuming her, making her ache even more, knowing that he was going to take care of it.

She heard his growl and knew he was about ready to come. She could feel it. He was swollen to near bursting but was holding back, waiting for her to join him. The thought of him intensely full, solid, hard and enlarged inside her, with her inner muscles clamped tight on him, was driving her over the edge.

"Harder, Dalton. I need you harder," she whimpered, not believing she was requesting such a thing, but at the moment not caring as long as he delivered.

He did, holding tighter to her thighs, leaning over her, bending her body forward for deeper penetration, and making sensations erupt inside her until she couldn't take any more. He began surging, pounding harder and faster into her like a jackhammer. And that's when she let loose, actually saw stars flying around her, caught a glimpse of the moon falling from the sky. Had Miami just experienced an earthquake? Was that why the floor seemed to be moving? His name poured from her throat in a gurgle the same time hers flowed from his. He thrust harder just seconds before his body bucked.

"Jules..."

She felt pleasure in every bone in her body. A delicious calm settled over every inch of her, and she felt his tongue, wet and hot, licking a zigzag path across her back while he continued to hold tight to her hips, staying lodged deeply inside her. She expected him to pull out of her, but he didn't and seemed in no hurry to do so.

"I love the feel of being inside you, Jules," he whispered hotly against her neck.

And as much as she didn't want to admit it, she loved the feel of him being inside her, as well. All she had to do was close her eyes to remember the feel of being taken by him. The feel of her backside resting tight against the hairy cushion of his groin while his shaft filled her so completely. Those hard and fast thrusts, the feel of his fingers fondling her breasts while pumping inside her. The angle of his penetration had been perfect, precise, so well defined she felt shivers going up her spine with aftershocks of pleasure.

"Ready to go another round?"

His question told her in more than words it would be one of those nights. Already, she could feel him getting hard again inside her. "Sure. Why not?" His chuckle sent more sensuous shivers through her.

"I need another condom."

It only took him a minute, and when he pulled out of her to handle that part of things, she missed the feel of him being embedded deep inside her. Moments later, he turned her around to face him. "This time I want to be looking at you when you come."

"Why?"

He smiled. "I want to see what I do to you."

His arrogance was in high gear. She decided to shift it down a little. "Just like I want to see what I do to you."

He lifted her up, and she wrapped her legs around him as he pressed her back against the wall, entering her all at once, surging deep, again filling her completely. He stared at her, penetrating her gaze with the same intensity he was penetrating her body. "I have a voracious appetite. After this, I'm going to be hungry."

That was understandable. "Did you order food for later?"

He smiled again in a way that made her toes curl. "Don't want food. Just you. I intend to eat you, Jules."

Jules's mouth curved into a smile. She liked the thought of that happening.

Nineteen

Dalton eased to the edge of the bed, sat up and glanced over his shoulder at the woman sleeping soundly. What a night. They'd made love for hours, and she'd driven him insane with both desire and complete satisfaction. He'd had sex with plenty of women in his day, had had orgasms galore. But never before had sex left him feeling like this. Gratified. Fulfilled. So damned contented.

When did an orgasm have the ability to rip him into pieces…the same way he'd wanted to tear into her dress? They had been the most earth shattering and intense that he'd ever experienced. Orgasmic power was something he'd always controlled, but tonight, she had truly been dominating.

He braced the palms of his hands on the bed and leaned back, tilting his face toward the ceiling and closing his eyes. He also felt confusion and frustration, but neither could top the masculine pleasure still radiating through parts of his body. Jules Bradford was definitely something else. He'd never known a woman quite like her.

After making uninterrupted love in that private room a number of times, they had dressed and managed to sneak out of the club hopefully unseen, since everyone's attention was drawn to the live entertainers on stage. But he was aware that although he hadn't seen Stonewall, the man was there, somewhere in the club. He had to have known where Dalton was and with whom.

"What time is it?"

Jules's voice intruded into his thoughts, and he opened his eyes and eased back in bed. What would her attitude be like this morning? They had done some pretty far-out things last night. Had probably broken the Guinness World Record with some of the positions they'd tried.

He glanced at the clock on the nightstand. "A little after six."

"Why didn't I spend the night in my hotel room?"

He looked over and smiled. "Because we hadn't gotten enough of each other yet."

She closed her eyes and actually smiled. "You're right. We hadn't had enough. I was in a pretty bad way."

Like him, she'd been insatiable. Most women wouldn't admit to that, and he liked her blatant honesty. But he was curious about what had driven her last night to need sex as much as he did. "Pretty bad way? Why?"

"Too much work and not enough playtime. I won't let that happen again."

There was no way that he would admit that he'd been in a bad way, as well, and had been since meeting her. He hadn't wanted any other woman in his bed, and any women he'd slept with anyway had left him wanting. Definitely lacking.

"So why did we come to your hotel room instead of going to mine?"

He lifted a brow. "Don't you remember?"

They had been riding the elevator up to her room on

the tenth floor when suddenly they began making out again right there in the elevator. That resulted in them bypassing her floor, and while she was recovering from another orgasm, he'd decided they should continue on up to his room. They'd barely made it to his room before they were taking off their clothes.

"Yes, I remember now," she said, nodding. "At least now that you're out of my system, I can start functioning like a normal person."

"Was I in your system?"

"Yes, like an annoying ache."

Being an ache he could handle, but he wasn't sure he liked the annoying part. "Where?" he asked, resting on his side to turn toward her.

"Where?"

"Yes, where was the ache? In your head, your teeth, back?"

"Doesn't matter."

"It does to me." He pushed the bedspread aside to uncover her. She was naked. Beautifully so. When she saw where his gaze was fixed, she tightened her thighs together. Too late.

"Does it bother you that I like looking at you there?"

She released a soft chuckle. "Kind of late for me to be bothered, isn't it? Especially after last night."

He had to agree with her there. Last night, he'd done more than just look. He'd touched, tasted, thrust inside like a lust-crazed maniac on an effing marathon. He wanted to see how long he could stay hard inside her and how many times they could come. And speaking of come…

He reached out, and his fingers caressed the folds of her womanly core before sliding inside to begin stroking her clit. Touching her there sent erotic sensations straight through to his fingertips. "What do you think you're doing?"

Now she thought to ask. Her voice was choppy, her breathing uneven and her legs eased open a little to give him better access. "Using my fingers to turn that annoying ache into a pleasurable one. Mmm, you're wet."

"You honestly thought I wouldn't be?"

No, he hadn't thought that. This basically proved he was no more out of her system than she was out of his. One all-nighter hadn't done the job, apparently. And when she let out a rasping moan, he knew it was time to take things to the next level.

He reached onto the nightstand where several condom packs were spread out. Some his. Some hers. He grabbed one and proceeded to sheathe himself. With an urgency he hadn't counted on but refused to back away from, he eased toward her and placed his body over hers. Capturing her hands in his, he held them over her head, drawing her luscious-looking breasts upward to mouth level.

He seized her gaze as he entered her, stretching her wide and sinking deep. For the first time ever, he actually felt the heat in a woman's womb, and it propelled him to begin moving, thrusting inside her. Riding her hard.

"Oooh, Dalton…"

She wrapped her legs around his waist, and he felt the tips of her fingernails dig into his back after releasing her hands. He stared into her eyes, glazed with lust and darkening with need. The thought that she still wanted this, needed this, as much as he did made him feel both possessive and invigorated. And he felt something else. Passion. Deep passion.

At that moment, he needed more than anything to

kiss her. Sliding his tongue between her parted lips, he began devouring her mouth with a greed he only experienced with her. And what was destroying his strong hold on reality was the way she was returning the kiss, with an intensity of fervor that equaled his own.

He loved her taste, and it would have suited him just fine for it to continue without any interruptions, but the need to breathe made such a thing impossible. She inhaled sharply the moment he released her mouth and when she exhaled, his name was said on a breathless sigh. "I can't take much more," she whispered.

He wasn't sure he could, either, but something within him drove him to try. Deciding to give her mouth a reprieve, he lowered his head to her breasts and slid a hardened nipple between his lips. Sensations tore through him, and he began sucking hard as his shaft continued to pump into her.

"Dalton!"

"Being inside you feels so good," he crooned as he continued his thrusts with an urgency he felt in every part of his body. He did know that what they were experiencing wasn't the norm. No two people should be able to fire up bedsheets the way they were and make multiple orgasms a standard practice.

And then something exploded within him, shot him off to a high plane, and his entire body hammered and bucked in pure ecstasy. And his guttural groans filled the air. Uncontrollably. Unashamedly. He was open in a way he'd never been before. For the first time in his entire life, he felt vulnerable. It took some doing for him to gain enough strength to lift his head, and when he met her gaze, he could only whisper her name. "Jules…"

His tongue swiped across her lips, and he said her name again. Easing his body off hers, he clutched her close and brushed a kiss against her temple. "Sleep," he said softly.

And while she slept, he would stay awake and try to figure out what the hell was happening. Specifically, why the thought of Jules making love with any other man was just something he could not accept.

FBI Agent Marcel Eaton returned the smiles of the people who greeted him in a conference room at Granger Aeronautics—Jace, Caden and Shana. "Where's Dalton? Still at lunch?" he asked, taking a seat at the long table.

Jace responded, "No, he took a trip out of town and won't be back until the weekend. You mentioned something to Shana about having new information on Brandy's death."

"Yes, and I appreciate all of you seeing me on such short notice."

Brandy Booker had been a young and vibrant administrative assistant in the executive department, whose suicide several weeks ago had shocked the entire company. What was disturbing was that after reading the suicide note, her mother felt Brandy had been forced to write it and that she'd not taken her own life but had been murdered. However, there was no evidence to support the mother's claim, and the authorities were still ruling the death a suicide. What was even more disturbing was that right before Brandy's death, she was caught on a Granger Aeronautics security camera on more than one occasion going through Dalton's office as if she were searching for something. Jace and the Granger Aeronautics security team had been scheduled to meet with her and question her about it on the same day they'd learned of her death.

Marcel, who had worked to expose trade-secret violators at the company a few months earlier, had been apprised of the suspicions surrounding both Brandy's death and her possible connection to the trade-secrets corruption. Bruce Townsend, who was a computer whiz and worked on occasion for Shana and Jules, was having Brandy's work computer analyzed to see if it had been wiped clean from some remote location.

Marcel glanced over at Shana. "Did you ever discover why Brandy's father's employment with Granger was terminated?"

It had been discovered that both Brandy parents had worked for the company, although Brandy didn't reveal that on her employment application. Her parents divorced and her mother had left the company to pursue a career in nursing, but her father had gotten fired a year later.

"Yes. Neil Booker was fired when he assaulted a female employee in one of the break rooms when she ended their affair. I guess he wasn't too happy about her dropping him," Shana said.

"Apparently," Marcel said, shaking his head. "We were able to search Brandy's apartment and didn't find anything but this," he added, placing what looked like an office key in the middle of the table. "Does it look familiar?"

Jace frowned as he picked up the key and studied it. "No, it doesn't."

"Well, we ran it through your security team and discovered it's a key to Dalton's office."

"A duplicate key?" Shana asked, leaning forward to stare down at the key. "So that's how Brandy got into Dalton's office when he swore he locked the door before leaving every day."

Marcel nodded. "Yes, and the big question is how she got hold of this copy."

Caden leaned back in his chair and rubbed his chin thoughtfully. "If you're thinking that maybe she and Dalton had an affair and she lifted it off him without his knowing it, then don't fall for that assumption, Marcel. Dalton said he's never been involved with Brandy, and I believe him. Trust me. If Dalton is ever involved with any woman, he has no problem admitting it."

"I believe him, as well," Marcel said, "but that's not what concerns me. I want you all to notice the age of the key. It's well worn and looks nothing like the ones you're using now. It's an entirely different brand."

Jace stood and pulled out his key ring. Caden did the same. Their keys were a shiny bronze color, and the one that had been in Brandy's possession was a tarnished silver.

"True, so what does this mean?" Jace asked with concern on his face. "Why would Brandy have an old office key in her possession?"

"One that obviously still works," Shana pointed out.

"Yes, one that still works." Marcel looked at Jace and asked, "Did you ever find out the names of any employees who occupied Dalton's office before he did?"

Jace hesitated before answering. "Yes. According to what I've been told, the only other person who occupied that particular office was my mom. After her death, it was closed up until Dalton began using it a few months ago."

Marcel's brow rose. "Your mom worked for the company?"

Jace sighed. "Yes, for a short while. From what I remember, she began complaining about getting bored at home and said that she regretted never having had the chance to use her college degree in marketing."

"So she was brought in as part of the marketing team?" Shana asked her husband.

Jace shook his head. "No. I asked Dad about it once, and he said he and Granddad decided to give Mom the glorified title of marketing analyst to keep her busy and away from Sutton Hills when they weren't there."

Caden's brow furrowed. This was the first time he'd heard any of this. "Why would they want to keep her away from Sutton Hills when they weren't there?"

"Evidently, during that time, she had it in for Hannah, and Hannah threatened to quit unless Mom's attitude improved," Jace explained.

"Who's Hannah?" Marcel asked.

"Our housekeeper. She's actually more than that. She's been with us for more than fifty years."

Marcel didn't say anything for a minute. "I had our investigative team work with your security guys, and it seems that key," he said, pointing to the one on the table, "would be the same key that opened Dalton's office years ago."

Jace frowned. "If that's true, how did Brandy get my mother's old office key?"

Twenty

"So how was Miami?"

Jules continued eating her breakfast, refusing to meet her father's eyes. "Nice. I needed it."

"Evidently. You had originally said you'd be returning Saturday, but I got your text message that you were taking an extra day."

The additional day had been Dalton's idea, but she would never admit that to her father. As far as she knew, no one was aware she and Dalton had spent the past week together. And what a week it had been with a man who was bold enough to have a colorful tattoo of Sonny the Cuckoo Bird, the mascot for Cocoa Puffs cereal, right on his lower hip. Jules thought it was a pretty erotic place for a tattoo.

She was a woman who enjoyed sex, and his presence had definitely served a purpose. Today she felt relaxed and back in control. Alert. Ready to tackle anything that came her way. Although the extra day had been Dalton's idea, she had agreed one hundred percent. Surprising what a few nights of nonstop sex could do for you, which had been a testament to just how horny she'd been. He'd been determined to transform that annoying ache into a pleasurable one, and he had done so. Possibly too well. And what was also surprising was how much better they got along once the issue of sex had been resolved.

They'd both agreed that what happened in Miami would stay in Miami, and there was no need to continue things in Charlottesville. Miami was one and done. They were out of each other's systems, and that was all that mattered.

"Have you talked to your sister yet?" her dad asked, interrupting her thoughts.

"No. It was late when I got in." Last night all she'd wanted to do was take a shower and go to sleep. It had been the best sleep she'd had in months. While in the shower, she'd noticed passion marks over a good percentage of her body. Luckily, none of those places could be seen when she was wearing clothes.

"So you haven't heard about the new development Marcel uncovered with respect to that girl who committed suicide?"

Jules's brow lifted as she took a sip of her coffee. She remembered the incident Shana had told her about. The suicide had come as a shock, and the mother had suspected foul play, but nothing had been proven. And then there was the issue of whether she'd been connected to that trade-secret scandal Marcel had exposed earlier in the year, when several Granger employees had been arrested. What had made the woman a suspect was that the security camera at Granger Aeronautics had captured her searching Dalton's office after hours.

"No, I haven't heard about it. What did Marcel uncover?"

"They discovered how she was getting into young

Granger's office when he was careful about locking the door every night before leaving."

"How?"

"It seems she had a key. One that once belonged to Sylvia Granger."

"Dalton's mother?"

Her father stared over at her for a minute before saying, "Yes, Jace, Caden *and* Dalton's mother."

Jules quickly picked up her fork and began eating her eggs. Why had she singled Dalton out? Her father was too perceptive and was probably wondering the same thing. "How did the woman get the key?"

"No one knows, but everyone finds it interesting that she had it."

Jules didn't say anything, but she found that piece of information interesting, as well.

Caden looked his brother up and down. "Glad you returned from Florida in one piece."

A side of Dalton's lips curved into a smile when he dropped into the chair across from Jace's desk. Caden was occupying the other chair in the room. Okay, he thought, he would play his brother's silly little game. "Any reason I was not supposed to return in one piece?"

Jace chuckled. "With both you and Jules in Miami, we were concerned you might return all shredded. Ripped into pieces."

The words shredded and ripped made Dalton remember the dress Jules had worn to the club that night. That had been the beginning of the most pleasurable six nights of his life. He had to fight back a throaty growl trying to break through the memories. He shifted in his chair and cleared his throat. "What makes you think our paths even crossed?"

"Didn't they?" Caden asked, studying him closely.

Dalton shook his head. "What is this? Get into Dalton's business day?"

"Why not? You certainly like getting into ours enough," was Caden's comeback.

"I concur," Jace added.

Dalton shrugged. "That was before the two of you married. There's no need to get into your business now, because your lives are boring as hell."

Caden laughed. "You think so?"

"Yes."

"Hate to disappoint you," Jace said, smiling while twirling his pen between his fingers. "And you never answered the question about whether yours and Jules's paths crossed."

If he refused to answer, they would take that as a yes. So he decided to tell them a lie. It wouldn't be the first time. "Sorry to disappoint you guys, but I didn't see Jules."

"Not at all?" Caden pressed.

Dalton rolled his eyes, refusing to answer. "I hope the reason you summoned me here, Jace, was not to interrogate me about Jules."

Jace tossed his pen on the desk and nodded. "You're right. This meeting has nothing to do with Jules. We thought we'd bring you up-to-date on Brandy Booker. Marcel discovered whose key she was using to get into your office."

"Let me guess. She'd made a duplicate," Dalton said drily.

"No. Only the company security team can duplicate the keys, and there was never a work order for one."

Dalton shrugged. "Doesn't mean anything if you

know someone in the right places. Brandy was a looker. Pretty damned hot, too."

Caden frowned. "And, of course, you know this. I hope you didn't lie to us about not having an affair with her, Dalton. Especially after I came to your defense with Marcel."

Dalton stretched his legs out in front of him. Brandy had flirted with him a lot of times. Had even thrown out hints regarding her availability and eagerness to please. Although he'd flirted back with her on occasion, the last thing he was interested in was an office affair. He figured Brandy for the clingy type, and things wouldn't have boded well when he dropped her, which he would have done eventually...like a hot potato. "Relax, Caden, I meant it when I said Brandy and I never slept together. Hell, I never even kissed her. She and I became friends, nothing more."

Jace snorted. "Instead of *friends*, maybe the two of you should have remained employee and employer."

Dalton smiled. "Oh, like you and Shana? And please don't tell me your situation with Shana was different, because it wasn't. Especially not when she's starting to walk around with a big stomach."

He knew his statement had been a stark reminder to his oldest brother of just what he and his now-wife had been doing months ago, probably during working hours in addition to those nighttime hours. Sounded like the teapot was calling the kettle black.

"Never mind him, Jace," Caden piped up. "Just tell him about the key."

Following Caden's advice, Jace said, "The key Brandy used to get into your office was Mom's."

Dalton lifted a brow. "Mom's key?"

"Yes."

"How did she get Mom's key?"

Caden sighed deeply. "That's a good question, one that we're trying to figure out."

At the sound of the buzzer on Jace's desk, he pushed the button and said, "Yes, Christine?"

"Mrs. Shiloh Granger is here to see Mr. Caden Granger. Should I have her wait in his office?"

Dalton watched a huge smile spread across Caden's face. "No, you can send her in here," Caden answered for Jace. Then to Dalton and Jace he said, "We have a lunch date. She's early."

"Then she should wait it out in your office," Dalton said, deciding to rib his brother. He'd pissed Jace off, so he might as well get Caden, too.

"Go to hell, Dalton," Caden said.

Dalton couldn't help but laugh. His brothers were so effing protective of their women. He was glad he wasn't involved like that. His mind drifted to Jules. He would admit he'd been possessive of her, which was so unlike him. That had been proven last week, especially on those days when they had gone out on the beach and she'd worn probably the skimpiest bikini she could find. Men stared, and the women gave her hateful looks for grabbing their men's attention. He'd been giving the men brooding looks for even glancing at Jules, but what man in his right mind would not have? However, that was then. He was back on familiar ground, and the only thought he was having of Jules was just how good she'd been in the bedroom. Now that she was out of his system, it was out of sight, out of mind. He was over his obsession with her.

He and his brothers stood when the door opened and Shiloh Timmons Granger walked in. Dalton would admit she was a beautiful woman. But Caden had fallen for the woman when the two of them were kids, wearing braces, climbing trees and doing all those things kids do on Sutton Hills. Both families had known the two were destined to get together when they were older, and it had been okay with everyone until Sheppard was sent to prison for killing Sylvia Granger. Then the Timmonses had forbidden Shiloh and her older brother, Sedrick—who had been Jace's best friend at the time—to have anything to do with the Granger children. They hadn't wanted Shiloh and Sedrick to associate with the offspring of a criminal. That hadn't bothered Dalton one iota, but it had bothered Caden and Jace because they'd lost their best friends. Shiloh's bastard of a father, Samuel Timmons, had been a holy terror, threatening her over the years with what would happen if she and Caden ever reconnected. And he probably made the same threats to Sedrick. Their mother, Sandra Timmons, had been a weakling, just like her children, doing anything Samuel had said. But Dalton would at least give Shiloh credit for taking a stand against her father and seeking Caden out when they got older.

"Sorry I'm early. I didn't mean to disturb the meeting," Shiloh said, smiling brightly.

"No problem, baby, we were through, anyway."

Dalton frowned. *They were?* When Caden headed to the door with Shiloh, Dalton asked, "Hey, what's next? Did Marcel say how they're going to find out where the key came from and how Brandy got hold of it?"

Jace shrugged. "I'm not sure, and he didn't say. I'm hoping Bruce Townsend will be able to locate all the information that was wiped off Brandy's hard drive. Marcel also mentioned they had checked surveillance videos from around Brandy's apartment to see if any gentlemen had visited her in the past six months or so."

"I hope you won't be one of them," Caden said, grinning at Dalton.

Dalton rolled his eyes. "I told you what the deal was with Brandy and me. Shiloh, you might want to get him out of here before he makes me mad enough to hit him."

Shiloh laughed. "Then, by all means, let me get him out of here. Did Caden remind you both about his concert at the end of the year?"

Dalton chuckled. "He didn't have to. An announcement was made on radio and television like he's some kind of celebrity or something."

Of course, he'd meant it as a joke, because his brother *was* a celebrity. Caden was a Grammy-award-winning saxophone player, who had sold out concerts worldwide. He'd given it up temporarily to keep their grandfather's deathbed promise. Shiloh had talked him and his band into headlining Charlottesville's annual Live-It-Up Ball to benefit cancer research.

"He *is* a celebrity," Shiloh said, grinning. "*My* celebrity."

Dalton hoped Caden and Shiloh weren't about to get all mushy on him now. He could handle only so much of such nonsense. "So where are you two going for lunch?" Jace asked the couple.

"We're meeting Sedrick and Cassie at Shelburne," Shiloh said.

Dalton glanced inquiringly at Caden. It was no secret that Sedrick hadn't taken the news of his sister marrying Caden well. "Sedrick?"

"Yes. Sedrick and I are trying to work out our differences," Caden said easily.

Too easily, Dalton thought. "Why bother?"

"Well, enjoy your lunch," Jace said, obviously hurrying them along. As soon as his office door closed, he turned a deep frown on Dalton. "What was that about?"

Dalton rolled his eyes. Shiloh's father, Samuel, had died last year of cancer, but as far as Dalton was concerned, her mother and brother were bad enough. "I don't like Shiloh's family, and I'm surprised you and Caden can even try to get along with them. They treated us like crap when Dad was sent to prison. Damn it, Jace, Sedrick was your best friend, and he didn't defy his father when he ordered them not to have anything to do with us. The only one who acted like she had any sense was Shiloh."

Jace rubbed his hands down his face. "Have you ever thought that maybe there's another side to the story?"

"Yeah, right. What other side is there? Sedrick's father gave the order, and he obeyed by dropping your friendship like a hot potato. And as far as Sandra Timmons being a victim, I'm not buying it. She could have left the old geezer. She could have walked away and taken Sedrick and Shiloh with her. I believe she was just as bad as he was, and I don't trust her, either. As much as I like and admire Shiloh, I can't stand her family."

Jace didn't say anything for a long moment. In a way, Dalton was right; Jace had felt utterly betrayed when he was sixteen and lost his best friend without a fight. He truly hadn't expected Sedrick to toe the line like he had. Shiloh certainly hadn't. She sent Caden notes, secret messages and birthday cards every chance she got.

"I've gotten over it, Dalton, and so should you."

Dalton wished he could, but he and his brothers had been made to feel like shit during that time, and all because people wanted to believe his father had been guilty of a crime he hadn't committed. That would make finding his mother's real killer all that much sweeter.

That automatically made him think of Jules. Why was she back in his mind? Hadn't he just said she was out of his system? "I have work to do," he said, standing to his feet. "It was nice to take a few days off, but I need to catch up on some things."

Before he reached the door, Jace asked, "Did you notice Stonewall on your trip?"

Dalton glanced over his shoulder and couldn't help but smile. "He was there but stayed inconspicuous as much as possible, which I appreciated."

Jules had appreciated it, as well. The man was the only one who knew their secret. Well, it really wasn't a secret, just no one else's damned business. There was a difference. "See you later, Jace."

Twenty-One

Jules glanced across her desk at Manning and smiled. "You've been busy."

Manning leaned back in his chair. "Just doing what you're paying me for."

They both knew that was a lie. He was an over-achiever. When you gave Manning an assignment, he always went above and beyond. She looked at the stack of files on her desk. "I need to begin reading."

"And I need to get out of here in a few hours. Dad has a doctor's appointment today."

She lifted a brow. "He's okay?"

Manning smiled. "Yes, he's doing great. This is just a routine checkup. Getting them to move from Boston was the best thing I could have done."

Jules agreed. Making the decision to move to Charlottesville from Boston had been hard on Manning, because that meant leaving his parents behind, with the responsibility falling on the shoulders of his younger sister and older brother. He'd soon discovered his frequent trips back home hadn't been enough, and when he saw the opportunity to make his parents' dream of one day owning a restaurant a reality, he made it happen. Now the senior Carmichaels were happy and so were Manning and his siblings. His sister, Deborah, had even relocated to Charlottesville and was working on her master's degree at the University of Virginia.

Two hours later, Jules stood to stretch her muscles, specifically to get the kink out of her neck. It was her opinion that the police officer that'd been called to the scene had done a terrible job recording details. The impact of Imerson's hitting that utility pole had been so great that he'd been killed instantly. One thing she found interesting was the officer's notation of there being two sets of tire tracks at one point. That could have meant a couple of things. Either someone had tried dodging Imerson on the road if he'd been driving erratically, or Imerson might have been trying to flee from the second car and lost control of his vehicle. Of course, for now, the latter was just a theory.

Another thing she found interesting is that no one had tested Imerson's blood-alcohol content. It had been the officer's opinion that testing was unnecessary since the victim's body reeked of alcohol and a half-empty bottle had been found open on the front seat of the car. It was merely speculation on Jules's part but for her, the entire scene was too tidy. What if someone had staged things to appear as if Imerson had been drinking heavily? According to the police report, an unidentified caller had reported the accident but hadn't stuck around until the police arrived. She found that interesting, too. As far as the police were concerned, the case was pretty cut-and-dried, so there had been no investigation into the anonymous caller. In that case, why had the police report been sealed? The only reason that made sense was to hide the number of red flags that should have been investigated more.

She refilled her coffee cup and glanced out the window. She couldn't help but take a moment to daydream, remembering her time last week in Miami. The state attorney's office had called earlier that day to let her know the jury had found Marcos Rodrigo guilty. As far as she was concerned, there was no other verdict that could have been delivered. The prosecution had presented a fantastic case, but when the mother, Carla Rodrigo, had taken the stand with her heart-wrenching testimony, that had pretty much nailed it.

Jules went back to her desk and sat down. She wished those were the only thoughts she had about Miami, but they weren't. She couldn't forget the days and nights she had spent with Dalton. Once they had finally gotten out of bed that first morning and showered, she was able to see that he didn't have just a hotel-room suite like she had. The man had the penthouse that could have held at least three suites the size of hers comfortably with room to spare. Needless to say, that's where she had spent most of her days and nights. There was no need to let all that space go to waste. It had been his suggestion, and she saw no reason not to go along with it.

Pretending had been nice. It had given them a chance to put out of their minds their dislike for each other and concentrate on satisfying their bodies' hunger. And that hunger had bordered on being downright greedy. Ravenous. To the point where they had made quickies a very fashionable pastime. She had to hand it to him; the man definitely knew how to please a woman between the sheets. Although she still didn't care for arrogant men, at least he could back up the attitude with skill.

Jules took another sip of her coffee, consumed in her memories. Hot. Racy. Sexy. She figured it wouldn't hurt to give in to them a few minutes longer, and she leaned back in her chair. Not only had her nights been spectacular, but her days with Dalton on the beach had been pretty fantastic, as well.

She wondered what he was doing now. More than likely he had returned to the office today as she had. And…more than likely he had moved on…like she should be doing. They had agreed that Miami was not to be repeated, and she had no reason to think he wouldn't keep his end of the deal, like she intended to keep hers.

But still, the memories were nice, and nothing was wrong with indulging in them.

"I'm glad we could all get together and do lunch," Sedrick Timmons said, smiling over at Shiloh and Caden. "My hours are crazy at the hospital."

"I can imagine," Caden replied, taking a sip of his wine and studying his brother-in-law, the heart specialist.

He would admit that he had been surprised when Shiloh mentioned her brother's invitation to lunch today. Growing up, Sedrick had been Jace's best friend, just like Shiloh had been his. Yet when Shiloh had chosen to defy her father's orders, Sedrick had not.

In fact, Jace admitted to not even recognizing Sedrick at first, when he'd arrived at the hospital after their grandfather's heart attack. And then, only a couple of months ago, Caden could clearly remember attending the open house for Shiloh's wine boutique and the discomfort of Sedrick staring him down with blatant dislike and hostility in his eyes.

But, to be fair and to give the man credit, the animosity could have stemmed from the fact that Sedrick hadn't wanted Shiloh to get back with him after what he'd done all those years ago, which Caden would admit had been shitty. But he and Shiloh had worked out their differences and put the past behind them. Caden hoped this invitation meant Sedrick was ready to do the same.

"Before the waitress comes back with our meal, there are a few things I need to clear the air about, Caden. And an apology to you tops the list." Sedrick paused a moment. "As you know, I was upset by the way you treated Shiloh when you were to be married the first time, but the two of you have worked things out and are finally happily married. All I have to do is look at my sister to see how happy she is, and if she's happy, then I'm happy."

"And I am happy, Sedrick," Shiloh said, taking Caden's hand. "I couldn't be happier."

"I can tell," Cassie Mayfield, Sedrick's girlfriend, said, with a huge grin on her face. "You're practically glowing."

"Thank you," Shiloh said, smiling.

"Your apology is accepted, Sedrick. And I promise to take care of Shiloh, and to always make her happy."

"That's all a big brother can ask."

The conversation then went to other areas until the waitress brought their food. The atmosphere was pleasant, but although Caden had accepted Sedrick's apology, there was something that still bothered him about that night at Shiloh's grand opening. He could understand Sedrick's hostility toward him somewhat, but what was up with the Greene family? Namely Michael Greene, his wife, Yolanda, and their son, Ivan, who was currently running for mayor. Granted, at the time, Caden hadn't known about his mother's affair with Mr. Greene, but even if he'd known, why would the family hold animosity toward him for what his mother and Michael Greene had done? Hell, he'd only been fourteen at the time. Had the hostility he'd seen in their eyes had anything to do with the affair, or was it something else altogether?

"How's your father doing?"

Caden lifted a brow and glanced over at Sedrick, surprised he'd asked. "Dad is fine. We go see him fairly regularly."

"That's good. I understand he's doing great things while in jail."

Honestly, his father's imprisonment was a topic he didn't want to discuss with Sedrick. His bitterness wasn't as deep as Dalton's, but he hadn't yet let go of the way the Timmonses had treated them when their father went to prison. "That might be true, but he doesn't belong in prison."

"Oh."

Caden heard doubt in that *Oh*. "And we plan to hire someone to prove his innocence." Sedrick nodded, and for a brief moment, Caden thought he saw an odd expression cross Sedrick's features.

Caden turned to his meal, convinced he'd just imagined it.

Dalton reached for his cell phone when it rang. He glanced at it quickly, not recognizing the number, but that didn't mean anything. "Dalton Granger."

"Mr. Granger. This is—"

"I know who this is," Dalton cut in, recognizing the voice. "Percy, I thought we agreed that you would drop the 'Mr. Granger,'" he said, leaning back in his chair.

"It's hard. You own the company."

"My *family* owns the company. How are things working out for you in the systems and technology department?"

He and Percy Johnson had attended the same high school, and although they hadn't been what one would consider close friends, they had played on the same football teams since middle school. Percy had been a damn good quarterback in high school and had gotten a scholarship to attend South Carolina University. He surprised everyone and turned it down when his girl-friend Tina got pregnant. He'd done the honorable thing by staying here and getting married.

Dalton had run into Percy waiting on tables in a nightclub he often frequented, the same club where he'd met Jules the first time. He had been holding a conver-sation with Percy, catching up on old times, when Percy mentioned he had recently gotten a degree in computer technology, graduating at the top of his class, but was having a hard time finding a job. Percy had been work-ing during the days at Cullum Meat Plant as a forklift operator and moonlighting at night as a waiter.

The one thing Dalton would never forget was that Percy had been one of the few kids at school who hadn't given him a rough time about his dad being in prison. In fact, Percy told him that he thought Dalton's father was innocent. That had meant a lot to Dalton at the time and was something he would never forget. That was the main reason he'd given Percy a job at Granger Aeronautics, right there on the spot. That had been a few months ago and, from what he heard, Percy was a hard worker and an asset to the company.

"Things are just wonderful, Mr...." Percy cleared his throat. "I mean, Dalton."

Dalton shook his head. "Let's agree that it's okay for you to call me Mr. Granger while at work if that makes you comfortable. But otherwise, it's Dalton."

"That's a deal." There was a moment's hesitation before Percy said, "I'm sitting in the parking lot, and so I guess officially I'm not at work." He paused. "Dalton, the reason I called is because I noticed something unusual. I just got this job, and I don't want to be a snitch or anything but…"

Dalton sat up straight in his chair. "You noticed what?"

"A program on one of the computers that shouldn't be there."

How could there be a program on a Granger Aeronautics computer that shouldn't be there? "You sure?" Dalton asked.

"Positive. Unless you are familiar with this type of stealth program, you wouldn't be able to detect it."

"But you can?"

"Yes. I might have just gotten my degree last year, but I've been messing around with computers for years. Besides that, I used to work for a company that did that sort of thing, legally, to monitor their employees. This one is more high-tech, and it's not monitoring anyone. It's taking information from somewhere in the building."

"Have you mentioned this to anyone else, Percy?"

"No."

"Good. Let's meet tonight, away from the office, and talk more about this. What about meeting at that nightclub where you used to work?"

"That's a good place. Percy Jr. has a football game after school, so would seven o'clock be okay with you?"

"Seven is fine. I'll see you then."

When he clicked off the phone, Dalton thought about getting security involved but then changed his mind. Security hadn't detected the spy devices implanted in

Shana's office earlier in the year. Not to mention that someone had tried hacking into her computer around the same time, and it had been someone from within the building. That's one of the reasons Jace had asked him to supervise security with the company and, as far as Dalton knew, everyone was doing their job and things were running well. But was there someone in the department who was compromising things? Someone with the ability to undermine his entire team of technical experts? He couldn't help but remember that Vidal Duncan had been able to embezzle money from the company for years without being detected, so Dalton knew such a thing was possible. Besides that, he mustn't forget that the person who'd tried hacking into Shana's computer had never been identified. It was assumed it was one of the employees who had been arrested. What if it wasn't, and what if the person was still working for Granger? The one benefit to working for the USN was knowing that anything was possible and that new technology, both good and bad, was being created every day.

He picked up the phone to call Jace and then put it down. Before taking the matter to Jace and Caden, he needed to first determine just what kind of program Percy had detected. He checked his watch and figured he had enough work to get through until his meeting at seven.

"Boy, did I need that," Shep said, releasing Carson's lips. He hadn't known she was visiting him today, and when Ambrose had come to the library to get him, Shep had been anxious to get to the room where he knew she was waiting. As usual, Ambrose had left them alone for an attorney-client consultation, when the guard had known it would be more than that.

Shep knew Ambrose always allowed them more private time than was strictly permitted, thus giving them the opportunity to engage in conjugal visits if they so desired. But, so far, he hadn't taken advantage of that. Carson deserved more than a quickie based on lust, and he intended to make sure she got what she deserved, even if it meant waiting until he was eligible for parole. She'd always told him she could wait because she loved him, and he knew with every bone in his body that he loved her. He'd admitted to his sons that he loved her the last time they had visited. They hadn't seemed surprised, because he knew Carson was beautiful both inside and out, and they knew it, too.

"And why did you need that, Mr. Granger?" she asked in a teasing tone. "Bad day?"

"The worst. Milligan and Davis were at it again today. I swear they're worse than Striker and Stonewall ever were."

"But with your help they will come around," she said encouragingly.

"I hope so." He then led her over to the table.

"So what did you find out?"

"According to Striker and Quasar, Jace and Caden have eased into their roles as husbands quite nicely."

Shep smiled, pleased and happy with the women his sons had married. "Nothing suspicious happening?"

"No. And, as you requested, Roland now has someone inconspicuously keeping an eye on their wives as they go about their daily routines, which isn't hard to do with Shana still working at Granger and Shiloh running the wine shop. It was easy for one of Roland's guys to become a frequent customer."

Shep nodded. "What's going on with Dalton?"

"I understand that Dalton went out of town last week and, of course, Stonewall followed."

Shep didn't say anything for a minute as he leaned back in his chair. "Now that they know about them, are my sons making things difficult for Striker, Quasar or Stonewall?"

"According to Roland, not at all, although Dalton and that little red high-performance toy of his make things challenging for Stonewall at times."

Shep grinned. "I can just imagine. You said Dalton was out of town last week. Where did he go?"

"Miami. Specifically, South Beach. Seems he followed a woman there."

Shep looked surprised. "Dalton? Following behind a woman? Must have been some woman."

"Yes. It was Jules Bradford."

"Jules Bradford? Shana's sister?"

"The one and only."

Shep looked confused. "But when I talked to Shana's father a few weeks ago, he mentioned that the two of them didn't get along, and that they practically hated each other's guts."

A smile curved Carson's lips. "That might be true to some extent, and I have to agree with what he said based on the one time I was in their presence. However, I think they might have recently reached a compromise...or entered into a truce situation of some sort."

Shep nodded slowly. "That should be interesting,"

he said, standing from his seat to take Carson back into his arms.

Carson went willingly. "I happen to agree."

Twenty-Two

Dalton walked into the nightclub and tried putting to the back of his mind what had transpired the last time he'd been here—the incident with Jules when she had deliberately given him her ass to kiss. Didn't matter now. That was water under the bridge since he had actually kissed that same ass just last week. Kissed it, licked those luscious cheeks and made love to them in ways that he got hard just thinking about. Now was not the time for an erection. He had business to deal with. Granger business. Besides, Jules was no longer in his system.

Moving around the tables while ignoring interested looks from various women, he made it to the booth in the back where Percy sat waiting. Dalton slid into the seat across from him. "You've been waiting long?"

Percy smiled wryly. "No. Actually, I just got here. I was hoping you wouldn't be early. My son's game ran into overtime."

Dalton nodded. "Who won?"

"We did," Percy said, smiling proudly. "I think he's going to be a good football player."

"Just like his dad."

"Thanks."

The waiter came to take their drink orders, and it was only after the man left that their conversation resumed. "So tell me what you know, Percy."

"Like I said, Dalton, I don't like to think of myself as a snitch, but you were good enough to give me a job, and my devotion is to you and your brothers. I wouldn't want anything to be going on with your family's company that you don't know about. Especially something that can affect it negatively."

Dalton nodded. "That's not being a snitch, Percy. That's called being loyal, and I know my brothers and I appreciate you for it."

"Thanks. I'm a newbie in the department, pretty much still in training. I don't think anyone, even Mr. Castor, knows of my past association with you. Nor do they know of my intensive background in technology. I deliberately didn't mention either. The former is because I didn't want anyone saying the only reason I got the job is because of my connection to you...although that's true. And the latter is because I don't want anyone thinking I'm coming into the company with the attitude of a know-it-all. So basically, I'm learning what they are teaching me and moving on from there."

Dalton knew John Castor was head of the IT department where Percy worked. He seemed like a likable guy who'd been with the company a good twelve years. He'd met Castor at several department-head meetings, and he always seemed alert, up-to-date on modern technology and on-point in making sure Granger's computers and software were high-tech and state-of-the-art.

The waiter delivered their drinks. After he left, Dalton said, "I think that playing it safe is a smart strategy. The technology field can be pretty competitive."

"I know. Anyway, Mr. Castor assigned me to look at a computer that had been brought in for repairs. The secretary said the keys were sticking and that when she typed one letter, another appeared."

Percy paused a moment to sip his drink. "I know I was only supposed to check out the keyboard, but I became fascinated by the model of the computer as I'd never worked on one like that before. It was pretty high-tech—especially for simple word processing—and I wondered why the keys would be sticking on that particular model. In fact, it should have been installed with a slider program. With a slider, all you need is a light stroke for the keys to operate. Also, the slider has a memory function that retains memory of certain key-strokes. Follow me so far?"

Dalton nodded. "So far, yes."

"That made me even more curious, so I checked out the hard drive to see whether the slider program had been installed, and I came across another program that was removed from laptops back in the nineties, because it was obsolete after the Y2K scare. So I wondered why this computer, a very new model, had it. It took me less than an hour to figure out the program actually was a type of filtering program that can erase data. I mean, wipe it out altogether. It can also transfer data from one computer to another from a remote device."

Percy paused, and Dalton knew he was giving him time to absorb all he'd told him so far. He'd been a kid, but he remembered the Y2K scare, and the belief, at the time, that with the changeover to the new millennium, computers worldwide would cease functioning. That didn't happen, of course, but that didn't stop corporations and financial institutions from buying into the scare. The only ones to benefit from the scare were the computer programmers, technicians and virtually anyone who knew anything about computers.

What really concerned Dalton was the last part of what Percy had said. He believed some type of filtering program had been installed on that particular computer that could erase data. Hadn't Bruce Townsend claimed that's what happened to Brandy's computer? That somehow it had been wiped clean?

"And you say it can be wiped clean from a remote location?"

"Yes. Without anyone ever detecting it. Sometimes it's all but impossible to trace."

Dalton leaned back in his seat. "Where is this particular computer now?"

"Back on the floor."

"In what department?"

"Accounting."

A feeling of unease settled in Dalton's stomach. Was that how Vidal had managed to steal money from the company without their knowing it? The man had been questioned and had refused to talk. And even with all the evidence stacked against him, his attorney had entered a not-guilty plea. Go figure.

"Don't mention a word of what you've told me to anyone, Percy. Not even to John Castor. At this point, no one is to be trusted until we figure out who put the program on that computer and why. Hell, there might be more of them placed throughout the building."

The thought of that really had Dalton's stomach in knots now. He couldn't wait to share this conversation with Jace and Caden. And it might be best if they had that meeting away from the office. Like he'd told Percy, at this point no one could be trusted.

Twenty-Three

Cuddled with Shana on the sofa while watching a movie on television, Jace glanced at his cell phone when he received a text message. Shana saw the way his brows bunched. "Something wrong, Jace?"

He glanced over at her, shaking his head. "Hell, I hope not. I just got a text from Dalton. He wants to meet with Caden and me at his place tomorrow morning at eight."

Shana raised a brow. "Did he say why?"

"No, and he asked us not to call tonight and ask questions. He will fill us in on everything we need to know in the morning."

When another text message came through, Jace glanced over at Shana. "Now he's telling me to make sure I bring you."

Shana smiled. "Now, don't I feel special? I wonder what this is about."

"We'll find out in the morning. Whatever it is, he evidently doesn't want to discuss it tonight."

Shana's smile faded, and undisguised concern showed in her eyes. "I hope it doesn't involve Jules."

"Why do you think it would?"

She shrugged her shoulders. "When it comes to Dalton and Jules, who knows? Did you ask him whether their paths crossed while he was in Miami?"

"Yes, I asked him, and he said no. But he was lying."

"Really? What makes you so sure of that?"

"Because I know Dalton. He could look you right in your face and lie…but he can't hide the way his jaw twitches when he's doing it. I don't think he's even aware of it. That's how I could catch him in a lie every time while growing up."

He adjusted their positions on the sofa to place her legs across his. "What about Jules? Did she mention anything to you about seeing him in Miami?"

Shana shook her head. "No, but I have a feeling she did see him. I didn't ask her anything about it when I talked to her on the phone today, and she didn't volunteer any information. I get the feeling she's being secretive about something, but I'm not sure it's about Dalton. It has something to do with a case she's working on."

"I thought she decided not to take on any new cases until after the holidays."

"Apparently, she changed her mind. Makes me wonder why. What about you and your brothers? Have you decided how you're going to go about reopening your father's case?"

"Yes, we're meeting with Carson on Friday at the office to see what she recommends. Dad trusts her. Hell, he's admitted to being in love with her, so I guess that says it all. I'm happy for him but also sad for him, as well. He deserves to be with her full-time. That's why it's important that we find my mother's real killer."

When Jace received another text message, he looked up at Shana and said, "Caden got the same text message from Dalton and wants to know if I know what's going on."

He texted his brother back and said, Your guess is as good as mine.

"So are you headed back to your place now?" Stonewall asked when Dalton walked out of the nightclub a couple hours after meeting with Percy.

Dalton met Stonewall's gaze and shrugged. "Not sure. Why do you want to know? Are you getting tired of following me around?"

"No, just asking," Stonewall said, grinning and falling into step beside Dalton. "And thanks for South Beach. I needed it."

Dalton chuckled to keep from admitting that he had needed it, too. He glanced at his watch. By his standards, it was still early, although most people would have gone to bed by now. After his conversation with Percy ended he had texted his brothers. Then he'd hung around, had a couple of beers and flirted with a few of the women. He hadn't been tempted to take one to a hotel, although several had invited him over to their place. He'd turned them down. That didn't necessarily mean he didn't want sex tonight. It just meant he didn't want it with them. He forced to the back of his mind the thought of the one woman he did want it from. She was supposed to be out of his system but, if that was the case, why were his thoughts consumed by her? And why hadn't he been able to put last week behind him?

"You're restless, Dalton."

He glanced over at Stonewall. "Restless?"

"Yes."

Dalton figured he would agree if being restless and being horny meant the same thing. What was so damned frustrating was that after a week of practically nonstop sex like he'd had in Miami, horniness was the last thing he should be suffering from. "You have a steady woman, Stonewall?"

If Stonewall was surprised by his question, he didn't show it. "No. I don't have a steady woman."

Dalton nodded. "Ever had a woman get into your system?"

"Can't say that I have."

"Then count your blessings."

They made it to Dalton's car, and he looked across the top of it to see all the bright lights of the nearby businesses. Some were tall buildings. Symmetrical. Well proportioned. Ripe with curves. His jaw tightened. Was he analyzing those damned buildings or remembering Jules's body? He thought his cravings for her were a thing of the past. Evidently not. It seemed that instead of working her out of his system, he'd embedded her deeper within it.

"Headed back to your place now?"

For a minute, he'd forgotten Stonewall was standing beside him. "I really don't want to."

Stonewall didn't say anything for a minute. "You need her address."

He didn't bother asking Stonewall who *her* was. "Do I?"

"Yes. You don't have it."

Dalton wondered how Stonewall knew that. And he was right. He didn't have Jules's address, because he'd never been to her home before. Just her office. "You got her address?"

"No, but I can get it."

"Then do it."

Dalton didn't care that he and Jules had agreed not

to pursue anything further once they returned to Charlottesville. On their last night together, she'd made it pretty damned clear that there would not be a repeat of Miami. However, at the moment, he didn't care that he was probably the last person she wanted to see, or that the courteous thing would be to call her first and not just drop by unexpectedly. But he was too horny to be courteous. Besides, he wanted the element of surprise on his side.

And he also wanted something else.

Jules rubbed her eyes, tired of reading yet another document. She had remained at her office well after Manning had left to take his dad to the doctor and decided sometime after seven to head home with the last of the files. Once there, she had showered, put on her pj's and decided to sit on the sofa in front of her fireplace and do some more reading.

By now, she knew that Imerson had worked alone out of an office on North Sampson, which was a ritzy area in Charlottesville. That meant his clientele was high-end and could afford the exorbitant fees he probably charged. Clients like Richard Granger.

Imerson had a good track record of solving cases other PIs couldn't, and since he worked alone, it took him a little longer. But he had a reputation for being thorough. Jules couldn't help wondering what he'd uncovered about the Sylvia Granger murder that could have gotten him killed…if that was the case. Sheppard Granger certainly thought that it was.

She had planned to read until ten o'clock and then stop to watch her favorite television show. But the show had been preempted by media coverage of a small earthquake in California. With nothing else to do, she had continued reading. It was either that or let those memories of her days and nights in Miami get the best of her.

An hour later, she was tired of reading but not sleepy enough for bed. She could call and chat with her father but figured he was occupied with Mona. And, of course, Shana probably had her hands full of Jace. She smiled at the thought. Naughty, naughty thoughts.

Jules figured she would enjoy a glass of wine and surf the television channels for a decent movie, and she was about to head for the kitchen to get the wine when there was a knock at her door. No one would be visiting her at this time of night and definitely not unannounced. She quietly padded across the room to retrieve the Glock, which she kept in a decorative ottoman beside the fireplace. In her line of business, you could never be sure who might come calling.

She eased to the door and looked out the peephole. WTF? Dalton! How dare he show up at her place? And how did he know where she lived? She was certain Shana would not have told him. And even worse, he was reneging on their agreement. She snatched open the door. "What do you think you're doing, coming here?"

He stood leaning in the doorway the same way he walked...with casual arrogance. He acted like he had every right to show up at her house at this hour, unannounced...not that it would have mattered if he had called first. The point was that he should not be here.

His tie was loose around his neck, and his sleeves were rolled up. The jacket of his Armani suit was thrown over his shoulder and, to her downfall, he looked too sexy for words. Tall, dark and predatory. Way too predatory, and she couldn't help noticing his focus was entirely on her.

"You plan on shooting me, Jules?"

She realized then that she was holding her gun, although it wasn't pointed at him. "I might," she said, placing the gun on a table near the door. "I thought we had an agreement, Dalton."

"We do."

"Then why are you here?"

Instead of answering, he said in a deep, husky tone, "Invite me inside, Jules."

A part of Jules wanted to slam the door shut in his face at that request. But then another, the one that recognized an electrical current flowing between them, wouldn't allow her to do that.

"I brought you something." She watched as he pulled a bag from behind his back. A bag from Parker's, known for their delicious apple pies. When they were in Miami, why had she mentioned her addiction to them?

"I thought you would like a slice."

She frowned. He hadn't thought anything. He had known she would want a slice. But that was no reason for him to default on their agreement. "I was just about to have a glass of wine."

"Then think of just how more enjoyable your glass of wine will be with this," he said, holding up the bag.

"Hmm, you're right." She snatched the bag from his hand and was about to slam the door in his face when he stuck out his foot and stopped her.

"I forgot to mention that I come with that bag."

Devious bastard. She should have known he hadn't appeared on her doorstep with a Parker's apple pie just because he was a nice guy. Dalton Granger had an ulterior motive for just about everything he did.

She looked at the bag and then back at him. Both, she knew from experience, were sinfully delicious. She licked her lips while wondering which she preferred tonight.

"Jules?"

She gave him an assessing glance. "I'm thinking."

"Fine, you're a thinker and I'm a doer, but we need to do it inside because it's cold out here." And then he brushed past her and walked into her home.

She frowned and closed the door behind him. "I don't recall inviting you inside."

He chuckled. "You're holding my entry card in your hand," he said, indicating the Parker's bag. "I'd like a glass of wine, as well, and there's enough apple pie for us to share."

When she gave him a dirty look, he smiled and said, "I see you're probably not too keen on sharing the pie."

"There's no *probably* in it," she said, heading toward her kitchen.

He followed. "Don't you know there's pleasure in sharing?"

That one particular word stopped her short. *Pleasure.* She placed the bag on the kitchen counter and turned around. "Why are you here, Dalton?" *Like I don't know.*

He leaned against the breakfast bar that separated her kitchen and dining room areas. "I've been thinking about you."

Her lips twitched. Had that admission come grudgingly? Definitely sounded like it. "And just what have you been thinking about?"

"Do I have to tell you?"

No, he didn't, but she wanted to hear it, anyway. "Yes, tell me, Dalton. What have you been thinking about?"

He held her gaze. "How good it felt being inside you."

She believed at that moment her heart missed a beat. And if that wasn't bad enough, a deep throb had started at the apex of her thighs. That's what she got for asking. "We agreed that—"

"Do you think I don't know what we agreed, Jules?" He rubbed his hand across his head, clearly frustrated. "Do you think I want to be here?" he asked testily. "But damn it, I like being inside you. I love the feel of your muscles clamping down tight on me while I thrust in and out of you. I love how easily your nipples slide between my lips and fit under my tongue. And I definitely love the feeling I get when my head is buried between your legs. And your taste…"

Trying to pretend that she wasn't affected by his words, she opened the cabinet door to retrieve two wineglasses, while squeezing her legs together tightly. She fought the urge to put the glasses aside and cross the room to him, strip off her pj's and spread her legs, because she loved the feeling she got whenever his head was buried between them, as well. And *his* taste…

"Jules."

She jumped. He was standing right there in front of her. When had he crossed the room? She should be piqued he had done so, but at that moment, she was so filled with awareness of him that she couldn't. He was staring down at her, focusing on her with an intensity that should disturb her. But strangely, it didn't. Instead, she knew how it felt to be totally desired. Wanted. She would even go so far as to say craved. She knew, because as much as she didn't want to admit it, whenever she thought about him, she experienced those same things. Although she doubted she would have given in to such a weakness as making a booty call like he was obviously doing. But, she had to admit, the thought had crossed her mind a couple of times since she'd returned from Miami.

She stared back up at him, feeling the heat radiating off him. She heard a scraping sound and realized it came from him pulling one of her chairs back away from the table. Then she watched as he eased down into it, facing her. "You liked doing it *this* way, Jules."

He'd spoken in a sexy tone, reminding her of the time in Miami one night when they had been on the hotel room's patio. He had sat naked in a chair, and she had sat naked, straddling him while he thrust in and out of her. She had definitely liked that position. While sitting in the chair facing him, she was able to look into his face and see each and every one of his expressions. She hadn't experienced anything as erotic in her entire life. And it seemed each and every thrust had met its mark, hitting right on her G-spot. She didn't want to remember just how many orgasms she'd had that night.

"Don't you?"

His question hung between them, brushing against her skin, soaking memories into her flesh. Her self-control was slipping, and she didn't like it. When he calmly sat back in the chair and slowly eased his legs apart, she saw what he wanted her to see. His huge erection.

She closed her eyes for a moment, trying to breathe in slowly as she fought to regain her control. A racy, hot fire was inching through her body, wrapping around her like a cape. Tightening like a band around her, making it impossible for her to escape a need Dalton could so easily generate within her.

"You might as well open your eyes, because it's not going anywhere."

She opened her eyes, and it seemed the moment she

did so, lust, as edgy and intense as it could get, took over her mind, and all she could do was stare at him, especially at his bulging crotch.

"You're thinking too hard, Jules."

Yes, she probably was. "And you're getting too hard, Dalton."

He smiled. "Making it just right for you," he said, answering easily.

She shook her head. "This is crazy."

He chuckled. "No, this is man wanting woman and woman wanting man. Nothing crazy about it."

Jules sighed, not so sure. "I don't even like you."

"You could have fooled me in Miami, and I'm sure, given how I felt a few months ago, I could have fooled you, too. Sex has a way of changing people."

"Not people," she countered. "Attitudes."

"Same difference. And have you finished thinking yet? Because when you stop thinking, then I can start doing."

He had said she was the thinker and he was the doer, and considering her time with him while in South Beach, she believed him. "Yes, I've finished thinking."

Dalton nodded slowly. "And what have you decided?"

Jules briefly considered how she would say this and decided to just be frank. "I've decided to see whether this chair is as sturdy as the one in Miami."

She wasn't sure what she saw first—the darkening of his eyes or the sexy smile that curved his lips. "There's only one way to find out," he said huskily.

Twenty-Four

Dalton concluded that although Jules might be the thinker and he the doer, when it came to this, they were of one accord. He could barely sit still watching Jules strip off her clothes in front of him. It amused him that whenever he'd seen her enter a nightclub, she'd always worn some sort of scandalous, barely there outfit. But here in the comfort of her home, beneath her robe, she was wearing flannel pajamas. However, he had to admit they were a cute pair, and she looked sexy in them.

"We really should be talking, Dalton."

He watched her, captivated by how she was slowly easing her pajama bottoms down her legs. "Talking about what?"

"Why this shouldn't be happening."

In that case, she wasn't about to hear a peep out of him.

"Dalton?" she called out to him when he hadn't responded. Now his gaze was fixated on the area between her thighs. And from where he was sitting, it was at eye level. He forced his gaze to her face. "Yes?"

"I said we should be talking."

"We should be doing just what we're doing."

She rolled her eyes when she began unbuttoning her shirt. "You would say that."

Hell, he didn't know a man alive who wouldn't... considering the view he was getting. And when she tossed her flannel shirt aside and stood stark naked in front of him, his gaze latched on to her breasts. He thought the same thing now he'd thought the first time he'd seen them, tasted them, fondled them and sucked them. Her breasts were perfect.

His gaze dropped back to the apex of her thighs. He could feel his entire mouth tingle and couldn't wait to get his tongue on her clit.

"You're not going to take your clothes off?"

Instead of answering her question, he said in a low growl, "Come here."

Their gazes met, held. He knew that by nature, Jules didn't like to be ordered around. But she knew what walking over to him could mean. *Pleasure beyond measure.* However, he wasn't surprised when she asked why. Like she really didn't know.

"I want to taste you."

He saw the flare of desire that lit her eyes. She was no longer thinking. She was ready to become a doer, as well. He watched as she shortened the distance between them. But she did not shorten it enough. "Closer."

She took a few more steps. That still wasn't good enough. "Closer, Jules."

"If I come any closer, I'll be in your face."

Exactly. "Come closer and spread your legs."

He certainly had a way with words, Jules thought, moving closer. And when he grabbed hold of her thighs, leaned forward and rubbed his face right in her center, she felt weak in the knees. And then she felt him lift-

ing her off her feet, hefting her up by the hips so that
his mouth was right there.

And the moment she felt his hot tongue slide inside
her, she screamed out an orgasm. She was sure he could
taste it, but he didn't stop working his tongue inside
her, holding tight to her thighs, securing her firmly
against his mouth.

Suddenly, his tongue went deeper, touched that particular spot, and she could feel new sensations invade
her body, spreading from where his mouth was to other
parts of her. She began writhing against his mouth, and
that seemed to make his tongue delve deeper still. He
was consuming her like he intended her to be his last
meal. Instinctively, she arched her back as she became
caught up in the most intense degree of lust that could
ever exist.

And then she was screaming again, but he wouldn't
let up. He didn't let up until the last wave of her orgasm
had washed through her. It was only then that he eased
her back down to let her feet touch the tile floor. And
she watched as he licked his lips. "You taste better than
any wine that's ever been created."

Those words stayed with her while she watched him
stand up and begin removing his clothes, and while she
watched, she felt hunger build up inside her body once
again. He was supposed to be out of her system, like
she was supposed to be out of his. What in the world
had gone wrong? Something had definitely backfired
on both their parts.

When he had removed every stitch of his clothing
and had sheathed his erection in a condom, he sat back
down in the chair. "Now we'll see how sturdy this chair
is."

She swallowed deeply. "We haven't already?"

"We haven't come close."

She looked down and saw that his erection appeared larger than ever. And she knew at that moment that was what she wanted. Without waiting for an invite, she moved toward him and straddled his lap, widening her legs just inches above his shaft. She wanted to be looking in his face when they made the connection. She wanted to see every single expression of both greed and pleasure.

"Ready?"

She held his gaze. He didn't know how ready she was. "Yes, ready. All systems go."

"Then, baby, let's blast off."

And when she banged down on him, his shaft automatically thrust inside her. She could actually hear him grit his teeth, moan some unintelligible words, curse under his breath and growl deep in his throat, while thrusting in and out of her. And she simultaneously rode him with flawless precision and perfect timing. She held tight to the back of the chair, which gave his mouth access to her breasts, and all she could do was throw her head back and moan.

He continued thrusting inside her over and over again. She heard the chair squeaking, and at one time thought they might fall out of it and tumble to the floor, but it held firm…at least almost until the end. A leg was the first to go, but Dalton still didn't stop; he just shifted his angle to put pressure on the remaining three chair legs.

And that was when she screamed, which was at the same time he threw back his head and shouted her name. He jumped up. Holding tight to her hips that were wrapped around him just seconds before the chair went crashing to the floor. He still didn't stop. Pressing her against the table, his thick pulsating shaft continued to beat down, pound into her in long, deep and feverish strokes.

Her entire body shivered; her mind went blank except for the feelings tearing through her. How could her self-control compete with this? And when her body joined his in yet another spasm, she knew she was in serious trouble. She hadn't counted on this. Hadn't counted on Dalton Granger being the one man she couldn't seem to get enough of. His yin to her yang…at least where sex was concerned.

Moments later, when they were able to breathe again, he pulled her into his arms and licked the side of her face before whispering, "Let's take this to the sofa."

Too weak to resist, and doubting she would have even if she could, she wrapped her arms around his neck when he lifted her. They paused momentarily to grab his pants off the back of one of the chairs. "I need more condoms."

And as she looked at the broken chair on her kitchen floor, she knew what she needed was another chair. A sturdier one.

"Are you trying to kill me?"

Jules's lips lifted in a smile. "Is that the *doer* whining?" she asked, easing her body off Dalton's.

He frowned as he pulled up into a sitting position on her sofa. "Hell, I'm not whining, just asking a question."

"One I don't intend to answer. I believe you're the one who showed up tonight at my place for a booty call. At least my sofa stood the test. You owe me a new kitchen chair, by the way."

Dalton chuckled. "You'll get it. It was worth breaking." He glanced around at all the papers spread on the coffee table. Papers he had shoved out of the way when he'd taken her on the sofa. That was before she began taking him. Riding him senseless into a new day. He leaned forward to straighten up the papers, and his hands froze when he saw what the documents were about. "You've got information on Marshall Imerson?" he asked, glancing over at her.

She nodded and adjusted her position on her sofa, wondering how many couples sat naked while talking on a sofa like it was a normal thing. But she didn't feel like going to the kitchen for clothes. Besides, they hadn't made it to her bedroom yet.

"Yes, and it wasn't easy. The records were sealed."

Dalton's brow lifted. "Sealed?"

"Yes."

"Why?"

"Good question. I believe it's because of the shitty way the initial police report was handled. There were so many red flags that, as a cop, I would have pursued. However, the police officer on the scene didn't."

Dalton didn't say anything for a minute. "Tell me what you've found out so far, and this time I *am* interested in what you're thinking."

So now he's interested in my mind and not my body. Jules smiled at the thought and told him just what she'd deciphered from the police report so far. "The former cop in me thinks it's clearly a cover-up, but there's no way to prove it. I intend to take a road trip later today and visit Imerson's wife, Leigh. She moved away not long after the accident."

"To where?"

"Steeplechase. I want to see if perhaps there's another file somewhere, or if he mentioned anything about the case to her."

"Sounds like you're going to be busy today, but then so am I. I've called Jace and Caden for a meeting at my place this morning at eight."

Jules's brows drew together. "Why?"

Dalton released a deep sigh. "It seems that the trade-secret scandal is deeper than we assumed."

"How so?"

Dalton shared with Jules what Percy had told him just that night. "Wow," she said, shaking her head. "When will it end?"

"Don't know. As long as there's greed in the world, people will do what they think they need to do to get rich quickly and illegally." He glanced at his watch. "Time sure flies when you're indulging in pleasure."

Jules chuckled. "Is that your way of saying it's time for you to leave?"

Dalton grinned. "I'm sure Stonewall wishes that was the case."

Jules sat up straight. "Stonewall? Stonewall followed you here?"

"Yes."

"And he's sitting out in front of my place?"

"More than likely. It's a wonder he didn't break the door down all those times you screamed. I guess he could decipher an 'I need help' scream from an 'I'm having an orgasm' scream."

Jules frowned over at him. "I can't believe you allowed him to follow you here."

"Baby, he's the one who led me. I didn't know where you lived."

Jules's frown deepened. "And he did?"

"Obviously. I'm here, aren't I?"

She opened her mouth to say something about him being a smart-ass, when she suddenly found herself lifted into his arms when he stood up. "Show me your bedroom, Jules."

"What if I told you I don't want to?"

"Then I would be forced to make you change your mind."

"Think you can?"

"Think I can't?"

She drew back and stared up into his face. "Your arrogance is showing, Dalton."

He gave her that smile that made her heart go *thump*. "We're wasting time, Jules. You have a busy day ahead of you, and so do I. So what do you say?"

She couldn't say anything with the feel of his erection pressing against her buttocks. "I don't think you can make me change my mind, but now is not a good time to prove it."

Twenty-Five

"Just when I hoped we had put the trade-secret scandal to rest and we could turn our attention to getting Dad out of prison, this happens," Jace said in disgust, pacing Dalton's living-room floor.

"We'll get Dad out of prison—nothing about that has changed," Dalton said, taking a sip of his coffee. "Especially since…"

When he stopped talking in midsentence and began studying the contents in his coffee cup, Caden asked, "Especially what, Dalton?"

"Nothing."

Jace's and Caden's gazes met again, and Dalton knew he'd almost made a slip. He'd promised Jules he wouldn't let anyone know of her involvement in investigating their dad's case just yet. "So what do we do about what Percy told me?"

"Percy Johnson," Caden said thoughtfully. "He was a couple of years behind me in school, but I remember him. Great quarterback. And you hired him to work for us?"

"Yes, and I'm glad I did."

"I'm glad you did, too," Shana said. She had begun pacing when Jace stopped.

Dalton glanced over at his sister-in-law. Was it his imagination, or had her stomach nearly doubled in size since the night of her dinner party?

"I remember him, as well," Jace said. "He was all-star even in middle school. He could throw a football farther than any quarterback I knew. I'm surprised he didn't make pro. I heard he got a full ride to some university in South Carolina."

"He did but turned it down."

Jace raised a brow. "Why?"

"He got his girlfriend pregnant." Dalton chuckled softly. "I'm sure you know how that works."

Shana spoke up rather quickly and said, "We need to let Marcel know what's going on." Dalton was convinced she'd spoken so quickly to diffuse her husband's wrath. In other words, to give Jace time to reconsider kicking his ass.

"I agree we need to let Marcel know," Caden chimed in.

"And Bruce, as well. There might be a connection with that computer and the one Brandy used," Shana tacked on.

"That's what I was thinking," Jace said, pacing again. "Certainly sounds like it."

Dalton thought it amusing that when Jace began pacing, Shana stopped, and when Shana stopped, Jace would begin. How could two people be so in tune with each other? That was weird. But hadn't he and Jules been in tune with each other those days and nights in Miami and last night, as well? Even now, the sounds of their moans and groans mingled together in his mind to make perfect harmony. And the way their bodies were so in sync when they made love. The rhythm was majestically perfect.

He hadn't left her bed until almost six this morning and had rushed through traffic to get here and shower before his brothers arrived. The last thing he needed was for them to get in his business, especially when it concerned Jules.

He jumped when a finger was snapped in front of his face. "What did you do that for?" Jace, Shana and Caden were staring at him like he was some oddity.

"Hate to interrupt your daydreaming, but Shana was asking you a question," Jace said. "She called out to you several times."

Dalton's brows pinched together. Had she? So what if he had been daydreaming? He was allowed to do so every once in a while. "Sorry, Shana, what did you want to know?"

"Is it possible for Bruce and Marcel to talk with Percy Johnson today? They will want to know exactly which computer he was working on. Knowing Marcel, he'll want to investigate with as few people knowing as possible, like the last time. He'll only inform those at Granger he feels he can trust."

"Good idea, and I suggest they talk to Percy away from the office, especially since we don't know who else might be involved," Dalton said. He then looked over at Jace. "How well do you know John Castor?"

Jace shrugged. "I don't know him any better than you do. He's been working for the company close to twelve years. He's married. Two kids in high school."

"So he was hired after Dad left," Caden said, as if thinking out loud to himself.

"Yes. And he did come to Shana's dinner party," Dalton said. "I saw him there."

Shana nodded. "I'll find out everything I can about him," she said. "As well as everyone who works in his department. That information will be available to you within forty-eight hours, if not sooner."

Jace nodded and glanced around at everyone in the room. "What's going on at Granger is pretty serious, but we still need to meet with Carson on Friday to discuss how to proceed in getting Dad's verdict overturned. And the only way we can do that is to hire someone to find the real killer."

Dalton took a sip of his coffee and said nothing. Little did they know that Jules was already working on it. He couldn't wait to see their reactions once they found out what she'd been doing in her spare time.

"Thanks for seeing me on such short notice, Mrs. Imerson," Jules said as the woman led her toward the rear of the house where the enclosed patio was located.

"No problem, Ms. Sweet, although I'm not sure what I'll be able to tell you. Marshall never brought work home, and he never discussed any of his cases with me."

The woman gestured Jules to a chair that overlooked a huge lake. In the distance, the tops of mountains could be seen above the branches of tall oak trees. The patio was completely glassed in, and heat was provided by an old-fashioned brick fireplace.

"I hope you don't mind sitting out here, but I love looking out over the water. It's so peaceful," Leigh Imerson said, taking the chair across from Jules.

"Yes, it is," Jules agreed. The drive from Charlottesville had been a peaceful one, as well. She'd taken the scenic route away from the hustle and bustle of traffic. The only traffic she had to be concerned with were the occasional riders taking their horses out for exercise.

She arrived in Steeplechase right before lunchtime, and since she hadn't eaten breakfast, she'd made a pit stop at one of the local diners. Steeplechase was one of those beautiful, quaint cities where you would want to retire, because there was no way for you not to be drawn to the cobblestone streets, bike paths and walking trails. And she'd seen the numerous horse farms that overlooked the Blue Ridge Mountains.

Sitting at the diner while enjoying lunch gave her a chance to unwind...and relive last night's memories. A part of her was convinced that last night had been a mistake, and she should not have slept with Dalton again. But then, honestly, who slept? That was why when she returned to Charlottesville later today, she intended to go home and crash. What if Dalton showed up later, figuring after Miami and last night that she was open to having some sort of an affair with him? Of course, she didn't want to have an affair with anyone and needed to let him know that. The last thing she wanted was for him to think things about their relationship just because they'd messed around a few times. Okay, it was more than a few times, but still, that was no reason for either of them to start getting any crazy ideas.

"Would you like some tea, Ms. Sweet? I just made a pitcher of my mango tea."

Jules had never drunk mango tea before and decided to try it. "Yes, thanks. I would appreciate a glass."

"Then please excuse me for a minute."

Jules watched as the woman stood to head to the area of the house she assumed was the kitchen. Leigh Imerson was an attractive woman who appeared to be in her midfifties. But even with her sparkling smile, Jules saw sadness in her eyes. Marshall Imerson had died almost four years ago, and Jules assumed the sadness was still for him.

She recalled that she and Shana would often return home from one of their high school functions to find their father sitting in the living room alone. And although he would smile brightly when he saw them, there had always been a degree of sadness in his eyes.

From what Manning had found in his research, it seemed that the Imersons had married right out of college. Marshall had gone to work for the Charlottesville Police Department for a short while before becoming detective…similar to the paths both she and her father had taken, Jules thought.

Imerson had been a good detective and transitioned into the role of private investigator with ease, building a successful company. Everyone thought he was a fun-loving family man, and those who'd been interviewed after the accident had never seen him take a drink. But their statements hadn't been enough for the police to investigate further.

Jules glanced around, deciding she liked this house. It was spacious and sat on what had to be at least five acres of land. The furnishings were nice, and the artwork was a mixture of contemporary and abstract. For someone who was supposed to have been facing financial ruin, which was purported to be the cause of Imerson's drinking problems, it seemed that Leigh Imerson had done pretty well for herself after her husband's death. Manning was spending the day investigating just how deeply in debt Imerson had been, or whether that rumor had been anything more than a smokescreen.

"I baked some chocolate chip cookies this morning and thought you might like a few to go along with your tea," Leigh said, entering the room carrying a tray with cookies and glasses of tea.

Jules stood to help her. "Why, thank you, Mrs. Imerson. Cookies and tea sound nice."

"You're welcome and please, call me Leigh."

"And you can call me Jules," Jules said as she selected several cookies off the tray.

Deciding she needed to broach the reason for her visit, Jules said, "I read the police report on Marshall's auto accident, Leigh. It claims he had been drinking the night he died. The report indicated that a liquor bottle was on the seat beside him, and that he'd smelled of liquor."

The smile faded from Leigh's face. "I know what that police report says, but it's not true. Marshall did not drink."

"But how do you explain the liquor bottle in the car and him smelling of liquor?"

Leigh shook her head with a look of confusion clouding her eyes. "I can't explain it. All I can say is that someone deliberately tried to ruin Marshall's reputation, and I don't know why."

Jules took another sip of her tea before asking, "Did you tell anyone what you thought? That you didn't believe the police report?"

"Yes, but the chief of police at the time claimed he had proof."

"What about a BAC test? Why didn't you request one to verify Marshall's alcohol concentration level?"

"I did and was assured one would be done. However, after I had Marshall cremated, I found out someone had dropped the ball and the test hadn't been done."

Jules wondered if someone had dropped the ball or had deliberately made certain that the test was never done. Was that the reason the police report had been sealed? Because of a monumental screwup? "At the time of his death, Marshall was working on an investigation for Richard Granger. Did you know that the report went missing after your husband's death?" she asked.

Leigh shook her head. "No. Like I told you earlier, Marshall never discussed work with me, and he never brought any work home as far as I know. So I have no idea where that report is or what happened to it. I even told that same thing to the man who came asking about it a few months after Marshall's death."

Jules's brow bunched. "Do you remember the name of the man?"

Leigh nodded. "Yes. His name is Ivan Greene, and he's currently running for mayor of Charlottesville."

Jules tried to keep surprise out of her face as she bit into her cookie.

Twenty-Six

Sitting at his dining room table, Dalton listened as Marcel interviewed Percy. Hearing the man's account a second time, as well as focusing in on the questions Marcel was asking, made Dalton realize just how serious the situation was and just how fortunate they were that Percy had been so attentive to certain things. Things that might otherwise have gone unnoticed.

His brothers and Shana had returned when Percy and Marcel had arrived. Bruce Townsend was there, as well. Marcel was the one asking questions, but Bruce was furiously jotting down notes. Jace was pacing, Shana was typing something on her tablet and Caden, who had obviously missed lunch, was hungrily snacking on a bag of chips he'd grabbed off the kitchen counter.

A short while later, Dalton watched Marcel draw in a deep breath, evidently satisfied with his line of questioning. Then Bruce began asking questions of Percy, and it seemed the two men began speaking a different language with all that computer mumbo-jumbo.

Bruce turned to Jace. "I need to get inside the accounting department, preferably after hours and without anyone knowing. Even security."

The Granger Aeronautics security team worked twenty-four hours a day, and everyone in the room knew it. What Bruce was asking was close to impossible. Jace glanced over at Dalton. "Can you make that happen?"

Dalton nodded. "Yes. I'll need to organize a few things but I'll let you know when and how tomorrow."

"All right," Jace replied. And then he asked Bruce, "Did you ever find out whether information had been wiped off Brandy's hard drive?"

"Not yet. But if Percy actually saw that program, that will answer the question for us."

"How can someone manage to wipe a computer clean from a remote location?" Caden asked, obviously baffled by what he'd heard.

"With so much modern technology out there, it's not impossible to do," Bruce replied.

"I concur with Bruce," Marcel said, rubbing a frustrated hand down his face. "The agency spends a lot of time investigating computer fraud and abuse. Just when we think we have a handle on it, some new software is developed. But this is more about abuse," he added. "This might be more than about trade secrets. Granger handles government contracts, so this security compromise is especially worrisome."

Dalton could tell it bothered the others in the room, as well. He hoped the FBI would get to the bottom of it and put all those involved behind bars. And speaking of bars...

"When do Vidal Duncan, Titus Freeman, Cal Arrington and Melissa Swanson go on trial?" Dalton asked.

Caden glanced over at him. "Funny you should ask.

I got a call from Duncan's attorney before I left the office. The man specifically asked for me. I guess he knew better than to call Jace."

"What did his attorney want?" Jace asked in a voice that had turned to steel.

"He didn't say. I figure he's going to try to work on some sort of plea deal for Vidal."

"Not with my help," Jace said angrily.

Marcel understood Jace's attitude. "As far as Arrington is concerned, he's finally decided to start talking to save his skin since Melissa Swanson is telling everything she knows. And Titus Freeman claims he's suffering from amnesia and can't recall a thing. I think his attorney is trying to come up with an insanity plea."

Caden shook his head. "You also got another call after you left the office, Jace. I hate it when you forward your calls to me."

"Who was it?"

"Your ex-wife."

"Evil Eve," Dalton said. "She's probably pissed that she wasn't invited to the wedding."

Jace rolled his eyes. "She's lucky she's not sharing a jail cell with Vidal. She still might if he decides to name her as a collaborator in my kidnapping. She's not out of the woods yet."

"And I think she knows it," Caden said. "I believe she wants to talk to you and convince you that she's an innocent woman."

Dalton chuckled, thinking the former Eve Granger probably didn't know the meaning of innocent. "Evil Eve coming to town is interesting," he said aloud. "It's showtime."

* * *

After returning home from Steeplechase, Jules took a three-hour nap. When she woke up, it was to find it had already grown dark outside. Hungry, she decided to order takeout and figured Chinese sounded good.

She had called Manning earlier and asked him to pull a report on Ivan Greene as well as his parents. What if Imerson had discovered the senior Greene's alibi wouldn't wash and they hadn't been on a cruise at the time of Sylvia Granger's death as they'd claimed? And from all accounts, Ivan would have been twenty-six or twenty-seven at the time. What if he'd learned of his father's affair with Sylvia and had gone to the boathouse to confront his father's lover? What if things had turned ugly? Violent? Deadly?

With the election in a few weeks, Ivan Greene's face was everywhere—on television and billboards—encouraging voters to vote for him for mayor. A native son. Harvard graduate. A person who truly cared for the betterment of the city. Typical politician with promises galore. According to the polls, he was leading his opponent, so he might just end up being Charlottesville's next mayor.

Jules was about to look up the number for the nearest Chinese takeout restaurant when her phone rang. It was Dalton. Should she answer it? *Sure, why not answer it? If you don't feel like being bothered, just let him know.* At that moment, she definitely didn't feel like being bothered. He had crept into her thoughts too many times today. Memories of each and every time they'd made love had overwhelmed her at some of the oddest moments. Made her hot, made her smile, made her want to drown in his flavor. That was too much Dalton

Granger to suit her. Definitely more than she'd experienced with any other man she'd been involved with.

She answered the phone. "Yes, Dalton?"

"Busy day?"

Her shoulders eased a bit. Why did hearing the sound of his voice do that to her? And why did his voice have to sound so soothing…and sexy? "Yes, it was busy. What about yours?"

"Crappy is more like it. My house was filled with a lot of people most of the day. Jace, Caden, Shana, Bruce, Marcel and Percy—all trying to make heads or tails of what's going on with the company and all that technology exploitation."

"I'm sure Marcel or Bruce will figure it out."

"Hell, I hope so. For once, I'd like to be a part of a company that's not in the red and not faced with greedy employees trying to steal from it. And on top of everything else, Caden mentioned that Evil Eve is coming to town."

Jules knew that Jace's first wife was named Eve but that Dalton preferred calling her Evil Eve.

"Any particular reason why?"

"I think she's afraid Vidal is going to name her as an accessory, and she wants to convince Jace she wasn't involved."

Jules snorted. "Depends on what you mean by involved. I'd think having an affair with Vidal constitutes involvement."

"Eve doesn't think the way most people do."

"Well, Jace isn't the one she should be convincing of her innocence. I'd think she should be worried about the prosecutors."

He paused a minute. "What are you doing for dinner?"

"Nothing." And just in case he had any ideas about joining her, she quickly put them to rest. "I ordered takeout. Chinese."

"Oh. And how did things go with your interview of Leigh Imerson?"

She hesitated, not yet ready to tell him what she'd found out. First she wanted to read the report on Ivan Greene that Manning was pulling together. But still, it wouldn't hurt hearing what he knew about the man. "It went well. She said her husband didn't bring work home or talk about any of his cases with her."

"So she was a dead end."

I wouldn't say that. "For now, I'm moving on to the next person on my list, Ivan Greene. What do you know about him?"

"Nothing, really. He's running for mayor, and if you want to believe the polls, he has a strong chance of winning. I'm sure you know his father supposedly had an affair with my mother."

"Supposedly? Don't you believe it?"

"Doesn't matter. Dad evidently received proof in the way of pictures. All I know is the man I saw with my mother that one time at the boathouse wasn't Michael Greene."

"And you don't know who the man was?"

"We were never officially introduced, Jules," Dalton said drily.

He sounded agitated, somewhat annoyed. She wondered whether talking about his mother and bringing up her affairs bothered him. "I'm sure that you weren't introduced, Dalton. But I just wondered if perhaps you remembered anything about the guy."

"That was a long time ago."

"Think you'd recognize him if you were to see him again?"

"What are you planning to do? Let me pick him out of a police lineup?"

"That might actually be possible."

"I was just teasing."

"I knew you were. No need to be testy."

"I'm not."

"Yes, you are. Look, my takeout has arrived," she lied. "I'll talk to you later." And without waiting for him to respond, she hung up the phone.

"Did she just hang up on me?" Dalton muttered, clicking off his phone and placing it back on the table. Jules sounded moody, and moody women had always been a total turnoff for him. But then, he had no right to be judgmental, since he wasn't in the best of moods himself.

Like he'd told her, his day had been crappy. Having people in and out of his house wasn't something he was used to, and he wasn't overjoyed about the reason they'd had to meet behind closed doors in the first place. And then, while they were assembled, Jace figured it would be a good time for Marcel and Bruce to meet Striker, Quasar and Stonewall. He felt it was important for everyone to know who was working on the same team. It had been a smart idea, but the day had been tiring and the meetings had seemed to last forever.

He had called to invite Jules to dinner, which he now saw was a mistake. So maybe her moody attitude was a blessing in disguise. Like him, she probably didn't want anyone in her personal space. They had spent last night together, but there was no need to overdo things by seeing her again today or even again this week. Or next week, for that matter. During his lifetime he'd dated a lot of women, but he'd never been a man who wanted an exclusive relationship with one.

And why had Jules asked about his mother's lovers? He hadn't known about Michael Greene until Jace and Caden mentioned the man to him. And he'd been truthful when he'd said that he wasn't sure he would recognize the man he'd seen his mother with that day in the boathouse if he were to ever see him again.

Moving toward his kitchen, he grabbed a beer out of the refrigerator and figured that he might as well order takeout himself, and Chinese wasn't a bad idea. Tonight he would give Stonewall a break and stay in for a change. Besides, he needed to come up with a plan to get Bruce into the accounting department of Granger without security knowing anything about it. It would be hard, but not impossible.

What Percy had uncovered with that computer was also a breach of security, and since he was the top dog in charge, all he had to say about that was *not on his watch.*

He stood in his kitchen and finished off the beer before tossing the can in the recycling bin. Shoving his hands into the pockets of his slacks, he leaned back against the kitchen counter. When had his place begun feeling lonely? He was probably thinking that way because it had been crowded with several people earlier and was totally empty now. And why did his mind wander and focus on a particular woman?

Jules was a distraction he didn't need now. He had things to take care of. And he understood how she'd gotten wrapped up in what she was doing, her own little investigation. All he'd ever needed or wanted from her was a physical connection. He'd had it—quite a few times—so he was good to go. He didn't need en-

tanglements, long-term or otherwise. And he didn't
need Jules.

Dalton's chest contracted in a long, deep sigh. His
life was turning to shit, and he didn't know why. The
company he and his brothers had promised their dying
grandfather to take on had been infiltrated by crazies,
and for the first time in his life, he was allowing a
woman to get under his skin. And if he wasn't careful, the next thing he'd be doing is ending up like his
brothers.

Damn it, that wouldn't be happening, and if the only
way to ensure that it didn't was to avoid her, then he
would. He refused to let any woman push him to lose
control. The repercussions would be disastrous. And
this way, his brothers didn't have to know that he and
Jules had ever hooked up. Right now they were just
speculating that that is what had happened, and they
could continue to do so. The more they stayed out of
his business, the better.

Twenty-Seven

"Honestly, Ms. Sweet, I'm not sure why you're here. What is it you want to know?"

Jules glanced around the lavishly decorated living room. It was immaculate, with all-white furniture that matched the white carpeting. It also matched the uniform of the maid who had escorted her inside, as well as the white Mercedes parked in the circular driveway. That was too much white. Too sterile for her taste. Too pristine. But Ivan Greene, mayoral candidate, looked right at home standing out in his tailor-made dark suit against all that white.

He hadn't offered her tea or cookies as Leigh Imerson had done, which led her to believe he didn't expect her to stay long. "Honestly, Mr. Greene, you aren't the one I asked to talk with. I was expecting to meet with your parents. I was surprised to find you sitting here waiting on me, instead."

She could tell from his expression that he wasn't used to being around those who spoke their minds. "And I honestly can't imagine what they could tell you, either. How about you telling me what this is about?"

Not before he answered a question of her own. "Do

you always designate yourself as your parents' spokesperson?"

He shrugged. "I've found it necessary to run interference for them since I began running for political office. Early on, for some reason, my opponents thought my parents would expose some imaginary secrets they could use as ammunition to hurt my campaign."

Jules held his gaze. "And they can't?"

Ivan Greene frowned. "There aren't any secrets to expose. What you see is what you get. Now, let's not waste our time. What exactly are you here for? Why did you want to meet with my parents?"

"It's about the Sylvia Granger murder." He didn't blink, which meant he'd known the nature of her visit. She couldn't be concerned with *how* he knew for right now.

"Then you're definitely wasting your time wanting to meet with my parents. They were out of the country on a cruise when that unfortunate incident happened."

"Were they?"

"Yes. You can check with the cruise line, but that was close to fifteen years ago, and there's a possibility their records don't go back that far. You might want to check with the man who was Sheppard Granger's attorney at the time. I understand he verified my parents' alibi."

She nodded. "So I understand, but I prefer not having a second party verifying any alibis I'm interested in. You never know when someone is not being honest. And I'm sure you're aware that at least one of your parents, specifically your mother, might have been a suspect had Sheppard Granger revealed the fact that your father had an affair with his wife, Sylvia Granger."

She watched his jaw twitch, letting her know he didn't like being told that. "Let's be real, shall we, Ms.

Sweet? We both know why that was never brought up in court. Granted, I understand my mother went to see Sheppard Granger while he was out on bail and asked him not to mention it because of their alibi, and he agreed. But only after his attorney checked out my parents' alibi. But then, Sheppard was a smart man. He'd known that mentioning his wife's affair with my father would have given the prosecution even more reason to argue that Sheppard Granger had a motive for killing his wife. He did the smart thing in leaving my parents out of it. And besides, like I said, they were on a cruise at the time Sylvia Granger was murdered."

"How convenient."

"Yes, and how lucky for them not to get caught up in that scandal. They were on that cruise trying to restore and rebuild their marriage. As you can see, it worked. My parents have been married a little over forty years now."

"That's admirable, considering the fact your father's affair with Sylvia had your mother angry enough to hire a private investigator to prove her suspicions were true and then send proof of the affair to Sheppard Granger."

"Only because Sheppard Granger needed to know what kind of woman he was married to. Sylvia Granger was evil, and she used my father to get what she wanted."

Jules raised a brow. "Which was?"

"A way to make her husband jealous, I imagine. I understand Sheppard had begun spending more time with Granger Aeronautics and less time with Sylvia. I heard she was beginning to feel somewhat neglected."

Jules didn't say anything for a minute. "You seem to know a lot about how she was feeling, Mr. Greene. Let's see, you were around twenty-six or twenty-seven back then, right? An attorney fresh out of Harvard Law School, who went straight to work with Miller, Wyatt and Barnes."

Then, without missing a beat, she asked, "And where were you the day Sylvia Granger was murdered?"

His gaze darkened with suppressed anger. "I wish I could say I was on that cruise with my parents, but I can't. I was here in town, but in court that day. All day. That can be verified."

"I'll make sure that it can. And what about your visit to Leigh Imerson? Not long after her husband's accident, you were inquiring about his investigative report on Sylvia's murder. Why were you interested? Were you afraid some damaging information was in that report? Whom were you trying to protect? Your parents or yourself?"

"I have no idea what you're talking about."

"Really? Well, personally, I think that you do know what I'm talking about."

His jaw twitched again as he leaned forward on the sofa. "Let's cut the bullshit, Ms. Sweet. You're a PI who goes by the name J. B. Sweet, but you're really Juliet Bradford, and your sister is married to Jace Granger."

She wasn't about to try to figure out how he had discovered that, either. "The fact remains that I am a PI. A darned good one, who plans to prove Sheppard Granger didn't kill his wife and expose the real killer."

"As far as I'm concerned, the real killer is in jail. Sheppard Granger killed his wife, so trying to prove otherwise is a waste of your time."

Jules stood, smiling. "No problem. I have time to waste. Thanks for seeing me in your parents' stead. Hopefully, next time I have a question, I'll get a chance to talk to them."

"I'd advise you not to hold your breath waiting for that to happen."

Jules met his gaze without blinking. "Oh, you might be surprised at what I can make happen, Mr. Greene. And I'll keep in mind the fact that you didn't tell me why you sought out Ms. Imerson after her husband's accident, which means I'll be doing even more digging for answers. Goodbye, and I wish you the best in the election."

She then turned and headed toward the front door but paused to say casually, "Oh, there is something else I'm curious about. You and your parents ran into Caden Granger at a party a couple of months ago, and I understand that the three of you weren't all that friendly toward him. Any reason for that? Even if he is Sylvia Granger's son, he was a child during the time of his mother's affair with your father. Why the animosity?"

Ivan's eyes blazed in fury. "Yes, he was a child then, but he's a full-grown man now."

"Meaning?"

"I guess that's for me to know and for you to try to figure out, Ms. Bradford."

Dalton approached the security station in the main lobby at Granger Aeronautics. The man at the desk watching the monitors on all the floors and elevators was George Gillum, a sixtysomething man who would be retiring next year. Not only did Dalton need to get George engaged in a conversation for about thirty minutes, but he also needed to switch off the video in the elevator that Bruce would be using. In the event it was played back later for some reason, they needed no evidence that Bruce had been on site.

Percy had visited accounting earlier and marked the

computer in question. The computer had been assigned to a young woman by the name of Ramona Oakley. Single, pretty and a dedicated employee of five years. She had a good work record, good attendance and a bubbly personality. It was rumored that last month she had begun dating an older man.

The woman sounded a lot like Brandy Booker. Dalton couldn't help remembering when Brandy had mentioned to him that she was dating an older man, one who was at least twenty years older than she was. He couldn't help wondering if perhaps there was some older man out there preying on the younger women who worked at Granger. First Brandy and then Ramona? Were there others? For some reason, he had a nagging suspicion it was the same man. That was a possible angle he would mention to Marcel.

George Gillum glanced up with surprise when Dalton approached. "Mr. Granger, I'm surprised to see you down here."

Dalton gave the older man a megawatt smile. "Yes, I thought it would be nice to get to know the employees, those we consider essential to the company. And you are first on my list."

George beamed, evidently feeling pretty darned important. "Thank you. I appreciate that. Do you want to know what I do every day?"

That was the last thing he wanted, Dalton thought. He didn't want George focused on any of those monitors for now. Not for at least thirty minutes. "No, that won't be necessary. But I need to know how things are going with you personally. I know you've been with the company close to twenty-five years." Dalton deliberately went to stand in front of the monitor that scanned the accounting floor to prevent George from seeing it.

"Yes, and it was your daddy who hired me. Good man, that Sheppard Granger. And he did what you're doing now. Got to know his employees. He knew I liked strawberries, and every once in a while he would bring me some that were grown right on your family estate."

Dalton couldn't help but laugh. "So Dad was the one sneaking into my grandmother's strawberry patch. I think she thought it was my brothers or me."

George chuckled. "Sorry about that, but they were so good." Then the smile eased from George's face. "They stopped coming when your dad left." He paused a moment. "Just so you know, I never believed your father capable of harming anyone."

Dalton nodded. "Thanks. That means a lot."

"I send your father a card every holiday to let him know I'm still here."

"That's kind of you to do that. I understand you're retiring sometime next year."

"Yes," George said, his smile returning. "My wife, Cora, and I plan to take one of those Mediterranean cruises. For fourteen whole days. At least, we hope to do so. We've both been saving our money to make it happen, but she had to have a hip replacement earlier this year, so we need to try harder to reach our financial goal."

Dalton decided then and there that regardless of whether George reached his financial goal for the trip, he would make the cruise happen for him and his wife… as a retirement gift from Granger.

He ended up talking to George way past what was needed, because he was enjoying conversing with him so much. George was proud of his two daughters and couldn't help boasting about his four grandsons. Dalton wished there were more employees at Granger like George, those who felt a deep loyalty to the company.

When his cell phone vibrated, he knew it was Bruce sending a signal that he was through with what he needed to do. "Well, George, I won't let this be my last time visiting. I enjoyed our talk."

A smile spread across the older man's features. "I enjoyed it, as well, Mr. Granger. Reminded me of old times with your daddy."

A few moments later, when Dalton walked toward the elevator, he decided that he would also pay a visit to the strawberry patch next time he visited Sutton Hills. Since George liked strawberries, there was no need to let any of them go to waste.

Ben Bradford eased out of bed to sit on the side. For some reason, Jules was on his mind. His daughter was up to something, and it didn't take a genius to figure out what. She was planning to find out who really killed Sylvia Granger. And knowing Jules, she would find that person or die trying...and it was the latter that had him worried. Especially after what Shana had shared with him regarding what Sheppard had told his sons. He had reason to believe the last PI trying to prove his innocence died a questionable death. There was no way in hell Ben would let his daughter be at risk. But then, he knew that Jules had a mind of her own. She always had and always would.

If he thought there was some way he could talk her out of pursuing this, he would. Or at least try. Jules knew this, which was probably the main reason she hadn't mentioned anything to him or her sister about what she was doing. And she wouldn't until she thought they needed to know. Right now she was keeping quiet as a church mouse.

"Ben, are you all right?"

He glanced over his shoulder at Mona as she pulled herself up to a sitting position in bed. He would never tire of looking at her. She was simply beautiful. He eased back in bed and drew her into his arms. "Yes, baby, I'm fine. I was just thinking about Jules."

"Jules? What about Jules? She's okay?"

She better be, he thought. *Anyone who hurts a hair on my daughter's head will have to answer to me.* "I'm sure she is. I haven't heard from her in the last couple of days. I know she's busy working on a case."

Mona pulled away slightly and looked up at him. "A case? But I thought she said she was getting some rest until after the holidays."

"I think she changed her mind. A case was brought to her attention that she feels she needs to handle."

"Oh." Mona went back into his arms and cuddled closer to him. "Is that why you're frowning?"

Ben didn't say anything for a minute. "And how did you know I was frowning?"

Mona went completely still and didn't say anything. Ben drew back to look into her face. "When were you going to tell me you'd gotten your sight back?"

Mona drew in a long, deep breath. "Not until I was certain it was back. All I'm getting is occasional flashes. I don't want to get too optimistic. How did you know?"

Ben smiled. 'I'm an ex-cop and an ex-detective, re- member? Picking up on most things comes second na- ture to me. But I couldn't help noticing you weren't using your wand as much as you normally do. And a couple of times, I caught you staring at me as if you could see me."

"At times I can see you." She blushed when she added, "Mostly when we make love and...I lose myself."

"What do you see then?"

"You above me. Loving me. You started out being a bright flash of light, and then one night, there was more. I saw you. I saw your features clearly. It was in a flash but I saw them, Ben."

"When?"

"While we were in New York."

He nodded. "Why didn't you tell me?"

Mona smiled. "I know you, Ben. You would have made a big deal out of it, and I didn't want that, especially if I'm hoping for too much."

"Have you told your doctor yet?"

"Yes. I made an appointment to see him as soon as we got back."

"And?"

"And he thought what happened was good. But he still warned me not to get my hopes up yet. He thinks we'll know something more definite in another month or so."

Ben pulled her back into his arms and held her tightly. "I told you my feelings on the matter. Even if you never regain your eyesight, Mona, I love you just the way you are."

Mona started to reply, but the look on her face said, *How can I reply to that?*

"You can't," he said, letting her know he'd read her mind.

She leaned up and kissed his cheek. "I am a lucky woman."

"And I'm a very lucky man."

* * *

"Sheppard Granger didn't take our advice, and his sons have hired a private investigator. She's snooping around."

The person on the other end of the telephone paused a moment then said, "That's unfortunate. We've gotten rid of one private investigator who tried to prove Granger's innocence, and we can definitely get rid of another. Continue to keep me posted."

Twenty-Eight

Bruce glanced around at the people gathered in Dalton's living room, waiting to hear what he had to say. "It was just as Percy said. Software was installed on that computer that was set to wipe everything out from a remote location." He paused a minute. "It's my guess that whoever is behind this doesn't know we're on to them—otherwise, the computer would have been wiped clean by now."

Marcel nodded. "In a way, that's a good thing. Hopefully, we can put a trace on it."

"Good luck with that," Bruce said, shaking his head. "The culprit is high-tech, way beyond us. You had better believe he or she has covered any tracks very well."

Jace leaned in closer, his jaw tight and his body stiff. "Are you saying there's no way we can find out who's behind this?"

"No, I'm not saying that, but I don't want any of you to think it's going to be easy or quick. Whoever is on the outside is using someone on the inside, and identifying that person may be our only key."

"We've done that already," Caden said. "At least we

know who uses that particular computer. But what do we know about her?"

Dalton spoke up. "She's a young woman by the name of Ramona Oakley. She's single, pretty and is friends with a lot of people in the company."

Everyone stared at Dalton. Caden rolled his eyes. "Why doesn't it surprise me that you would know all that?"

Dalton smiled at his brother. "Yes, why doesn't it?"

"Is there a reason we should find all that important, Dalton?" Jace asked wryly.

"Yes, when you add in the fact she's dating an older man."

"Like Brandy," Shana said, smiling, following Dalton and making the connection. "Are you thinking that whomever Brandy was involved with may be the same guy Ramona is seeing? Given that both computers were tampered with in the same way?"

"Yes, that's what I'm thinking," Dalton said, grinning.

"That *could* be a link," Shana said.

"I agree," Bruce said, nodding. "It's worth checking out. We might not be able to put a trace on the person who tampered with the computer, but we can speak with the woman in question."

"Let's not be so quick to put all our apples in one basket," Marcel warned. "I wouldn't just check on what we can find out about Ms. Oakley, but on every single person in that department."

Shana nodded. "Consider it done."

Jules glanced up from the document she'd been reading and smiled up at Manning. "Ivan Greene's alibi isn't as tight as he thinks it is. According to this, he might have been in court that day, but the judge granted a long recess. And it was during that block of time that Sylvia Granger was murdered."

She paused a moment and then asked, "Did we ever hear anything back from that cruise line on whether Michael and Yolanda Greene were actually on the ship the entire week in question? I know Sheppard Granger's attorney at the time supposedly checked it out, but I can't guarantee he did a good job, or that he checked it out at all. We're not taking anyone's word for anything."

"We haven't heard anything yet. The woman I spoke with indicated records that far back were in storage and they would need time to retrieve them."

"Well, stay on top of them. We don't have a lot of time."

"Will do." Manning stood there for a minute and stared at Jules.

She frowned. "Is something wrong?"

"You tell me."

"Tell you what?"

"Is anything wrong?"

Jules leaned back in her chair and crossed her arms over her chest. "What makes you think something is wrong?"

"For starters, for the past three nights, you've practically slept here. Like you're afraid to go home or something."

"Why would I be afraid to go home?"

"You tell me."

"Emanuel." Whenever she called him by his full name, she let him know she meant business. "There is nothing to tell you. I had a lot of reading to do and I decided to stay here and do it. Last night, I fell asleep while reading, which is why you came in early and found me asleep on the couch over there."

"You've never done that before."

"I've never had a case like this one before. Usually, on criminal cases, I'm called in to either keep people out of jail or to help put them there. I've never handled an investigation in which someone is already in jail and I'm trying to prove he's innocent. And what's so sad is that if Sheppard Granger is indeed innocent, fifteen years were taken from his life."

Manning didn't say anything as he continued to stare at her. "Are you sure that's all it is?"

She broke eye contact with Manning and gathered the papers on her desk into a neat stack. "Yes, I'm sure that's all it is. Now, if you don't mind, I need to get some more work done. I lost time when I left to go home to shower and change clothes."

"Hey, you're the boss. You can do whatever you want to do."

She glanced back up at him. "Including firing you."

He chuckled. "Now, that's something you can't do. But I'll leave you alone so you won't be tempted to try."

When Jules heard the door close behind Manning, she released a long, deep sigh. Manning had hit too close to home to suit her. It wasn't that she was afraid to go home—she just didn't want to risk Dalton showing up unannounced again. It had been over a week since she'd seen or talked to him, and at first she'd been fine. But now she was feeling pressure, and of what she wasn't sure. All she knew was that if he were to show up, she wouldn't ask him to leave. And the thought of her being that weak had her frustrated as hell, deeply annoyed with herself.

She'd never let any man get under her skin, but he

had somehow done just that. It just didn't make sense. If it was only about sex, then she would have gotten enough to last awhile. She definitely shouldn't be itching for more. Had it really been *that* good?

Yes, she concluded. It had been *that* good. Just thinking about how good had her pulse racing and every single cell in her body craving more of the kind of ecstasy only Dalton Granger could deliver.

She stood and walked over to her window. Cold showers weren't working for her, and there was no way she could go back to her toys after experiencing a man like Dalton. Even Shana had asked her yesterday if she was all right. Her sister still didn't know that she was working on Sheppard Granger's case. Maybe it was time to tell her. Jace and Caden, as well. Especially since Ivan Greene's alibi wasn't wrapped up too tightly.

She glanced away from the window when her cell phone rang. Recognizing her sister's ringtone, she crossed the room to click on her phone. "Shana?"

"Yes, it's me. I was just checking on you."

Jules slid into her chair. "And I was just thinking about you. There's something I need to talk to you about. And I want Jace and Caden included in this conversation, as well."

"What about Dalton?"

To say Dalton was already aware of what she had to say would mean explaining some things she would rather not broach with her sister. So instead, she said, "Yes, include Dalton if he's available."

"He's available. We all are. Right now. We met at Dalton's place to cover some business we preferred to handle away from the office. Bruce and Marcel left a few minutes ago, but we're still here. Can you drop by now, or do you prefer we come to you?"

"I can drop by," Jules said. She glanced at her watch. "It shouldn't take me long to get there. Let's say in about twenty minutes."

"We'll be here waiting."

Jules clicked off the phone, knowing she had to prepare herself both mentally and physically to see Dalton again.

Jace stopped pacing long enough to ask, "Did Jules say why she wanted to meet with us?"

Shana smiled up at her husband. "No, she didn't."

"And she didn't have a problem with his being here?" Caden asked, nodding toward Dalton.

Shana shook her head. "No, she didn't have a problem with Dalton being here."

"Excuse me, but this is *my* house. I'm sure if she had a problem with it, she would have suggested the three of you meet with her someplace else," Dalton said.

"No need to get touchy. I was just asking since the two of you don't get along," Caden responded, stretching his legs out in front of him.

At that moment, an image of how well he and Jules got along entered Dalton's mind…right along with an image of how she'd looked when he'd last seen her. She'd been naked in her bed. Her skin had felt warm beneath his fingertips, and her parted lips had just whispered his name.

He stood and began pacing, almost bumping into Jace a couple of times. "Will one of you sit down?" Caden demanded, frowning. "You're making me dizzy."

Dalton glared at his brother. "It's *my* floor. I have the right to wear out the carpet if I want to."

Jace lifted a brow. "And why are you wearing out the carpet?"

"Yes, Dalton, why are you?" Caden asked, too. "You seem kind of nervous about something. Is the fact Jules is coming over making you twitchy for some reason?"

That got Shana's attention. Although she didn't say anything, she stared at him in a way that made a prickling sensation spread over his skin. "I am not nervous. I just have a lot on my mind."

"Don't we all," Jace said, giving up the floor to slide onto the sofa next to his wife. "I keep thinking about everything Bruce said earlier. And Marcel brought up some good points. We can't target just one person. Everyone is a suspect. Right now the only people we can really trust at Granger are each other."

When the doorbell sounded, anxiousness suddenly filled Dalton's body. It had been over a week since he'd last seen Jules, but he had thought about her every single day, dreamed about her every effing night. Already, blood was pumping through his veins, and his body was on fire, craving something he was trying to prove to himself that he could do without. And damn it, he was failing miserably, especially when he could already pick up her scent. Not Amarige specifically. This time, it was the feminine scent of a woman. A woman his body remembered mating with. A woman his tongue remembered tasting. A woman his—

"Are you going to get that, Dalton? After all, it is *your* house."

He blinked and glared at Caden. Instead of giving his brother the satisfaction of a response, he headed for the door and opened it. And there she stood. Dressed in a maxi dress, jacket and boots, looking sexier than should be allowed during daylight hours. Why was he so glad to see her? Why were his mind and body telling him he had missed her? That he had been miserable for the past week? That he had wanted her, even though he'd tried convincing himself he hadn't?

"Jules."

"Dalton," she said, parting lush crimson lips into a semblance of a smile. "How are you?"

"Okay, what about you?"

"Fine."

"Damn it, Dalton, aren't you going to let her in?" Jace called out.

Dalton stepped aside. "Come on in. The natives are getting restless."

All eyes were on Jules as she stood in the middle of Dalton's living room about to disclose why she had asked for this meeting. She could handle all pairs of eyes…except one. Curiosity was not lining the dark depths of Dalton's pupils. What she saw nearly took her breath away, had goose bumps forming on her arms and had the area between her thighs tingling with a sensation she recognized very well.

"Jules, you wanted to meet with us," Shana prompted.

Jules smiled at her sister. "Yes." She paused a moment and then said, "I know that no one asked or hired me to do so, but I decided to prove that Sheppard Granger did not kill Sylvia."

"What?"

"Why?"

"How?"

All three questions were thrown to her at once. The only one who hadn't asked anything was Dalton, because, of course, he knew what was going on. But that didn't stop him from keeping his intense stare on her as if he had x-ray vision, making her feel naked even while fully clothed.

"I think I can sum up all your questions in one response. Because I am a private investigator. That's what I do for a living, and I'm good at what I do. Besides that, my sister is now a Granger. If your lives are in danger, then so is hers. The thought of that doesn't sit too well with me. And although I've never met your father, my dad has, and he feels that Sheppard is serving time for a crime he didn't commit."

"So you've taken it upon yourself to prove his innocence?" Caden asked, arching a brow.

"Yes. Already, I've started my investigation and—"

"Started an investigation?" Shana asked with panic in her voice.

"Yes."

"You do know what Dad thinks happened to the last private investigator, right?" Jace asked, taking Shana's hand in his.

"Yes, I know. And I've looked into that situation, as well."

Shana leaned forward in her seat. "Sounds like you've been quite a busy little beaver, Jules. I think you need to fill us in on a few things."

Jules heard the censure in Shana's tone and knew her sister didn't like the thought of her taking on the investigation. "Okay, then. I had Manning do the legwork for a few things during that week I was in Miami." Bringing up Miami made her force away erotic images that had suddenly sprung forth to the front of her mind.

"Who's Manning?" Caden wanted to know.

"Her administrative assistant," Shana answered.

Jules continued. "When I got back, I read the reports,

and the first thing I found odd was that Marshall Imerson's accident report had been sealed."

"Sealed?" Jace asked, frowning.

"Yes, sealed. But Manning was able to get a copy, anyway. The ex-cop in me found a lot of things in the report inconsistent, and there were things I felt should have been looked into further, like the fact that a BAC had not been done. It was determined that Imerson was intoxicated at the time of the accident because an open liquor bottle was on the seat beside him, and he smelled of liquor."

"That didn't necessarily mean he'd been drinking," Caden pointed out.

Jules smiled. "Precisely."

"I decided to meet with Mrs. Imerson, his widow, so I drove to Steeplechase.

"She moved there a few years ago when her son went off to college." Jules then went into the details of her conversation with Leigh Imerson. "She was bothered by everyone's belief that her husband was drinking when she was adamant that he didn't drink. She also indicated that he didn't bring work home, so she didn't know about an extra file he might have kept."

Jules paused a moment and leaned back against the breakfast bar. "But what I found interesting is that I'm not the only person who wanted to know whether Imerson kept an extra file. It seems that not long after the accident, she was approached by someone else about it."

"Who?" Shana asked, leaning in even closer.

Jules met her sister's gaze. "Ivan Greene."

Twenty-Nine

Un-fucking-believable, Dalton thought. That piece of information was something Jules had not shared with him when they talked on the phone. Ivan Greene? Mr. Want-to-be Mayor himself?

Dalton had sat back and listened to the information Jules was sharing with his siblings and Shana… checking Jules out from head to toe while she did so. The other people in the room had been so busy lapping up every little detail Jules was providing that he doubted they even noticed he was doing so.

But the instant that thought entered Dalton's mind, Jace glanced over at him with that I-know-what-your-ass-has-been-up-to look on his face…so maybe someone *had* noticed.

"I went to see Ivan Greene yesterday."

Dalton's head jerked around so fast it was a wonder it didn't snap. He stared at Jules. "You did what?" he asked, his voice rising a little louder than it should have. "You went to see that asshole?"

"Oh, he finally speaks," Caden said drily, his eyes zeroing in on his brother. "You've been so quiet sitting over there, Dalton, that I'd almost forgotten you were here."

"Yes, I went to see him yesterday," Jules said, refusing to look at Dalton or Caden. "I asked for a meeting with his parents, but he wouldn't let me talk to them. He met with me, instead."

"What did he say?" Jace asked, rubbing his chin.

"A lot of BS if you ask me, but mainly that his parents were on a cruise at the time your mother was killed, and that he was in court all that day. I'm still checking on his parents' alibi, but as far as I'm concerned, his doesn't hold water."

"Why not?" Dalton asked, definitely now focused on what Jules was saying.

"Because although he was in court, the judge granted an unusually long recess during the time of your mother's death."

"Which makes him a prime suspect," Caden said thoughtfully.

"Not without a motive," Shana interjected.

"If he needs a motive, then I'll give him one," Dalton said angrily, not liking the fact that Jules had confronted Greene by herself. If he was the killer, then the man was stone crazy, and crazy people would do just about anything. "His father was fooling around with Mom, and his mother finds out. I understand Ivan and his mother have a close relationship." *Like I thought I had with my mom.* "If he felt our mother had wronged his mother, I can see him meeting with Mom, confronting her and threatening her if she doesn't stay away from his dad," he went on.

"But how did he get your father's gun?" Shana asked.

Dalton glanced over at her, letting out a frustrated sigh. "Good question."

"I'm not saying Ivan did it," Jules said, reclaiming everyone's attention. "All I'm saying is that I think he has some connection to the whole business. I asked why he was interested in Imerson's investigative report, but he wouldn't tell me. He danced around the question, but I let him know I planned to keep digging until I came up with answers. A good cop—or ex-cop—doesn't operate on assumptions but on facts, and I intend to further my investigation and get those facts. I just thought I'd let you know what information I'd accumulated so far."

"You've done a lot. We appreciate it, and you will be compensated," Jace said, standing up and speaking for everyone.

"That's not necessary."

"It *is* necessary," Jace countered. "We are planning to meet with Carson tomorrow at the office, and we still plan to do that. If you don't mind, I'd like you to join us at that meeting. It's at two o'clock."

"Thanks. I'll be there."

"And just as long as you know, Jules," Shana said as she stood, "I'm not exactly overjoyed about your handling this investigation, but I know if anyone can find the real killer, it will be you. And, in a way, that's what terrifies me, because that person is someone who's determined not to be found."

Thirty minutes later, Jules was less than a mile away from Dalton's home when her cell phone rang. She knew who was calling. "What do you want, Dalton?"

"You. Turn around and come back." And then he clicked off the phone.

Jules's hands tightened on the steering wheel. *Just who does he think he is to issue an order like that? Do I look like someone who's happy to be at his beck and*

*call? Do I look like someone who lets a man say jump
and then merely ask how high? Do I—*

She then made a quick U-turn convincing herself
that she would go back but only to give Dalton a piece
of her mind and nothing else. She arrived and parked
her car next to Stonewall's. He glanced up from whatever book he was reading.

"I forgot something," she muttered when she walked
past his car.

He smiled. "Whatever you say."

She frowned and continued toward Dalton's front
door. As soon as she lifted her hand to knock, the door
opened, and she gasped when she was pulled inside and
the door slammed shut behind her.

Thirty

Dalton backed Jules up against the door, grabbing her wrists and holding them high above her head while molding his hard body to the softness of hers. However, he made sure to hold her where she couldn't knee him in the groin as she'd threatened before.

"What do you think you're doing, Dalton?" she said angrily, while looking him dead in the eyes.

"What does it look like I'm doing? I want you. I told you to come back, and you did."

"I didn't come back for this. I came back to give you a piece of my mind."

"Really?" He smiled. "I definitely want a piece... but not of your mind. I want this," he said, and ignoring her gasp, he released one of his hands to reach under her dress to the apex of her thighs. It wasn't his imagination—he was certain her thighs parted to give him easy access.

Her heart was thumping hard. He felt it against his chest. He also felt the stiff nipples pressing against him. So why was she trying to fight what they both wanted? He leaned in close and began licking the side of her neck and collarbone. "Missed me?"

"Hell, no!"

He used his fingers to push her thong aside to get to her womanly folds. "You didn't miss me?" he asked again, inserting his fingers inside her and going straight for her clit. Her breathing against his ear changed, but between one bated breath and the next, she managed to say, "No."

Oh, so she wants to play hard to get, does she? He leaned in and captured her lips, sliding his tongue easily into her mouth and then kissing her the way she liked, the way she'd always enjoyed. His tongue moved around her mouth, reacquainting itself with areas he'd grown to love, craved to taste. Then she decided to join in the play, tangling her tongue with his, sucking on it in a way that made his shaft throb, while his fingers continued to massage. Her juices wetting his fingers were telling him what her mouth refused to admit.

But he would try one more time. He broke off the kiss, kept stroking her while he stared at her and asked in a deep, husky whisper, "You missed me?"

He felt her shiver, saw the stubborn look in her gaze, and when she used her tongue to provocatively lick her lips, the throb in his shaft turned to an ache.

"It depends," she said, lifting her chin in defiance.

"On what?" Stroking her intimately was causing her scent to invade his nostrils, reminding him of what he'd gone more than seven days without. What he so desperately wanted now.

"On whether you missed *me*."

Hell, yes, he had missed her. He could honestly say he had never missed any woman like this before and definitely wouldn't confess to one if he had. But he would confess to Jules because, damn it, he *had* missed her. Not just the sex, but her. Seeing her, talking to her, touching her, holding her…

"Well?"

He stared deep into her eyes, holding tightly to the darkness of her irises. "Yes, I missed you. And just so you don't doubt my words, let me prove just how much."

He removed his hand from beneath her dress and while she stared at him, he licked the wet fingers, inserting each one into his mouth and voraciously sucking on them before licking them clean. And then he clutched her close and leaned in to kiss her again, taking her mouth like a hungry person, feasting on her tongue like it would be his last chance to ever do so. She returned the kiss with as much hunger as he. As their moans mingled, the sound seeped into his being, the same way her scent was doing, firing him up, making him want her even more.

He withdrew from the kiss and pushed the jacket from her shoulders. He went for the buttons of her dress with lust driving his fingers. When he revealed a sexy red bra, he smiled. His favorite color. He would appreciate her wearing it later, but now he was driven to taste her and undid the front clasp of her bra, watching with ravenous eyes as her breasts spilled free. The tip of his tongue tingled when his gaze latched on to her nipples, dark, hard and luscious-looking. With a growl from deep in his throat, he lowered his head to slide one rigid peak between his lips, and then he began sucking in earnest.

"Dalton…"

His name was a breathless whisper from her lips as he continued to taste her, remembering he had dreamed of doing this very thing to her during his past few sleepless nights. Without missing a beat, he moved from one firm nipple to the next, sucking hard, liking how she was clutching his head to hold him right *there* as he hungrily consumed her.

But he wanted more, and he lifted his head to stare into her gaze, seeing her eyes diluted with lust, the way he knew his own were. Without saying a word, he eased the maxi dress from her shoulders and worked it down past her hips and her booted legs. He made a decision right then to keep her boots on. Bending down, he came to eye level with her red thong. Damn, he liked that thing. After pulling the flimsy scrap of lace down her legs, he tossed it aside.

What was it about her *here*, this part no longer shielded by the thong, that filled him with a need the likes of which he'd never experienced before? He wanted her so badly he was almost weak in the knees. Going without her for a week had been torturous. How could he have become addicted to anyone, especially this woman? The thought that any woman could literally bring him to his knees was breaking him down inside. But not enough to try to break free of whatever spell she'd cast on him.

Grasping hold of her thighs, he slid his tongue inside of her, sank his mouth into her deep, locking it in place over her feminine mound. What made him want her so much? Was it this? Her taste? Or the way her body fit so perfectly with his when they made love? And when had he begun thinking that fucking a woman had anything to do with love? But he closed his eyes, deciding he didn't want to think anymore, that he just wanted to savor this, relish her in a way he'd never appreciated another woman. He moaned as his tongue continued to lap her up, lick and taste a mouthful of her as if he couldn't get enough.

And when he felt her thighs begin to tremble, felt her hands dig deep into his scalp and heard the initial sound of a woman about to come, he latched his mouth on to her even tighter, shoving his tongue deeper and moving it in a circular motion right against her G-spot, until she screamed his name. Over and over again.

"Dalton..."

When he felt the last spasm retreat from her body, he pulled his mouth away and got to his feet to sweep her into his arms. He needed her in his bed. Now.

Moving through the living room, he quickly headed to his bedroom and tumbled down on the bed with her, only to sprint back to his feet and start tearing away at his clothes while staring down at her. And there she lay, staring back at him with firm breasts and those pointed nipples he loved to lick, a navel that he loved to kiss and the area between her legs that he loved to taste. And naked except for her boots.

"You're ready, I see," she said after he removed his slacks and briefs.

Yes, he was ready, and his erection was letting her know it. "For you, always."

His lips tightened at the words he'd just said. There had never been an *always* with any woman. Why was she different? At that moment he wasn't sure—he just knew she was. The only thing he was sure about was that he had to get inside her. His shaft was throbbing, not just for release but also for her. He reached into his nightstand and pulled out a condom packet. Opening it with his teeth, he sheathed himself while she watched.

When she began removing her boots, he said huskily, "Leave them on."

He held her gaze steady when he moved closer to the bed. "I want your back to me, Jules."

Without saying a word, she twisted her position and turned around, tilting her rump to him. *Mercy.* He joined her on the bed, grabbed hold of her hips and thrust hard inside her, going to the hilt in one single plunge. He growled and threw his neck back, feeling the muscles in his throat almost pop. When he began moving, his thrusts were fast and hard while his hands held her in a firm grip. The sound of flesh slapping flesh and the feel of his testicles hitting against her backside were sending him over the edge, but he refused to take the dive without her.

He felt her first signs of an orgasm when her buttocks began shaking like a volcano, and he continued to pump inside her as she screamed his name, releasing the same pent-up passion he'd endured for the past week.

And then his body exploded, sensations ripped through him, seemingly tearing him into pieces, making his heart pound in a way it had never pounded before. It was as if, for the first time ever, he had found something that was…his.

He pushed that thought to the back of his mind, not ready to deal with such thoughts now of all times. When it came to women, he didn't get possessive. He didn't…

"Dalton…"

She whispered his name, breaking through the clouds suffocating his mind. And he turned her around to him; he stared at her and felt his heart begin pounding even more. And that was when he leaned in, cupped her face in his hand, whispered her name and kissed her. Hard. Needing this kiss the same way he'd needed to connect his body with hers earlier. He should regain control, but at the moment all he could do was continue to lose it. He would deal with the reason why later. For now, he needed this.

He needed her.

Thirty-One

Jules nudged Dalton awake and looked down at him. "What's for breakfast?"

He slowly opened one drowsy eye and then two before staring at her as if she were an apparition. "Jules?"

"Yes, that's the name I prefer going by," she said, glancing around his bedroom. "Nice place, Dalton, although you should think about adding more pictures on your walls." She looked back down at him. "Now, what's for breakfast?"

He rubbed a hand down his face. "You stayed the night?"

She thought that was a dumb question. "No, I showed up this morning naked. Stonewall let me in, and I found you here in bed naked, with several opened condom packets on your nightstand. Looks like you had a wild night."

"Smart-ass," he muttered.

"What did you say?" she asked, leaning down toward him, her hair falling in his face. "Could you repeat that? I'm sure I misunderstood what you said just now."

Suddenly, he reached out and grabbed her around the waist, flipped her on her back and then hovered over her. Now it was him looking down at her. "Did I invite you to stay last night?" he asked, like the very thought of such a thing was foreign to him.

"No, I forced myself on you. Hid my clothes and locked us in here."

"Jules…don't play with me," he said in a warning tone, leaning toward her.

She stared up into his face. Although he still had that drowsy look, his jaw had tightened, and his eyes were like steel. What in the world was wrong with him? She'd heard about not being a morning person, but this was kind of ridiculous. She used her arms to shove him back, not caring that he almost tumbled off the bed. "And don't you play with me," she said in the same warning tone.

Pulling herself up, she pushed her hair back from her face and glared at him. "What is wrong with you, Dalton?" she snapped.

He rubbed a hand down his face. "Nothing." Her question seemed to slap him out of whatever stinky mood he was in. "It's just that…"

When he didn't finish what he was about to say, she inched closer to him. "What?"

"I'm not used to this."

"You're not used to what?"

He shrugged. "Waking up and finding a woman in my bed."

Jules's eyes narrowed. "Just to set the record straight, you didn't *find* me here, you *put* me here. In your bed. Leather boots and all. And except for the few times I demanded a potty break, you've pretty much kept me here."

His voice actually made the sound of a growl. "Do you have to be so damned sassy?"

"And do you have to be so damned arrogant?"

Jules stared into his eyes and saw beyond the moodiness and confusion. She saw nervousness. A high level of discomfort. Why? "I'm going to ask you for the third time, Dalton. What's wrong with you? Why are you so tense?"

"And I told you," he said, moving to lie down in the bed beside her to stare up at the ceiling. "I am not used to waking up...*with* a woman in my bed."

"If I recall, you woke up with me in your bed several mornings in Miami."

"That wasn't *my* bed. It was the hotel's bed. No women spend the night in *my* bed."

She frowned over at him while stretching and hated to admit that *his* bed slept a whole lot better than hers. "So what happens to them? They sneak out on you before sunrise?" Although she asked, she couldn't imagine such a thing happening.

"No. I have this rule. No woman sleeps in my bed."

She froze. "So where do they sleep when the two of you get together?"

He shrugged again. "Their own bed. A hotel room. But definitely not here."

She stared at him. "Let me get this straight. Are you saying that you don't have a problem sleeping in *their* bed, but you have a rule against them sleeping in *yours*?"

"Yes, that's exactly what I'm saying."

She smiled. "Then I'm glad I made you break that rule. Of all the idiotic things I've ever heard. That's being downright selfish."

"No, that's being smart."

"Then I guess you were pretty damned dumb last night, huh?"

She saw the flash of fire that swept into his eyes but wasn't fast enough to get out of his way. She tried sprinting from the bed, but he caught her around the waist and tugged her back. "I need to do something about your sassiness," he snarled.

"And I need to do something about your arrogance," she snarled back.

They stared long and hard at each other, and then it suddenly occurred to them that their breathing pattern had changed. They were breathing out a different kind of fire. Not one of anger, but one of desire. Jules wasn't sure who made the first move, and she didn't care. All she knew was that suddenly her back was on the mattress, and his hands were touching her everywhere. His mouth followed as his teeth raked across the skin his hands had stroked.

She sucked in a shallow breath. His touch was filling her with a longing she had never imagined. Her entire body tingled with awareness, and shivers escalated down her spine.

"You never said whether or not you missed me, Jules," he said, his voice feeling like corn silk on her skin. He had paused from sucking on one of her nipples, but his hands were still planted firmly between her legs.

"Didn't I?" she asked, barely getting the words out.

"No, you didn't. And I think I sufficiently proved how much I missed you last night."

Yes, he had. Almost too much. And in the most raw, sexual way. Primitive at its best. All last night and the early part of this morning. Before daybreak. "I owe you."

"And don't think I won't collect."

He used his knees to spread her thighs and a moan escaped from her lips when he entered her, pushing his engorged shaft inside her to the hilt. And he looked down at her, laced his fingers with hers when he began riding her hard. He established a rhythm. She didn't know the lyrics, but she understood the melody each and every time his hips slammed down into hers. They were making music, composing a song. One that would blow up the charts. It had a crazy beat and an intense tune.

She needed to lose herself in this particular song, and he was making it happen with each and every stroke. Strumming her like a guitar. Beating down on her like drums. Playing her like a finely tuned piano. And when her body exploded at the same time his did, she felt she was experiencing more than sensuous music. Dalton had played the entire song using every single instrument.

And moments later when he moved his weight off her and pulled her gently into his arms, kissing the side of her flushed cheeks, she felt drained, exhausted but pleasured in every inch of her body.

Jules woke up an hour or so later to find Dalton staring down at her with tension in his face. This time was worse than before. "I hope you're on the Pill."

She wiped sleep from her eyes and yawned. "And if I'm not?"

Dalton frowned. "Please say that you are."

"Why, aren't you ready to become a daddy?"

"Jules…"

"Okay, I'm on the Pill. What happened? Broke another rule?"

"Yes," he said grudgingly, lying back down and staring up at the ceiling fan over his bed and feeling as though his entire effing mind was about to detonate.

How had he let this happen? Unprotected sex. A woman spending the night in his bed. Jeez.

No woman had gotten laid in his bed, had ever been invited to his house, not even for a quickie. He didn't give out his address and rarely gave out his phone number. For him, most encounters were one and done, pound and gone. He might take someone out to dinner and then to a hotel, or to her place if he was invited, but that was as far as it went.

Maybe if he were to go back to sleep and wake up, it would all be a bad dream. But deep down, he knew there was nothing bad about what he'd experienced with Jules…except the unprotected sex part.

"Well, I'm on the Pill, and I don't have a cold."

He glanced over at her. "What the hell does a cold have to do with anything?"

"Plenty. How do you think Shana got pregnant? She and Jace *were* using protection, but Shana was taking antibiotics, so her Pill didn't work."

Dalton rolled his eyes. "Oh, is that what happened?"

"Yes. Didn't Jace tell you anything about it?"

"He told me she was pregnant and, trust me, that was enough."

"Now you see how accidents can happen," she said, easing out of bed.

Dalton tried not to notice her naked body when his shaft began throbbing again. "Not an accident. Carelessness."

"Doesn't matter—it wasn't intentional. Like I'm sure if something goes wrong and I end up pregnant, I won't blame you." She smiled over at him. "I will at first, but then I'll get over it."

He sprinted from the bed and grabbed for her, but this time she was too quick and slammed the bathroom door before he could reach her. In a way, he was glad. He needed the solitude to think…bash his head against the bedpost a few times. To figure out what in the hell was happening to him. Breaking one rule was bad enough, but then a second? Both in the same night and with the same woman. Shit. How crazy could one man get?

She cracked open the door and poked her head out. "Hey, why don't you have extra toiletries in your bathroom, just in case you have an overnight guest or something?"

Dalton drew in a deep breath. Hadn't he told her he didn't have overnight guests? "Because I don't. Sue me."

"Lucky for you, I keep a little overnight bag in the trunk of my car. You never know when I might have to take a flight at the last minute. Would you be so kind as to go out to my car and get it? I would go, but I don't want Stonewall to see me naked."

Hell, he didn't want Stonewall to see her naked, either. "Fine. Where are your car keys?"

"In my purse. I think it's still at your front door where you made me drop it." She pulled her head back into the bathroom and closed the door.

He got up and grabbed his bathrobe off the back of a chair, glancing at the clock on his nightstand. *Shit.* That time couldn't be right. He slid his feet into his bedroom shoes. "Jules, it's almost eleven o'clock," he called out to her, hoping she'd heard him through the closed door.

She opened the door and poked her head out again. He could hear the shower going. "I know, and today is when we're meeting with your father's attorney. At two. I haven't eaten since lunch yesterday."

Her eating schedule was the last thing on his mind. Jace and Caden were probably wondering where he was. Why he hadn't come into the office today. It was a wonder they hadn't called.

He moved quickly through his living room and found her purse right where she had dropped it. He remembered he hadn't given her time last night to get inside the door before he was all over her. The memories of taking her against the door sent ripples of pleasure through him.

He opened the front door and peeped out. The parking lot of his condo appeared almost empty, with most people away at work. The only cars were his, Stonewall's and Jules's.

Stonewall. Of all the times he wished he didn't have a bodyguard, today was it. Stonewall's windows were up, and since they were tinted, he had no idea whether the man was awake or napping. Hopefully, Stonewall wouldn't notice him. Tightening his bathrobe against the biting cold, he walked past Stonewall's vehicle, opened Jules's trunk and grabbed the overnight bag.

He thought he had made it without being noticed when Stonewall rolled the window down, looked over at him and smiled. "Morning, Dalton. Sleep well?" Dalton ignored the man and kept walking until he was back inside his condo and then slammed the door shut.

"Dalton, I need my stuff," Jules called from the bathroom. "We have less than three hours to make that meeting, and I have to go home, change clothes and grab something to eat."

He walked back to his bedroom and knocked on the bathroom door. He barely heard her above the shower as she called, "Just leave the bag on the vanity."

He opened the door and was about to do just that when he saw her in the shower through the glass door. They had showered together in Miami. So why was seeing her in *his* shower, using *his* water and *his* soap causing such a possessive reaction from him? Why was he thinking that everything in this place was *his*... including her?

He placed the bag on top of the vanity and slid out of his robe. Surprise shone on Jules's face when he snatched open the shower door and stepped in. She backed up. "What do you think you're doing?"

"About to take you in my shower," he said directly, reaching out and pulling her to him.

She placed her wet hands on his chest. "We don't have time."

He pushed her back against the shower wall and lifted her hips as she wrapped her legs around his waist, the water spraying down on them. "We're going to make time."

Thirty-Two

They were late. Not much, but late, nonetheless. And when they walked in together, all eyes turned their way. "Sorry I'm late," Jules said, sliding into one of the first empty seats she saw.

Leaving me to fend for myself, Dalton thought. "Sorry I'm late, as well." And because he figured there was speculation circling around the room because he and Jules had walked into the conference room together, he said, "I bumped into Jules downstairs and helped her get through security."

He figured that lie had gone over well with Carson, but with Shana and his brothers, he wasn't sure. In a way, it hadn't exactly been a lie. He'd been bumping into Jules for most of the past twelve hours.

"No problem. We haven't started discussing anything. Just chitchatting," Carson said, smiling. She then turned her attention to Jules. "I understand you've been busy."

Jules nodded. "Yes, I have. Has anyone filled you in?"

Carson shook her head. "No. I'd prefer that you do

it. As an attorney, I prefer not to hear important information secondhand."

Jules nodded and began talking. Dalton noticed how attentive Carson was to what Jules was saying, only interrupting to clarify a few points. He watched as she jotted information down on a notepad, but otherwise her gaze stayed glued to Jules.

When Jules had finished covering everything, Carson pushed her notepad aside. "Although Ivan Greene and his parents, until they are fully ruled out, should be considered persons of interest, we can't place all our attention on them. I would love to know what Imerson had in that report, as well, but we can't waste time going backward. We have to build our own report, and hopefully in that process we will find out some of the same things he did."

"And they were things that got him killed," Shana said pointedly, staring across the table at her sister.

"Yes," Carson said, nodding. "Sheppard certainly believes that, and from what you've garnered from that police report, Jules, there might be something there. If so, I hope you understand the risk you're taking by becoming involved in this case."

"The work I do does involve a certain amount of risk so, yes, I understand."

"And I hope you understand there's a strong possibility that once I share everything with Sheppard, he might not want you handling the investigation."

Jules nodded. "I've thought of that, too, considering how protective he is of everyone, and I can understand and appreciate that. But regardless, Carson, I intend to finish what I started, with or without Mr. Granger's blessing. And you can tell him that." She paused briefly and then added, "Respectfully, of course."

Carson grinned. "I most certainly will." She leaned back to relax in her chair. "So now, is there anything any of us can do to help move the process along?"

"Yes, there is," Jules said, pulling out her cell phone to check the notes she'd made earlier.

Dalton had been with her then. He'd watched her, fascinated by how her fingers had moved on her smartphone, although he didn't have a clue what notes she'd made. All he could think about while watching her was how those same fingers had gripped him, stroked him and led him to her mouth.

The thoughts made him shift in his chair. They had left his house at the same time today and had grabbed something to eat at one of the restaurants nearby. He felt the least he could do was feed her since he had been responsible for her missing two meals. And he had to admit he'd been pretty damned hungry himself.

"First of all, Jace and Shana."

Dalton could tell his brother and sister-in-law were surprised when Jules called out their names.

"Yes?"

"Yes?"

"I would like a list of everyone who attended your dinner party. I understand there were some people there you didn't know because of uninvited guests tagging along, but I want a list just the same."

Jace nodded. "No problem. And just to make you aware, there were video cameras in place that night."

Dalton sat up straight. "Video cameras?"

Jace shifted his glance to Dalton and smiled. "Yes, video cameras." He paused as if he wanted that to sink in with Dalton before swinging his gaze back to the others. "It was Quasar's idea."

"And a good one," Jules said, nodding.

She wouldn't think so if there had been a camera out on the patio that night, Dalton thought. He cleared his throat. "Where were the cameras located?"

Jace shrugged as he glanced back at Dalton. "They were strategically positioned in various places."

Cut the crap, Jace, Dalton wanted to say. "Exactly where?"

Jace smiled. "Here and there. Is there a particular place you're interested in?"

Dalton figured his brother knew what he was getting at, since he had walked in on him and Jules kissing on the patio. "We'll discuss this later."

Jules, who at some point had caught on, hurriedly said, "And Caden?"

"Yes."

"I retrieved my audio notes when I interviewed you regarding that attempt made on your life. You mentioned how the Greenes were treating you rather poorly at Shiloh's wine boutique open house, and you led me to believe others were doing so, as well. I'd like names."

Caden nodded. "The only other person whom I recall acting like a bit of a jerk that night was Sedrick Timmons. Everyone else was pretty friendly."

Jules lifted a brow. "Dr. Sedrick Timmons? Shiloh's brother?"

"Yes, but I will admit he thought he may have had a reason to feel some animosity toward me. He wasn't too keen on Shiloh and me getting back together. He spent quite a bit of time hanging out with the Greenes that night, and I'm sure they were filling his head with lies about me."

"Lies about what?"

"I have no clear idea, but I can speculate now that it might have had something to do with the affair between Michael Greene and my mother. As you know, I didn't even know anything had been going on between them at the time, and I didn't find out until during our interview."

"Yes, I remember that. What about Shiloh and Sedrick's mother, Sandra Timmons? From Manning's research, I see she and Sylvia Granger were good friends at some point. I will need to interview her as well as Sedrick. Maybe Sedrick can shed some light on why the Greenes were so hateful to you that night. Ivan Greene certainly wouldn't tell me when I asked him about it. I've also compiled a list of people who were members of the country club that your parents were close friends with at one time. I intend to interview them as well as try to determine why they were so quick to believe your father was guilty."

Jules then glanced back over at Jace. "And I'll need permission to review Granger employment records of one of your former employees, namely Michael Greene."

"That won't be a problem," Jace said evenly. "Just say when."

"Thanks, and one other thing."

"What?" Jace asked.

"I need access to the boathouse."

After the meeting, Shana pulled Jules aside. "You did a great job in there. I'd forgotten how meticulous you are during your investigations. You don't believe in leaving any stones unturned, do you?"

Jules smiled. "Not on my watch."

Shana studied her sister. "Where were you last night?"

Jules lifted a brow. "Why you want to know?"

"Because Dad was looking for you. He was concerned since he hadn't heard from you in a few days."

Jules drew in a deep breath. "I know. I need to call him. I've been super busy."

"That's what I told him, but I think you're the person who should tell him why. I'm not sure how he's going to feel about you handling the Sylvia Granger investigation and the risks involved."

Jules waved away her sister's words. "I'll be fine."

"Jules, we can't help but worry. Take care of yourself." Shana turned to walk off but then stopped and leaned in to whisper, "And that's an awesome-looking hickey on the right side of your neck."

When Jules blushed and quickly slapped her hand over that part of her neck, Shana chuckled and said, "Gotcha. I was just teasing. There's no hickey, but the mere thought that you believed there was lets me know what you were doing last night. I just have to figure out with whom."

"So, Dalton, you were late for our meeting with Carson because you were delayed getting Jules through building security?" Caden asked, coming to stand beside his brother.

"That's what I said, isn't it?"

"Yes, but it's what you're not saying that has me worried."

Dalton shook his head. "You know, Caden, since you've been married you haven't made much sense. Maybe you need to get back into playing your sax to calm your mind."

"I do play my sax, and my mind is calm. I'm not the one who's worried about where those cameras were located at Shana's dinner party."

His brother's comments reminded Dalton he needed to talk to Jace. "Whatever. Now, excuse me for a minute." He quickly walked over to catch Jace before he left the room.

"Jace?"

"Yes?"

"About those video cameras?"

Jace leaned back against the table. "What about them?"

"Were there any positioned out on the patio?"

Jace smiled. "I figured that's what you were worried about."

Dalton rolled his eyes. "Well, were there?"

Jace rubbed his chin. "Umm, let me think."

"Cut the crap. You know if there were or not."

"Yes, I do know, and there weren't. But there were cameras positioned to show who came and went off the patio, just in case private meetings were taking place. Like the one you and Jules were holding."

"We weren't holding a private meeting that night. And we merely kissed. No big deal."

"Really? Then why were you so concerned about whether or not you were captured on video?"

"Just safeguarding my privacy."

"What about your privacy, Dalton?" Shana asked, joining them.

"Nothing," Dalton quickly replied noticing, in his peripheral vision, that Jules, who'd been talking to Caden, was leaving.

At that moment, Sarah Pecorino, one of the executive administrative assistants, entered the boardroom appearing flustered as she approached Jace.

"Sarah, is there anything wrong?" Jace asked.

"Sorry to disturb you, Mr. Granger, but there is

someone here to see you. Security has detained her, and I told them to let her know you were in a meeting. However, they say that she's very insistent."

Dalton turned his head to keep from chuckling, knowing immediately who was demanding Jace's attention. Evil Eve had arrived in town. And Dalton could tell from Jace's expression that he knew, as well, but his brother still questioned Sarah.

"Who is she?"

Ms. Pecorino raised her chin. "I spoke with her, and she told me to tell you she's Mrs. Jace Granger."

"Well, she told you wrong, Sarah. As you can see, the only Mrs. Jace Granger is standing right here beside me," Jace said, indicating Shana.

"I know, sir, and she said you would say that. And she told me when you did to remind you that she was the first."

Thirty-Three

"What are you doing here, Eve?"

She had been standing by the window and turned around. Dalton watched the smile on her face die when she saw that Jace hadn't come alone. She lifted her chin. "Jace, didn't Caden tell you I was coming?"

"I told him," Caden said somberly, leaning against the door.

"Well, then," Eve said, using her hand to smooth down the skirt of her designer suit. "I wanted this to be a private meeting between Jace and me."

"You stopped getting what you wanted from me a long time ago. Anytime I deal with you from now on, it's a family affair. You've met my brothers, and this," Jace continued, pulling Shana to his side, "is the *only* Mrs. Jace Granger. So I wish you would stop using my name. Now, I'm asking you again on behalf of everyone. What are you doing here?"

Instead of answering, Eve smiled and took a chair at the table, one that was not offered to her. "Jace, I can understand your being upset with me. But why was I detained in security?"

"I don't think you do understand. If you did, you

wouldn't be here. And as far as security goes, after your last visit I gave them strict orders not to allow you back inside this building."

Eve chuckled. "Please don't blame that nice young man sitting at the front desk. I tailgated another visitor," she said without remorse. "But I didn't get far. I didn't even make it to the elevator before he caught me. And the reason I'm here is because I recently remembered something important. Something Vidal told me that you might find interesting."

"I doubt I'd be interested in any of your and Vidal's pillow talk," Jace said.

"I think you might be interested in this since it's about your precious Hannah."

Caden, who had been leaning disinterestedly against the door, suddenly straightened. So did Dalton, who had been glancing periodically at his watch and wondering where Jules had gone. Now he, too, was at full attention.

Eve smiled at seeing the three reactions when the woman's name was mentioned. "Ahh, so Hannah still has her tight hold on you guys. Like always, I see."

"Whatever Vidal told you about Hannah is probably a lie, and you can keep it to yourself," Dalton said angrily.

"Tsk, tsk, tsk, Dalton. You and your brothers always thought Hannah was so precious, so upright, so damned sacred," Eve admonished with a smirk.

"Dalton is right, Eve, there's nothing you can tell us about Hannah that will change that," Jace said. "Now, we'll have security escort you out. Remember what I said about never coming back. If you do, I'll have you arrested for trespassing."

When everyone followed Jace's lead and headed for the door, an angry Eve sprang from her seat. "Wait! You

294   *Brenda Jackson*

all need to know that your grandfather Richard and your precious Hannah were having an affair…which is probably why he left her so damned much in his will, and—"

"He left you, the ex-granddaughter-in-law, nothing? Not a single dime for having to put up with the Grangers?" Jace said angrily. "Is there nothing you won't stoop to? And, what my grandfather and Hannah did was their own damned business."

"That might be true, but it won't look good if word gets out just what was going on at Sutton Hills. You know how people like to gossip. Richard's dead, but dear, sweet Hannah is very much alive and enjoying all that stuff good old Richard left her. I don't think Granger Aeronautics needs such a scandal, do you? It will die down eventually, but just think of the sensationalism until then. However, I'd be willing to keep my mouth shut about it for…let's say a million dollars."

The room became deathly quiet as everyone stared at Eve, who merely stared back with a smirk on her face. When the silence lengthened, she said, "It seems you might need to have a family meeting to discuss this. Just keep in mind that the price might go up if I have to wait too long."

Finally Jace spoke, his voice nearly trembling in anger. "There's nothing to discuss. I can't believe you're trying to extort money from us."

Eve waved her hand. "Granger Aeronautics has plenty of money to spare and still have enough for any future Grangers to have a good life. So spare me the sad song."

Jace didn't say anything, and it appeared that he was actually considering the idea. "So for a million dollars you're offering to keep quiet?" he asked, as if for clarification.

Triumph gleamed in Eve's eyes. "That's right. I want a million, or else I will tell everything I know. And, of course, I will embellish the parts that I don't know. Just think how such a scandal might rock the company, shake the shareholders, especially when you're trying to get the company back on its feet. So do we have a deal?"

Jace stared at her, and the anger and loathing he felt toward his ex-wife were apparent, not in his features or in his stance. But it was radiating off him in waves, and there wasn't a person in the room who didn't feel it. Except, of course, for Eve, who was gloating too much to notice.

Then Jace asked in a loud voice, "Did you get all that, Herb?"

A voice answered from a speaker system somewhere in the room. "Yes, Mr. Granger, we got it all, loud and clear."

"Thanks." Jace then glanced over at Eve, who had a shocked look on her face. "Extortion is a federal offense. Thanks to my security team, we have all the proof we need about your despicable behavior. The authorities have been notified and are on their way." He and the others turned to leave.

"Jace! Wait! Surely you aren't going to let anyone arrest me?"

When there was a knock on the door, Dalton opened it, and two federal agents walked in. Jace glanced back over at Eve. "You think not? Watch me."

Dalton was furious and rounded on his brothers the minute the three of them were alone. "The two of you knew what had been going on with Granddad and Hannah and didn't say anything? You didn't tell me?"

Caden leaned back against the table, seemingly not

bothered by his brother's outrage. "Just like you didn't tell us what was going on with Mom and some man?"

Emotions he couldn't swallow almost choked Dalton, who needed a moment to breathe in deeply before saying, "That was a low blow, Caden. I told you guys why I didn't say anything. I had promised Mom."

"Well, have you thought that maybe we made promises, too, Dalton?"

Dalton glared at him. "Did you?"

Caden shrugged. "No. But I was here, and you weren't. You could have come back home on occasion like Jace and I did."

Jace decided it was time to step in. "Look, Dalton. The old man confided in me because he felt I needed to know. And, like I told Eve, what Granddad and Hannah did was nobody's business."

"And nobody told me," Caden said. "Not Granddad or Hannah. It was just something I sensed whenever I came home. The old man seemed happier. Not as reserved. More relaxed."

Dalton nodded. "And Hannah?"

Caden smiled. "The usual Hannah. Happy. Merry. Cheerful. It seemed some of her was rubbing off on him."

Dalton couldn't imagine the old man happy, cheerful and merry. "How long had it been going on?"

Jace sat down on the table's edge. "Not sure. It started at some point after we all left for college. I figure they were both two lonely people. Hannah was always someone he could trust. Talk to and confide in. They had both lost their spouses, whom they'd loved deeply, so I can understand them falling in love."

Dalton's head snapped up. "In love? What makes you think they were in love?"

"Because Granddad told me so," Jace said. "He loved Hannah, and she loved him. Not everybody has sex just for the hell of it."

"Sex! They had sex?" Dalton asked as if horrified, as if he couldn't fathom such a thing. Just like he couldn't imagine Richard Granger happy, cheerful and merry, he couldn't imagine him being interested in sex, either.

"I don't know what they had, Dalton," Jace said, rolling his eyes. "It might have been nothing more than companionship between them."

Yes, Dalton thought, nodding. *Companionship*. He could accept that a lot better than the other idea. "Is Hannah aware that both of you know?"

Jace leaned back on his palms. "She knows that I know. We talked within a week or so of the funeral. I walked into the kitchen one night and found her sitting at the table crying. I told her I knew and that I also knew that they genuinely loved each other."

"I think she has an idea that I know, although we never discussed it," Caden responded.

"You think Dad knows?"

"We've never discussed that, either," Jace said. "But, then, we had no reason to. Dad and Hannah are close... and so were Dad and Granddad. But I have a feeling Dad knew."

"And Hannah really loved the old man?" Dalton asked, as if he found the thought totally beyond his comprehension.

"Yes, they loved each other. She took his death hard but kept it inside. More than once, when she stayed overnight at the estate instead of going home, I would get up and find her crying."

Dalton shook his head. "Damn, I had no idea."

"And just because Granddad was elderly and set in

his ways didn't mean he didn't need someone to love. Everyone needs someone to love."

Dalton snorted. "Speak for yourself."

Jace studied his brother a minute and then asked, "At the reading of the will, when Granddad bequeathed Hannah all that property, that trust fund and all those other assets, you didn't think anything then?"

"No," Dalton said honestly. "I thought she deserved everything she got for putting up with our asses all those years. She was always there for us. I love Hannah."

"We all do," Caden said softly.

Then changing the subject a little, Caden said, "I'm glad security recorded every aspect of our conversation with Eve. She was entirely vindictive."

"Evil," Dalton added. "She certainly lived up to her name today."

"That was a smart move on your part, Dalton," Jace said. "We can thank you for having security send Eve to a room that was already set up for surveillance."

"I agree," Caden chimed in.

That meant a lot coming from his brothers. "Thanks. I figured she was here for a no-good purpose, and I wanted us to be prepared." Dalton glanced at his watch. "Well, I need to go."

Jace arched a brow. "Go? Need I remind you that you came in late today, just in time to attend that meeting?"

Dalton smiled. "No, you don't need to remind me. But just remember. I saved the company from a scandal. There's no doubt in my mind that Eve would have done just what she threatened to do. But who cares who Granddad had an affair with while he was living? Furthermore, why didn't he and Hannah bring their affair out in the open?"

"Probably for privacy reasons. The fewer people who knew, the less they would have to deal with gossip and people's opinions," Jace said. "I assume he didn't want to put Hannah through that."

"So what's going to happen to Eve?" Caden asked, pushing away from the table.

"Do you care?" Dalton asked.

Caden shrugged. "In a way, I do. I used to think she was a nice person."

Dalton snorted. "Boy, did she have you fooled. She saw you as the gullible brother. I saw right through her the first time Jace introduced us." He looked at his watch again. "Look, guys, I have to go. I'm getting an early start on the weekend," he said, heading for the door.

"With anyone we know?" Caden called out.

"None of your business." Dalton grinned, throwing the words over his shoulder as he dashed through the door.

Thirty-Four

"So what do you think?"

Jules looked over at Manning and Bruce. The two men were standing beside her as they glanced at the investigational wall they'd erected for the Granger case. But leave it to them working together to construct a state-of-the-art wall that was actually a two-hundred-inch touch-screen display that could also be controlled from her computer or smartphone.

"Manning, you know just what I need. And Bruce, you're a computer genius. Don't you want to come work for me full-time instead of splitting your time between Shana and me?"

Bruce threw his head back and laughed. "Shana asked me the same thing when I created *Greta*."

Jules gave him a pointed frown. "Oh, she did, did she?"

Greta was an automated search engine that was great for investigative work. Like Shana, Jules had her office network installed in her car. That way she could use voice commands to tell *Greta* what information she wanted and, within minutes, *Greta* was reciting everything Jules needed to know.

"Yes, she did. And speaking of Shana," Bruce said, glancing at his watch, "I have a meeting with her and Marcel in an hour, so I'm out of here."

Jules nodded. "How's that investigation going involving trade-secret violations at Granger?"

"Crazy. Really crazy. This even has me stumped."

"You, the computer whiz?" Manning asked, chuckling.

"Yes, even I can be stumped sometimes. But what's weird is how a computer can be wiped clean remotely. Computers could always be wiped clean, that's not the issue. It's how someone can target a computer from a remote location without being detected. How that happens is what's bothering me."

Jules leaned back on her desk, intrigued. "But in order to do that they'd need inside help initially, right?"

Bruce nodded. "That's what I'm assuming." He looked at his watch again. "You know, you can call on me if you need any technical help with this particular case. I've gotten to know Jace and his brothers, and I think they're swell guys. If they believe their father is innocent, that's good enough for me."

An hour or so later, Jules had placed all the information she had gathered on her wall. In her column for suspects the only three photos were of the Greene family, but she was certain more would be added once the investigation intensified.

Featured in the column of people she wanted to talk to were Sandra Timmons, Sedrick Timmons and various members of the country club Sylvia and Sheppard used to frequent. Also on that list were Dalton and his brothers as well as Sheppard, Hannah and a few Sutton Hills employees who worked there at the time Sylvia was murdered. It had been a long time ago, but she needed to talk with everyone to see if they recalled anything unusual about that day.

Over the weekend, she intended to watch the dinner party video Shana had promised to drop by her place later. She still had a copy of the wine boutique grand opening video Shiloh had given her when Jules was investigating the attempt on Caden's life. At the time, she hadn't found anything suspicious, but it wouldn't hurt to take a second look.

Anything to keep her busy this weekend and away from Dalton.

She had felt his intense gaze on her during the meeting with Carson. It was bad enough that they'd walked into the meeting together, but she doubted anyone had believed his lie about helping her through security.

Jules stretched, thinking that at some point during the early part of next week she needed to get into the boathouse. None of the Grangers seemed eager to talk about that possibility when she'd brought it up earlier at the meeting. She'd heard from Shana that none of the brothers had been back to the boathouse since their mother's death. Nor had they been back to the house where they'd lived with their parents. When Sheppard had gone to jail, the house had been locked and never reopened.

She glanced over at her desk when the buzzer sounded and moved quickly to push the button. "Manning, I thought you'd left already."

"I was about to, but now you have a visitor."

"Who is it? Dad?" she asked expectantly. She'd been thinking about what Shana had told her earlier, and knew that at some point she needed to go visit her father and let him know of her decision to investigate Sylvia Granger's murder.

"No, it's not your dad. It's Dalton Granger. Should I send him in or send him packing?"

Jules expelled a deep breath, knowing it wouldn't be a pretty picture if the latter were to happen. Both men were muscular and about the same height, weight and build, and the idea of them taking each other on was too much to contemplate. "No, it's fine. Send him in. I'll be the one to send him packing."

"Do you want me to hang around for a while?"

Jules shook her head. "No. I can handle Dalton."

Jules knew her statement was a lie even when she'd said it. It was becoming quite obvious that Dalton was the one man she couldn't handle.

"So you think you're going to send me packing?" Dalton asked, walking into her office as if he had partial ownership of the place. Jules doubted she would ever get used to his arrogance.

"I don't recall your having an appointment to meet with me, Mr. Granger," she said, not moving from behind her desk. So, okay, it was kind of crazy to act so formal with him now, considering that at some point during the night she had fallen asleep with one of her nipples in his mouth. It was the first time she'd ever been sucked to sleep.

"I didn't think I needed one."

"I can believe that. You're ballsy enough to show up just about anywhere, unannounced and uninvited."

"Yes, that's me," he said, grinning. His expression changed when he glanced over at her display on the office wall. "What the hell is that?"

She followed his gaze. "My investigative wall."

"And my picture is up there?"

She smiled, seeing how such a thing irritated him. "Yes, and so are Jace's and Caden's."

He crossed his arms over his chest. "Why?"

"Because having a visual chart of everyone involved with your mom's death helps me keep track of things. And I want to hear your account of what happened that day and the days before and after."

"It's all in the court records. A police detective talked to us."

"But did you tell him everything?"

Dalton didn't say anything for a minute, remembering the day of that interview. The man had been nice, but tenacious. However, no question the detective asked, no matter how he'd asked it, was going to make him break the oath he and his brothers had made the day before. "I told him what I thought he needed to know."

"In other words, you didn't tell him everything. I know for certain you didn't mention seeing your mom with another man."

No, he hadn't. "Hell, if I hadn't told my own father, I definitely wasn't going to tell a cop whose job it was to find my dad guilty."

"I've been a detective, Dalton, and that's not the way things go."

"That depends on what police force you're working for. And why is Hannah's picture up there? And Patrick's and Clyde's?"

Patrick Crestwood had been with Sutton Hills as ranch foreman for over forty years and had mentioned to Jace that he planned to retire next year. His son Clyde had already been groomed to take his place.

"All active employees of Sutton Hills at the time of your mother's death could have important information," Jules said evenly. "There's no telling what they might know. Who knows? There might be even more secrets to discover."

Her words made Dalton remember what had transpired earlier with Eve. He slid into the chair in front of Jules's desk. "Have you talked to Shana since leaving the meeting today?"

"No. Why?"

"You missed the action with Evil Eve."

"So she *did* come to town."

"Boy, did she ever."

Dalton then told Jules about their meeting with Eve and her extortion scheme. When he finished, Jules shook her head. "That's unbelievable. Did she actually think she could get a million off you guys that easily?"

"I guess so, especially by throwing Hannah in the mix. She knows how we feel about her. Hannah helped my brothers and me retain our sanity through the craziness of my father's trial. She means the world to us, and if you mess with Hannah, then you mess with all three of us."

Jules nodded. "And to think Hannah and your grandfather were involved."

Deciding he didn't want to get into that discussion, Dalton cut her off. "Whatever. So what do you have planned for tonight?"

"Going home and watching a video or two."

"What movies?"

"No movies. The video of Shana's dinner party and the grand opening of Shiloh's wine boutique."

"Think you might notice something you haven't seen before?"

"I might. It's worth a shot."

He didn't say anything for a minute. "Mind if I join you?"

Jules clearly understood that watching a video with her wasn't all he had in mind. Rather than call him out on it, she countered, "You might find the videos boring."

He held her gaze, and she wondered what it was about him that made her ache inside whenever he looked at her that way. "I'll take my chances, Jules."

At that moment her cell phone rang, and she cringed when she saw it was her father calling.

"What's wrong?" Dalton asked when he saw her reaction to the call.

"It's Dad. I haven't told him about my involvement in the investigation, and I should. I'd rather he heard it from me than someone else." She quickly picked up the phone. "Hi, Dad. Yes, I'm fine. Dinner?" she asked after a few beats. "Tonight?"

She paused a minute. "Well, I had planned to stay in and watch a couple of videos," she said, knowing he would think the same thing Dalton had.

"Pork chops? On the grill?" Jules's mouth began tingling, and she subconsciously licked her lips. She glanced over at Dalton and saw how his gaze followed the movement of her tongue.

"That sounds pretty tempting, Dad, but I'm going to have to pass tonight. What about lunch tomorrow? My treat. I'll call in the morning and let you know where. Goodbye. I love you, too."

She clicked off her phone and returned Dalton's stare. She couldn't believe she'd actually given up the chance to savor her father's mouthwatering grilled pork chops just to watch a couple of videos with the man sitting across her desk.

But then, she knew as well as he did that watching videos wasn't all they would be doing.

Jules had been right. Watching those videos wasn't all she and Dalton would be doing. She slowly entangled her body from his and tried not to wake him. Easing out of bed, she slid into the dress shirt Dalton had discarded and left him sleeping, closing the door behind her.

She and Dalton had left her office at the same time, but he'd made a pit stop at a pizza parlor for takeout, and she'd swung by Shana's place for the video. By the time he had arrived at her house she had showered, and she answered the door in her bathrobe, wearing nothing else underneath. He had dropped the pizza box on the nearest table, swept her off her feet and taken her into her bedroom.

Now here she was, three hours later, making her way to the kitchen for cold pizza. She felt exhausted and well rested at the same time. How that was possible she wasn't sure; she only knew that it was.

Releasing a long breath, she microwaved a couple of pizza slices while she grabbed a soda from the refrigerator. Moments later, she sat at her kitchen table trying to figure out just what was going on between her and Dalton. It was as if they were addicted to each other. It was ridiculous to think such a thing was even possible, but how else could one explain their desire to be together as much as they were?

Even now, she imagined she could actually feel his breath on her throat, and the way her body would relax against his after they'd made love. And then there was the way she felt whenever his mouth touched any part of her body, or whenever he was inside her. He took her the way a man took a woman he desired. And she enjoyed his scent, which was all over the shirt she was wearing. His shirt.

After eating her pizza, she grabbed the rest of her soda and went into the living room to watch the dinner party video. The first thing she noticed was that the quality was good, and she appreciated that. She had seen a lot of grainy videos in her day.

Grabbing her notepad from the coffee table, she relaxed on the sofa. Shana would be giving her a list later of those who had attended the party, so chances were good that Jules would be watching this particular video again.

She found it amusing when she watched the brothers' facial expressions when Dalton arrived at the party. And seeing him in the video reminded her of just how good he'd looked that night.

All right, Jules, stay focused. You're not watching the video to check out Dalton. You can go into your bedroom to do that if you're so inclined.

Settling back against the sofa cushions, she jotted down notes. So far nothing and no one seemed suspicious. Most of the people she saw spent a lot of time at the food table, which was understandable since Hannah had made an awesome spread that night.

She lifted a brow when she noticed the arrival of the man who'd tried hitting on her that night. Gary Coughlin. She was trying to recall what he'd told her about himself beyond his name. He had said that he was fairly new to town and had come to the party with a friend who was a business associate of Jace. Someone named Ron. CEO of Zimmons Aviation Supply Company. She also recalled him saying he was a divorcé. She jotted all that information down for Manning to verify later.

She hated having a suspicious mind, but it came with the territory.

A few minutes later she became curious when the video showed Coughlin reentering the party from the patio. That was probably during the time he'd left her out there with Dalton. She saw what looked like a smile on his face when he went straight to the coatrack, got his coat and left the party without saying good-night to anyone…not even the man he'd come to the party with, someone whom she could only assume was named Ron. *Interesting.*

"So this is where my shirt ran off to."

Jules turned in the direction of Dalton's voice, and her breath caught. He stood there, leaning against her coat closet door, shirtless but wearing a pair of dress slacks. The sight of him made her mouth water. Hadn't they made love for nearly three hours straight? So why were her hormones kicking up and acting crazy again? It could be because at that very moment her five senses were on full alert and focused on him. And all that sexiness had her head spinning.

"You want it back?" she asked, knowing that even if she gave it back, his aroma would still be on her skin.

He chuckled, and the sound sent a distinct warmth bubbling through her. "That would leave you naked, and I love seeing you naked, Jules."

Not as much as I love seeing you naked, she thought, even as she figured that more sex was the last thing either of them needed right now. Sexual hunger she could deal with, but sexual addiction was way too crazy to think about.

"I'm finished watching the video of Shana's dinner party."

"Did I miss anything?"

She decided not to mention her suspicions about Gary Coughlin until she checked out a few more things. "I don't think so."

"Well, I did miss something. I missed you in the bed when I woke up."

She smiled. Is this the man who had just told her the other day that he didn't like waking up to women in his bed? But then, it wasn't his bed in there; it was hers. "You needed your rest."

She patted the seat beside her. "Now, come sit down, and let's watch the next video. Since you weren't at the open house at the wine boutique it might be useful for you to review it with me."

"And afterward…"

Jules grinned. "You can go home if you like."

He moved across the room and slid in the seat beside her, pulling her into his arms, leaning close to whisper into her ear. "And what if I don't want to go home?" He ended the question with a warm lick beneath her ear, across her cheek and down her neck, making the muscles between her legs tighten in arousal. "Then I guess you can stay."

"I'll make sure you won't regret the invitation."

She just bet he wouldn't and felt her hand trembling slightly when she picked up the remote. Like the other video, the quality was good, and she tried shifting her focus away from Dalton and to the video by jotting down details on her notepad. She made note of the times people arrived and departed from the party at the wine boutique. She noted several people had attended both Shiloh's open house and Shana's dinner party.

"That's Sandra Timmons," Dalton said in a tone that let her know the woman wasn't one of his favorite people.

She nodded. "I recognize her from the picture we have of her. She's a nice-looking lady."

"Whatever. And that's Sedrick, her asshole of a son."

Jules remembered Sedrick Timmons from his picture, as well. "I don't see a family resemblance between him and Shiloh."

"Probably because he looks like his father and she looks like…"

When he stopped in midsentence, Jules decided to fill in. "Her mother?"

Dalton shrugged. "I don't see any similarities between the two women."

"Probably because you like Shiloh but don't like her mother."

"Maybe."

The video kept rolling. It was cute to see Shiloh's reaction to Caden when he walked in and how she pretended not to look at him when she was doing just that. And there was Caden, openly staring at Shiloh, making his interest quite obvious.

"Go get her, Tiger," Dalton said, also picking up on his brother's predatory demeanor. "Wait! Zero in on that guy and woman standing over by the buffet table."

Dalton's sudden outburst almost scared Jules. "What guy? What woman?"

"That one," he said, pointing, getting off the sofa to move closer to the screen. "The woman in the blue dress."

"Her name is Nannette Gaither," Jules told him. "Shiloh's working with her on the city's annual ball for cancer research. The same function Caden is headlining. I joined them for lunch one day, and she seems nice, just a little too chatty for my taste."

"I don't care about her. I want you to zero on him— the man she's with."

Jules froze the screen on a close-up of the man in question. "I believe he's Nannette's fiancé. I can check with Shana to be certain. Why does he interest you?"

Dalton came back to the sofa and sat down, his gaze not leaving the television screen. She reached out and felt his body trembling, feeling his anger. "Dalton, what is it? What's wrong?"

He didn't say anything for a minute. "That's him."

"That's who?"

He drew in a deep breath and shifted his gaze from the television to her. "I wondered if I would remember him. If I would be able to recognize him if I ever saw him again…and honestly, I never thought I would. He looks different, older, gray around the temples, a little weight around the middle, less hair, but it's him."

She swallowed tightly. She knew the answer to her next question but figured she needed to ask it, anyway. Not for her, but for Dalton. "Who is he, Dalton?"

He reached out and gripped her hand. As he stared into her eyes, she saw the hurt, the pain and the agony of the past trying to drown him when he said, "He's the man who was with my mother at the boathouse that day."

Thirty-Five

Dalton leaned back in the recliner and stared at Jules. He had managed to slip out of bed without waking her, deciding to sit in the chair and watch her sleep.

And think.

He thought he'd purged all the guilt inside him when he'd confessed to his father that he'd known about his mother's affair. But seeing that man on the video had affected him in a bad way, and Jules had been right there to help see him through it.

She had held him tightly, telling him everything would be all right, and that what had happened was in the past, that his mother's mistakes were not his. Jules had even talked him out of leaving right then to find the man and confront him.

He'd wanted to tell the guy he had been at the boathouse that day, hiding out in the closet. That he'd seen them naked, kissing in bed. He wondered how many other times the two had met there, right under his father's nose at Sutton Hills? How had the man even gotten on the property without anyone knowing about it?

Jules made a sound, shifting in her sleep and kicking off the covers, something he noticed she did a lot. Dalton crossed the room and slid the covers back over her naked body. And then he stood there, leaning against the bedpost to look at her.

It had been raining earlier, practically pouring by the time she had turned off the video. He'd swept her into his arms and carried her into the bedroom. And then she had tried to do what time hadn't been able to do—purge all the guilt from him. She had made love to him in ways they had experienced before, but something about tonight had been different. It had meaning. A deeper definition. It had been perfect.

And during those moments of being inside her, he hadn't felt one iota of guilt or anger. He'd only felt pleasure and a gratification that had been so strong it had affected him in ways he thought he wouldn't survive. But he had survived just to indulge again and again, while the sound of torrential rain beat down on her roof, washing the shingles and simultaneously washing his soul.

He had needed that. For the first time, he didn't see Jules as just another woman he had sex with, but as the *only* woman he wanted to have sex with. And for some reason the thought of that didn't send him into panic mode, didn't make his dick fall off or his fingers rot. What he felt was inner peace, a desire to be with a woman in a way he'd never thought possible.

A peace that could only be had with her.

She was the first woman who'd ever made him consider an exclusive relationship, basically abandoning his lifestyle as he now knew it. That was a lot to think about, and he couldn't do it here. What he told her was true. He wasn't a thinker—he was a doer. But this was one time he had to think and not act, because failing was not an option. He had to get it right.

Glancing around, he spotted her notepad and pen.

Tearing off a sheet of paper, he began writing, first assuring her that he was okay and that he had not left to go find Nannette Gaither's fiancé, but was going back to his place to think some things through and would call her later. He ended by telling her that he hoped she had a nice lunch with her father.

After placing the note on the pillow where his head had lain a short while before, he quietly dressed before tiptoeing from the bedroom.

Ben glanced over at his daughter. "Are you okay, Jules?"

Jules looked up from her meal and met her father's concerned eyes. In a way, she wasn't okay because Dalton wasn't okay. She was certain that he was better than he had been last night, but she knew he wasn't one hundred percent.

Seeing that man in the video had taken a toll on him, and she could just imagine what he'd been thinking. At the time he'd been a child, not fully realizing what the man and his mother had been about. But now, as a grown man, he knew all too well. She had pulled him into her arms and held him while his body shook with a hurt that should have been buried long ago.

And later he had made love to her, as if doing so would release all the anguish from his body. When she'd awakened that morning, she'd found the note on the pillow saying he was okay and just needed time to think.

"Jules?"

She drew in a deep breath. Over the years, her daddy had always been the one she could take her troubles to and talk things out with. He never judged, and he never condemned. He always listened and offered advice only when she asked for it.

"I'm glad we're doing lunch, because there's so much I need to tell you, Dad," she said softly, not knowing where to begin.

"I'm listening, Jules."

She loved this man so much. The man who'd always been there for her and Shana. The man who was still there for them. Benjamin Bradford was the daddy every girl should have. "I've taken on Sheppard Granger's investigation to find out who killed his wife."

Ben didn't say anything for a minute. "He hired you?"

She shook her head, smiling wryly. "No. In fact, he's probably not going to like it when he finds out. He believes the other PI on the case, a few years back, was murdered."

"That's what I heard, too. The thought of that doesn't bother you?"

She chuckled softly. "I'm an ex-cop, Dad, and I was a detective for two years."

Ben nodded. "Yes, I know."

"Risks come with the territory, with the job I do. I can handle it."

"I know you can handle it, Jules, I'm just asking you to be careful."

"I will." She paused a moment and then told him what she'd learned so far. Her father agreed that Ivan Greene's flimsy alibi was worth further investigation.

When the waitress delivered their dessert, she said quietly, "And then there's Dalton," she said.

Her father glanced up at her before taking a sip of his coffee. "You two still at it?"

Definitely not the way he was probably thinking. "I haven't told anyone, not even Shana…but Dalton and I are no longer…"

"Enemies?"

Her father finished her thought for her when it seemed she couldn't. "Yes, we're no longer enemies."

"Oh? And what are you?"

This was her dad, so she couldn't come right out and say that they were lovers, that Dalton was the man she went to when she needed to get laid, the man whose body she could do all kinds of naughty stuff with. "Friends."

Ben nodded. "I see."

In a way, she was sure that he did. "We watched a video together last night."

"So he's the reason you gave up my grilled pork chops?"

Jules smiled. "Not really. I needed to watch those videos. Both were work-related and part of the Sylvia Granger investigation. One was of Shana's dinner party, and the other was the grand opening of Caden's wife's wine boutique."

"Did you learn anything?"

"Yes. But first, I need to share something with you. When Dalton was about ten or eleven, he discovered his mother was having an affair. He didn't fully understand what all that meant at the time, and she swore him to secrecy. He thought it was cool that he and his mom had a secret. After she died and he got older, he realized just what sort of secret she'd made him keep."

"That was cruel for her to do that to a child."

"Yes, it was. For years, he'd felt guilty and believed that by keeping his mother's secret, he had betrayed his father."

Ben nodded. "I can understand him thinking that way. But again, he was just a child at the time."

"Well, last night while watching the video, he recognized the man his mother had been with years ago, and it affected him in a bad way."

"The man was at Shana's dinner party?"

"No, he attended Shiloh's open house, but Dalton wasn't there that night which is why he didn't make the connection until he reviewed the videotape."

Ben took a sip of his coffee. "I hope Dalton isn't thinking about confronting the man."

Dalton had suggested that very thing last night, but luckily, she'd been able to talk him out of it. "He did at first, but now I don't think he will."

"So what's next?" her father asked.

Finishing off her apple pie, Jules placed her fork down by her plate. "Now I add the man's name to my list of people I want to talk to."

Back at her office, Jules stood in front of her investigation wall. A picture of Vance Clayburn was now pinned up along with the others she needed to interview. As her father had reminded her, just because the man and Sylvia Granger had been lovers did not mean he had a reason to kill her. But what if Sylvia had wanted more from the relationship and had threatened to tell the man's wife? Jules's research indicated that Clayburn had been married at the time of the affair.

So far, she knew that Clayburn was a sixty-one-year-old divorcé, which suggested a thirty-year difference in his and Nannette Gaither's ages. He'd made his billions years ago in Silicon Valley. He later branched out and acquired a number of small industrial companies and began growing them into multimillion-dollar corporations. It was announced a couple of years ago that he would be expanding one of those companies to Charlottesville, thereby boosting the local economy and employment rate.

The man lived in a gated community in one of the wealthiest areas of Charlottesville. Jules wasn't surprised by that because, despite his wealth and influence, he had always kept a low profile and avoided the spotlight like the plague. It had been very difficult to get the one photo she did have. She wouldn't be able to surprise him and just drop by. He would need to know she was coming and give her clearance to enter his property.

Sitting down at her desk, Jules glanced at her watch. It was close to six in the evening, and she hadn't heard anything from Dalton. She hoped he hadn't changed his mind and sought out Clayburn, after all.

She tapped her fingers on her desk a few times before quickly making her decision. She would drop by Dalton's place for a quick second to check on him. It wouldn't be the first time she'd gone there unannounced. Besides, he'd shown up at her office and her home unannounced himself.

Grabbing her purse from her desk drawer, she headed for the door.

Thirty-Six

In bare feet, Dalton crossed the living room and opened the door without first looking out the peephole. Jules's scent was her signature, and it could penetrate walls and doors. And there she stood on his doorstep looking delicious enough to eat. She definitely looked good in her jeans, flats and pullover sweater with her hair unbound and swaying around her shoulders. "Jules."

"Dalton. I don't need to come in. I just wanted to check to make sure you were okay."

"I'm fine, but come in, anyway," he said, stepping aside.

She entered and turned around in the middle of his foyer. "Your note did say that you had a lot to think through, but when you hadn't texted me or anything, I got worried."

He nodded. What he had to think through had nothing to do with the man who'd been his mother's lover and everything to do with Jules. But she didn't know that.

"Yes, and I'm fine. I was about to call you after I shaved."

She smiled. "I noticed you hadn't done that."

He rubbed his stubble. "For a minute, I thought I

would go for the rugged look, but figured my brothers would have something to say about it," he said, leading her toward the living room.

"Speaking of your brothers, have you told them?" she asked, following him to the living room.

"About that man in the video?"

"Yes."

"No, not yet. To be honest, I haven't thought much about it."

"You haven't thought much about telling your brothers?"

"No, or about that man in the video, for that matter," he said, gesturing for her to sit down.

"Oh, I assumed when you said you had a lot to think through that you would be making decisions about that," she said, sitting down on his sofa.

He remained standing and shoved his hands into the pockets of his jeans. "What you said last night was true. I can't blame myself for the things Mom did. And I agree with you in that I think it's something Jace and Caden need to know about. I'm sure it will help in the investigation."

"Yes, but if that's not what's been consuming your mind all this time, what exactly did you have to think about? I've been worried about you all day." She spoke with a confused expression on her face.

He slowly began walking across the ceramic-tiled floor toward her and came to a stop right in front of where she sat. She lifted her head to look up at him. That's when he said, "I needed all that time to think about you, Jules."

Jules was even more confused now because what Dalton had just said didn't make sense. And why was he staring at her like that? As if he were seeing her for the first time?

"Think about me?" she asked, making sure she had heard him right.

"Yes, you."

She was even more confused. "Why?"

"Because I've decided I want an exclusive relationship with you."

Jules's heart skipped a beat, and she had to draw in a deep breath, not sure whether she should be flattered or not. His tone had made it seem that it was solely his decision to make and that that settled the matter. Boy, was he wrong. "And what if I decide I don't want an exclusive relationship with you?"

"Then I think you have a problem."

Jules had to fight to keep from grinning. He thought that *she* would be the one who had the problem? She shook her head. He'd just taken his arrogance to another level.

"And why would it be me with the problem?" she asked, hardly able to wait to hear what he had to say.

"Because I won't allow any other man to touch you, kiss you or make love to you ever again."

Her brow shot up the minute he said the word *allow*, and anything else that followed fell on deaf ears. *"Allow?"* she said, slowly rising to her feet. He had been standing so close that he had to back up for her to be able to stand. "Did you just say *allow*? And just how do you even think you have a say in the matter?"

"You know who I am," he said as if that explained everything.

She glared at him. "Yes, I know. You're a man used to having his way with women. A man who thinks all he has to do is speak, and the woman will obey. A man who assumes he can tell me what I can do or not do with my body and with whom. A man—"

Dalton had heard enough, and pulled her to him, covering her mouth with his. He felt her body tense, but only for a second before she began returning the kiss with the same hunger. They had kissed many times before, but never like this. He wasn't sure who was trying to eat whom alive. Him or her. All he knew was that the more he tasted her, the more he wanted.

He was feeling more than just heat. He was feeling something he'd never felt before. The moment their mouths broke free to breathe, he swept her off her feet and began kissing her again while heading to his bedroom. When they reached the bedroom, he dumped her on the bed. Before he could move away she reached out and pulled him down, too.

"Don't think because we're doing this that it means anything," she said.

He had news for her. It meant everything. She might not like the idea of being exclusive, but her body was telling a different story. Why couldn't she see this was meant to be? He had, and he had accepted it as such... although it had taken him almost an entire damned day to do so.

Instead of wasting his breath disagreeing with her, he decided to put his energy to other uses. Like taking off her clothes. When he'd finished, not to be outdone, she began taking off his. Tugging his T-shirt over his head and tossing it aside and then straddling him to undo the fly of his jeans.

"Need help?"

She glanced at him. "No, I got this."

And when she pulled out his engorged erection, he knew that she did. And when she went down on him, covering him with her mouth and then locking her lips tight, his eyes rolled back in his head. Her mouth was deadly. Was she trying to give him a heart attack?

The sight of her head between his legs and the feel of being fully lodged inside her mouth was too much. When she began bobbing her head up and down, he wasn't sure how much longer he could last, throbbing inside her mouth.

And then before he could blink, she had released him to pull her body up to straddle him, positioning herself over him perfectly before plunging downward. Whether she entered him or he entered her, he wasn't sure. All he knew was that their bodies were connected as tightly as could be. There was no doubt in his mind that he was embedded deep inside her. Beyond the hilt.

She only went still for a minute before lifting her body slightly to begin riding him. She had ridden him before, but never like this. Never with this intensity. Or with this degree of force. Or strength. And she wouldn't stop. Or let up. She had more energy than the Energizer Bunny.

And when he felt he couldn't take any more, was certain he was about to take his last breath, he screamed her name at the same time his hips bucked upward. Hers slammed downward, and the impact triggered an orgasm he wasn't sure he would live to see to completion. But he did see it through, and every sensation known to man…and some man might not have experienced yet… surged through him. He would have been knocked flat on his back had he not already been there.

And he knew she felt the enormity of what he'd experienced, as well. It was there in the eyes looking down at him, in the way she was breathing, the way her nipples were still hard. How in the world did she think he would allow her to do this with another man? There would never, ever, be another man for her. Only him. And it was more than just wanting an exclusive relationship with her.

That startling fact rammed through his brain, scorched the cells there, when he comprehended what that meant. The one thing that had happened to him, that he'd thought, swore, declared, avowed never would. He had fallen in love with her.

The dawning of that idea had him reaching up, running his fingers around her lips in shocked silence. Then he tumbled her off him and into his arms and then shifted his body so they could lie sideways facing each other. While she was trying to get her breathing back under control, he stared at her as if seeing her through a different pair of eyes. In a way, he was.

"Jules…"

After drawing in several slow breaths, she answered. "Yes?"

He caught himself, knowing he couldn't tell her what he felt. He would botch things up if he did. What he would do was wait until he found the right words to make sure she fully understood the depth of his feelings. So instead he said, "You didn't give me a chance to take off my jeans."

She chuckled. "Now we're even."

He lifted a confused brow. "Even?"

"Yes. The first time you made love to me in this bed, you didn't want me to take my boots off."

A smile touched his lips. "No," he said, remembering. "I didn't." In fact, he'd taken her a couple of times that night before finally removing those boots. There had been something erotic about making love to a woman with her boots on.

She was about to say something, but he figured whatever she wanted to say could wait until later because at that moment, he wanted to kiss her again.

The next morning Dalton opened the door to his brothers and their wives. Jace frowned. "Texting me about a meeting for eight in the morning at your place is becoming a habit, don't you think?"

Dalton smiled. "Nothing like a little family get-together in the morning. Come on in. I'm glad you could make it this time, Shiloh."

She grinned. "Thanks for inviting me *this time*, Dalton."

"You would have been bored to tears at the last meeting. It was Granger Aeronautics stuff." When everyone had made it into his living room, he said, "Grab a seat, everyone. Jules is in the kitchen making coffee."

Shana blinked. "Jules is here?"

Dalton fought back another smile. "Yes, she's here."

"Kind of early for visitors, isn't it?" Caden asked.

Dalton knew he wasn't referring to them but to Jules. "Depends on who the visitors are. I have something to tell everyone. Jules and I both do."

"Oh, hell, please don't tell us you got her pregnant," Caden said in his Dalton voice with all the dramatics. "But, then," he said, reverting back to his Caden voice, "that's not possible because the two of you aren't an item. You two can't stand each other. You're bloody enemies. Right?"

"Tell your husband to shut up before I hit him, Shiloh," Dalton said, trying not to smile. "I'll go help Jules with the coffee."

Dalton quickly left the room. When Caden had jokingly asked the pregnancy question, Dalton had almost stopped breathing. Jules would probably be pregnant if she hadn't been on the Pill. But he would admit the thought of her pregnant with his baby didn't make him crazy like it once would have. He rather liked the idea, which only proved just how far gone he was.

Jace sat up straight on the sofa beside Shana. "Are you saying Dalton actually spotted the man who had an affair with Mom at the boathouse on one of those videos?"

Dalton nodded. "Yes, that's exactly what she's saying." Once he and Jules had come out of the kitchen with the coffee, he'd given Jules the floor before anyone could ask any nosy questions about their relationship. When she started by saying she'd asked them to come by this morning because of a new development in the on-going investigation, everyone in the room had a one-track mind.

"And he was at our party?" Jace asked, reaching out for Shana's hand.

"No," Dalton said, getting out of his seat to stand beside Jules. "He was at Shiloh's open house for her wine boutique."

"What?" Caden and Shiloh said simultaneously with startled looks on their faces.

"*Who* is he?" Caden asked, his eyes filling with confusion.

Dalton glanced over at Jules, nodding for her to continue the story. "He is Nannette Gaither's fiancé. Vance Clayburn."

"Vance Clayburn?" Caden said, jumping up out of his seat. "That night at the opening, I *knew* I remembered him from somewhere, and I even asked him if we'd met before, and he said no. Now it's all coming back. It's been years, but I'm certain I've seen him before."

Jace lifted a brow. "Had you, like Dalton, seen him before with Mom?"

"No," Caden said, shaking his head. "Not with our mother, no," he said, with a grim look on his face. He then turned to his wife, who was sitting on the sofa. "He was with yours, Shiloh. And they were kissing. Neither of them saw me."

Shiloh looked shocked. "Kissing? My *mom* and another man?"

Caden nodded. "Yes, your mom and another man. I had come over to your house to see if you wanted to go riding and figured you were in the stables so I headed right over there. That's when I walked in on them."

"But...but you never told me about it."

Caden drew in a deep breath and sat back down on the sofa, pulling Shiloh into his arms. "Because it was years ago, when we were in our early teens. Before Mom died. I was just a young guy, and I was probably thinking more about seeing you than anything else. Anyway, the truth is I had honestly forgotten what I'd seen. Until now."

Thirty-Seven

The plot thickens, Jules thought, back at her office a few hours later, standing in front of the investigation wall. Using the touch screen, she moved the image of Sandra Timmons to the side where the suspects were shown. Could Sandra have killed Sylvia in a bout of jealous rage? After all, it now seemed they had been having an affair with the same man.

Jules turned when there was a knock at her office door. "Yes?"

Manning came in smiling. "I got that information you wanted on the Gaithers, and you're right. They are strapped for money, big-time."

Jules nodded. "No wonder Nannette needs a rich husband."

"And I can't find anything on a Gary Coughlin. I questioned Ron Zimmons and he said he didn't know the guy. They arrived at Shana and Jace's party at the same time and walked in together."

"Umm, interesting. Pull a still shot of him from the video. I want to give Coughlin's photo to Marcel to see if the Bureau can ID him."

After Manning left, Jules returned to studying her

wall, but her gaze shifted to Dalton's profile. When Shana had pulled her aside after the meeting and told her that she had a hickey on the side of her neck—a real one this time—she had dashed off to the nearest bathroom to check for herself. Shana had been right. No wonder everyone had been looking at her strangely.

She'd spent the night at his place on Sunday, and then she had gone home to get dressed for work after the meeting, making sure she'd worn a turtleneck sweater to the office. Manning could be just as observant as Shana.

She turned when the buzzer on her desk went off. She walked over and pressed a button. "Yes, Manning?"

"Shiloh Granger is on line one."

"Thanks."

Jules paused before clicking over. "Hi, Shiloh. Everything okay?"

"I was just wondering if you had been able to reach my mother. You said you wanted to interview her."

Jules sat down behind her desk. "I did try her after our meeting this morning, but her secretary said she wasn't taking any calls."

"Margaret is instructed to tell everyone that... everyone but Sedrick, me and a few others. I called Mom myself, and she has agreed to see me, although she has no idea what our discussion will be about. Would you care to join me, since I will want to ask her the same questions you probably have?"

Jules smiled. "I'd definitely like to join you. What time?"

"Let's say in an hour? Can you meet me at Shady Pines, my family estate? You won't be able to go through the security gates without me."

"No problem. I will be parked outside the gates, waiting for you."

* * *

Carson glanced across the table at Sheppard. "So there you have it. Jules Bradford has decided to reopen the investigation into Sylvia's death, with or without your blessing."

Sheppard leaned back in his chair and pursed his lips. "I'd prefer that she stay out of it, Carson."

"I figured you would feel that way, but I think her mind is made up. Shana is her sister, and she wants to find the real killer before he gets crazy."

"As far as I'm concerned, the person who killed Sylvia is definitely crazy. She was murdered fifteen years ago, and if the person is fearful the investigation is being reopened, that means he will do anything to make sure that doesn't happen. That young lady is risking her life for me."

"Her future father-in-law."

"What? Things are *that* serious?"

Carson chuckled. "Yes, but I doubt either of them knows it yet. But it was pretty obvious to me and, I think, to others in that meeting."

She paused a moment and then said, "I got a call from Jace this morning, and he wanted me to let you know two things."

"Which are?"

"First it seems Eve Granger came to town Friday and was caught on tape trying to extort money from Granger Aeronautics."

"How?"

"By threatening to go public with the fact that Hannah and your father were involved. She asked for one million dollars."

Sheppard let out a whistle. "Is she crazy?"

"Apparently. But, like I said, she was caught on tape, and the Feds came to arrest her."

Sheppard nodded. "Good. I hate the fact that Jace ever married her in the first place. She caused him nothing but heartbreak. And as far as Dad's and Hannah's involvement, what they did was their business. How did Eve find out?"

"I think Vidal Duncan told her. It's my understanding that Jace and Caden already knew, but Dalton clearly did not."

"How did he handle finding out?"

"According to Jace, he was upset at first that everyone knew but him, but then he was fine with it. Your sons adore Hannah."

"Yes, and she adores them." Sheppard leaned closer to her. "You said there were two things. What's the other?"

Carson paused a minute and then said, "While looking at videos of Shana's dinner party and Shiloh's open house, Jules might have stumbled across something interesting."

"What?"

"The man Dalton saw Sylvia with that day at the boathouse? Dalton was with Jules the night she was watching the video, and he pointed him out to her. His name is Vance Clayburn."

"Vance Clayburn?" Sheppard asked, startled.

Carson watched his expression. "Yes. Do you know him?"

Sheppard's expression may have been unreadable to others, but Carson was able to see the anger that tightened his jaw and shadowed his eyes. "Yes, I know him."

"How?"

"His computer company once put in a bid to provide computer services at Granger Aeronautics."

"You are Ramona Oakley, right?" Marcel asked, greeting the young woman who walked into his office.

Nervousness showed on her face. "Yes, but I don't know what this is about. I've never gotten into any trouble, not even a parking ticket. Except for that one time I received a citation for swimming topless on the beach, but that was four years ago. Why would anyone from the FBI want to talk to me?"

Topless on the beach? Marcel cleared his throat. "Please have a seat, Ms. Oakley. I'm Marcel Eaton, Special Agent for the FBI, and my division is handling the trade-secret violations at Granger Aeronautics. I would like to ask you a few questions."

"All right, but I don't know what I can tell you. I was shocked like everyone else when Mr. Freeman, Mr. Carrington and Ms. Swanson were arrested. Who would have thought? And then for one of the company attorneys, that man named Vidal Duncan, to try to kill Jace Granger. He had to have been demented or something to think he could get away with it."

She paused to take a deep breath and then asked, "So what would you like to ask me?"

Marcel leaned back in his chair. "Just the routine questions to get a feel of what you do at Granger. And, if you don't mind, I'd like to record our conversation."

She smiled. "I don't mind being recorded. I think that's cool. And telling you what I do at Granger Aeronautics is easy. I work on payroll, and I love my job, crunching all those numbers, and knowing at the end of the week everyone will get a paycheck because I've taken my job seriously and made sure they get paid,

and on time. There are ten of us in my department."
Ramona paused to take a breath.

Marcel nodded, thinking the young woman was definitely chatty. Almost too chatty. He decided to get down
to the reason she had been asked to come in. "Ms. Oakley, we recently checked several computers in your work
area, and it seems that yours has software on it that was
not installed by Granger."

Ramona Oakley blinked, startled. "That's impossible. I don't put anything on my computer. It's against
company policy. Everyone knows that. The only thing
I do every once in a while is listen to my music. That's
permissible and makes a long day go by faster."

"You download your music onto the company computer?"

"No. That's not permitted, either. Granger provides
us with unrestricted music channels. I enjoy pop music,
and that's the site I listen to."

Marcel nodded. "And how do you listen to your
music?"

"With headphones, of course," she said, looking at
him as if he was dense.

"Granger provides you with special headphones?"

"No, we use our own. I have a special pair. At least
they were special up until last week. The guy who gave
them to me as a gift dumped me for no reason at all, so
they aren't special any longer."

Marcel lifted a brow. "He dumped you?"

"Yes, can you believe that?"

It depends, Marcel thought to himself. "The two of
you had a big fight or something?"

"No, and that's what's strange. I thought things were
going well. I guess he decided to stop cheating on his
wife."

Marcel lifted another brow. "He was married?"

"So he said. And that's why we couldn't be seen in public and had to do things discreetly."

"And you didn't have a problem with that? The wife? Doing things discreetly?"

"No, of course not," she said, shifting into a more comfortable position in her chair. "It's not like I want a husband or anything. Heck, I'm only twenty-five. I like being single and having fun. Besides, he was nice to me. He liked buying me things."

Marcel drew in a deep breath, thinking that there definitely wasn't any shame in her game. "And one of the things he bought you was a pair of headphones?"

"Yes. Said he got them while vacationing with his wife in Dubai a few months ago."

"Do you happen to have the headphones with you?"

"Yes. I take them everywhere I go. They're great at the beach because they're waterproof," she said, searching her purse for them. "Here they are."

Marcel took the headphones from her and immediately knew there was something familiar about them. It didn't take him but a second to remember that a similar pair was found in Brandy Booker's belongings. "I'm going to have to hold on to these for a while, Ms. Oakley."

She looked surprised. "Why?"

"I'll need our technicians to check them out."

"Why? They're just headphones."

"We'll verify that and return them to you. Is this the only pair you have?" Marcel asked.

"Yes. He only gave me that one pair."

"And what was his name? The man who—"

"Dumped me? Go ahead and say it. I don't mind."

Marcel cleared his throat. "What's his name?"

"John Wayne."

Marcel's brows bunched together. "John Wayne?"

"Yes, isn't that neat? His parents named him after the actor."

Probably not his real name, Marcel thought but decided to keep that to himself for now. "Where did the two of you meet?"

"In the park, not far from where I live. He was walking his dog."

"So he lives in your area."

"No. He said he liked driving over to our park. He thought it was a lot more interesting."

I bet, Marcel thought to himself. Half an hour later, he finished going through all the questions he had for Ramona Oakley. "That is all for now, Ms. Oakley," he said, standing.

She stood, as well. "For now? Does that mean you might be calling me back in?"

"Possibly."

"That's neat. I like talking to you. How old are you, Mr. Eaton?"

He moved from behind his desk to escort her out of his office. "I'm fifty-seven."

"You don't look it."

"Thanks."

"Are you married?"

"Yes, for twenty very happy years." He decided to throw that in just in case she was getting any ideas. "I'm the father of triplets who just entered college this fall."

Before she could ask him any more questions, he quickly said, "Have a good day, Ms. Oakley."

Thirty-Eight

The housekeeper of the Timmons estate escorted Shiloh and Jules into the family room. And, just like the rest of the house Jules had seen so far, it was massive and too elegant for words. She turned to Shiloh in awe. "And to think you once lived here."

"Yes, but don't be too impressed. It wasn't a home filled with love, and I stayed away as much as I could. I found my solace at Sutton Hills," Shiloh said, sitting down on one of the sofas.

"And with Caden?" Jules asked, sitting down, as well.

Shiloh's smile displayed more than a hint of happiness when she said, "Yes, and with Caden." She was about to say something else when the sound of footsteps could be heard on the marble floor.

"Shiloh, sweetheart, imagine my surprise when..." Sandra Timmons's smile and words died slowly when she saw Jules. "I didn't know you had brought a friend with you."

Both Jules and Shiloh stood. Shiloh smiled over at Jules. "Yes, I did. Mother, I'd like you to meet Jules Bradford. She's Shana's sister."

Sandra Timmons arched a brow. "Shana?"

"Yes. Jace's wife."

"Oh."

Do you have to make your disappointment so obvious? Jules thought, studying Shiloh's mother. Sandra Timmons was a beautiful woman for her age, and Jules wondered how much of it was original and how much was courtesy of a plastic surgeon. She definitely looked the part of a wealthy matron, from the sophisticated and stylish pants suit she was wearing to the style of her hair, with not a strand out of place.

When it was obvious that Mrs. Timmons wouldn't make the first move to display Southern hospitality or graceful manners, Jules decided to do so. Crossing the room, she extended her hand. "Nice meeting you, Ms. Timmons." She did not add the cliché of, *And I've heard a lot about you*, although it would have been true.

"Yes. Thanks. Welcome to my home."

The handshake was flimsy and over rather quickly; it certainly didn't make her feel welcome. "Thank you," Jules said politely.

"The reason I'm here, Mom, is to ask you some questions. And the reason I brought Jules with me is because she has a few questions to ask you, too."

Confusion lit Sandra Timmons's eyes. "Questions? I don't understand."

"Jules is a private investigator, who has reopened Sylvia Granger's murder case."

Jules watched the flash of shock that appeared in Mrs. Timmons's eyes. It appeared so quickly that anyone not watching her closely would have missed it.

"Reopen the case? B—but why?"

Jules thought she would be the best person to answer

that. "Because I don't believe Sheppard Granger killed his wife, and I intend to prove it."

The woman was speechless, that was pretty obvious. And it took her a few seconds to recover. With a stiffened spine, she said, "Evidently, you also believe in fairy tales, Ms. Bradford, because everyone knows the truth. Sheppard killed Sylvia."

"Really? And you know this how? Were you there, Ms. Timmons?" Jules asked curtly.

The ice that suddenly formed in Sandra Timmons's eyes was like a glacier. "No, I was not there, Ms. Bradford, but Sylvia was one of my closest friends, and she confided in me about some…personal things. I knew just how mean Shep had been to her, accusing her of god-awful things and believing everything that their housekeeper was telling him."

Jules opened her mouth to speak, but Shiloh beat her to the punch. "If you and Sylvia Granger were such close friends, Mom, how is it that the two of you were having an affair with the same man?"

Dalton walked into the conference room to find his brothers, Shana and Bruce already seated around the conference table. "What's this meeting about?" he asked, sliding into the first available seat.

Jace rubbed the back of his neck. "Not sure. Shana got a call from Marcel, and he asked that we meet him here."

"I thought we decided not to discuss any business here at Granger since it seems that even the paper clips have ears," Dalton said, picking up a paper clip that lay on the table and analyzing it.

"Marcel asked Bruce to use his magic scanner to

double-check and make sure this room is bug-free," Shana said, grinning.

Dalton glanced over at Bruce. "Hey, man, the Feds need to put you on their payroll."

Bruce chuckled. "I'm on Shana's and Jules's payrolls, and that's good enough for me. Besides, you know how the government is these days. Like everyone else, they are trying to do more with less. I don't mind helping out my country."

"And speaking of Jules…" Caden said.

Dalton was expecting questions, but wasn't about to give any answers. "Mind your own business, Caden," he said in a firm voice.

"Why? You never do," was Caden's quick comeback.

Jace thought he would have to intervene when there was a knock on the door. "Come in."

Marcel entered. "Glad all of you were able to make it at such short notice. Thank you," he said, sitting down. "For the past week or so, my team and I have been doing extensive background checks on everyone in the accounting and computer technology departments. This morning, I got around to interviewing Ramona Oakley, the young woman whose computer was infected with that spyware."

"How did that go?" Shana asked, taking a sip of water.

"It was pretty interesting. I think we might be on to something."

"What?" Jace asked, the intensity of his gaze showing he was on full alert.

"This," Marcel said, placing the headphones he'd confiscated earlier from Ramona Oakley in the middle of the table.

Caden lifted a brow. "Headphones?"

"Yes, headphones. Ms. Oakley used them on occasion to listen to music while working. She did indicate she only visited music sites Granger deemed unrestricted. Take a close look at them, Bruce," Marcel suggested.

Bruce picked them up and studied every inch of them before he began to dismantle them piece by piece. When he didn't find anything unusual, he put them back together. "Now, let's see what I missed," he said, reaching for his briefcase and placing it on the table.

Bruce opened what was referred to as his briefcase of toys, software and hardware specifically created to combat computer espionage. Taking out what looked like nothing more than a miniature flashlight, he scanned the headphones. When the scanner began flashing, he looked over at Marcel, smiled and said, "Bingo. Whatever is in here cannot be seen with the naked eye. And it's my guess that once the device makes contact with a computer, the spyware is automatically downloaded and activated."

"Damn," Caden said, shaking his head. "How did she get it?"

"Her boyfriend," Marcel responded.

"The older man?" Dalton asked.

Marcel nodded his head. "Yes. He recently dumped her, but she should count her blessings."

"Why?" Shana asked, staring down at what looked like a fancy pair of headphones.

"Because that same type of headphones was found in Brandy Booker's apartment when it was searched." He then tossed another set on the table. Hers are identical except in color.

Jace leaned back in his chair. "Are you saying…?"

"Yes," Marcel said, nodding. He glanced over at Dalton. "I think your hunch might have been right on the money. The same older man who was dating Brandy, and used her to install the spyware on her computer, is more than likely the same man who used Ramona Oakley for the same purpose. My job is to find out who he is."

Sandra Timmons's features went into shock. Some people were good at masking their emotions, but she was not. Jules thought it might have had something to do with the way her mouth seemed to drop, almost falling to the floor. But it didn't take long for her to recover and put that iron face back into place. "I have *no* idea what you're talking about."

"Really?" Shiloh asked, moving to stand in front of her mother. "Well, let me tell you what I'm talking about. You were seen with him."

"Him who?"

"Vance Clayburn."

Again, another shocked look. It was there one second and gone the next. Mrs. Timmons attempted to look thoughtful. "Vance Clayburn. I believe that's the man Nannette Gaither is engaged to marry. Why would you think that—"

"You were seen with him. Years ago. In our stables. Caden saw you, and don't you dare call my husband a liar."

Sandra Timmons opened her mouth to do just that and then thought better of it. She closed her mouth tightly and then switched her gaze from Shiloh to look out the windows where those same stables could be seen. It was obvious she was trying to hold her emotions together. Either that or she was trying to get her lie straight before she told it, Jules thought.

"Well, Mother?"

It was obvious Shiloh wasn't cutting her mother any slack. She wanted answers, and she wanted them now. When Sandra Timmons's gaze came back to rest on Shiloh, there were emotions etched across every inch of her features.

"We need to talk privately, Shiloh."

"No, Mom, we don't. You might be a murder suspect if you don't—"

"Suspect for murder! What are you talking about?" Sandra Timmons asked in a panicky voice.

It was Jules who spoke. "You and Sylvia Granger were involved with the same man, Ms. Timmons. For all we know, you could have killed her in a jealous rage."

"That's insane. I would not have killed Sylvia—she was my best friend. She didn't even know Vance and I knew each other, and she told me she only messed around with Vance to—"

When she didn't finish, Jules pressed. "To what?"

Sandra Timmons drew in a deep breath before narrowing her gaze at Jules. "Ms. Bradford, you aren't the police, and I don't have to answer any of your questions."

Jules smiled. "You're right, I am not the police, but I believe I have enough information to give them a reason to reopen Sylvia Granger's murder case. Things aren't like they used to be. Police departments have special task forces in place just to handle cold cases, and they will be relentless in their questioning and pursuit of the truth. And you will have no choice but to tell them what they want to know. So you can either deal with me or with them. The choice is yours but, no matter what you decide, I will eventually find out the truth."

Sandra Timmons looked faint for a moment, but then

recovered herself. "I'd prefer to have a private conversation with Shiloh."

"Sorry, Mom. It will be in your best interest for Jules to hear whatever you have to say, as well."

Sandra Timmons glanced over at her, and Jules knew the woman was not convinced of that. But finally, she relented. "Vance and I met while in college. We were hoping our parents would allow us to marry, but they didn't. They already had other partners picked out for us."

"Arranged marriages?" Shiloh asked.

"Yes, you could say that. In our circles, at our station in life, we did what our parents ordered. Over the years, we'd run into each other on occasion. We knew both our lives were miserable, but..."

"You were committed to remaining married," Jules finished for her.

"Yes," Sandra Timmons said quietly. "We were committed to remaining married."

"So how did he become involved with Sylvia Granger?" Jules asked.

Jules watched as Sandra Timmons dropped gracefully onto the sofa and she and Shiloh sat down, as well.

"Sylvia used him."

"For what reason?" Jules heard herself asking.

"She wanted knowledge of his business. For what reason, I don't know. I never confided in her about my history with Vance and, like any other man she saw and wanted, she figured she could go after him. I detested her for that."

Jules wondered if Sandra Timmons realized she was giving herself even more of a motive to get rid of Sylvia Granger. "You detested her?"

As if realizing what she'd said, Sandra Timmons

corrected herself. "But I got over it quickly. If I had shown my anger to her, she would have wondered why. Besides, Vance was a grown man who could do what he wanted."

"Were there any other men that you know Sylvia was involved with besides Vance Clayburn?"

"There was Michael Greene, but she joked about using him, too."

"Using him how?" Jules wanted to know.

"She didn't elaborate, and I didn't ask."

Jules then asked, "Where were you on the afternoon Sylvia Granger was killed?"

The anger in Sandra Timmons's gaze was undeniable. "You would like to pin her death on me, wouldn't you? Well, sorry, you can't. I didn't kill her."

"Then tell us where you were"

Sandra Timmons nervously began twisting her hands together. "I was nowhere near Sutton Hills."

"Then why won't you say where you were?" Shiloh asked her mother.

Sandra Timmons stood again, but Jules and Shiloh remained seated and watched her begin pacing. "I was somewhere else...with someone."

"Who?" Jules asked. "And where?"

Sandra Timmons was annoyed. That much was obvious. She was also frustrated and nervous. That was obvious, as well. She then turned and faced Jules and Shiloh. "I was somewhere with Vance."

Now Shiloh stood on her feet. "Why, Mom? I knew there was not a lot of love, if any, between you and Dad. So why sneak around? Why didn't you get a divorce if you wanted to be with Vance Clayburn?"

Sandra Timmons shrugged. "It would not have been that easy. Our parents established the terms of our marriages, and there was no way I could ever get out of it with enough money to support you and Sedrick. They made sure of it."

"So you were willing to sneak around, betray Dad, take chances and even let a woman you considered your close friend sleep with him?"

"What happened between him and Sylvia wasn't his fault. She tricked him. Used him. He explained things to me, and I forgave him."

Jules nodded. "And are you forgiving him for marrying Nannette Gaither, Ms. Timmons? You're free, and so is he. If you and Vance Clayburn have this great love affair, why aren't the two of you together now?"

Before she could answer, Shiloh asked a question of her own. "And why *did* you and Dad begin hating the Grangers? Why did Dad start treating Caden and his brothers like they were the scum of the Earth and forbid Sedrick and me to have anything to do with them? Why?"

Sandra Timmons sat back down, but Shiloh remained standing. She looked at her daughter. "That was my fault. Samuel began suspecting I was having an affair. He just didn't know with whom. One day he returned unexpectedly from a business trip, and I came home and found him here, sitting in a chair upstairs waiting. He knew I had been with someone and was full of accusations. At first I told him there was no one else, but he got mean, hateful and almost violent. I knew I had to tell him something. Give him a name." She paused a moment. "So I told him I was having an affair with Sheppard."

"What?" both Jules and Shiloh exclaimed simultaneously.

"You led Dad to believe you and Mr. Granger were having an affair?" Shiloh demanded.

"Yes," she said nervously, wringing her hands.

"No wonder Dad hated Mr. Granger. But there was no reason to treat his sons the way he did."

Sandra drew in a deep breath. "Samuel felt justified. Anyone could see how close you and Caden were becoming, closer than ever. We knew that would eventually lead to a romance of some sort between the two of you. Samuel refused to let that happen. He refused to accept the son of the man he assumed was my lover as a future son-in-law. When Sheppard went to jail, he saw the perfect opportunity to force a wedge between the two of you. But he even went further. He wanted to make sure Jace, Caden and Dalton were ostracized by the community, as well. He set up this vindictive campaign to hurt them."

"And you let him," Shiloh said in disgust.

"Why didn't you tell Mr. Timmons the truth, Mrs. Timmons? Give him Vance Clayburn's name? Why did you continue to allow your husband to assume Mr. Granger was your lover?" Jules asked.

She didn't say anything for a minute. "It made perfect sense at the time. Sheppard went to prison for killing Sylvia, and it was reported in the news that another woman was involved. Samuel assumed I was the woman. He believed Sheppard killed Sylvia to be with me and thought his going to jail was his just reward. I thought it was the perfect solution. I could keep Vance's name out of it, since Sheppard wouldn't be around, anyway."

Jules was stunned. What she was hearing was unbelievable. It was bad enough that a man had been in prison almost fifteen years for a crime he hadn't committed, but he'd also been wrongly accused of taking part in an affair he probably knew nothing about. And Sandra Timmons was standing here admitting that she had seized an opportunity to benefit from Mr. Granger's incarceration.

"Why were you protecting Vance Clayburn, Mom? Why?"

Sandra sprang from the sofa. "I had to. If your father had found out the truth that..."

Shiloh lifted her brow when her mother's voice faltered. "That what? If Dad found out the truth about what?"

"It doesn't matter. He found out, anyway," Sandra Timmons said softly, anguish forming in her features.

"What did Mr. Timmons find out?" Jules asked, determined to find out for herself.

Sandra Timmons walked to the window, glanced out and stood there a moment before turning back around. Instead of answering Jules, she spoke directly to Shiloh. "He found out...when you were in that bad accident a few years ago and you needed a blood transfusion. The only person who could give you the blood to save your life was Vance."

Jules watched as shock tore into Shiloh's features, and she held on to a table for balance. "What are you saying, Mom?"

Regret shone in Sandra Timmons's eyes when she said, "Vance Clayburn is your father."

Shiloh crumbled to the sofa beside her, and Jules reached out and took her hand as Sandra added, "So now you know why Vance is marrying Nannette. He hates me and will do anything to hurt me. Mainly because he had a child I never told him about...until I needed him to save your life."

Thirty-Nine

A few hours later, Jules stood in front of her investigation wall. Though she wished she had gone home after leaving Shady Pines, she hadn't. She had come here. Knowing what she knew now she was determined more than ever to free Sheppard Granger.

She rubbed her hand down her face and remembered what had happened after Sandra Timmons's announcement. Shiloh had gone into shock. Sandra Timmons had fled the room, and Jules had had to handle things from there.

Shiloh only wanted Caden at that point, so Jules had contacted him right away and asked him to get over to Shady Pines immediately.

Caden had arrived in what Jules knew was less than half the time it would normally have taken to get to Shady Pines from downtown Charlottesville. He had walked into the room and gone immediately to his wife, who was still sitting on the sofa in a daze.

Jules watched and felt a sharp tug at her heart as Caden, without asking any questions, kissed his wife on the lips before sweeping her into his arms. Moments later, just before leaving, he thanked Jules for calling him, and then they were gone. He hadn't taken time to ask questions or seek answers. It was as if he knew what Shiloh needed, and the first thing was to get her away from Shady Pines.

Jules shook herself, trying to step away from the ugly scene she'd been a party to at the Timmons estate. If she lived to be a thousand she would never forget the admissions she'd heard from Sandra Timmons.

She came back to reality. She took a look at her own life, accepting that she had fallen in love with Dalton. There was no need to deny it, because it was true. But if nothing else, she knew from their time together on Sunday that Dalton would never see her as anything but a sexual object. One he was now trying to possess by wanting them to be exclusive. She couldn't let him do that. She wanted the kind of love Shana had with Jace, the kind Shiloh had with Caden. Since there was no way Dalton could or would ever provide that kind of love to her or any woman, she might as well cut her losses and move on.

She needed to concentrate on this investigation and not become distracted. And Dalton was a distraction. A delicious one, but a distraction, nevertheless. Next time she saw him, she would let him know her decision—it would be best if they didn't see each other again.

She checked her watch. It was late, and there was so much at stake right now. Manning had left for home hours ago, and she'd told him she wouldn't be long in leaving the office herself. But she was still here. She had stayed back to finish up her notes on the meeting with Sandra Timmons and to review everything she knew about Vance Clayburn. Sandra Timmons claimed the two of them were together somewhere on the day Sylvia Granger was murdered. Was that true? Jules would certainly check that alibi. Where had they been? Was she telling the truth or was she protecting Clayburn again? It wouldn't be the first time she'd gone out of her way to protect him. She'd even let her husband believe she was having an affair with Sheppard Granger to protect him. And, of all things, the man was Shiloh's biological father. What a mess.

It was getting late, and she was tired. The first thing on her agenda tomorrow morning would be to go talk to Mr. Clayburn himself. And she would refuse to be put off. Grabbing the files off her desk and her coat from the rack, she drew in a deep breath and left her office, heading for home.

Bruce studied all the computer components on the table in front of him. He had received verification that Brandy Booker's computer had been wiped clean, as he'd suspected.

It was late, but he just couldn't let this problem go. He was convinced things were just as he'd explained to Marcel and the Grangers earlier today. Someone had created this spyware and installed it in a set of headphones. So far, only two pair of headphones had turned up, and both had been owned by employees of Granger. Were Granger employees being targeted for some reason? But what if—and he was allowing his imagination to run wild—what if other corporations had been targeted? What if they didn't know about it? What information was being collected and why? And who would benefit?

He picked up his phone and dialed a private number only he and one other person knew. They could connect with each other when one of them needed to bounce an idea off the other. His friend lived in DC and worked for one of those federal agencies most people didn't even know existed.

As soon as the person came on the line, he said, "I need you to put your thinking cap on. I want to run an idea by you, and I need you to confirm whether it has merit."

Jules let her head fall back after looking out her peephole. Dalton was standing there. There was no doubt in her mind that she would let him in, but wasn't it just earlier that day in her office that she'd decided to stop seeing him because he was a distraction? But it was about more than being a distraction. She had fallen in love with a man who didn't want or deserve her heart.

So why was she thinking that she would break it off with him another day? Not tonight, not when her heart was pumping fast just knowing he was standing on the other side of her door. Not when there was this deep stirring in the pit of her stomach at the thought of just what he would do once he got inside.

The latter is what had her opening the door, taking a step back and saying, "Come in, Dalton."

His gaze raked over her as he stood there in the doorway. "Miss me?"

So now he wanted to collect, she thought. Okay, she would be honest with him. "Yes, I miss you."

A smile spread across his lips. And it happened just the way she had known it would, just as she'd been hoping. Expecting. He slammed the door shut behind him, swept her into his arms and headed for her bedroom.

A short while later, when Dalton slid off Jules to lie beside her, he gathered her into his arms and whispered against her damp cheek, "I think you're trying to kill me."

Smiling ruefully, she snuggled closer to him. "I was just thinking the same thing about you."

Dalton knew he would never, ever tire of this. A willing woman. An insatiable woman. A very beautiful woman.

A woman he loved.

"You're not dozing off to sleep on me, are you?" he asked, leaning over and nudging her.

Her lips curled into a smile as she reopened her eyes. "While you're in my bed with the stamina of a bull? Never." She paused a moment and then added, "Although I did have one hell of a day."

He tightened his arms even more around her. "So I heard. We were at the office, ending our meeting with Marcel and Bruce, when Caden got your call. It's been years since I've seen him move that fast. Didn't know he still could."

"His wife needed him. And he came. Took charge. Swept her into his arms and saved the day."

Dalton kissed her cheek. "Are you getting sappy and romantic on me?"

Jules shrugged. "I guess I am." She glanced up at him. "Is that bad?"

He shook his head. "No, it's just not you."

"And it's not you, either."

But it could be, he thought. *It could be both of us*. Dalton knew now would be a good time to tell her how he felt about her, but knew she wasn't ready to hear it. Or accept it. For one, she probably wouldn't believe him. She would have to see his transformation gradually. He would love her forever. And only her. That was a lover's vow. One he intended to keep.

"Have you heard from Caden?" she asked, cutting into his thoughts.

He decided to change the subject somewhat. "Yes. He called back later to tell us what happened, and I gotta say we were all stunned when we heard the news. There is a lot to process, especially for Shiloh, but Caden did assure us several times that Shiloh was okay."

"I knew she would be," Jules said seriously. "She just needed Caden. And she's going to need some time to figure out what happens next, as far as her *family* is concerned."

"Yes, and at some point, she's going to have to deal with the fact that Samuel Timmons wasn't her biological father. Personally, I'm glad he wasn't."

Jules shook her head. "And to think Sandra Timmons allowed her husband to believe she was having an affair with your father to safeguard her secret. And what is even sadder is that I honestly think she believes your father killed your mother."

"That just goes to show how demented she is," Dalton said, glancing down. He hadn't covered their bodies, and he enjoyed seeing them lying together like this. Naked. Limbs entwined.

"She claims she and Sylvia were close friends."

"I always thought they were. But who remains close friends with a woman who sleeps with your former lover?" He couldn't help looking at her breasts and thinking she had the sexiest nipples.

"You have a point there. But according to Sandra Timmons, she never told your mother of her and Vance's history. And since she hadn't told Vance of her friendship with your mother, she forgave him for it."

"Big heart," Dalton said sarcastically.

"I'll say." She paused for a minute. "There was something else she said that I want to investigate further."

"What's that?" Dalton asked, feeling himself getting hard again.

"That your mother was using Vance Clayburn to gain information about his business. Why would she want to know about a computer business?"

"You got me. Let me know when you find out. But for now, all I want to do is this." He leaned down, tightened his hold and kissed her.

Forty

The next morning Jules walked into Vance Clayburn's office and was surprised when his secretary smiled and said, "He's expecting you, Ms. Bradford."

Really? This ought to be interesting. Jules followed the woman into Vance Clayburn's office.

"Come in, Ms. Bradford. Please have a seat," Clayburn said, offering her a chair across from his desk. "I got a call from Sandra Timmons last night. I figured after your meeting with her that you would probably have a few questions for me."

"Thank you for seeing me, Mr. Clayburn," she said, sitting down in the chair. "And you're right. I do have some questions for you. Several, in fact."

He leaned back in his seat. "Fire away. I have nothing to hide."

Jules nodded. "Do you mind if I record our conversation? Makes it easier when I need to write up my notes."

"I don't have a problem with it. Like I said, I have nothing to hide."

"That's good to hear," she said, starting her mini-recorder. "Now then, before we get started I just want to let you know that I am reopening the Sylvia Granger murder investigation. I have questions for several people, and my first question for you is where were you on the day Sylvia Granger was killed?"

A smooth smile touched his lips. "That's easy enough to remember. I was with Sandra Timmons."

"Would you care to elaborate? Where were you?"

"At a hotel in DC. We were there for two days. We heard about Sylvia's death on the news the day we checked out of the hotel."

"And when did the two of you check in to the hotel?"

"We checked in to the hotel the day before Sylvia Granger was killed."

"Do you have proof the two of you were together during that time?"

"That was close to fifteen years ago, and I certainly haven't kept receipts from that time, but if I have to prove it, then I can...and I will."

Jules leaned back in her chair. "I must ask some personal questions of you, Mr. Clayburn. Did you and Sandra Timmons often have romantic rendezvous?"

He held her stare. "On occasion. After college, we went our separate ways and married other people, but then we ran into each other years later in New York. By then, she and Samuel had a son. I was in New York on a business trip, and she was there with her mother-in-law on a shopping spree. We happened to be staying at the same hotel. Sandra's mother-in-law was a sound sleeper and, well, Sandra managed to get away once she was asleep for the night. She came to my room. The spark we felt for each other had never gone away. I can assure you that neither of us planned this. I will say that I think it was during that time that Shiloh was conceived."

Jules didn't say anything for a minute, and then she

asked, "When was the next time you saw Sandra Timmons again after that time in New York?"

"Not for a long, long time. I happened to be in Charlottesville on business about fourteen years later. I looked her up. We got together."

Jules nodded. "And how long were you in Charlottesville at that point?"

"Around six months."

"You went out to Shady Pines during that time, didn't you?"

He held her gaze. "Yes, and Sandra told me we had been seen together by someone. In the stables."

"Yes, you were."

He shrugged. "I only went there because I knew Samuel was out of town, and I wanted to convince Sandra to leave him. She'd confided that he'd become abusive and was becoming worse. I saw her bruises and tried persuading her to leave him. But she refused. She said he would take her children away, and she couldn't let him do that. I got angry. Very angry."

And he was getting angry just talking about it. Jules could hear it in his voice. "Is that why you got involved with Sylvia Granger? Out of spite?"

Jules thought she actually saw pain in his features. "No, not out of spite. The fact that she was refusing to leave Samuel for me, when I knew she loved me, was hard for me to accept. I was hurt. Deeply. I would have ended my marriage for Sandra, but she refused to leave an abusive husband because of her children. He had already threatened to fight her for custody if she ever tried to leave. Of course, at the time, I didn't know one of the children was mine."

He didn't say anything for a minute. "As for Sylvia Granger, she is the one who sought me out, not the other way around. I guess you can say she got to me when I was most vulnerable. She had an agenda, and she used me. She didn't know my history with Sandra and, at the time, I didn't know that she and Sandra were close friends."

He paused a moment and then said, "But it was just that one time. At the boathouse."

"How did you get on the estate without anyone knowing about it?"

"We got there by boat."

"Boat?"

"Yes. The boathouse is on a waterway that feeds into Mammoth Lake. Sylvia owned a small boat that she kept to go back and forth to the marina."

This information was critical. Jules wondered whether this was how the killer had gotten on and off the estate without being seen. She would need to investigate this location right away.

He glanced at his watch. "Now, Ms. Bradford, I hope I've answered your questions satisfactorily. I do have another appointment in a few minutes."

"I'll try to be quick, but I do have a few more if you don't mind." She knew he wanted to say that he did mind, but he probably figured if he answered all her questions now, she wouldn't have to come back.

"Fine, what additional questions do you have for me?"

"Ms. Timmons indicated that Sylvia used you, and you just basically said the same thing. Could you elaborate on that?"

"At the time, I owned one of the largest computer companies in the Silicon Valley, and she wanted to know everything about it."

Jules lifted a brow. "Why?"

"She didn't ever really say, but I found it interesting that she would take any opportunity to discuss my business."

"Was there anything specific she was interested in?"

He shrugged. "Several things, but mainly my expectations regarding Y2K."

"Y2K? I remember reading about that when I was in college."

"Then you know it was the disaster that never was."

Jules nodded in agreement then paused a minute and asked, "Ms. Timmons is certain Sheppard Granger killed his wife. Do you share her sentiments?"

"No, I do not."

She angled her head and stared at him, somewhat surprised by his answer. "Would you care to share your opinion about who did?"

He was quiet for a moment. "Of course, no one asked me, because no one other than Sandra ever knew about my one-time affair with Sylvia, and no one knew that we had met several times prior to that so Sylvia could 'learn' more about computers. But, had I been asked, I would have told them the one person who had a motive for killing Sylvia was the Grangers' housekeeper, Hannah."

Jules kept the surprised look from her face. "And why do you think it was Hannah?"

"Because she and Sylvia didn't get along. And I understand the two women had words earlier that day and that Hannah had threatened her."

Jules's brows bunched. "Hannah had threatened Sylvia?"

"So Sylvia claimed. Of course, I wasn't there to hear it myself. Sylvia was upset and said she didn't care that

Hannah had been with the Grangers for years. She had to go. It was either her or Hannah."

Jules didn't say anything for a minute as she thought about what Vance Clayburn had just said.

"Makes sense, don't you think?"

His question invaded her thoughts. "What makes sense?"

"That Hannah killed Sylvia."

She leaned forward. "And why would that make sense, Mr. Clayburn?"

"It would explain how Sheppard Granger's gun came to be in the boathouse. If he didn't take it from the Granger estate, then who did?"

Jules's mind was in a complete turmoil by the time she returned to her office. Vance Clayburn's question was still burning her ears. *If he didn't take it from the Granger estate, then who did?*

That was a good question, but the possibility that Hannah had been involved was hard to come to terms with—it was completely mind-boggling.

But what *if* everything Vance Clayburn had said was true? What if Hannah had threatened Sylvia, and Sylvia had tried to get Hannah fired? That would certainly give Hannah a motive. The woman had been with the Grangers for years and was considered part of the family. And if she believed Sylvia was unfaithful to Sheppard and had confronted her about it, then…

She grudgingly moved Hannah's profile to the suspects' column of her investigative wall, trying to push to the back of her mind what Dalton had just said days ago… *Hannah helped my brothers and me retain our sanity through the craziness of my father's trial. She means the world to us, and if you mess with Hannah, then you mess with all three of us.*

She didn't want to think about how the Grangers would feel when they discovered their beloved Hannah was now a suspect. She'd given Manning the task of verifying Clayburn's and Sandra Timmons's alibis. Had they really been in DC at a hotel together when Sylvia was murdered? If anyone could confirm that, it would be Manning.

When her buzzer went off, she moved to her desk. "Yes, Manning?"

"You have guests."

She frowned. "Who is it? I'm not expecting anyone."

"Michael and Yolanda Greene are here."

Surprise lit Jules's eyes. "No one else? Not their son, Ivan?"

Manning said quietly into the receiver, "Not unless he's invisible."

"Funny. Give me a second before sending them in."

Jules couldn't help wondering what had brought the Greenes to her office. But first she had to get rid of her investigation wall. Using her remote, she turned off the screen. And, just in time. The door opened, and a couple she knew to be Michael and Yolanda Greene walked in.

She crossed the room to greet them. "Mr. and Mrs. Greene. I'm glad you're here."

"We know you came to the house to see us, but Ivan forbade you from talking to us. We decided to come to you, since we have nothing to hide."

Jules nodded, remembering that was the same thing Vance Clayburn had said earlier. "Then would you mind answering a few questions?"

"Not at all," Michael Greene said. "We told Ivan that

we wanted to be open and honest, and he understood, but he thinks he has to protect us."

"From what?"

"People who want to ruin his chance to be mayor."

"Oh, I see." It sounded to her like Ivan was trying to protect himself...or at least his political career. "Please have a seat."

"So what do you want to know?" Yolanda Greene asked. She and her husband were holding hands, as if giving each other support.

"I know about the affair between you, Mr. Greene, and Sylvia Granger. Further, my assistant was able to verify your alibi about being on a cruise at the time of the murder." She looked over at Yolanda Greene and saw pain etch her features.

"Were you aware that Sylvia was involved with another man at the same time?" Jules continued.

Michael Greene's features tightened. "No, but it doesn't surprise me. Sylvia only wanted an affair with me to gain information."

"About what?"

"My work at Granger Aeronautics."

"Could you tell me about what that work involved?"

"I was manager of the information systems department. Today, most businesses refer to it as the computer technology department."

Jules nodded. "What did Mrs. Granger want to know?"

"She was interested in a lot of computer stuff, which I admit I should not have shared with her...like what the company was doing to protect themselves from Y2K. What computer programming we were using. What software was out there to combat such a thing."

Jules didn't say anything. So far, according to what

she knew, the two lovers Sylvia Granger was reported to have had were both connected to the computer industry, and her main point of interest had been Y2K.

"Did she say why she was interested? It seems like an odd thing for someone like her to take an interest in," Jules remarked.

Michael Greene shook his head. "No. I figured she had been hit with the Y2K scare like a lot of people at that time. Our affair only lasted for a few months, and then she dropped me. Then Sheppard Granger found out, and I was fired immediately."

"And where did you and Sylvia meet when you got together?"

"At different hotels in the city."

"Never at the boathouse?" Jules asked.

Michael Greene shook his head. "No, never at the boathouse." He paused a minute and then added, "I made a mistake with Sylvia Granger, a terrible mistake, and I almost lost Yolanda because of it. We've worked hard over the past fifteen years to rebuild our marriage and have put that time behind us."

Jules nodded. "I can respect that, but at the same time, an innocent man has been in jail for over fifteen years and—"

"He's not innocent," Michael Greene said.

"You don't think so?"

"No. He knew about my affair with his wife, and that angered him. If she had had another lover besides me, that would make him even more angry, angry enough to kill her."

Jules was quiet for a minute. "I watched the video this past weekend of the grand opening of Shiloh's wine boutique and saw both of you behave very rudely to Caden Granger. Why was that? Caden and his brothers were just children when their father went to jail. What are you holding against them?"

"I think I can best answer that."

Jules's gaze moved from the Greenes to the doorway. Ivan Greene stood there with an angry Manning holding him back.

Forty-One

"Do you want me to throw him out, Jules?" Manning asked seriously.

She shook her head. "No, let him come in, especially if he can give me an answer to my question."

When Manning released Ivan, he rushed into the room. "Mom. Dad. I told the two of you that I would handle things."

"And we told you that we didn't mind talking to her. We have nothing to hide."

"That's not the point."

Jules crossed her arms over her chest. "Then what is the point, Mr. Greene? Why don't you tell me why you and your parents treated Caden so shabbily that night at Shiloh's open house? And, while you're at it, how about telling me why you were so interested in Marshall Imerson's report on the Sylvia Granger murder?"

He glared at her. "Why are you so interested in that report?" Ivan fired back.

"Because that report probably contained information proving that Sheppard Granger did not kill his wife," Jules responded.

"And I believed it contained information proving

otherwise, and that Marshall was killed before he could prove it."

Jules lifted her brow. "Marshall? Sounds like you knew Imerson personally since the two of you were on a first-name basis."

"I did. Fresh out of law school, I was a court-appointed attorney. My first case was defending a woman who'd been arrested for killing her boyfriend. Marshall was a detective on the case, and with his help, I was able to prove the woman had been abused and was defending herself. She was cleared of all charges, and Marshall and I had been friends since. He was older, and I considered him something of a mentor. With his help, I understood how law enforcement worked, and I got to know a lot of the guys around the precinct. They were invaluable whenever I worked a case."

He paused a minute and then said, "Marshall and I stayed in touch over the years, even after he went into business for himself as a private investigator. Imagine my surprise when he came to me and told me he had been hired by Richard Granger to find out who had killed his daughter-in-law and that my parents were the primary suspects."

He paused again. "I couldn't believe it. I had just finished law school a few months after Sheppard Granger's trial and had no idea my father had been involved with Sylvia Granger. I assumed the reason he'd left Granger Aeronautics was of his own choosing, not that he'd been fired. I also didn't know about my parents' marital problems even though my sisters did.

"After Marshall dropped this bombshell on me, I asked my parents about it, and they told me the truth. Mom told me about the PI she'd hired and the pictures she'd sent to Sheppard Granger showing Dad and Mrs.

Granger together. She also told me that she'd told Sheppard Granger that she and Dad had a solid alibi proving neither of them had anything to do with his wife's death. I think Sheppard believed their story, but Richard Granger did not. He was determined to find a scapegoat for his son and decided my parents would fill the role."

"That might not have been the case, Mr. Greene," Jules said. "Are you sure this isn't circumstantial evidence?"

"I had no reason to think otherwise. No one knew about my father's affair with Mrs. Granger, but to get his son out of jail, Richard Granger was determined to make it public information. When I heard that Marshall had been killed in a questionable accident…especially when it was well-known that he didn't drink…I knew someone was behind it. Someone didn't want Marshall's information to be made public. I'm sure Marshall discovered some incriminating information on Sheppard Granger, and Richard Granger arranged his accidental death."

Jules just stared at Ivan, and it was easy to tell by his expression that he truly believed what he said. "Mr. Greene, have you ever considered that perhaps the information Marshall Imerson discovered proved just the opposite? That Sheppard Granger did *not* kill his wife? And just to go back to Caden Granger for a moment, you still haven't explained why you and your family were so hostile to him."

Ivan hesitated a minute and then said, "When Richard died, I assumed my parents' secret was safe again. Then Richard's grandsons came to town, and rumors quickly began flying around that they, like Richard, intended to prove that Sheppard Granger was innocent. All I could see was them reopening the case and using my parents again as a scapegoat for what their father had done. We have no reason to be friends with people who want to ruin our family name."

Especially when the scandal could hurt your chances of becoming mayor, Jules thought. "Well, I happen to think that Sheppard Granger is innocent, and I have the information to prove it."

The intercom on Dalton's desk buzzed. "Yes, Ms. Pecorino?"

"Mr. Granger, Bruce Townsend is here to see you."

Dalton threw aside the papers he was reading. "Please send him in." He stood when Bruce walked in. "Bruce, what's going on? You here to search my office for one of those headphones?" he joked.

Bruce chuckled. "No, but last night I watched that security video of Brandy Booker searching your office, and there's one particular picture that she seemed interested in."

"Yes, that one over there," Dalton said, pointing to a framed painting on the wall. "She brought a camera and took several shots of that particular picture. Don't know why. There's nothing to it but a painting showing fireworks for a Fourth of July celebration."

Dalton leaned back against his desk and continued, "Marcel and his people checked it out. In fact, I just got it back a few weeks ago. They said it cleared their inspection, so they have no idea why she was interested in that one more than the others."

Bruce nodded. "Mind if I borrow it again?"

"Not at all." He watched Bruce take the painting off the wall.

"Thanks."

Before he opened the door to leave, Bruce turned

around. "By the way, did anyone ever find out who had this office before you moved in?"

Dalton nodded. "Yes. My mother. It was locked for years before I decided to move in here. The Feds found a key in Brandy's belongings, and it turned out to be my mother's key to this office."

"How did Brandy get it?"

"That's what Marcel is trying to figure out."

Manning walked into Jules's office. "Vance Clayburn was telling the truth. Hotel records verify that he and Sandra Timmons were together at a hotel those two days in DC."

Jules nodded. "Okay, then we can move them from here to here," she said, using the touch screen to shift their profiles to another area of her chart. "That means we need to concentrate on Ivan Greene for now until we determine where he was during those hours of recess that coincided with the time Sylvia was murdered. And I've got a new angle to investigate," she said, smiling.

Manning asked, "Y2K?"

Jules shrugged. "Why not? Both Michael Greene and Vance Clayburn claim that Sylvia Granger's interest in them was due to their knowledge of computers, and she asked questions specifically about Y2K."

"I was too young to really remember the big scare," Manning said.

"So was I, but I've been thinking over what I heard about that period of time. It was believed that with the arrival of the new millennium, entire computer systems around the world would crash and literally cause chaos worldwide. Everyone was freaking out at the thought of that happening, and during that time, most major corporations, banks and other financial institutions were at the mercy of any company that employed computer programmers, software engineers or anyone who had a solid knowledge of computers."

"Boy, that must have been scary," Manning said.

"And it should have been, but I don't think anyone really thought about the possibilities that issue could present. What if some computer-savvy individuals got together and decided to take advantage?"

Manning lifted a brow. "By doing what?"

"By installing their own software into computers. Software they could command and update without ever being detected."

A frown touched Manning's features. "Was that possible?"

"In the computer age, anything was possible."

"And you believe that actually happened at Granger?" Manning asked, rubbing his chin.

"That's a possibility we have to explore. I need the name of the computer company Granger Aeronautics hired to handle the Y2K scare."

Manning glanced back at the wall. "No problem. It shouldn't take long for me to get that." He paused a minute then said, "So you think Sylvia Granger's death might have been bigger than just a jealous husband, jealous lovers or jealous wives."

"Yes. I don't think it's a coincidence that both of her lovers feel she used them to obtain Y2K information. But that doesn't mean I'm shifting my focus from Ivan Greene."

"I hope I'm not interrupting, but I brought lunch."

Manning and Jules glanced up to find Dalton standing in the doorway with a huge bag in his hand. As he crossed the room to place the brown bag on her desk, he glanced over at her wall.

She braced herself as Dalton stopped dead in his tracks, a deep frown on his face. "Why is Hannah listed as a suspect?"

Jules glanced over at Manning. "Leave us alone for a minute, will you, please?"

Concern showed in Manning's gaze. "You sure?"

She smiled. "Positive."

He nodded, gave Dalton what Jules could only perceive as a warning look and left the room, closing the door behind him. She then turned her attention back to Dalton. "Thanks for lunch. To answer your question, she's there based on information I recently received."

He placed the bag on her desk and asked, "What information?"

"Why don't you sit down and I'll tell you?"

"I'm okay standing."

"Suit yourself," she said, sliding into her chair and reaching for the bag. "Smells like Chinese, and I'm hungry. Thanks."

"Stop stalling, Jules. Let's finish this discussion so we can get on with lunch."

He was right. She was stalling. "Did you know your mother and Hannah didn't get along?"

"They probably had their differences from time to time. Dad and Mom didn't get along all the time, either, but he didn't kill her."

"Did you know Hannah threatened your mother?"

"So did Dad."

"He did?"

"Yes. The night before she was murdered. We all heard them yelling, but we agreed not to mention it to the cops. But even making a threat in the midst of a frustrating argument doesn't mean he meant to kill her. And the same goes for Hannah."

"I'm just checking everyone out, Dalton. That's my job. But have you ever wondered how your father's gun got out there in the boathouse? Who would have access to it besides your dad?"

"I have no idea, Jules. But no matter what that inquisitive mind of yours is telling you, Hannah did not kill my mother."

"Do you know where she was on the day your mother was killed?" Dalton didn't say anything for a minute, and his anger was obvious. "After lunch, I'm heading over to Sutton Hills to question Hannah. Would you like to join me?" she asked.

Dalton held her gaze. "Wild horses couldn't keep me away."

After a quick lunch they arrived at Sutton Hills in record time, given that Dalton had suggested they ride in the same car. His. This was Jules's first time in his red death trap, and she wasn't sure she would survive.

He assisted her from the car. "You okay?"

"Yes, but I left my heart back at the intersection of Bond Road and Duval Boulevard. Did you have to speed all the way over here?"

He shrugged. "I figured you'd want to get here as soon as we could."

"Yes, but in one piece would have been nice."

"And speaking of nice," he said, sweeping his gaze over her, "you look good as usual. Did you know red is my favorite color?"

She glanced over at his car and then back at him. "I figured as much, but I hope you don't think I decided to wear this red dress today because of you."

He smiled and pulled her into his arms. "I can hope, can't I?"

Leaning down, he placed a kiss on her lips and then surprised her when he took her hand and led her to the massive front door. Pulling out a key, he opened it and ushered Jules in. "Hannah?" he called out.

It wasn't long before Hannah appeared from the back. Not for the first time, Jules recognized that Hannah was a beautiful older woman and could see why Richard Granger had fallen in love with her.

"Dalton! Ms. Bradford! Had I known you were coming, I would have prepared lunch."

Jules smiled. "Thanks, but we've eaten already. I hate to impose on your time, and you may not have heard, but I recently reopened the Sylvia Granger case and—"

"You did?"

Was that nervousness she heard in Hannah's voice? "Yes, yes, I did."

"That's good news if Shep will be released from jail," she said.

"Yes, it sure would be. I'm checking on a few things, and I'm here to ask you a few questions if that's all right."

"Me?" She looked at Dalton and then at Jules. "I don't understand. Why would you want to ask me any questions? I'm sure I can't have much to say that would shed any light on the matter."

Detecting anxiety in her tone, as well, Dalton reached out and took her hand. "It's just routine, Hannah. She had to ask Jace, Caden and me some questions, too. Come on, let's sit in the living room and get this over with."

Bruce studied the portrait he'd taken from Dalton's office. Already, he had scanned it for bugs, magnetic cameras and hidden spyware. Now he was searching the internet to determine the artist's name and when the scene had been painted. To be honest, he wasn't impressed with the artwork. But there had certainly been something about the painting that had interested Brandy Booker. And he was curious as to what that was.

Forty-Two

"What do you want to know, Ms. Bradford?"

Jules noted that Hannah's nervousness had increased and wondered whether Dalton had picked up on it, as well. "Mainly I'd like to know about your relationship with Sylvia. Did the two of you get along?"

Hannah glanced over at Dalton, and he gave her a supportive smile. "I won't lie to you. She wasn't the easiest person to get along with, but I did my best."

Jules nodded and decided to get straight to the point. "Sylvia mentioned to someone that you had threatened her and that you were afraid of losing your job here at Sutton Hills. Apparently, she was going to fire you."

Hannah's spine stiffened. "Yes, she said she was going to fire me. But she said that often enough that I just ignored it."

Jules didn't say anything for a minute. "And did you threaten her?"

"I knew what she was doing behind Shep's back, because I'd overheard her phone calls. I told her that I was going to tell him if it didn't stop. I guess maybe she saw that as a threat."

"And on the day she was killed, did the two of you argue?"

"Yes, we did."

"Can you tell us what about?"

She paused again. "It was about how she was treating Shep. I overheard her arguing with him the night before and again the following morning, after the boys went to school. It was terrible that morning. She refused to give him the divorce he had asked for. He had proof she was unfaithful. He was hurt. Broken. I'd never seen him so miserable, and it seemed as if she was determined to make things even worse for him. Seeing him that way broke my heart. He was a good man and didn't deserve that. She didn't deserve him."

"What happened after that?"

"He got in his car to leave, and I heard her tell him to meet her at the boathouse at noon or else."

"Or else what?"

"She didn't say, but he did tell her he would be there at noon. I was angry with her. She had hurt Shep, and he didn't deserve that. She got dressed, and I confronted her. We argued. She said she was going to demand that Shep fire me when they met later that day. She told me to start packing. Then she got in her car and left for the boathouse."

Jules glanced over at Dalton. He had been quiet and listening attentively. She wondered what he was thinking. She looked back at Hannah and saw the tears glistening in her eyes as she studied her hands. "Hannah, do you know how the gun got to the boathouse?"

Hannah glanced back up at Jules, and it was a long moment before she answered. "I took it there. I followed her. I was angry that she had hurt Shep so much. I confronted her, and she laughed at me. Even when she saw the gun, she told me I didn't have the guts to use it. And she was right. I didn't. I couldn't. No matter how much she had hurt Shep, or how much I hated her at that moment, I couldn't forget she was Jace, Caden and Dalton's mother. I put the gun down and left."

"You put the gun down where?"

"I left it on a table near the door."

Jules didn't say anything. She'd read the police report; according to Sheppard Granger, he arrived at the boathouse at noon and found the gun lying on the floor. He made the mistake of picking up the gun. Whoever had shot Sylvia had wiped their prints clean before putting it on the floor in a place where Shep would be sure to see it.

"Did you see *anyone* go to the boathouse after you left?"

"No. No one. I went straight back to the house and got back to work in the kitchen."

"Have you told anyone else what you told me today?"

Hannah nodded. "Yes, I told both Richard and Shep. I called Richard as soon as I got back here and told him what I'd done. I would have told the police about it, but neither Richard nor Shep would let me. They said they knew I didn't kill Sylvia, and that's all that mattered."

Hannah then turned to Dalton. "I'm so sorry, dear. I didn't kill her, but for those few minutes that day, I wanted to. In a way, I wish I had. Then I would be the one in jail instead of your father."

Without saying a word, Dalton went over to Hannah and pulled her to him. It was then that she began sobbing in his arms.

A short while later, after leaving Hannah, Jules suggested now would be a good time for her to check out the boathouse. She was surprised when Dalton offered to come with her since she'd heard none of the Grangers had been there since their mother's death.

He said nothing as she moved around quickly, going from room to room, making notes and taking pictures with her cell phone. All evidence that a murder had taken place had been removed long ago. With the furniture covered in drop cloths, the place was eerily silent.

As they left the boathouse about twenty minutes later to head back to Dalton's car, Jules asked, "Did you often access the boathouse via the water?"

"Yes. My parents owned a boat at one time, and sometimes their friends would come to visit in boats of their own. Are you thinking that perhaps that's how the killer got away without being seen?" he asked, opening the car door for her to get in.

Jules shrugged. "It's a definite possibility. Clayburn claims that's how your mother got him to the boathouse without being seen."

When Dalton slid behind the steering wheel, he glanced over at her and said, "Hannah was telling the truth. She didn't kill my mother."

Jules snapped her seat belt in place. "What makes you so sure?"

"Hannah might have been mad enough to confront my mother. Even mad enough to think she could threaten her, which is why she'd taken the gun. But my mother was right. She didn't have the guts…only because she has too much of a heart."

Forty-Three

"I love it when you do this," Jules moaned with closed eyes while Dalton massaged her feet. The past three days with him had been simply wonderful. They spent their nights together and woke up to make love each morning. She had worked late all three days, compiling her notes, moving people around on her wall and conducting more interviews. Today, Dalton had shown up at her office to take her to dinner. They never made it to the restaurant since the sexual heat between them had been unbearable. So instead, he had taken her home, stripped them both naked and made love to her. Then they had showered together and ordered takeout.

Now with a full stomach and dressed in a pair of jeans and a T-shirt, she was sitting on the sofa with Dalton. He had arranged their positions so her feet were in his lap while he massaged them.

"I love your hands on me," she said softly, opening her eyes and looking at him.

A smile curved his lips. "Where?"

"Everywhere."

"I like hearing that."

"I could get used to this."

Dalton leaned over and kissed her lips. "So could I."

Jules stared into the dark eyes staring back at her. They were talking about more than the massaging of her feet, and they both knew it. "Could you really, Dalton? Get used to this? One woman? One pair of feet in your lap? One relationship?"

"Only if that woman is you."

A knot caught in Jules's throat. Was he talking about exclusivity again or something else? She didn't want to jump to conclusions but…

She was about to ask for clarification when her cell phone rang. The ringtone indicated it was Bruce. Earlier she had left a message for him to call her. She glanced over at Dalton. "I need to get this."

"Yes, Bruce? I know it's late but can you meet me at my office? In around thirty minutes?"

A few seconds later she smiled and said, "Great! I'm on my way."

She clicked off the phone. "That was Bruce. While putting together all the information I've been gathering this week from persons of interest, something kept coming up."

"What?"

"Y2K. Both Greene and Clayburn believe your mother only initiated affairs with them to find out information about it. I have a hunch about something that I want to discuss with Bruce tonight."

Dalton pulled himself up off the sofa and then reached out his hand to her. "Then come on. Let's go."

Marcel pushed the documents he was reading aside when his phone rang. "Special Agent Eaton."

"You are the federal agent who handled everything

that went down at Granger Aeronautics a few months ago, right?"

Marcel leaned back in his chair, wondering whom he was talking to. "That's right. What can I do for you?"

"I remember seeing your name in the newspaper when Jace Granger was kidnapped. I need someone to talk to, to tell them what I know. I've got journals, and I've made audio recordings. I've got names. But my life is in danger, and the lives of those I care most about have been threatened if I don't do what they want. I have a feeling these people are about to get rid of someone who's working to expose what they are doing and—"

"Who *is* this?"

"I can't tell you now."

"Can we meet and talk? If someone's life is in danger, I need to know."

The caller paused and then said, "I can't come to your office. They will know."

Marcel knew of a place he used whenever he met with informants. It was late but he could have his men in place to make sure no craziness happened. "Are you familiar with the Wiltshire area?"

"Yes."

"There's an abandoned warehouse in the center of the complex. Can you meet me there in half an hour?" Marcel asked, already out of the chair and sliding into his jacket.

"Yes."

And then there was a click, and the caller was gone.

"Okay, Bruce," Jules said, sitting down in her office chair while Dalton took the sofa. "Based on information I've obtained this week, this is what I believe." She then told Bruce her idea about Y2K, the same thoughts she had shared with Manning.

"Funny you should think that about Y2K. I got a painting off the wall in Dalton's office a few days ago. It was the one Brandy seemed interested in those times she searched his office. I discovered the artist, Jeb Peters, was one of those who helped promote the Y2K scare back then."

"Why?" Dalton asked.

"He was one of those people who refused to use or acknowledge technology. He thought Y2K was real and would be God's punishment to a world too dependent on technology. Which is why he also believed it was a passing fad."

Dalton shook his head. "Boy, was he wrong."

"Based on what I found out about that painting, I checked with a contact I have in DC and what I was told pretty much backs up what you're thinking, Jules. Homeland Security believes there was a group of computer-savvy individuals who got together during the Y2K scare and decided to take advantage," Bruce added.

"How could they do that?" Dalton asked.

"Like Jules said, during the Y2K scare, it was believed that with the arrival of the new millennium, the entire computer system would crash and cause chaos. People's fears were out of control because most people didn't know enough about computers, and they would believe almost anything. I can see how someone savvy could take advantage of the situation. In fact, it would have been fairly easy to do."

"I agree," Jules added. "All they would have to do is install their own software onto another computer or computers. Software they could command and update without ever worrying about it being detected."

"And you believe that actually happened?" Dalton asked, rubbing his chin.

Jules met his gaze. "Yes, and to be completely honest, I have a hunch that's what happened at Granger Aeronautics, which would explain the ability to wipe out those hard drives. And I believe those headphones were a way to update the software or transfer it to a new computer, which would need to be done every so often."

"I totally agree," Bruce said, rubbing the back of his neck. "I tried calling Marcel on the way here but he had just left his office, so I couldn't reach him. I will have to fill him in on everything later."

"Damn," Dalton muttered. "A network of people?"

"Yes, and all of them computer savvy. Experts," Bruce said, sliding into the chair across from Jules's desk. "Not sure how many, but it's my guess that over the years, it's grown to include new members and even more sophisticated technology. No telling what information they are pulling out of computers."

"Or putting in there," Jules added. "Or how far they will go to make sure nobody finds out about them."

"And you think my mother somehow got involved in such a network?" Dalton asked Jules.

"Yes, and I believe that's why she was killed. That picture on the wall was a clue she deliberately left behind, but nobody was able to make a connection until now," Jules said. "I asked Manning to find out the name of the company that was hired to handle the Y2K scare at Granger Aeronautics. It's a company by the name of Triple H Computer Company. I've spent the last several days doing extensive research on them and as hard as it is for me to believe, I think I've made a connection between them and your mother's death."

"You've certainly been a busybody, Ms. Bradford. Unfortunately, your curiosity is going to cost you."

Jules, Dalton and Bruce turned and saw a familiar couple standing in the doorway with guns aimed directly at them.

Forty-Four

"Un-fucking-believable," Dalton muttered through shocked lips.

"Just as I suspected," Jules said, not shocked at all.

Bruce stared at the guns leveled at them, and for the time being, he decided not to say anything.

"Don't start the party without me," a third person said, entering the room also brandishing a gun. "We have not been followed," he said to his colleagues.

Jules stared into the faces of Harold and Helen Owens…and Gary Coughlin.

When he saw her staring at him, he winked and said, "Yes, sweetheart, it's me. You may remember me as Gary Coughlin but please, call me Garrett Herbert. I'm Harold and Helen's silent partner at Triple H Computers."

"We need the three of you in the center of the room, so don't try anything. I would hate to kill any of you in here. The blood would leave a nasty stain on such gorgeous floors," Helen Owens said. "Now move."

Jules wished she had time to pull her Glock out of her desk drawer, but decided not to take a chance. But she did have time to activate the audio record button located on the underside of her desk without detection.

"Now where were we?" Harold Owens said, grinning as the three of them stood in front of Jules's desk. "Oh, yeah, so now you know our computer company is the one involved with Y2K at Granger Aeronautics. And, just as you suspected, we were involved in Sylvia's death. Why don't you appease their curiosity, Helen?"

"Certainly, dear."

Dalton stared at the elderly couple, who seemed far too old for this sort of thing. Who did they think they were? Bonnie and Clyde? And what about Garrett Herbert, the man Jules had flirted with that night at Shana's party? Considering the ages of the three, he figured that he, Bruce and Jules should be able to overtake them easily. But then, the three were packing some serious-looking weapons. He wouldn't do anything stupid to put Bruce and Jules at risk. He just hoped like hell that Stonewall had put things together and had called the police.

"Dalton," Helen Owens said, grabbing Dalton's attention. "That mother of yours was really a piece of work. The computer network was my idea. I figured I would involve a few women who were smart enough to want to make more millions than they already had. But all most of them wanted were their tea parties, social clubs and charities. The only one I felt comfortable inviting in was Sylvia. She liked the idea. But then she got greedy. Thought she could run the show because she was younger. She didn't know the first thing about computers, but she was a threat, nevertheless. Figured one day she would try to take things away from Harold and me. And I couldn't let her do that."

"So you killed her," Jules said, making a statement rather than asking a question.

Helen's gaze shifted from Dalton to Jules. "Yes, I killed her, and I took great pleasure in doing so. I was the one building my network, the one driving the business forward. Sylvia Granger had forgotten I was the star. Not her."

Dalton couldn't believe what a monster this woman must be to stand there and openly admit to killing his mother. Yes, he could see that even now Helen Owens was the star, and that Harold and Herbert were just two of her yes men.

"Homeland Security will bring you down," Bruce said. "They are on to you."

Helen waved his words away. "Let them try. They will fail just like the FBI did. They have been trying to crack us for years. Now we're too big. Our network stretches too far and wide. We are in places you wouldn't even think of. I plan to take over the world."

"The world?" Dalton asked, thinking the old broad had really lost her marbles. He knew all about how to set high goals, but this was ridiculous.

"Yes, and I know you're thinking I'm just a crazy old woman, Dalton. But I'm also a smart one. And I'm ruthless. My players know this. Sylvia might have been the first casualty, but she wasn't the last. Others have thought the three of us are old and past it. But they soon found out a bullet knows no age limit."

"And who's responsible for killing Brandy Booker?" Bruce asked.

"I am," Garrett Herbert said proudly. "She started out doing what she was told, but then she began asking too many questions. All she had to do was find the information from that picture on the wall. I even gave her a key to make things easy for her. And I told her where to look, but she didn't follow orders. At least with Ramona Oakley, I didn't need her to do anything that raised her suspicions."

"How did you get the key?" Jules asked.

"I cleaned out Sylvia's purse after I killed her," Helen said, as if killing people was something she did every day.

"And what was so special about that picture?" Dalton asked, carefully trying to inch closer to Jules.

"I can answer that," Bruce said. "All this time, everyone assumed it was a painting of the Fourth of July with all the fireworks going off in the sky, but it was a New Year's Eve celebration for the new millennium. If you look closely, you can see Y2K written in one of the firecrackers. Sylvia was smart enough to leave that clue behind. Evidently, at some point, she knew not to trust you three."

"Enough talking," Harold said. "Both you and Helen have told them too much. But since they have to die, anyway, I guess it doesn't matter."

"And how are you going to explain our deaths?" Jules asked. Like Dalton, she was hoping Stonewall had put two and two together and right now all she knew was that she had to stall for time.

"Easy," Helen said. "Each one of us is taking you to three different places. We have other players waiting to assist. They have orders to kill you and dispose of your bodies so you will never be found. I wish I had thought of doing that to Sylvia."

"Instead, you framed my father," Dalton said angrily.

"Which was so easy to do," Helen said, smiling. "I saw that gun on the table and figured I would use it. Sylvia mentioned Sheppard was on his way to the boathouse for a meeting, which fell right into my plans. After shooting her, I wiped my prints from the gun and put it in a place where Sheppard couldn't miss seeing it when he walked in. What happened worked like a charm."

Trying to keep the conversation going, Jules asked, "And you got off Sutton Hills how?"

"By boat. Simple, really."

"Enough talking," Herbert said, smiling. "Before I turn you over to the players, Ms. Bradford, I plan on enjoying you the way I had intended that night Granger so rudely interrupted us during the dinner party."

"Over my dead body," Dalton said in a threatening tone.

"Trust me," Helen chuckled. "That can be arranged. By morning, you *will* be dead."

"Since you plan to kill us, anyway, you might as well answer a few questions that have me puzzled," Jules said, trying to stall. "Why kill Marshall Imerson?"

"I can answer that," Harold Owens said. "He found out too much."

"Enough talking," Herbert said again. "We need to get going. I'll handle the PI."

Knowing he needed to stall even more and because he wanted Jules to know how he felt in case he didn't make it, Dalton said, "Before we leave, I have something to say to Jules, since this might be my last chance."

"Trust me, son," Harold said, chuckling. "It will definitely be your last chance."

"Then I have something to say to her." He turned to Jules. "I love you. I thought I would have time to show you, to prove it to you and convince you of just how much I do, but if these clowns are really serious, I just wanted you to know how I felt."

Jules stared into Dalton's eyes. Even from a distance, she could feel anger and rage pouring from him, but she saw something else. At first she thought he was just stalling for time, but all it took was a look in his eyes to see he was dead serious. Tears filled her eyes. "Oh, Dalton."

"How touching," Herbert sneered. "Now, let's go. Move it, Ms. Bradford."

"Drop your guns. You're under arrest."

Shots rang out, the first coming from Herbert's gun. Jules was thrown to the floor, and she was aware of Dalton's body covering hers. Bruce had managed to pull out his gun and was protecting them both.

Jules glanced up and saw her entire office swarming with people. Marcel and his men were there, as well as Stonewall, Striker, Quasar, Roland and a few other men she didn't know.

"Are the three of you okay?" Marcel asked, rushing over and helping them back to their feet.

"Yes, we're fine," Dalton said, pulling Jules into his arms. "I thought I had lost you."

She shook her head, smiling. "And I thought I'd lost you. Did you mean what you said? Or just stalling for time?"

Dalton leaned over and kissed her on the lips. "I meant every word."

"Good, because I love you, too. I love you so much, Dalton."

A woman's scream snatched their attention, and they glanced over to Helen Owens. "These handcuffs are too tight," she hollered at the young federal agent who had cuffed her. "Don't you know I'm old enough to be your grandmother?"

"Oh, now she wants respect," Bruce said, shaking his head.

"And by the way," Jules said to the three criminals. "Just in case you want to deny anything you said in here tonight, you've been recorded. Every single thing you said is on tape."

"And just so you know," Marcel added, "Homeland Security has taken over all your computer stores across the country and is searching them right now. They've already arrested some of your players, and I understand a lot of them are talking. So you and your network are being shut down, Mrs. Owens."

She lifted her chin. "No matter. I am still the star."

Marcel rolled his eyes. "Get her out of here."

Taking Jules's hand in his, Dalton approached Stonewall, Striker and Quasar, who were standing together, staring in fascination at Jules's wall.

"I was hoping you had figured out what was going on, Stonewall."

Stonewall nodded. "Didn't take me long when I saw the older couple and remembered them from Shana's dinner party. I couldn't see any reason for them to be here, and I called Roland right away. I also called Striker and Quasar. I figured they were close by and could get here before Roland in case I needed backup."

"Well, I appreciate you guys being here."

At that moment, Jace, Caden and their wives rushed through the door. Shana grabbed her sister. "Are you okay? Striker called and told us what was going down. We were so scared."

"I'm fine," she said and then glanced up at Dalton. "The man I love was with me the entire time."

"Love?" several voices said simultaneously.

"Yes, love," Dalton said. "And I love Jules, as well."

Jace and Caden just stared with dropped jaws. "Please close your mouths," Dalton said, grinning. "The two of you can fall in love—so why can't I?"

"It's not that we thought you couldn't," Jace said, recovering from shock. "We just figured you never would."

"I thought so, too," he said, looking down at Jules. "But she is a woman a man can't help but love." He leaned over and kissed Jules's lips.

"Thanks for calling Marcel, you guys," Dalton added.

"We didn't call Marcel," Shana said. "I wonder who did."

Marcel grinned. "I got a call this evening from an informer. He came with journals, audio and enough information to help shut down the whole network. Seems like he took it upon himself to infiltrate the organization to help blow their cover."

"Who was it?" Caden asked.

"Me," a deep voice said. They all turned around.

"Sedrick!" Shiloh exclaimed, rushing over to her brother. "But how? What are you talking about?"

"After Dad died, Harold Owens approached me with his crazy idea, but I wanted no part of it. Then they threatened to harm you and Cassie if I didn't cooperate. I knew that I had to do whatever I could to shut them and their organization down. The first thing he and his group asked me to do was to make sure Richard Granger didn't survive his heart attack."

"You're kidding. Granddad?" Jace asked.

"Yes. But Richard died because his heart gave out, not because I gave him the injection to kill him, which they had ordered me to do. But they didn't know that."

394   *Brenda Jackson*

"They actually wanted you to kill Granddad?" Caden asked, not believing what he was hearing.

"Yes. Richard was determined to free Sheppard, and they figured sooner or later he would find out too much. They also killed Marshall Imerson. I recently got wind that they were going to kill Jules."

"B-but I had no idea," Shiloh said, smiling up at her brother.

"That was my plan. That's why I tried keeping you and Cassie at a distance and acted like a jackass to drive both of you away. Harold and Helen were always watching and listening. Trying to find my weakness. But no matter how mean I was to you, you put up with it, and Cassie refused to leave me."

"Because I love you. And Cassie loves you, too," Shiloh said, reaching up and patting her brother's cheek.

"I love you, too. And I love Cassie. I can't wait to get home tonight, tell her everything and apologize. I think I'm going to take a few days off from the hospital and take her somewhere. And propose."

Shiloh gave her brother a big hug. "That's great, Sedrick, and it's about time."

"Well, we appreciate your contacting us tonight and unloading all those goodies," Marcel said. "Dr. Timmons even has a list of names of some of the players. Thanks to him, we have a good chance to arrest most of those involved."

Marcel paused a minute and then added, "We got here as quickly as we could, but it's those guys over there who were already poised and in place to handle things." He tilted his head toward Stonewall, Striker and Quasar. "They are something else. I wish they would come work for me."

"Sorry," Roland Summers popped his head in to say. "They're already taken."

"Maybe we can negotiate," Marcel said, grinning.

"Or possibly work together from time to time," Roland countered.

"She killed Mom," Dalton said, a short while later as he stood alone with his family and Jules in Jules's office. His gaze was on Jules as she stood a few feet away, showing Shana her wall.

"So now we know what happened," Jace said. "Dad will be set free."

"Yes," Caden said, nodding his head. "Dad will be freed."

Dalton glanced over at Jules and smiled. "Excuse me, guys. I need a little private time with my lady."

He then crossed the room and pulled Jules into his arms. "Everyone seemed fascinated by your wall."

"I am fascinated by the man who has a Cocoa Puffs tattoo and enjoys making love to me with my boots on."

Dalton threw his head back and laughed. "And I am deeply in love with a woman who looks totally gorgeous in red and who can make my heart throb with any outfit she wears...especially with a pair of stilettos."

Taking her hand, he pulled her into the supply closet next to her office and closed the door. "Privacy at last."

"Not much and not for long," Jules said, smiling up at him. "I love you."

"And I love you." Dalton then leaned down and laid one hell of a kiss on the woman he loved.

Forty-Five

The next morning the following headlines appeared in papers across the country:

Virginia Socialites are Ringleaders in a 5 Billion Dollar Computer Fraud Operation.

Arrests Made in Fifteen-Year Computer Network Scandal.

Senator John Monroe Arrested as Part of Computer Fraud Scheme with More Arrests to Come.

Fifteen-Year-Old Murder Solved—Sheppard Granger Set to be Released from Jail.

The last article was what held Dalton's attention while sharing breakfast with Jules the next morning. He had refused to let her out of his sight. They had had to go to FBI headquarters to give statements, and afterward, they had gone to his place. The moment he had closed the door behind them, he had taken her into the bedroom. There, he had undressed them both, licked every inch of her body, buried his head between her legs and given her an orgasm like no other. He'd then joined their bodies together while telling her over and over just how much he loved her.

Jace, Caden and their wives were on their way over to his place. And then, in what Dalton thought of as a Granger Convoy, they would caravan to the prison to bring their father home. Warden Smallwood had already contacted Jace. Both the FBI and Homeland Security had delivered papers overnight for Sheppard's immediate release. Others would join in the convoy with them, including Stonewall, Striker, Quasar and the other men whose lives Sheppard Granger had helped turn around.

A huge celebration was planned at Sutton Hills... and a wedding. Sheppard had made it known that he wanted to marry Carson as soon as it could be arranged. Already, his friend and former cellmate, Reverend Luther Thomas, had been contacted, and Hannah was busy preparing a wedding feast. According to Warden Smallwood, the media was camped outside the facilities, and a call from Hannah that morning to Jace confirmed the same thing was happening at Sutton Hills. Roland assured Jace that his men would protect the Grangers' privacy.

"You talked to your dad, right?" Dalton asked Jules.

"Yes. There is more good news. He's excited that the doctor confirmed yesterday that Mona's sight is returning. He expects it to be at one hundred percent in a month or so. Maybe before then. And he's glad everything turned out the way it did for your family. He sends his best regards to all of you."

He reached out his hand and captured hers. "*Our* family."

He then slid out of his chair and onto his knee in front of her. "Juliet Bradford, will you marry me?"

She stared down at him, not believing what he was asking. "B-but...but..."

"Just say yes."

She threw her head back and laughed. "Yes!"

When he stood up, she jumped out of her seat, off her feet and into his arms, straddling him with her legs. His hands supported her as they kissed, their tongues mingling in a way that made him want to explore her mouth forever and always. He was drowning but at the moment, he didn't care. He just needed this closeness with her, a closeness he'd never been able to have with any other woman. A closeness he knew he could only have with her. Now he understood. His brothers had tried to explain things, but he hadn't believed them. He needed to experience this kind of love for himself. Now he was.

He broke off the kiss to catch his breath. Breathing hard, he placed his forehead against hers. Listening to the sound of her breathing, just as labored as his own, had him hoping neither one of them had a heart attack from too much of this.

"When?" she asked in a choppy voice. "When do we get married?"

He lifted his head a little to look into her eyes. "As soon as possible. I want the world to know you're mine and mine alone."

She chuckled. "Definitely not today. It's your father's day. His day with Carson."

He nodded. "Yes, this is Dad's and Carson's day."

"Not next month. It's Caden's charity concert. But definitely while Shana can still fit into a bridesmaid's dress."

"Is that possible?"

She pinched him. "Ouch!"

"That's my sister you're talking about. And speaking of babies…do you ever want any of your own?"

"I'm ready when you are."

She leaned back and stared even more deeply into his eyes. "Thank you. But not for a while yet. I want to enjoy my niece or nephew for a while."

"*Our* niece or nephew."

She shrugged. "I guess I'll share him or her with you."

She began disentangling herself from his arms, or at least she tried. "We need to get dressed. Everyone will be here in an hour or so. Today is a big day. I finally get to meet my future father-in-law. I'm looking forward to that."

"I know he's looking forward to meeting you." He took a firm grip on her hips and guided her gently toward the bedroom. "There will always be things we make time for. Making love will always be one of them, and baby, that time has come."

Sheppard Granger stood and looked out the prison library window. As far back as he could see through the gates of Delvers, newspaper reporters and television cameras lined the street. He shook his head. This was unreal. Almost unbelievable. Today, after fifteen years, he would walk out through those gates a free man. All because his family and good friends believed in him. Especially his sons. The three he'd fathered, and those he'd adopted as his own over the years.

"It's almost time, Sheppard."

He didn't have to turn around to know Ambrose was there. He nodded, and then his eyes widened when he saw the convoy headed toward the prison. Cars in a line as far back as he could see; there were at least fifty, maybe more. Of course, Dalton's little red death trap led the pack.

He turned around. "I know it sounds crazy, but I'm going to miss this place."

"No, it doesn't sound crazy. I believe the Man upstairs had a job for you to do here. You've done it, and now, Sheppard Granger, it's time for you to go home."

A smile touched Sheppard's face. "Yes, it's time to go home. I'm marrying a beautiful woman, the woman I love, and I have a grandbaby on the way. It's time for me to go home."

Crossing the room, he gave the man who'd looked out for him for a long time a bear hug. "You and your family will always be welcome in my home. Remember that."

Ambrose nodded. "Thanks. I will remember that."

Then Sheppard walked out of the room without looking back.

Dalton Granger glanced around, noting the hundreds of people assembled in the rose garden of the Granger estate. He hadn't expected a small wedding. Not for his dad. But for any man to have twenty best men was a little bit much, especially on such short notice. But here they all stood: Jace, Caden, Dalton, Stonewall, Striker, Quasar and fourteen others—all men whose lives Sheppard Granger had helped turn around at both Glenworth and Delvers. Some had gone back to school; many even to college, and others were business owners—successful men in their communities. All thanks to his dad.

Roland had walked Carson down the aisle, and Dalton thought she looked absolutely beautiful. She was wearing a beautiful blue dress, knowing blue was his father's favorite color. Seeing the tears that had formed in his father's eyes had almost been too much for Dalton. But all he had to do was look out among the guests to see that his own future wife was crying enough for both of them.

When Dalton had introduced Jules to his father, Sheppard had pulled his future daughter-in-law into his arms and thanked her profusely for all she'd done to make this day possible. He then gave Ben a big bear hug like the two were the best of friends. Dalton had a feeling the two men would be.

"I now pronounce you man and wife," Rev. Luther Thomas said, pulling Dalton's thoughts back to the business at hand. "Sheppard Granger, you may kiss your bride."

Dalton watched as his father pulled Carson into his arms and gave her a whopper of a kiss. Wow! He didn't know the old man had it in him. He guessed being locked up for fifteen years would have that kind of effect on you.

After a long kiss, the newlyweds turned to the guests as the reverend said, "I present to you, Sheppard and Carson Granger. May they have a long and happy marriage."

"Welcome home, Sheppard."

He crawled into bed beside his wife. "Welcome to Sutton Hills, Mrs. Granger." He leaned over and kissed her, not believing they were together after all this time. Next week they would leave for a while. She'd never been to Hawaii, and he wanted to take her there. Besides, he needed to get his bearings, take time for everything to sink in. And eventually things would, because he would have Carson by his side.

"Thanks for believing in me, Carson."

A smile touched her lips. "And thanks for being a man who was worth believing in."

He reached out to touch her and ease the straps of her pretty black negligee down her shoulders. He had waited five years to make love to her, and he couldn't wait a minute longer.

Using the tips of his fingers, he touched her everywhere and heard her sharp intake of breath when his fingers moved to certain areas, letting him know her hot spots. Before the night was over, he was going to make sure her entire body was hot.

Leaning in, he kissed her again, and when he released her lips, they were both panting for breath. "I love you, Carson," he whispered against her moist lips.

"And I love you," she said, staring up at him.

He eased his body over hers, joined their hands together, entwined their fingers and knew he was finally home. Desire and love filled him, and then he felt himself filling her. She arched her body into him, giving him the opportunity to go deeper, and he knew when he began moving inside her that his life was now perfect.

He held her gaze and saw the love in her eyes. It was the same love that had gotten him through the days and nights at Delvers, and tonight he intended to push them over the edge. There were no more limitations for them.

When she called his name as a spasm ripped through her, he felt it, and the strength of it pushed him over the edge, as well. He knew at that moment that this time, their first time together, had been well worth the wait.

Forty-Six

A month later...

"*T*his is Connie Moore reporting live from the Red Carpet of Charlottesville's annual Live-It-Up Ball to benefit cancer research. This year's entertainment is Grammy winner Caden Granger, who will be performing to a sold-out crowd. Tonight is particularly special, because it will be the first time his father, Sheppard Granger, will see his son perform. As most of you know, Sheppard Granger was released from jail after serving fifteen years for a crime he didn't commit. All the Granger men and their wives are expected tonight. It's no secret that the youngest Granger, Dalton, is engaged to be married. Sorry, ladies. Unfortunately, he's taken, and plans to tie the knot on New Year's Day.

"Everyone is excited and anxiously waiting for the Granger limo to arrive so we can all get a glimpse of those handsome men. In the meantime, here is our mayor-elect, Ivan Greene, arriving. Mr. Mayor, may we have a word with you?"

Ivan Greene smiled for the camera, showing a mouth full of dazzling white teeth. "Yes, Connie, I will always

*have time for the people of Charlottesville, and I'm
glad everyone came out to support such a worthwhile
cause tonight."*

*"Thanks, Mr. Mayor. And what do you think about
Sheppard Granger being released from jail after all
this time?"*

*Still smiling, Ivan faced the camera and said, "I'm
glad Mr. Granger was released. I, for one, never believed he was guilty..."*

"What the f—"

Jules slapped her hand over her fiancé's mouth before he could finish what he was about to say. They
were sitting in the limo with everyone and watching
the proceedings on the limo TV monitor. "Remember,
sweetheart, we are in the company of others," she said,
smiling. "And there are guests," she said, referring to
her father and Mona.

Dalton removed her hand from his mouth, kissing
her fingers, and then said, "Your dad and Mona aren't
guests. They're family. And please tell me, at what time
did Ivan Greene think Dad was innocent?"

Sheppard reached across the aisle of the limo and
placed a hand on his youngest son's shoulders. "Let it
go, Dalton. It doesn't matter anymore."

Jules glanced over at Dalton, saw that hard glint in
his eye and knew that he wouldn't let it go. *Oh, boy.*

"In a way, I don't blame Dalton," Caden said. "I
don't think I'll ever forget how the Greenes treated me
at Shiloh's open house. I might dedicate a song to them
tonight."

Dalton smiled. "Which one?"

"A musical rendition of 'Eating Crow.'"

"I got one better," Dalton countered. "How about
'Your Lying Heart?'"

Jace shook his head, grinning at his brothers. "I am so glad you're back, Dad. They are yours to tame."

When the limo pulled up to the red carpet, the driver opened the door, and everyone behind the ropes began screaming. Some for Dalton, some for Sheppard, others for Caden and some for Jace. Mostly for Caden. Jules knew men in black tuxes did things for some women.

Connie seized the opportunity to cop an interview with Sheppard. "Mr. Granger, I understand the state will compensate you for all that time you were unjustly incarcerated."

Smiling, Sheppard said, "That's what I understand. Any compensation will be going to the Sheppard Granger Foundation for Troubled Teens. Now if you will excuse me, my family and I need to get inside. I'm anxious to see my son perform tonight."

Sheppard and the others moved ahead, but Dalton hung back. It wasn't long before Jules figured out why. Ivan hadn't gone inside yet, and he was standing in a group surrounded by reporters while being interviewed.

"Hand me your lipstick," he said.

She lifted a brow. "What?"

"Hand me your lipstick."

"Which just happens to be your favorite color?"

He smiled down at her. "Yes, my favorite color."

She opened her purse and gave him the lipstick. She glanced back over at the mayor. Too bad he was wearing a white suit.

She watched Dalton ease his way through the reporters who were so busy listening to what the mayor was saying that no one noticed the word Dalton was writing on the back of the mayor's dinner jacket with her lipstick.

Dalton returned moments later, smiling. He handed

Jules's lipstick back to her and took her hand. "Now I can enjoy the evening."

She glanced over her shoulder just as the crowd of reporters around the mayor was disbanding. Her jaw dropped when she saw what Dalton had scrawled in flaming red on the back of Ivan Greene's white jacket: *Liar.*

She glanced over at Dalton and he winked, leaned close and whispered, "I wanted to write *Fucking Liar* but didn't have time."

She shook her head, fighting back a grin as they threaded through the other attendees who were also entering the auditorium. She knew that with Dalton she would never have a dull moment. He had told her about his time in the USN and his long-term affair with Lady Victoria, who was now married. He'd said he hadn't wanted any secrets between them.

Up ahead, she saw Sandra Timmons with Vance Clayburn. He had broken off his engagement to Nannette Gaither last month and had been seen around town with Sandra Timmons. According to Dalton, Shiloh was acknowledging Clayburn as her father. And Jules had heard about Sedrick's talk with Jace, explaining why he'd severed their friendship all those years ago. It seemed Samuel Timmons had threatened to send both him and Shiloh off to boarding school if he got wind that they were still friends with the Grangers. Jace understood and he and Shedrick were trying to rebuild the friendship they'd lost.

Dalton wrapped his arms tighter around her and pulled her closer. They would be getting married on New Year's Day at Sutton Hills. She was letting Mona and Carson plan their wedding. All she and Dalton wanted to do was show up.

Leaning over, he nuzzled her ear. "Let's play hooky from work all next week."

She glanced over at him. "And do what?"

He smiled, and she knew what he had in mind. "Sounds good to me."

He tightened his hand on hers, and all she could do was look forward to spending the rest of her life with him…the man she loved.

Epilogue

"Jules, you look absolutely beautiful," Shana said, staring at her sister with tears in her eyes. "Mom would be so proud of you today."

Jules smiled back at her sister. "Just like Dad and I were proud of you a few months ago. And now it's my time."

Shana nodded. "Yes, and now it's your time."

As Jules tried sitting still while Shana, Mona and Carson fussed with her veil, she took a moment to reflect on her life. She knew she loved Dalton, and he loved her and together they would have a beautiful life together. They wouldn't always agree, and there would be days he'd want his way. But in the end, the key word would be *compromise*. They'd done a lot of that over the past few months.

She glanced out the window and looked out over the Sutton Hills estate. Already Sheppard had had the boathouse torn down and another would be built in a different location. He and Carson had moved into the main house, and Jace and Shana and Caden and Shiloh were making plans to build their own homes on Sutton Hills property. She and Dalton had decided not to make any decisions about anything like that yet. For now they would live at Dalton's place. They would be flying out after the reception for a two-week honeymoon in Paris, and she couldn't wait.

She looked up at Mona, caught the woman's eye and winked. Everyone was thrilled that Mona's sight had returned in time for her wedding. Mona and her father would be marrying next month on Valentine's Day, and she couldn't wait. Her father and Mona deserved all the happiness in the world.

Carson glanced at her watch and smiled. "It's time. We don't want to keep Dalton waiting."

Jules laughed. "No, we don't."

Dalton Granger glanced around, noting the hundreds of people assembled for his and Jules's wedding. And the three men he loved the most, his father and brothers, stood beside him as his best men.

When the music began playing he watched Shana walk in ahead of her sister and when he saw Jules on Ben's arm, his heart stopped. She looked so beautiful in her white designer gown.

It seemed to take forever for her to reach him, and when she did she turned to him and smiled. He knew at that moment that she was the woman he'd been destined to marry. His very own Juliet. Unlike the other weddings he'd attended, this time he paid attention to the minister's words, and when he had to answer with an "I do," his voice was clear and precise because he meant every word.

When the minister said, "I now pronounce you man and wife. You may kiss your bride," Dalton pulled Miss

Whirlwind into his arms and kissed her, sealing their vows and making what was once a lover's vow a husband's vow. He would love her forever.

* * * * *

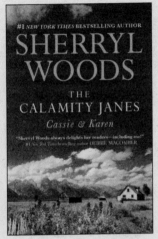

New York Times bestselling author

BRENDA NOVAK

**brings you a brand-new *Whiskey Creek* tale
of first love and second chances.**

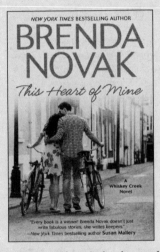

NEW YORK TIMES BESTSELLING AUTHOR

BRENDA NOVAK

This Heart of Mine

A
Whiskey Creek
Novel

"Every book is a winner! Brenda Novak doesn't just
write fabulous stories, she writes keepers."
—*New York Times* bestselling author Susan Mallery

As the daughter of a hoarder, Phoenix Fuller had a tough childhood. So when the handsome, popular Riley Stinson became her boyfriend in high school, Phoenix was desperate not to lose him—especially once she found out she was pregnant. She might have acted a bit obsessive when he broke up with her. But she did *not* run down the girl he dated next.

Unfortunately, there was no way to prove her innocence. Now, after serving her time in prison, Phoenix has been released. And all she wants is to get to know her son. But Riley doesn't trust Phoenix, doesn't want her in Jacob's life. He is, however, ready to find someone to love. And he wants a good mother for his son. He has no idea that he's about to find both!

Available now, wherever books are sold!

REQUEST YOUR FREE BOOKS!

2 FREE NOVELS
FROM THE ROMANCE COLLECTION
PLUS 2 FREE GIFTS!

YES! Please send me 2 FREE novels from the Romance Collection and my 2 FREE gifts (gifts are worth about $10). After receiving them, if I don't wish to receive any more books, I can return the shipping statement marked "cancel." If I don't cancel, I will receive 4 brand-new novels every month and be billed just $6.49 per book in the U.S. or $6.99 per book in Canada. That's a savings of at least 19% off the cover price. It's quite a bargain! Shipping and handling is just 50¢ per book in the U.S. and 75¢ per book in Canada.* I understand that accepting the 2 free books and gifts places me under no obligation to buy anything. I can always return a shipment and cancel at any time. Even if I never buy another book, the two free books and gifts are mine to keep forever.

194/394 MDN GH4D

Name	(PLEASE PRINT)	
Address		Apt. #
City	State/Prov.	Zip/Postal Code

Signature (if under 18, a parent or guardian must sign)

Mail to the **Reader Service**:
IN U.S.A.: P.O. Box 1867, Buffalo, NY 14240-1867
IN CANADA: P.O. Box 609, Fort Erie, Ontario L2A 5X3

Want to try two free books from another line?
Call 1-800-873-8635 or visit www.ReaderService.com.

* Terms and prices subject to change without notice. Prices do not include applicable taxes. Sales tax applicable in N.Y. Canadian residents will be charged applicable taxes. Offer not valid in Quebec. This offer is limited to one order per household. Not valid for current subscribers to the Romance Collection or the Romance/Suspense Collection. All orders subject to credit approval. Credit or debit balances in a customer's account(s) may be offset by any other outstanding balance owed by or to the customer. Please allow 4 to 6 weeks for delivery. Offer available while quantities last.

Your Privacy—The Reader Service is committed to protecting your privacy. Our Privacy Policy is available online at www.ReaderService.com or upon request from the Reader Service.
We make a portion of our mailing list available to reputable third parties that offer products we believe may interest you. If you prefer that we not exchange your name with third parties, or if you wish to clarify or modify your communication preferences, please visit us at www.ReaderService.com/consumerchoice or write to us at Reader Service Preference Service, P.O. Box 9062, Buffalo, NY 14240-9062. Include your complete name and address.

ROM15

BRENDA JACKSON

31433	A BROTHER'S HONOR	___ $7.99 U.S.	___ $9.99 CAN.
31625	A MAN'S PROMISE	___ $7.99 U.S.	___ $8.99 CAN.

(limited quantities available)

TOTAL AMOUNT	$ _____
POSTAGE & HANDLING	$ _____
($1.00 for 1 book, 50¢ for each additional)	
APPLICABLE TAXES*	$ _____
TOTAL PAYABLE	$ _____

(check or money order—please do not send cash)

To order, complete this form and send it, along with a check or money order for the total above, payable to MIRA Books, to: **In the U.S.:** 3010 Walden Avenue, P.O. Box 9077, Buffalo, NY 14269-9077; **In Canada:** P.O. Box 636, Fort Erie, Ontario, L2A 5X3.

Name: _____
Address: _____ City: _____
State/Prov.: _____ Zip/Postal Code: _____
Account Number (if applicable): _____

075 CSAS

*New York residents remit applicable sales taxes.
*Canadian residents remit applicable GST and provincial taxes.

MIRA®

www.MIRABooks.com

MBJ0515BL